**For two years she'd been dreaming of ways to nail
Josh Garland. . . . Tonight she was going to do it.**

Feenie crept toward the thirty-six-foot Grady-White her ex had christened *Feenie's Dream*. She'd recognize the boat anywhere—the pristine white hull, the shiny handrails. The logo painted on the side said *Sea Breeze*, but that didn't matter. She knew that boat right down to the teak cabinets, which she'd lovingly oiled countless times. It was *her* boat, or at least half of it was, and Josh had stolen it right out from under her. God, how had she been so gullible?

Feenie unzipped her sweatshirt, pulled out the camera she'd hung around her neck, and snapped a picture, then eased closer for a clearer view.

When Josh appeared she watched, fuming, as he activated the boat hoist, lowered *Feenie's Dream* into the water, and hopped aboard. Beer in hand, he swaggered to the helm.

She wanted to scream. She wanted to wrestle the keys from him and pitch them right into the bay. Not caring anymore whether he spotted her, she stomped closer and snapped another picture, muttering as the camera clicked. "You lying, cheating piece of—"

Her feet flew out from under her, and she splatted facedown on the ground. All the air rushed out of her lungs, and a hand clamped over her mouth.

"Don't move."

ONE LAST BREATH

LAURA GRIFFIN

POCKET BOOKS
New York   London   Toronto   Sydney

Pocket Books
A Division of Simon & Schuster, Inc.
1230 Avenue of the Americas
New York, NY 10020

This book is a work of fiction. Names, characters, places, and incidents either are products of the author's imagination or are used fictitiously. Any resemblance to actual events or locales or persons, living or dead, is entirely coincidental.

Copyright © 2007 by Laura Griffin

First Pocket Books paperback edition October 2007

POCKET and colophon are registered trademarks of Simon & Schuster, Inc.

Cover design by Lisa Litwack
Illustration by Craig White

Manufactured in the United States of America

10   9   8   7   6   5

For information about special discounts for bulk purchases, please contact Simon & Schuster Special Sales at 1-800-456-6798 or business@simonandschuster.com.

ISBN-13: 978–1–4165–3737–3
ISBN-10:   1–4165–3737–6

For Doug

For Doug

ACKNOWLEDGMENTS

This book would not have been possible without the encouragement and dedication of Kevan Lyon, who loved Feenie from the start and never once suggested I change her name. I'd like to thank Amy Pierpont and Maggie Crawford for giving priceless editorial advice, as well as Abby Zidle, who took on this project with enthusiasm and offered invaluable insights.

I'd also like to thank my late grandmother, Rubalee, who set a high bar for everything and inspired me to write romance novels when she observed that "it takes a hell of a man to be better than no man at all." I hope everyone finds theirs.

PROLOGUE

Reynosa, Mexico
5:25 p.m.

Detective Paloma Juarez opened her eyes and tried to focus. The darkness swirled around her, and she couldn't see anything, not a scrap of light. Her skull felt as if it had collided with a sledgehammer. The mist in her mind cleared, and she remembered it hadn't been a sledgehammer but a combat boot. Was her jaw broken?

Goddamn combat boots.

She tried to sit up, but her arms and legs felt numb. She was still bound. Giving up on movement for the time being, she rested her head on the floor and tried to orient herself. She was naked. The cool concrete pressed against her skin. The room smelled like chemicals . . . ammonia, maybe? The air felt muggy. She ran her tongue over sore, swollen lips and tasted blood.

His stream of questions had been endless. What had she given away? What had she managed to keep from him? Threats and blows had come after each question, followed by an icy rush of terror when her interrogator had reached for his belt. No amount of police training had prepared her for that.

Her breath rasped in and out. In a small, objective corner of her mind, she realized she was hyperventilating, beginning to panic. She had to come up with a plan.

Any minute, they might come back.

She squirmed against the concrete, willing her arms and legs to come alive. Soon they flooded with sensation, and her wrists and ankles burned where the bindings had cut through her skin. Ignoring the pain, she maneuvered herself onto her knees. The flesh was raw there, too, but that was the least of her problems.

She managed to stand. Surrounded by darkness, there was no way she'd find something to cut her bindings. She needed to escape the room, to put as much space as possible between her and her captors. She began hopping—tiny hops that stole the breath from her lungs and had her heart thundering.

She bumped against something hard and reached out her bound hands to touch it. It felt smooth, metallic. And curved. A storage drum? The room she'd been in earlier had looked like some sort of warehouse.

Voices approached, followed by some shuffling. A door opened, allowing a narrow shaft of light into the room. Paloma crouched behind the drum and tried to disappear.

"Where the fuck she go?" It was a male voice, the one called Ruiz.

"Gimme the flashlight."

Her body quivered with recognition at the second voice. The American. She shrank lower, praying he wouldn't find her.

She knew it was futile. The light swept over her.

"Got her," he said.

The flashlight shone in her eyes, bright and blinding. She couldn't see the man holding it, but she didn't need to. His face was permanently engraved in her memory banks. He had leathery skin and frigid gray eyes and a smile that had utterly unnerved her.

"Going somewhere?" he snarled. "We're not done with you."

"Please." Her voice sounded hoarse. "I already told you everything I know. Just let me go."

He moved closer, and she caught the familiar stench of sweat and tequila. The odor was stronger than before, and she tried not to think about what that meant.

"You'd like that, wouldn't you? But that's not the plan. I think you've got something left to tell us."

"No, I—"

Her face hit the floor with a *crack*. Something warm gushed from her nostril.

"I'm going to ask you one more time. And I want an answer. If I don't get one, you're gonna end up like your partner. Got it?"

Her heart lurched. "Where's Ben?"

A knee dug into her back between her shoulder blades. "Same place you're gonna be if you don't cooperate. Now. Who else knows?"

"I already told you—"

"I want *names!* Who else have you talked to?"

"I told you, I—"

A boot crashed into her rib cage, sending pain zinging through her body. She whimpered and curled into a ball, realizing her fate had already been determined. No matter what she said, they were going to kill her, just as they'd killed Ben. *Oh, God.*

She thought of Kaitlin—her plump cheeks, her swinging pigtails, her singsong voice in the morning: *See ya later, alligator!* And the last thing she'd said to her daughter that day: *After a while, crocodile!* Why hadn't she added *I love you?*

"Ten seconds . . ." he said.

Something cool and hard nudged at her temple. How had this happened? She was a *cop*. A *good* one. At least, she had been until today. Today she'd made mistakes. She and Ben had walked right into an ambush.

"Nine . . ."

She was going to die. The only thing she had left was the name. Her brother's name. Marco was the one person besides Ben who knew the most important detail of her investigation. And she was thankful Ben didn't *know* he knew. If he had . . .

She couldn't think about what they'd done to Ben. She had to think about her family. She had to protect them.

"Eight . . ."

These men couldn't find out about Marco. She had to end this before they came up with a way to drag it out of her.

"Seven . . ."

"Okay, okay!" she said. "I'll tell you! Please. Don't hurt me anymore."

The flashlight beam shifted, illuminating the patch of concrete next to her head. Blood had pooled there. From her nose? Her mouth? It hardly mattered now.

Hail Mary, full of grace. . . . Paloma saw her mother, eyes closed, clutching her rosary. *The Lord is with thee—*

"Six . . ."

Blessed art thou amongst women—

"Five . . ."

"Just let me sit up!" She took a deep breath. The flashlight beam shifted onto the bloodied toe of the black boot. Using all her remaining energy, she pulled herself onto her knees. Her ribs ached, and her nose throbbed, but her lips twitched into a smile.

"The name you're looking for is . . ." She paused,

swishing saliva and blood around in her mouth. She inhaled deeply and spat on the boot. "Fuck you."

Nothing happened. She enjoyed a minuscule moment of triumph. Then the boot swung back.

Mayfield, Texas
5:50 p.m.

Feenie Garland was having the day from hell.

It had started at ten that morning when she'd returned from her tennis match to find a note taped to the fridge: *Call caterer!* Her husband had failed to get further details, but it didn't take Feenie long to fill in the gaps. The caterer was sorry, but because of an unforeseen problem, she couldn't deliver the food for tomorrow night's charity auction. The problem? The woman's kitchen had been shut down by the health department. Now Feenie had ninety-six people coming to her in-laws' waterfront estate for a party and nothing to serve.

Her day took another nosedive at noon when the Texas swing band she'd booked called to say their lead singer had laryngitis.

Yeah, right. She'd bet her favorite pair of black stilettos that Swingtown had opted for a better gig. Or at least something that paid more than peanuts.

Charity auctions were always such a pain to organize. You had next to nothing to spend, yet you had to provide food and booze and entertainment that would make wealthy donors want to write checks. Sure, the ticket sales helped, but the real dollars rolled in when people got tipsy enough to plop down ridiculous amounts of money for less-than-amazing junk.

How did she always get roped into these things? She'd been a straight-A student, for God's sake, and editor of her college paper. Was this really the best use of her talents? Charity auctions and tennis tourneys? It might have been okay if only she had something more to focus on. Something that really mattered. Maybe if she had a baby . . . a pudgy, smiling baby to give her life focus. Maybe then she wouldn't feel so adrift.

"Earth to Feenie!" a voice snapped, interrupting her pity party.

"Sorry. What?"

Cecelia Strickland rolled her eyes. "I *said*, what about your mother-in-law's cook? Could she handle it?"

Feenie eyed her best friend across the break-fast table and scoffed. The idea of Dottie Garland's seventy-year-old cook catering a party for a hundred was ludicrous. "I don't think so. She's a great cook, but she's slow as molasses. We'd be better off doing it ourselves."

Cecelia raised an eyebrow.

"No way, Celie. Neither of us cooks worth a damn."

"Well," Cecelia said, tucking a perfectly high-lighted lock of blond hair behind her ear. Like Feenie, she hadn't showered or changed since tennis that morning. They were in full crisis mode. "We could call the club. Think they could do it in a pinch?"

Feenie pursed her lips. The idea had merit. The Mayfield Country Club wasn't known for its outstanding cuisine, but the auction planning committee—which consisted solely of Feenie and Cecelia—was desperate. Plus, the Garland family had practically founded the place, and Feenie's mother-in-law could use her influence with the manager. And the Mayfield Food Bank fund-raiser was a worthy cause. Who wouldn't want to help raise money to feed the hungry?

"That's a thought. It'll be a rubbery chicken breast and undercooked pasta, but who cares, right?"

"Not me," Cecelia said. "We're on the verge of Ritz crackers and Cheez Whiz here."

The phone rang. Feenie sprang from her chair to grab the receiver off the kitchen counter. Maybe the caterer hadn't been shut down after all. Maybe Swingtown's lead singer had made a miraculous recovery. She lifted the phone to her ear and prayed.

"Hello?"

"Hi, it's me."

"Oh." She heaved a sigh.

"You sound elated," Josh said.

Feenie gave Cecelia an apologetic look and took the portable phone into the living room. "Sorry. I'm having a nightmare day here. You won't *believe* what's happened with the auction."

"Can't talk now," her husband said. "I'm on my way to the courthouse, and Sanderson just called to tell me we've got a mediation tomorrow morning. I'll be here all night."

"Oh." Feenie felt deflated. She'd been looking forward to eliciting some sympathy from Josh over the auction fiasco. He typically didn't give a hoot about her charity work, but this event was at his parents' house, after all, and she'd expected at least a flicker of interest.

"It's okay," she said, trying to sound cheerful. She didn't want to add to Josh's problems if he was having another stressful day. He'd been working so hard lately. "I'll warm up some of that leftover lasagna for you when you get home." Thank heaven Stouffer's cooked better than she did.

"What?" he asked, obviously distracted. "Feenie, I can't talk right now. Really, I've gotta go."

"Never mind. We'll talk later. Don't work too hard, sweetheart."

She blew a kiss into the phone, but all she got back was a dial tone. Sighing, she returned to the kitchen, where Cecelia was hunched over a phone book.

She tapped a pink fingernail on the page. "Here's the number for the club. Want me to call, or should we get your mother-in-law to do it?"

The phone rang, and Feenie glanced at the caller ID.

"Josh again," she told Cecelia, cradling the phone on her shoulder. "Hey, sweetheart. What'd you forget?"

Instead of her husband's voice, she heard breathing. Heavy breathing. And panting. And moaning. The moaning sounded oddly familiar. Then a woman's voice: "Oh, baby! Oh, yes! Oh, baby! Oh, yes! *Ohhhhh* . . ."

Feenie gasped and dropped the phone.

Officer Marco Juarez hated domestics. It was always the same shit: Drunk man slaps woman around. Woman calls the cops, hysterical. Cops hightail it over and find everybody's kissed and made up, even though the woman has a shiner and a bloody lip. No matter what you said, the victim always resisted filing charges.

Maybe this call would be different. So far, it was, by virtue of the fact that it had come from a rich neighborhood. Juarez turned onto Pecan Street and drove past the tidy row of restored bungalows. He rolled to a stop in front of a yellow and white two-story, where a crowd had gathered in the driveway. He turned to his rookie partner.

"Follow my lead."

Peterson nodded eagerly and checked his weapon.

Juarez raised his eyebrows. "Why don't you start by talking to bystanders, see if we can get a feel for what's happening?"

"Got it," Peterson said.

Juarez slammed the door of the cruiser and walked up the driveway. Most everyone looked like your typical nosy neighbor. A white-haired man in aqua

Bermuda shorts stood off to the side with his arms crossed. He scowled as Juarez approached him.

" 'Bout time y'all got here. Gal's been at it twenty minutes now. She's hot as a firecracker."

Juarez looked up the driveway and spotted the "gal" in question. She had a head full of blond curls and wore one of those short, pleated skirts that barely covered her rear end. She was loading what looked to be a .22.

A deranged cheerleader?

With fluid ease, she tucked the slender rifle against her shoulder, aimed at something on the back fence, and fired. A shiny object burst into smithereens. A beer bottle? No. Several more objects were lined up on the fence posts.

Juarez glanced around. Suits and ties were strewn about the driveway. He eyed the upstairs windowsill, where a pair of boxer shorts had hit a snag on the way down. They fluttered like a battle flag in the evening breeze.

Former cheerleader, deranged *wife*, he decided.

"What's she shooting?" he asked the neighbor.

"Dunno. Think it's a vase or somethin'."

"It's a trophy," a woman put in. She was blond, thirtyish, and looked as if she'd just come off a tennis court. "Last year's club championship."

"You know this woman?" he asked her.

"She's my best friend."

"She intoxicated?"

The woman snorted. "Nope. Just pissed."

Juarez waited for more.

"She just found out what a prick she married," the woman said, as if that explained everything.

"Her husband inside?" Juarez touched his sidearm, and the woman frowned.

"You don't need *that*, for heaven's sake! No one's inside. Only thing in danger 'round here's those trophies."

Procedure called for him to draw his weapon anyway and disarm the subject, but Juarez wasn't much on rules and regulations, especially when they went against his gut instincts.

And his gut instincts at the moment told him the friend was right—this woman was armed, but she wasn't dangerous. Not yet, at least.

The wife reloaded, and Juarez watched. She was pretty, actually. Graceful. She knew how to handle a gun, too, and for some reason, the combination made his pulse pick up.

"Ma'am," he said, walking toward her. "I'm gonna have to ask you to put the gun down."

Instead of complying, she turned and glared at him. Her cheeks were flushed pink, and blond ringlets fell over her eyes. He put her at late twenties, five-five, a hundred and thirty pounds. He couldn't help noticing a very nice share of the weight was concentrated up top.

She turned back around, aimed the gun toward the fence, and fired, this time taking out a little brass statue. She was a hell of a shot.

"Ma'am." Juarez stepped closer and clamped a hand on the barrel. It was still warm.

"What?" she demanded.

"Put the gun down."

She huffed out a breath and laid the gun on the pavement. Then she crossed her arms over her chest and gave him a venomous look.

"Mind telling me what's going on here, ma'am?"

If possible, her cheeks flushed even more. "Target practice. Why? Is there a law against shooting golf trophies?"

He repressed a smile. "No, but there's a law against firing a weapon within city limits."

"That's a utility easement back there, so I don't see what the big deal is."

"What's your name, ma'am?"

She started to speak, then bit her lip. "Feenie. Feenie Gar—I mean, Malone."

"Okay, Mrs. Malone—"

"That's *Ms.!*"

Peterson appeared and retrieved the gun from the driveway.

"Okay, Ms. Malone," Juarez said. "Let's cool off for a minute, all right? Now, my partner here is going to hold on to your gun while we go inside and talk."

She looked him over then, her blue eyes simmering. Her neighbor had been right about the firecracker thing. This woman was hot, in more ways than one, and she had a defiant streak that Juarez admired.

"Look, Ms. Malone." He leaned in and lowered his voice. Several curious neighbors inched closer. "Whatever you're doing here, I'm sure he deserves it. But you're causing a disturbance, and I'd hate to have to haul you off to jail. There're kids watching."

She glanced at the crowd behind her and bit her lip again. She seemed to calm down fractionally, and some of the color faded from her cheeks. "Okay, Officer . . . ?"

"Juarez."

"Okay, Officer Juarez."

"Why don't we go inside now?" He surveyed the debris on the driveway. "Keep any other guns in the house?"

She tossed a look over her shoulder as she led him to the back door. "Sure. My husband collects them. The .22 is mine."

"Where does your husband store his guns, ma'am?"

She opened the screen door and ushered him inside. "In the safe, usually, but right now they're at the bottom of the swimming pool."

Juarez stopped short. "The swimming pool?"

"That's right. With his clubs and his flat-screen TV." She smiled sweetly. "I'm feeling much better now, Officer Juarez. Can I fix you some lemonade?"

CHAPTER

I

Mayfield, Texas
Two years later

Feenie stood in the middle of the vacant lot, straining to concentrate as the noonday sun blazed
down on her. It wasn't the heat, really, that made
concentration impossible, but the way the man next
to her was peering down her shirt.

"That's *Wolf,* no *e* at the end," he said helpfully,
leaning closer as she scribbled in her reporter's notebook.

Feenie stepped back, hoping he'd get the hint.
"Thank you, Mr. Wolf. And you said you've been with
Lansing Corporation how long?"

"Five years." He flashed his overwhitened teeth. "And I should tell you this development promises to be one of the most luxurious gated communities on the Gulf Coast. We've spared no amenities here."

The talking points were straight out of Lansing's media packet, and Feenie wondered why the PR department never bothered to tell employees to mix it up just a teensy bit so their quotes didn't sound so canned.

"This community will set a whole new standard for luxury retirement," he plunged on, reciting the press release verbatim. "We believe it's simply a question of when, not if, other developers will try and follow our lead. But of course, part of what we're offering is a spectacular waterfront view, and I should point out that properties like these are in limited supply now that the federal government has cracked down on development of coastal wetlands."

"I see," she said, taking notes. Wolf would be expecting her to write an article that would make people want to rush out and buy one of these expensive lots she was standing on. But she'd already been warned not to write a fluff piece, so as soon as she finished talking to this guy, she planned to place a few calls to the Army Corps of Engineers to see if she could get the other side of the story.

Feenie glanced up, and, no joke, Wolf was looking straight at her boobs. What a sleaze. She was beginning to understand why Mary Beth, her colleague at the *Mayfield Gazette*, had been so eager to drop this story on her desk. Mary Beth had claimed she'd had an emergency dentist appointment and couldn't make it to the interview, but Feenie now suspected the real emergency had been finding a way to avoid spending the afternoon with this creep.

Of course, even if Feenie had known the real reason she'd lucked into this assignment, she still would have come. It was an actual *news* story, slated for twelve inches of column space on page three. It was Feenie's first chance to write something besides obituaries and wedding announcements, and she couldn't afford not to leap on the opportunity.

Even if it meant spending the afternoon being ogled by a jerk with a fake-and-bake tan.

"Thank you for showing me around, Mr. Wolf. Looks like I've got everything I need here, and I really should be getting back to the office. It's been quite a pleasure meeting you."

She extended a hand, half expecting to get struck by lightning for uttering such a bald-faced lie.

"The pleasure's been mine," Wolf said, taking her hand and dropping his gaze again. This guy was unbelievable. And she wasn't even wearing anything remotely sexy today, just taupe slacks and a white button-down. If she ever had to interview Wolf again, she was definitely going with a turtleneck.

"Before you leave," Wolf said, still holding on to her hand, "I'd like to give you a better idea of the view we're talking about here."

She tugged her hand away, and he started walking toward a flight of wooden stairs leading up to an observation platform.

"I appreciate it, Mr. Wolf, but I really have to get back soon. My deadline—"

"Oh, this will only take a minute," he said over his shoulder.

The observation deck was flanked by empty lots. But only about fifty yards away was Fisherman's Grill, a crowded waterfront restaurant. Surely Wolf wouldn't have the nerve to put any moves on her in front of the entire lunch crowd. She huffed out a breath and followed him up the stairs.

"From this vantage point, prospective buyers can see what a magnificent view they'll have when they invest in a Lansing home. Without exception, all our lots are designed for sunset vistas."

Feenie glanced at her watch—another hint he probably wouldn't pick up on—and then took a cursory look around. Sunlight glistened off the water, and a quartet of brown pelicans soared overhead. The view *was* nice, she had to admit. And the breeze fifteen feet up felt coolly refreshing. She moved the damp hair off her neck and immediately regretted the gesture. Now Wolf was staring at her with a smug look.

"I notice you don't wear a wedding ring. How's a pretty girl like you manage to stay single?"

Okay, no points for originality. This guy was a loser, hands down, but she didn't want to alienate the primary source for her first actual news story. Maybe, just maybe, if she did a good job with this assignment, her editor would promote her from part-time stringer to full-time features writer. The position came with a salary and benefits, and Feenie sorely needed both. Her desk was awash in unpaid bills and overdue notices.

She forced a smile. "Too busy to date, I guess. Look, I hate to be rude, but like I said, I have a deadline, so—"

She lost track of the thought as she glanced past Wolf.

"No freaking way," she muttered.

Wolf turned to see what had grabbed her attention.

A thirty-six-foot Grady-White had just pulled up to the dock at Fisherman's. Feenie watched, mouth agape, as Josh Garland stepped off the boat and tied the bowline to a cleat. Then he held out his hand and helped a blond woman in an impossibly small bikini disembark.

"That lying *bastard!*" she hissed.

"You know Josh Garland?"

She tore her attention away from Josh. She was supposed to be conducting an interview, dammit, and she'd just lost all semblance of professionalism.

"Uh . . . yeah." Who didn't know Josh? He was the golden-haired hometown hero who'd gone off to break all kinds of football records as a wide receiver for UT. He was a local celebrity.

"So . . . he's your boyfriend?" Wolf persisted, clearly

wondering how this latest development affected his chances.

"No. He's just . . . no. Um, if you'll excuse me, Mr. Wolf, I need to get going."

Minutes later, Feenie charged across the dining room at Fisherman's and plowed straight through the double doors leading to the deck outside. She spotted Josh and his most recent plaything strolling up the pier. The girl was busy tying a gauzy cloth around her waist in a vain attempt to appear clothed. Josh had less flesh on display. He wore a silk Hawaiian-print shirt, khaki shorts, and leather sandals. This was his Tommy Bahama look.

Feenie strode up to him and fisted her hands on her hips. "Just how stupid do you think I am?"

Surprise flared in his eyes, but he quickly recovered. "Well, look who's here. Hey, Feenie. Long time no see."

"What the hell do you think you're doing, Josh?"

He draped a proprietary arm around the blonde's shoulder. "Not that it's any of your business, but we're about to have lunch."

He tried to sidestep Feenie, but she anticipated the move and blocked his path.

"Nice *boat*, Josh." She jabbed a finger toward the end of the pier. "Funny, I think I may have seen it somewhere before. Yes, as a matter of fact, I think it's *mine*. I think you *stole* it!"

The girl's eyes widened, and Josh burst out with a fake laugh. "Dream on," he said.

"I'm not blind," Feenie snapped. "I don't care what name you've painted on the side of that thing. It is *my* boat, and don't even try to act like it isn't!"

Josh sighed heavily. "Please excuse my ex-wife, Tina. She's a little delusional."

"Delusional?" Feenie shot back. "You're the one who's delusional if you think I can't recognize my own boat! You told me you lost that boat in a poker game! Let me remind you, this is a community property state, Josh. And let me also remind you that hiding assets during a divorce is a serious offense! Oh, wait! But you're a lawyer, so I guess you already knew that. Too bad you won't be able to plead ignorance when I take you back to court!"

Josh gave her one of his dismissive looks, and Feenie felt the familiar surge of indignation that had plagued her throughout her marriage.

"Don't mind her," he said in the girl's ear. And she really was a girl, twenty at the most. Feenie wondered where he'd picked her up. Maybe she was the receptionist at his law firm, just as Feenie had been once upon a time before she was stupid enough to get married.

"She's going through early menopause," he continued. "It makes her kind of *loco* sometimes."

Josh smirked, and Feenie realized he'd said that purely for her benefit. He knew full well she was touchy about the fact that she'd just turned thirty and her biological clock was tick-tocking away.

She shifted her attention to Josh's date and felt a

faint stirring of sympathy. "Fair warning, honey, this one's not a keeper."

Feenie turned on her heel and stalked off.

As Cecelia steered her blue Ford Explorer down the Garlands' street, Feenie twittered with adrenaline.

"I can't believe you talked me into this," Cecelia said. "You look like a cat burglar."

Feenie zipped her sweatshirt. It was black, just like the jeans and baseball cap she had on. "So what?"

"So if someone sees you poking around in the dark like that, you could get arrested. Or shot!"

Cecelia cast her a worried look as she neared the turnoff to the Garlands' waterfront estate. Josh's parents lived in a sprawling mansion at the top of the property, while Josh occupied the lavish guest cottage near the water. He'd lived there ever since the divorce.

Feenie checked her watch. It was after nine already, and she didn't have time for a lecture. Josh played poker at the club on Wednesday nights, and Feenie wanted to see his living quarters while he wasn't home. She allotted precisely two minutes to deal with Cecelia's cold feet.

"Celie, I appreciate your concern. But I know what I'm doing, okay? Now, are you in or not?"

Not the most persuasive sales pitch in the world, but Feenie knew it was all Cecelia needed. Ever since Josh had teamed up with some unscrupulous attorneys to screw Feenie out of everything in the divorce, she and Cecelia had been devising ways to get him back. Most involved maiming, but tonight's plan could work too.

Cecelia glanced over her shoulder, as if they were being chased by a fleet of police cars. "I don't like this, Feenie. This is trespassing! Home invasion! If Robert finds out, he's going to kill me!"

Cecelia's husband was an accountant, a real stickler for rules and regulations. Feenie gave Cecelia a pleading look.

"Oh, all right!" Cecelia said. "But make it snappy, okay? Ten minutes. I'll circle the neighborhood and come back. I want us long gone when Josh gets home."

Cecelia stopped the car in front of the Garlands' secondary driveway, which led directly to the guest cottage. Feenie hopped out before Cecelia could change her mind.

Thunder rumbled in the distance as Feenie crept up the drive. Feeling a few raindrops, she moved off the gravel and onto the carpet of St. Augustine grass covering the property. Soon the guest cottage came into view and, alongside it, a weathered boathouse. She ducked behind a clump of sago palms and surveyed the situation.

The driveway in front of the guest cottage was clearly illuminated by a pair of floodlights. Feenie spotted two vehicles: a yellow pickup truck sporting oversized tires and the silver Porsche Cayenne that Josh had been driving around town ever since he'd made partner—big shocker—at his father's law firm.

Shoot. Had he changed his poker night? Maybe he was hosting for a change. But she didn't recognize the truck, which looked like a Tonka toy on steroids.

She had two options. She could head back to the road and wait in the rain for Cecelia, or she could sneak a quick peek.

Her choice was obvious.

Inching up the driveway, Feenie studied the house. Lights glowed in the living room, which contained a pool table and a big-screen TV. The guys had probably gathered in there, which meant they'd never notice her. She tiptoed around the side of the house until she came to the water's edge. She stayed away from the fishing lights near the dock and approached the boathouse from the concrete bulkhead. Something splashed nearby, and she whirled around.

Just a fish. She needed to calm down.

Turning back toward the boathouse, she crept closer until two slips came into view, both illuminated by fluorescent lights. One slip contained the twenty-two-foot Boston Whaler that belonged to Josh's father. The neighboring slip housed the thirty-six-foot Grady-White that Josh had christened *Feenie's Dream*. She'd recognize the boat anywhere—the pristine white hull, the shiny handrails. The name painted on the side now read *Sea Breeze*, but that didn't matter. She knew that boat right down to the teak cabinets, which she'd lovingly oiled countless times. It was *her* boat, or at least half of it was, and Josh had stolen it right out from under her with that ridiculous poker game story. God, how had she been so gullible?

Josh suddenly emerged from the guest cottage. He wore khaki shorts and a navy golf shirt and was talking to a man now standing on the side of the dock closest to Feenie.

Feenie unzipped her sweatshirt, pulled out the camera she'd hung around her neck, and disabled the flash. She hoped the fluorescent lights would be bright enough to allow for a decent shot. She snapped a picture. The rain was coming down heavily now, so she eased closer for a clearer view.

She wanted hard evidence, something she could wave in front of a judge. The last time Feenie had been in a courtroom with Josh, she'd been hopelessly outmatched, thanks to his family's cadre of lawyers and the ironclad prenup she'd naively signed just before her wedding. Feenie thought of all the nights recently she'd spent at home eating ramen noodles and clipping coupons. Meanwhile, Josh had probably been out sipping margaritas on the deck of *her* boat with a parade of women. He could have the bimbos, but she'd be damned if he'd keep the Grady-White. She'd drag him back into court if she had to.

She watched, fuming, as he activated the boat hoist, lowered *Feenie's Dream* into the water, and hopped aboard. Beer in hand, he swaggered to the helm.

She wanted to scream. She wanted to wrestle the keys from him and pitch them right into the bay. Not caring anymore whether he spotted her, she stomped closer and snapped another picture, muttering as the camera clicked. "You lying, cheating piece of—"

Her feet flew out from under her, and she landed facedown on the ground. All the air rushed out of her lungs, and a hand clamped over her mouth.

"Don't fucking move."

CHAPTER

2

H er screams never made it past the hand. She
flung her arms back and tried to grab hold of
the person pinning her. The kneecap dug deeper between her shoulder blades, and a hand trapped her
wrists in a viselike grip. After minutes of thrashing,
she stilled and tried to catch her breath. It wasn't easy
with a giant hand smothering her. She wanted to bite
it, but she couldn't get an angle, and it was covered by
a leather glove anyway. She tried screaming again.

"Shut *up!*" the man snarled, tightening his grip.

Her heart hammered wildly as she tried to think.
What was happening?

A few possibilities came to mind, and she stifled
a sob. Cecelia was right. She never should have ven-

tured out here alone at night. At the very least, she should have brought a weapon. Mace was practically invented for situations like this, and she kept a vial in her nightstand. Why hadn't she brought it?

God, this man was heavy. His knee pressed firmly into her spine, and he seemed to be crouching there, waiting for something. What was he planning to do with her? And why didn't he move?

Maybe someone was coming.

She tried to listen. Shouts carried over from the boathouse, but she couldn't hear clearly because of the rain. An engine roared to life, and she recognized it as belonging to her boat.

Oh, Lord, were they leaving? If Josh and his friend left, she'd be totally alone with this maniac. She needed to get someone's attention. Fast.

She kept perfectly still. When the pressure at her back lessened a fraction, she summoned every ounce of strength she had and thrust her body sideways.

He didn't budge. Everything she could muster, and he didn't even flinch. The engine noise changed, signaling the boat reversing out of the slip.

She started to weep.

Would Cecelia get worried? Would she come looking for her or go get Robert? Maybe they'd find her in a ditch somewhere. Or washed up on the shore, all tangled in the salt grass.

Suddenly, the weight disappeared. The attacker yanked her to her feet. Feenie faced the boathouse with its two empty slips.

She let out a shriek, but then the hand clamped back over her mouth, and a powerful arm hooked around her waist.

"Feenie?" Someone called in the distance. "Feenie, where are you?" It was Cecelia, and she was getting closer.

The arm tightened.

"Can you swim?" he growled.

Was he going to drown her? She was torn between wishing Cecelia would find her and hoping she'd stay as far away as possible.

"Nod your head, yes or no," he ordered.

She remained silent, paralyzed with terror and getting dizzy from lack of air.

"Nod your head!"

She nodded yes.

The hand vanished, and she doubled over, gulping down oxygen. Then the ground disappeared, and she plunged face-first into the water.

Feenie peered over the photography editor's shoulder at the computer screen.

"Are you sure we can't enlarge it any more?" she asked. "I can barely tell anything from this."

Drew Benson surveyed the grainy image on the monitor. "How 'bout using a real camera next time?"

He was right. The camera had been on clearance at Wal-Mart, an idiot-proof point-and-shoot for $39.99. Feenie had bought it along with the black sweatshirt just before going to Josh's.

"Cut me a break," she said. "I'm an amateur here."

Drew looked her up and down and lifted his eyebrows in agreement. "Nice look you've got going, by the way."

"Thanks. I call it 'swamp chic.'"

After fishing the camera—and herself—out of the water, Feenie had made Cecelia take her to the newspaper office, hoping someone in the photo lab could develop her film. Cecelia had pitched a fit, of course, saying they should go straight to the police. But Feenie had talked her out of it. After all, what would she say? That she'd been sneaking around her ex-husband's house with a camera, and someone had the gall to confront her? It sounded ridiculous. Besides, a guy from the newspaper checked police reports every morning, and if she filed a complaint, it would be all over town by noon tomorrow. Feenie had had her fill of being grist for the local gossip mill during her divorce.

So now she was standing in Drew's office, dripping mud all over his linoleum floor. Her jeans were coated with muck and grass, and her hair had gone into extreme frizz mode.

Luckily, Drew had a pretty high threshold for eccentricity. He was the only man Feenie knew who wore a ponytail to work and still managed to be taken seriously. It probably helped that he was a genius with a camera. Feenie thanked her lucky stars he'd been working late tonight. If anyone could get a useful print out of her waterlogged camera, it was Drew.

Sure enough, he'd managed to develop her film and upload it onto the computer in less than an hour. Feenie had taken three shots, but the last two were hopelessly blurred.

She inched closer to the computer, and her tennis shoes slurped. "You're sure there's nothing else we can do?" she asked.

Drew used the mouse to zoom out. The picture of Josh standing aboard the boat filled the screen.

"Well, we can print this, but it won't help. The quality's terrible. Why'd you go at night, anyway? Would've been much easier to get a good shot during the day."

Obviously. But tonight was the only time Feenie had felt reasonably sure Josh would be gone. The Wednesday poker game was a fixture in his life, had been for years. And Feenie knew better than to show up during a workday. Josh was notorious for taking long lunches and leaving early for fishing excursions.

"I didn't think Josh'd be home," Feenie said. "Plus, with the fishing lights, I thought it'd be easy to sneak in close and get a good picture. I hadn't counted on the rain or the people."

Drew sighed. "I can enlarge this, but it won't help much. You'll get the boat and the figure in the foreground, but the rest is crap."

The photograph showed not one but two other people in the boathouse with Josh. Feenie didn't recognize either man. The first wore a T-shirt, jeans, and a baseball cap, and Feenie couldn't see his face because the hat cast a shadow over it. But Feenie didn't care much about him, anyway. What she really wanted was a clear view of the man in the background, the shadowy figure standing near the Boston Whaler. She hadn't noticed him at the time. Was he the guy who had attacked her moments later? The timing seemed off, but at the very least, his image would offer a clue. His hands were shadowed, so Feenie couldn't tell if he was wearing gloves or not. Her attacker had definitely been wearing leather gloves, either black or brown. That, plus the fact that he was strong as an ox, was about all Feenie knew about him.

She shivered at the memory. God, she'd never been so terrified. She'd felt utterly helpless; he could have snapped her neck like a Popsicle stick if he'd wanted to.

"Let's print it anyway," she told Drew. "At least we have a good shot of the boat."

Drew grinned. "You got it. And good luck with your ex. I hope you crucify him."

After wrapping things up, Drew offered Feenie a lift, and she gratefully accepted. Adrenaline had given way to fatigue, so she leaned her head back against the vinyl seats of his Toyota Tercel and closed her eyes for most of the drive. She was dying for a hot bath and a cold Corona.

The house on Pecan Street was her refuge. The 1930s-era three-bedroom home had captured her heart the moment she'd seen it. It had a wide front porch and two dormer windows on top, with a white picket fence surrounding the backyard and pool. After she and Josh had bought the place, she'd spent months going room to room, freshening dingy paint, refinishing woodwork, and polishing tarnished fixtures. Josh wasn't much of a handyman, but Feenie didn't care. She'd preferred doing everything herself, anyway. The place had been her baby, and she'd grown even fonder of it since her divorce. Not only was it the only thing of real value she'd taken from the marriage, but it was the sole remnant of her former life that she still enjoyed.

"Uh-oh," Drew said, jerking Feenie out of her daze.

Red and yellow lights swirled in the distance, and she spotted a fire truck parked diagonally across the street.

In front of her house.

"Oh, God," she muttered. Her palms started to sweat, as they always did when she saw or heard a fire truck. The only thing keeping her from having a full-blown panic attack was the conspicuous lack of flames or smoke.

Feenie glanced up and down the block and saw no signs of fire. Except, of course, the shiny red rig. What was it doing there? Had something happened to Mrs. Hanak? The seventy-five-year-old widow lived in the garage apartment. Feenie had taken in the tenant a couple of months ago to help with expenses. Mrs. Hanak seemed to get around okay, but Feenie knew she had some health issues. What if she'd had a heart attack? Or a stroke?

Then Feenie saw the tree.

The giant pecan that had once shaded the house's western exposure lay sprawled across the road. Its copious foliage peeked out from behind the fire engine.

"Damn," Drew said. "That thing's *huge*."

Feenie nodded, both relieved and horrified. Mrs. Hanak, bless her heart, was okay. But the tree obviously was not. It had probably been a hundred years old.

Drew rolled to a stop near the fire truck. Feenie thanked him for the ride and climbed out.

"Road's impassable, ma'am," a firefighter in a fluorescent orange poncho told her. "You're gonna have to move that vehicle."

"He's just dropping me off," she explained, waving Drew away. "I live here."

"Three-two-six Pecan Street?"

"That's me." She surveyed the damage with a knot in her stomach. "Was anybody hurt?"

He turned toward the massive pile of leaves and branches blocking the road. "Just the tree, ma'am. Took a bolt of lightning. Looks like she was a beaut, too."

A crowd of neighbors milled around on the other side of the truck. Mrs. Hanak stood beside the newlyweds who had just moved in across the street. She wore her yellow velour bathrobe and sneakers and had donned a plastic produce bag to protect her hair from the drizzle. Mrs. Hanak had her hair done weekly and was very particular about keeping it dry.

Feenie smiled halfheartedly and waved.

" 'Course, your kitchen's gonna need some work," the firefighter said.

"My kitchen?"

"Yes, ma'am. This here's just half the tree. Other half crashed right through your roof."

An hour later, Feenie had shed her soggy clothes and stood naked in front of the bathroom mirror. It was worse than she'd expected. Her lip was puffy, and both kneecaps were decorated with blue and purple polka dots. Turning and looking over her shoulder, she saw a fist-sized bruise in the dead center of her back where the assailant had pinned her with his knee. The face-plant onto the grass had left a magenta scrape on her chin.

Her answering machine droned in the other room. Two stern messages from her credit card company. Then a message from Cecelia wanting to make sure she'd gotten home okay and begging her to go to the police station in the morning. Feenie listened to the voices while cataloging her collection of welts and scrapes.

"Francis, it's Dad. Just calling to check in."

She closed her eyes and felt a stab of guilt. She needed to call her father. Last year, he'd sold the house Feenie had grown up in and retired to a waterfront condo in Port Aransas, and now their relationship was limited to phone calls and occasional visits. It had been weeks since Feenie had talked to him, and he tended to worry. But she couldn't deal with him just now. Instead, she had to deal with her reflection.

Did one of Josh's friends really do this to her?

Highly unlikely. Maybe Feenie wasn't the only one stalking Josh. Maybe some gal's husband or boyfriend had a reason to be lurking around. It was possible. Josh tended to let his libido run amok.

She turned on the faucet. As the claw-footed tub filled with scalding water, she let her mind wander to what was *really* bothering her. Besides the tree in her kitchen, she was worried about Josh. What had he been up to tonight, anyway?

He hadn't been going fishing, that was certain. No one went fishing in a thunderstorm. And who were those people with him? She knew his poker buddies, but the guys from tonight had looked totally unfamiliar. And Josh's friends weren't the type to drive jacked-up trucks with oversized tires. Nothing about the scene made sense to her.

She dumped some vanilla-scented gel into the bath. As she sank into the foam, she closed her eyes and tried to clear her mind of everything Josh-related. They'd been divorced nearly two years, and he still managed to suck up all her mental energy. Why did she let him do this to her? She needed to stop wasting time on him. She had a story to write, a career to pursue. And now her kitchen was wrecked. How on earth was she going to pay for that? She was pretty sure the insurance bill was one of the many sitting unopened and unpaid on her desk downstairs.

She needed a real job. Soon.

She couldn't lose her house. It embodied all the plans she'd ever made for herself. It symbolized adulthood, security, family. Although her marriage had been an obvious failure, she wasn't willing to give up on all the rest yet.

She'd long ago given up on Josh. He was a lying, cheating jerk who had humiliated her in front of everyone she knew. Feenie didn't know what he was up to these days, but she suspected it was something illegal. Drug running, maybe? Josh the stellar athlete had never been into drugs, at least not to Feenie's knowledge. But who knew what he was into now?

Whatever it was, she wanted nothing to do with it. Feenie didn't need any more trouble, and Josh Garland had already given her enough to last a lifetime.

When the alarm wailed in her ear the next morning, Feenie immediately thought of calling in sick. But her emaciated bank account and the tree in her kitchen changed her mind. As an hourly employee, she didn't get sick leave, so any morning she failed to clock in simply meant money out of her pocket. Suppressing a groan, she levered herself out of bed and tried to think of something in her closet that would conceal all her cuts and scrapes.

She decided on a rose linen pantsuit that was leftover from her charity luncheon days. It kept all her limbs hidden, and she could wear a sleeveless white shell underneath without looking too casual. Reporters weren't known for their fashion acumen, but Feenie believed in dressing for success. She might not feel successful, but she could at least look the part.

After working some magic with her makeup and popping a few aspirin, she grabbed her purse and headed for the front door. Because her garage had been converted to an apartment—Josh had wanted it for a home office—Feenie made a habit of parking in front. She supposed she should feel lucky her car hadn't been parked in the driveway during last night's rainstorm.

The sky had cleared, but the air outside still felt like a warm, wet blanket. Mrs. Hanak ambled toward the end of the driveway to collect her *Gazette*.

"Morning, Mrs. Hanak," Feenie said, manually unlocking her car door. In a former life, Feenie had been the proud owner of a convertible white Mustang. In her current incarnation as a semi-employed, debt-ridden divorcée, she drove a secondhand white Kia Spectra somewhat lacking in amenities.

She slid behind the wheel and pulled away before Mrs. Hanak could press her for details about her home repairs. She drove straight to the office, resisting the urge to pull into Southern-Made Donuts for a sugar boost. She had exactly nine dollars and twenty-six cents in her wallet, and she was saving it for her weekly lunch date with Cecelia.

The *Mayfield Gazette* was headquartered in a vintage building on Main Street. The newsroom and ad offices occupied the top floor, and the printing press lived downstairs. A receptionist in the first-floor lobby greeted visitors and controlled the flow of crackpots who stopped by routinely to complain about various and sundry offenses suffered at the hands of the liberal media.

Feenie climbed the stairs and headed for the break room. Drew found her there pouring a sixteen-ounce cup of the sludge that passed for coffee at the *Gazette*. Sometimes Feenie really missed her job at Josh's law firm. The work had been mind-numbing and thankless, but there had been a cappuccino maker in the reception area.

"Hey, Drew," she managed after a sip.

"It's your lucky day, Feen."

She wasn't feeling terribly lucky at the moment, but the look on Drew's face piqued her curiosity. "What's up?"

"I spent some more time on that photo," he said. "Managed to lighten up the shadows a bit with the computer."

"You're kidding," Feenie said. Drew was definitely racking up brownie points.

"Nope." His smile widened. "And I've got an ID for you."

Brownie points galore.

Feenie followed him into the photo lab, where several color pictures were spread out on a Formica counter. She recognized an eight-by-ten enlargement of the baseball cap guy from Josh's boathouse.

"Nice," she said. The photograph was grainy, but Drew had lightened it somehow, making the face visible beneath the cap. "Who is he?"

"That's the interesting part. I thought he looked familiar, so I checked our electronic archives," Drew said. "You're looking at a Mr. Rico Martinez. Better known on the street as Rico Suave."

"Rico *Suave?* That awful eighties singer?"

Drew grinned. "Nineties. And it's also the name of a young drug dealer out of Corpus Christi. We ran the kid's mug shot about a year ago when he was arrested for supplying dope to high school kids there."

"No way."

"He stood trial about six months ago, but got off on some kind of technicality. Police in Corpus botched the search of his apartment, if I remember it right."

"Are you sure it's the same guy?"

"Take a look for yourself." Drew pulled up an old issue of the *Gazette* on the computer screen. He toggled between the two pictures so Feenie could compare them. The mug shot showed a man with longish brown hair and a goatee. The guy in Feenie's photo was clean-shaven, but the eyes and nose were identical. It was either the same man or his twin brother.

"I can't believe it," she said. "What was he doing at Josh's boathouse last night?"

Drew raised his eyebrows.

"Shoot," she muttered. Now what was she going to do? Just last night, she had decided she didn't want anything more to do with Josh, and now here she was in possession of some truly damaging information about him. Not only that, but the information was potentially newsworthy, and she worked at a newspaper, for crying out loud.

She gave Drew her best pleading look. "I really appreciate you working on this. I just need one more favor from you."

He crossed his arms.

"Could you sit on this?" she asked, knowing she was asking him to go against every journalistic instinct he had. "Just for a few days? Let me check it out a little before we mention it to Grimes."

Feenie needed to gather some facts before she took her suspicions to the news editor. If she dumped this information on him now, he'd yank the story away from her and hand it to a veteran. Plus, if there was some kind of mix-up, she wanted a chance to sort it out. Maybe there was a perfectly good explanation for why a reputed drug dealer would be taking a late-night boat ride with Josh in the Gulf of Mexico.

Yeah, right. A little night diving, maybe? In the middle of a thunderstorm?

"I'll give you two days," Drew said, "as a personal favor. After that, Josh Garland's fair game."

Juarez watched her exit the newspaper building. She wore pink, head to toe, and she had a pair of sunglasses nestled between her breasts. She unhooked them from her shirt, slid them on, and unlocked the door to her piece-o'-crap-mobile.

She was going to be a problem, that was obvious. The extent of the problem remained to be seen.

Juarez shoved his key into the ignition and put his pickup in gear. She sat there a minute messing around with her lipstick, then her hair. Just when he thought she'd finished, she flipped open her cell phone.

"Shit," he mumbled. This woman was a piece of work. He'd known it two years ago when he'd watched her tuck that .22 into her pretty little shoulder. She was going to be a pain in the ass, no question about it.

She was a cute pain in the ass, though. She still had that hot little body. Just watching her got his blood going, and he remembered having the same reaction the first time he'd seen her.

Finally, the taillights glowed as she backed out of the space. Juarez pulled out behind her. Pain in the ass or not, she *knew* something. Wives and girlfriends always did. He hoped that something would lead him to Paloma. No one had seen or heard from his sister or her partner in two years, and Juarez had come to the grim conclusion that they were dead. He was too much of a realist to let himself believe otherwise. He'd been investigating Paloma's disappearance since the beginning, and all the evidence led back to Josh Garland. He'd either killed her or paid someone to do it for him.

Either way, the result was the same. Paloma was gone, and Juarez had to get up each morning knowing he could have prevented it if only he'd paid more attention. In a life filled with fuck-ups and missed opportunities, *that* fuck-up was worse than all the others put together.

The Kia rolled to a stop at an intersection, and Juarez hung back discreetly, making sure she didn't spot the tail. He probably didn't need to be so careful, but he couldn't help it. Although he wasn't a cop anymore, his training was second nature. Plus, he couldn't afford to get sloppy, not where Feenie Malone was concerned. He had to handle her in such a way that she'd give him what he wanted without even realizing she was being handled.

Juarez couldn't make things right again, he knew, but he could make them better. He could do what everyone else had failed to do so far—figure out what really happened to his sister and give his family some peace. And when he solved her case, when he found out who was responsible, he'd make sure they got what they deserved. He'd had two years to ponder just what that meant, and he had a vivid imagination.

Feenie started at the cop shop. Her first objective was to find out if local police had any record of Rico Martinez and his misdeeds. As Feenie walked across the parking lot, she dug her seldom-used press pass out of her purse and wiped the lint off it. She'd received the pass when she'd joined the *Gazette* staff a year ago, but so far, none of the funeral directors and wedding coordinators she habitually dealt with had demanded her credentials. Surely the Mayfield Police Department would be more attuned to security.

They weren't. Without even glancing at her ID, the receptionist-dispatcher directed her through a set of double doors to booking. Once inside, Feenie

stood before a chest-high counter and a glass window. She introduced herself to the balding guy sitting at a desk behind the counter and asked to check
a report. He didn't move, so she held up her media
pass.

He looked thoroughly unimpressed.

"Where's McAllister?" he wanted to know.

John McAllister regularly covered the police beat.
He subsisted on coffee, beer, and cigarettes and was
known for his crude jokes. He'd never told them in
Feenie's presence, but she'd heard them repeated in
the break room.

"I don't know," Feenie said. "I'm here to get some
background information, and I need to see some police reports."

Frowning, the cop heaved himself out of his chair
and plopped a plastic binder onto the counter.

"This here's the log. Help yourself." With that, he
returned to his desk and started rearranging papers.

Feenie opened the book. Every entry in the log
included a number, a few cryptic words, and a date
and time. It appeared to be a list of incidents arranged
in chronological order. She flipped to the back of the
book and scanned the dates. The log contained incidents only as far back as one week.

Unless Rico Martinez had been in trouble with
the Mayfield police during the past seven days, the
book was useless to her.

She cleared her throat. "Um, excuse me. Do you
know how I might look up something by person?"

The officer folded his arms over his belly and stared at her.

"You know, see if someone in particular has a record with the department?"

The cop got to his feet and shuffled over. He leaned an elbow on the counter and looked Feenie up and down. After letting his gaze linger on her breasts, he seemed to conclude that she merited further conversation.

"Who you looking for, darlin'?"

"His name's Rico Martinez. I want to see if he has a police record here."

"Rico Suave?" The cop looked surprised.

"That's right."

"Why you asking about him? He operates outta Corpus."

"Look, I just need to know if you have anything on him," she said. "I'm doing a background check."

"A background check, huh? That stuff's not just sitting around, you know. Someone's gonna have to look it up on the computer." The cop's eyes narrowed. "So, what's this about? Why didn't they send McAllister over here?"

"It's a joint assignment," she improvised. "Now, would you mind helping me?"

The cop set his jaw.

Feenie's patience was slipping. "It's a matter of public record, you know."

Clearly, Officer Beer Gut didn't care for pushy females.

"You want that information, you're gonna have to fill out a pee-ya sheet," he said.

"A pee-ya sheet?"

He reached under the counter and pulled out a piece of paper, which he slapped down in front of her.

"Public Information Act, dollface. Cripes. Who'd you say you work for? The Barbie Channel?"

Feenie fought back the urge to strangle him. She picked up the form, folded it in half, and tucked it into her purse. "Fine. I'll get this right back to you."

After spending three hours squinting at old newspaper articles on microfilm in the Mayfield library, Feenie was having a severe Tex-Mex craving. She unearthed the twenty-dollar bill she kept buried in her glove box for emergencies and headed for Rosie's.

Rosie's Tamale House had started as a truck that made the rounds at local construction sites. Word spread, and within three years of founding her business, Rosie had two trucks operating in town and a diner just across from the courthouse. Judges, lawyers, and county bureaucrats packed the place every weekday to fill up on handmade tamales and local gossip. Feenie and Cecelia joined the crowd every Friday at noon. Today was only Thursday, but Feenie desperately needed a tamale fix.

The aroma of homemade tortilla chips greeted her when she entered the restaurant. Her mouth began to water as she made her way to the back. The lunch crowd had dissipated, so her favorite booth was empty.

Feenie placed her order with the teenage waitress. Then she retrieved the PIA form from her purse. She'd never filled one out before, but it didn't look too complicated. She fished a pen out of her bag and completed all the blanks, wondering what her editor would do if he got wind of her little fact-finding mission. She might have to try a subtler way of getting information. At the moment, however, she couldn't think of one, because the waitress placed a steaming plate of tamales in front of her. Feenie took a bite, closed her eyes, and enjoyed a moment of pure bliss.

"That looks good."

Feenie's eyes flew open. A dark-haired man in a black leather jacket loomed over her table. He wore ripped jeans and scuffed black boots and about half a week's worth of beard. He looked like a member of Hell's Angels. To her horror, he slid into the seat across from her and picked up a tortilla chip.

"You should try the enchiladas," he said, casually dipping the chip into her bowl of *queso*.

Feenie managed to swallow the bite she'd been chewing. "Who are you?"

He seemed menacing, and the impression was confirmed when he met her gaze. His eyes were jet black, and his left eyebrow was bisected by a thin white scar.

Knife fight, probably.

He didn't answer, just looked her over with a slow, penetrating stare. Her throat went dry.

"You don't remember me, do you?" he asked.

"Um . . . no. Should I?"

"Marco Juarez," he said, extending a hand. "And I sure as hell remember *you*."

He remembered her? From what? His name didn't ring any bells, which seemed odd. Her world wasn't populated by biker guys, so she felt sure she'd recall meeting one.

"Feenie Malone," she said, taking his hand. It was big and warm, and she tugged hers loose almost instantly.

The waitress appeared, wearing a coquettish smile Feenie was sure hadn't been in place two minutes ago. "Hi, Marco," she said. "Get ya somethin'?"

He smiled back at the girl, and Feenie realized her mistake. He still wasn't handsome, but he no longer looked like someone from *Dog the Bounty Hunter*.

"Just a Coke," he said, winking.

That was it. Three words, and the waitress nearly swooned. When she disappeared, Feenie leaned back and folded her arms.

"That's pretty impressive, but don't you think she's a little young for you?"

He smiled again, and Feenie willed herself not to respond the way the waitress had. It was tough. The guy had great teeth, and there was something undeniably sexy about his shaggy hair.

"I still have no idea who you are." For lack of something better to do, she took a sip of her Diet Coke. The fizzy liquid cooled her throat and calmed her nerves a little while she waited for his explanation.

"I'm the police officer who came to your house a few years back. You were shooting up some statues, I think."

The day Josh had moved out. Or, more accurately, the day she'd thrown all his possessions out their bedroom window and laid waste to his trophies with her .22. She recalled the polite, well-groomed officer who'd come into her kitchen for lemonade. Add a few inches of hair and some black leather, and this was the same guy.

"You look different," she said, picking up her fork and returning her attention to the tamale plate. She didn't want to seem flustered. "I didn't know they let cops dress like that."

"I'm undercover, you could say. So, how's your husband doing? What was his name? Jeff something-or-other? Y'all work things out?"

"His name is Josh, and he's no longer my husband. So *no*, we didn't work things out."

"Sorry to hear that," he said blandly.

He didn't look sorry. In fact, he looked smug. And something about his gaze was sending warm little darts through her body. Was he flirting with her?

The waitress returned with his Coke, and Feenie asked for the bill. She wasn't really interested in rehashing the second-worst day of her life with an unkempt stranger.

"It's been nice chatting with you, Officer Juarez, but I really need to get back to work." She dug the twenty out of her purse, placed it on top of the check, and slid across the booth to leave.

"Wait," he said, slapping his hand down on hers.

His eyes bored into her, and she pulled her hand free.

"What is it you want, Officer Juarez?"

He smiled now, and the seriousness melted away. He leaned back and draped an arm over the seat. "Just thought I'd offer to give you a hand, that's all. I hear you're checking up on Rico Martinez."

She tried to mask her amazement. "Where'd you hear that?"

He shrugged. "Word gets around. I can help you get some information on him if you want."

"Why would you want to do that?"

His mouth curled up at the corner. "I feel sorry for you."

She didn't say anything, and he shrugged again.

"Suit yourself. Just thought I'd clear some of the red tape, but if you can't use the help—"

"I didn't say I couldn't use it." Not having a single inside source anywhere, she needed all the help she could get. Officer Juarez would be her first contact.

"Okay, then," he said. "Why don't you explain to me what you're looking for, and I'll see what I can find out?"

Feenie hesitated. She didn't know if she should trust this man, but she didn't have much to lose. She'd read everything she could get her hands on about Rico Martinez, but the newspaper articles about him had dried up after his drug trial six months ago, the Corpus Christi trial for which Rico—a part-time auto mechanic—had somehow managed to hire one of the most expensive defense attorneys in San Antonio. Now, wasn't *that* interesting? And if that weren't strange enough, the judge had conveniently dismissed the charges against him after the attorney had argued that there was a problem with the search of his client's apartment.

"All right," she said. "I'm trying to find out if Martinez has been in trouble recently."

He reached for another chip. "Any reason to believe he has?"

She paused again. She didn't want to give too much away and she certainly didn't want to tell the police her suspicions about her ex-husband. Not that she felt obligated to protect Josh—any trouble he was in was his own doing—but she didn't want to embarrass herself by starting unfounded rumors about a member of one of Mayfield's most prominent families. Her ex-father-in-law was a control freak, and Feenie knew he wouldn't hesitate to sue her if she messed with his family's reputation. She had to tread carefully where the Garlands were concerned—they had connections throughout the legal community in Mayfield and the entire county.

"No reason in particular," she said. "I just ran across something suspicious, and I thought I'd see if there might be a story there."

"Want to elaborate on that?"

"Not really."

He watched her, but his face was unreadable. "You know Martinez is dangerous," he said. "He's violent, he's trigger-happy, and he's not that bright. He won't like it if he finds out some eager young reporter's asking questions about him."

"Somehow I doubt Martinez subscribes to the *Gazette*," she said. Wow. Did he really think she looked young?

"He's probably not an avid reader," Officer Juarez said, "but he'd most likely find out if he was the subject of a news story with your name attached to it."

"If he's in enough trouble to merit a story, he's got bigger problems than bad publicity."

He cocked his head to the side. "Even if nothing

makes it into the paper, people talk. Martinez has connections. You sure you want to get into all this?"

She tried to look unconcerned, but she was getting a feeling of dread in the pit of her stomach. "Yes."

"Okay. I'll check out his rap sheet. See if anything recent pops up. You got any other names you want me to check out while I'm at it?"

Feenie had the vague feeling she was being pumped for information. She remembered the second man in her photo, but she didn't have an ID on him. She shook her head.

He leaned closer and rested his forearms on the table. "Anything else I can do for you?" His voice was low now, and it wasn't her imagination—Officer Juarez was definitely flirting.

Feenie's cheeks heated. "No. Thank you."

"How can I contact you?"

Any way you want.

He raised his eyebrows, and for a mortifying instant, she thought she'd said that out loud.

God, she needed a date. She dug a scrap of paper from her purse and jotted down her name and number. When was the last time she'd given a man her phone number? Bill Clinton must have been president.

"I lost my business cards," she lied. "Here's how to reach me at the *Gazette*. My home phone's underneath. I appreciate your help, Officer Juarez."

He looked mildly amused. "Just call me Juarez."

"Okay, Juarez. Thanks for the help."

• • •

Almost as soon as she settled into her cubicle the next morning, Drew walked past.

"Hey, Drew, can I talk to you a sec?" He turned, and she lowered her voice a notch. "Do you still have that print from the other night? The photo I took?"

"Sure," he said, stepping into her cube. "I haven't had a chance to work on that second guy yet. I'm not optimistic about getting an ID."

Feenie glanced around, but no one seemed to be eavesdropping. Of course, in a newsroom, you could never be sure.

"Mind if I hang on to those prints?" she asked.

"No problem. Just swing by the photo lab. Hey, and there're kolaches in the break room."

Feenie perked up immediately. With her kitchen inoperable, last night's dinner had consisted of a granola bar and a soft drink. She fetched a pastry and then stopped by Drew's desk, where he had discreetly left a manila envelope for her. She returned to her cube feeling as if her day was off to a good start.

"Malone! Get your butt in here!"

She froze, cream cheese kolache halfway to her mouth. She recognized the tone in her editor's voice but had absolutely no idea what she'd done to deserve it.

"What's he want?" Feenie hissed at Grimes's assistant, who sat just outside his office in the cubicle next to Feenie's.

"Beats me," Darla said, shrugging.

Besides answering phones and handling payroll, Darla's job included getting the early lowdown on absolutely everything that happened at the *Gazette*. For her to have no idea why Grimes wanted Feenie in his office was not a good sign.

Feenie shoved her breakfast and the envelope into the desk she shared with another part-time staffer. Squaring her shoulders, she stepped into the lion's den.

"Yes, Mr. Grimes?"

He stood behind his desk with his arms crossed. He wore his usual Men's Wearhouse tie, and his salt-and-pepper hair needed combing. An avid runner, Grimes had a perennial tan and had avoided the usual pooch most men had acquired by the age of fifty. He was attractive, actually, if you got past the presentation.

"Close the door," he snarled.

Feenie obliged and calmly took a seat in the chair across from his desk. With his demanding nature and occasional temper tantrums, Grimes reminded Feenie of her father. The best way to deal with him was to match his anger with tranquility.

"Is something wrong, sir?"

"Goddamn right something's wrong!" He reached for his breast pocket and pulled out what should have been a pack of Winstons. When he found himself holding a box of Nicorette gum, he scowled and tossed it onto the desk. "I just got off the phone with McAllister."

What did that have to do with her? Unless ... maybe McAllister's police contacts had told him about her little research project. Her editor hadn't authorized it. She hadn't worked on it on company time, but she'd used her press pass to make people think she was gathering information for the paper. Her stomach tightened, and she prayed she wasn't about to get fired.

"McAllister's down in Cozumel with some new girlfriend. He decided to extend his diving vacation another week." Grimes reached for the Nicorette gum and fumbled with the package. "I'd fire his ass if I could, but he has better connections than anyone else on this rag, and unfortunately, he's a damn good reporter."

Grimes popped a piece of gum into his mouth, and his temper seemed to subside.

"Congratulations, Malone. You've just been promoted to the police beat."

Feenie's jaw dropped. "You want me to cover *police?*"

"That's what I said, didn't I? It's only temporary, but if you make it work, I think we'll find something full-time for you when McAllister gets back. Meanwhile, I need you to double your hours so that we have something to put in the news section."

She couldn't believe her luck. Her pay was about to go up, *and* she'd have a legitimate reason to nose around the police station. "Thank you!" she gushed. "You won't be sorry!"

"I hope not." Grimes sank into his chair. "Your writing's come a long way since you started here, but you're still green when it comes to dealing with sources. Just check the log every day, write up a few crime briefs. If something big comes up, let me know ASAP so I can give it to someone else."

Ouch. "Okay, no problem."

"Just hold down the fort, all right? When McAllister gets back, we'll switch you to features or something."

"Thank you, sir," Feenie said, getting to her feet. She was already calculating what her next paycheck would look like if she doubled her hours. And a full-time salary ... the mere prospect had her grinning.

"And Malone?" he asked as she stepped toward the door. "Lose the pink suits, okay? The cops won't give you the time of day if you show up dressed like that."

Feenie looked down at her peach silk blazer and matching slacks. She still had bruises to conceal, or she never would have worn it. But not even receiving fashion advice from Grimes could dampen her mood at the moment.

She beamed a smile at him. "Thanks for the tip."

Feenie was seated on her living-room floor surrounded by bills and overdue notices when Cecelia strode into the house without knocking.

"Hey, what's up?" Feenie asked, noting the six-pack of Corona and the brown paper bag in her arms.

"What's up?" Cecelia asked. "You skip our lunch for the first time since . . . *ever*, and you're asking me what's up?" She plopped the beer onto the coffee table and handed Feenie the bag. "What's up with *you?*"

"I'm sorry about lunch, but there was nothing I could do about it. Grimes gave me an assignment, and I was so busy all day, I hardly had time to breathe."

Cecelia surveyed the room. "What's all this?"

"Just doing some bean counting. I've got bills stacked up."

Feenie plucked a beer from the cardboard holder, and Cecelia reached over and popped the top off with the bottle opener attached to her keychain.

"Thanks." Feenie took a long gulp and held the icy bottle to her neck. She'd changed into a tank top and cutoffs after work, but still she felt overheated. She was trying to cut back on electricity by laying off the AC.

Cecelia stared down at all the papers and looked worried. "What's going on, Feenie? You in some kind of financial trouble? If you need some money—"

"I don't." Feenie would die before she'd ever ask her best friend for a loan. Cecelia and Robert were having trouble in the fertility department, and they were saving money in case they ended up needing expensive treatments to get pregnant.

"I thought you were doing better ever since you got a tenant," Cecelia said.

"I am."

Cecelia pursed her lips, obviously not convinced. "How much rent does she pay?"

Feenie mumbled a number, and Cecelia's eyes bugged out.

"Feenie! That's practically nothing! You may as well let her live here for free! Please tell me you make her pay utilities."

Feenie rolled her eyes. "Give me a break, Celie. She's on a fixed income. And she's elderly. She's got all these expensive prescriptions . . ."

The look on Cecelia's face told her she thought Feenie was a total pushover.

"Just drop it, okay? I'm not having money problems."

Cecelia folded her arms over her chest. "Okay, then what gives? You've been avoiding me since the boathouse thing, you're obsessing over Josh, and, if I'm not mistaken, you've got an oak tree on top of your kitchen."

"It's a pecan."

"Would you *please* tell me what the heck's going on?"

Feenie moved some papers off the sofa and stacked them on her portable file box so there would be room to sit down. Then she opened the brown paper bag and smiled. "You brought me tamales?"

"Yes!" Cecelia exclaimed, sinking onto the couch. "Now, spill."

"There's really not much to spill. I've learned some interesting dirt about Josh, a tree fell through my roof, and my editor just gave me a promotion." Feenie pulled a foil-wrapped tamale from the bag. "Thanks for dinner, by the way. Don't you and Robert usually go out on Fridays?"

Cecelia accepted the tamale Feenie handed her. "Tax time. He's swamped with work. Could we back up a minute? What'd you find out about Josh?"

Feenie gave her an abbreviated version of the Rico Martinez story. Cecelia quirked an eyebrow when she got to the drug-dealing part but didn't appear that shocked.

"You don't look surprised," Feenie said.

Cecelia shrugged. "I guess I'm not, really. Nothing Josh does surprises me. He lied to you and cheated on you and robbed you blind. Why should I be surprised that he's associating with drug dealers?"

Feenie huffed out a breath. "Well, *I* was surprised, and I thought I knew him better than anybody."

Cecelia popped open her Corona. "No offense, Feen, but you've always had blinders on where Josh is concerned. You could've avoided your whole sorry marriage if you'd just paid more attention to his extracurricular love life while y'all were dating."

The truth stung, but Feenie forgave her for it. She and Cecelia had grown up together, and they'd always been brutally honest with each other—more like sisters than friends. Cecelia had played that role in Feenie's life ever since sixth grade, when Feenie's older sister, Rachel, been killed in a car accident. Her mother had died that day, too, on that horrible summer afternoon when Feenie's childhood had come crashing to a halt.

Cecelia, just a gawky twelve-year-old at the time, had helped Feenie muddle through the worst year of her life, and Feenie in turn felt a gut-deep loyalty toward her. Their friendship had been cemented long ago, and it would take a lot more than a few harsh words to put a crack in it now.

Plus, Cecelia was right. Josh had practically no scruples, a fact Cecelia had been pointing out for years. She'd always shown an amazing immunity to Josh's charms.

Feenie wished she could say the same about herself.

"Anyway," Feenie said now, "I'm still looking into it. My new job at the paper should help."

"Yeah, you said something about a promotion. Did they finally give you the features job?"

Feenie smiled. "Even better. I'm on the police beat. And while I'm covering that, I should be able to nose around some more about this drug thing."

Cecelia put her beer down on the coffee table, making a wet ring on top of Feenie's overdue phone bill. "Don't you think you should let this go?"

"Actually . . . no. I think Josh is up to his neck in something, and I want to know what it is."

"Let the police handle it, for heaven's sake!"

Feenie swallowed her last bite of tamale and wiped

her hands on a napkin. "What if they have no idea what he's doing?"

Cecelia shook her head. "Feenie, drop it, okay? You're obsessed. That guy has never brought you anything but misery, and this won't be any different. Plus, it's not your problem, for once. Someday Josh's luck will run out, and he'll get what's coming to him."

"Well, what if I want to help him get it? Besides, if one of Mayfield's most prominent lawyers is smuggling drugs, that's news. And I'm a reporter, remember?"

"Any shot you have of being a real reporter is going to disappear if you botch this up," Cecelia said. "Besides, you can't write an objective news article about your ex-husband. That's about the most blatant conflict of interest I've ever heard."

Feenie had thought long and hard about that very issue. "I can't write the story, but someone else can. If this story's as big as I think it is, just bringing it to the editors' attention could secure a permanent position for me on the news staff. That's something I can't ignore, Celie. I need this job."

"I still think this is a bad idea," Cecelia said. "How are you ever going to move on with your life if you spend every waking moment obsessing about your ex? Aren't you even the slightest bit interested in getting back out there and seeing what other fish are in the sea?"

The doorbell rang, and Feenie jumped up to answer it. She welcomed any excuse to cut short the Fish-in-the-Sea Speech, which she'd been hearing for nearly two years.

The excuse stood in her doorway wearing a black T-shirt, sunglasses, and jeans—no rips this time. He still hadn't shaved.

Feenie crossed her arms over her chest. "What are you doing here?"

Juarez removed the glasses. "You always this friendly?"

She didn't really know why she felt so annoyed with him. "I thought I asked you to call me."

"You did," he said. "Your phone's not working."

Great. Her phone service had been cut off. "How'd you know where I live?"

He leaned against the doorjamb and gave her a baleful look. Even slouching, he still looked formidable. It wasn't his height, exactly, because he wasn't particularly tall. But he had really broad shoulders and a certain . . . presence.

"I've been here before, remember?"

Her cheeks warmed. Why did he keep reminding her about that? He must get some twisted pleasure from making her squirm.

"Well, well," Cecelia said from behind her. "I didn't know you were expecting company, Feenie."

"I wasn't."

Cecelia thrust her hand out at Juarez. "Cecelia Strickland. I'm an old friend of Feenie's."

Juarez flashed the same smile that had turned the

waitress to mush yesterday. "Marco Juarez. I'm a new friend of Feenie's."

"I'm sorry, but have we met somewhere?" Cecelia tipped her head to the side. "You look really familiar."

"You must be remembering Feenie's domestic disturbance a couple years back. I was one of the cops who handled the call."

Cecelia's eyebrows snapped up. "Really?"

"Really."

She turned to Feenie. "Well, isn't it a small world?"

Feenie glared at Cecelia. She could tell her friend was about to make an exit.

"So nice to see you again, Marco," she said on cue. "Sorry I can't stay, Feenie, but Robert and I are going out."

"But—"

Cecelia winked at her. "I'll call you tomorrow."

Feenie gave up trying to keep Cecelia around. She'd obviously tagged Juarez as an eligible fish. Feenie watched with irritation as her best friend reversed out of the driveway. She was so busy giving Feenie a thumbs-up sign, she nearly backed into a tan SUV parked diagonally across the street. Feenie rolled her eyes.

When she turned her attention back to Juarez, he was smiling at her.

"You planning to invite me in?"

"You realize I don't even know you. For all I know, you're some serial killer posing as an undercover cop.

What makes you think I'm going to let you in my house?"

"Because I have information you want," he said simply. "And because you can trust me."

His eyes turned serious at the last part, and for some reason, her reservations faded. Maybe she was being stupid, but she *did* trust Officer Juarez. And she was very curious to know what he meant by "information."

She pulled the door back and nodded for him to come in. Not wanting him to see the mess in her living room, she led him into the dining area, where he had to duck his head to avoid the chandelier that dangled over the center of the empty space.

His gaze darted around, pausing briefly on her cleavage before meeting her eyes. "Not finished redecorating yet?"

"I'm a minimalist. What'd you find out?"

He smiled slightly. "Straight to the point. I like that."

Feenie folded her arms and tried not to look uncomfortable. It was almost dusk, and she was alone in a nearly dark room with a muscle-bound stranger. She definitely felt uncomfortable.

"Your hunch about Martinez was right on." His voice was all business now. "He's had a hard time keeping his nose clean since his trial. He was detained at the border recently, just missed getting arrested."

"What happened?"

"Some drug dogs homed in on his vehicle. It was a cargo van, apparently, full of plastic kid toys. A couple of agents turned the thing inside out, but they never found any contraband. Tried to sweat out Martinez and the truck driver, but they never got anywhere. Finally, they had to let them skate."

"So if he wasn't arrested, how'd you hear about this?"

Juarez shrugged. "I've got contacts. Certain people are keeping an eye on Martinez. They think he might be part of something big."

Whoa. Her instincts had been right, or at least not totally off the mark.

Juarez peered over her shoulder at the living room. "Do I smell tamales?"

She suppressed a sigh. She didn't really want to invite him to stay for a snack, but he'd just come through with some helpful information. There might be more where that came from if she could keep him talking.

"Cecelia brought me dinner," she said. "The tamales are gone, but I can offer you a beer."

"Sounds great."

Juarez followed her into the living room, where she picked up a longneck and handed it to him. The place was a wreck, and she felt embarrassed that her only furniture was a sofa and a table, both covered in papers. In addition to the cash assets, Josh had gotten nearly every stick of furniture in the divorce, although Lord knew why he'd wanted it, since he'd gone straight to live at his parents' guesthouse. He'd probably just taken it out of spite.

But the lack of furniture—and even air conditioning—didn't seem to faze Juarez. He took a seat on the arm of her couch. "Hey, you wouldn't happen to have a lime for this, would you?"

A lime? He didn't strike her as the high-maintenance-beer type of a guy, but she barely knew him.

"I could probably find one. Just a sec."

She headed into the kitchen, where she was confronted by a splintered tree limb. After picking her way around the broken branches, she fished a bottle opener out of a drawer and located a lime in the refrigerator. She cut a wedge and returned to Juarez, who was still sitting on the sofa arm.

"Here you go." She frowned down at his beer, which he'd already opened somehow.

"I found something else you might be interested in." He squeezed juice into his bottle and stuffed the lime in behind it. "Martinez got shot a while back. Something gang-related over in Corpus. Drive-by. Rico sustained a flesh wound, but a friend of his died in the shooting."

"I read something about that."

"Yeah, well, you may not have read the next part. It never became public. Police had some pretty good leads on who pulled the trigger. But before they could pick up the suspect, he turned up dead in an alley.

Pistol-whipped and shot. Four times, point-blank range."

Yikes. "You think Martinez killed him."

"It fits. A killing like that looks pretty personal." He furrowed his brow. "I told you in the beginning, you want to be careful here. Martinez is bad news."

"I appreciate it."

He swigged his beer and watched her, as if he was waiting for her to say something. "Want to tell me what this is about?"

"Nothing, really. It's like I said, I'm just doing some background stuff for a story."

"A story about Martinez or drug smuggling or what?" He looked intent now, and she knew she shouldn't say too much.

"Something like that."

He stood up and stepped toward her, his eyes darkening. Feenie eased away, but he didn't back off. "Let's get something straight," he said. "Information is a two-way street. I'll help you get some, but I'm gonna want something in return."

She looked up at him and felt her pulse jump. What kind of "something"?

"Um, Juarez, I think you've misunderstood—"

"Next time I see you, I want a better explanation for why you're asking all these questions. Got it?"

Feenie bit her lip. An explanation. Okay. But that still posed a problem. She'd been so excited to have a source, she hadn't counted on the quid pro quo. Grimes was right—she was totally green.

"Okay," she said, wishing her voice didn't sound so meek.

"Good." He smiled suddenly and handed her his half-empty bottle. "I'll be in touch. Thanks for the beer."

Juarez sat behind the wheel of his truck and flipped open the passport he'd snaked from her file box. *Francis Malone Garland.* He was in luck. The passport was four years old, so it would include several years of travel with her ex.

His cell phone rang.

"Juarez," he said, thumbing through the pages.

"Marco? Is that you?"

No matter how many times he explained that this was his *cell* number, his mother always acted surprised to hear his voice on the other end.

"Yeah, Mom. It's me."

The passport was filled with stamps, mostly Mexico—Cozumel, Cabo San Lucas, Puerto Vallarta. A few stamps from the Caribbean. It didn't tell him much at first glance, but he'd have to check out the dates and compare them to what he had on Garland.

"Where are you, Marco? It's almost eight."

Almost eight . . . What happened at eight?

"Kaitlin's been waiting for nearly an hour," she continued. "You promised to take her out for ice cream tonight."

Shit. How had he forgotten? He tossed the passport aside.

"I'm on my way, Mom. Tell Kaitlin I'll be right there."

"You can't take her out now! It's almost her bed-time!"

He pictured his niece waiting by the front door. He was such a jerk.

"Tomorrow's Saturday. So what if she's up a little late?"

"Marco . . ." His mother's voice had that familiar ring of disapproval.

"I'll have her back by nine. Promise. Look, I'm almost to your house." He threw his truck in gear and tried to come up with the shortest route to his mom's neighborhood. It would take him ten minutes at least, even if he sped the whole way.

"Oh, all right," she said. "I guess it wouldn't hurt—"

"See you in a minute."

He flipped shut his phone and eyed the passport sitting on his passenger seat.

Francis Malone Garland.

Feenie Malone.

His gut told him she wasn't involved, but he wanted to make sure. If he'd learned anything from being a cop, it was that you could never be too careful.

And you couldn't trust anyone. Not even pretty blond cheerleaders.

CHAPTER

5

Feenie jogged through her neighborhood, trying to ignore her throbbing muscles and the suffocating humidity. It was too late in the morning for a run, really, but the chocolate doughnut she'd picked up on the way to the office made it mandatory. She didn't regret treating herself, though. Working on a Saturday morning called for special indulgences. She'd put in three hours at the *Gazette* writing up a gas station robbery from last night, organizing her desk, and copying down names and numbers from McAllister's Rolodex. Whatever Grimes threw at her next week, she wanted to be ready.

She felt a stitch in her side and slowed her pace. It was hot. And running always seemed like such a masochistic sport. Tennis was more her thing, but Feenie had long since ceased to be a regular at the Mayfield Country Club. Running was free, and she made an effort to do that or swim several times a week. She still had ten pounds to shed from the twenty she'd acquired after her divorce, and losing the weight suddenly seemed like a priority.

It was Juarez's fault, damn him. If it weren't for him, she wouldn't be obsessing over her imperfect body. Not that he was ever going to see it.

Probably not, anyway.

God, was she really considering getting involved with him? He was practically a stranger. And he was *so* not her type. He was bossy and infuriating and entirely too . . . carnal. Any sane woman would stay away from him, which was just what Feenie intended to do after she finished using him for her story.

Or was he using her? She couldn't decide why exactly, but whenever he offered to help her, she got this needling suspicion that he was up to something. Yet another reason not to get mixed up with him any more than absolutely necessary.

Rivulets of sweat slid down her neck. Feenie distracted herself from the scorching temperature by admiring the pretty houses and waving at people out working in their yards. As she turned onto Pecan Street, the familiar buzz of a power saw filled the air. Her neighborhood was in transition, with many of the homes undergoing renovations as retirees sold out to young families. She wondered which house was getting a facelift this time.

She neared home and realized the buzzing noise was coming from her driveway. She halted in her tracks, almost getting clipped by a tan SUV pulling away from the curb.

Juarez stood outside her kitchen, wearing jeans and work boots—that was it—and holding a chain saw. Wood chips carpeted the driveway, and her dismembered pecan tree sat neatly off to one side. Leafy branches overflowed from two of her trash cans.

She was up the driveway in three strides. *"What* are you doing?"

He turned around, and heaven help her. His perfectly sculpted upper body was covered in a thin layer of sawdust and sweat.

This was why she was out jogging in the zillion-degree heat. Compared to this ideal specimen of humanity, she felt like a Gummi Bear.

"Hi," he said, dropping the saw onto the grass. He picked up the last few pieces of wood and placed them on the pile. Mrs. Hanak appeared out of nowhere with a glass of lemonade and a plate of oatmeal cookies. Juarez gave her one of his smiles and took the glass. He tipped it back and finished it in one long gulp, his Adam's apple moving as he drank. Feenie got butterflies in her stomach just watching him.

"Thank you, Mrs. Hanak. That hits the spot."

Mrs. Hanak beamed under the praise. She was wearing her best housedress.

Apparently, Juarez was an equal opportunity flirt. Feenie's temper festered.

"Well, we sure appreciate your help, Marco," Mrs. Hanak said. "That tree's just been sitting there for days now."

Mrs. Hanak shot Feenie a pointed look and shuffled back to her house with the empty glass. Juarez took a cookie from the plate he was holding and offered one to Feenie. When she just gaped at him, he shrugged and put the plate down.

She folded her arms over her sports bra, wishing she'd worn a T-shirt.

"I want to know what you think you're doing to my tree."

Juarez hooked his thumbs through his belt loops and stared at her. He looked like a Levi's ad, and she had to glance away to keep the butterflies from starting up again.

"I'm getting it out of your kitchen. Having a big hole in your house isn't great for security. Just ask Mrs. Hanak."

"Well, it's *my* house, isn't it? What gives you the right to just come over here and start sawing?"

He smirked. "Are you going to try and tell me you weren't planning to have it removed? I just did you a favor."

Okay, it was a favor. It had certainly saved her the trouble and expense of hiring someone. But still . . .

it took a lot of nerve to show up at someone's house with power tools.

He stepped close to her, and she smelled wood chips and a hint of sweat. The butterflies were back.

"Want to know something?" he asked in a low voice.

"Huh?"

"Your cheeks get red when you're pissed off. It's pretty hot." He reached over and tucked a curl behind her ear, and she flinched. "Why are you always so skittish around me?"

The smug look on his face told her he knew exactly why she was so skittish around him. Her eyes dropped to his chest, and she felt her throat constricting.

"I'm not. I just—"

He bent his head down and kissed her. Very lightly, just a brush of the lips. Every muscle in her body tensed.

"Relax," he muttered.

"I don't want to relax."

"Liar."

He wrapped his hand around her neck and tipped her head back. The next kiss was deep and seductive. He tasted wonderful, all tart and sugary, and she felt the heat coming off him in waves. He was standing close, but he touched her only with his mouth and his fingertips. She was kissing him back, she realized, and jerked away.

"Why did you do that?" she squeaked.

"You wanted me to."

He stepped back from her, and she felt instantly chilly, which didn't make sense, because it was hot as Hades, and she'd just been running. She was standing in her driveway in her workout clothes, for God's sake.

"I don't want you to do it again," she said, although at the moment, she couldn't think of one good reason why they shouldn't go inside and jump straight into bed.

He shrugged and picked up his saw. "Okay, I won't. Hey, you don't have a fireplace, do you?"

She blinked at him. "A fireplace?"

"Yeah, I thought I'd haul this wood off for you. If you don't have any use for it."

He'd just kissed her stupid in the middle of her driveway, and now they were talking about firewood?

"No, I don't have a fireplace."

"Great," he said. "Move so I can back my truck in."

She stepped aside.

He reached into his pocket and pulled out a business card. "And here's the number for a friend of mine. He does remodeling, and he's cheap. Drop my name, and he'll get your kitchen back together in no time."

She nodded.

"Until then, I'll put a tarp over the hole. It's not safe to leave it like this." He winked at her. "Pretty woman like you should be more careful."

• • • •

After loading his truck, Juarez slipped into the house. He heard the shower running upstairs as he walked into the living room and spotted the portable file box sitting in a corner. He quickly replaced her passport in the folder where she kept it and eased out the front door.

So far, everything about her checked out. She'd done plenty of traveling with her husband down in Mexico and the Caribbean, but it looked like vacation stuff. She hadn't been out of the country in two years, since her divorce, he guessed.

It looked as if she wasn't part of Garland's business dealings, but he still couldn't be sure. Based on everything he'd dug up about her so far, she was a model citizen. Sure, she had a less than stellar credit rating, but who didn't these days? Other than some sloppy bill-paying habits, she seemed to be a Girl Scout.

But then again, that might be a front. He needed to get closer to her.

Juarez started his truck and glanced at the upstairs window. This woman was smarter than he'd expected. And she was reluctant to trust him, which meant her instincts were good, too. If she kept probing, it wouldn't take her long to put all the pieces together.

He intended to be around when she did.

The last thing he needed was a reporter going public with information about Garland. He felt fairly sure he could keep a lid on any news stories Feenie might write, but she wasn't his only concern. Reporters were like buzzards—they attracted each other to a carcass. That meant the clock was ticking on his covert investigation.

The information he had from Paloma was sketchy, but he'd managed to fill in many of the gaps since her disappearance. Feenie Malone might be able to fill in the rest. Involved or not, she had access to key information. And he needed to get his hands on it before Garland got wind of what she was up to.

If he didn't, two years of painstaking work would be down the drain. He wasn't about to let that happen.

Feenie was jarred awake by the persistent hum of her cell phone. She groped around on her bedside table until she found the damn thing and mumbled hello.

"You asleep?" someone asked.

She pulled the phone away from her ear and checked the number. She didn't recognize it or the voice.

"Who is this?"

"Juarez. Are you really in bed? It's barely ten."

Feenie looked at the clock. "It's ten-fifteen, and I had a long day." A long week was more like it. "What do you want?"

Ever since the kiss in her driveway Saturday, she'd been irritated with him. The encounter had given him the upper hand, and she didn't like that. She needed to get things between them on a more professional footing.

"I need to see you. Meet me at Rosie's in fifteen minutes."

She paused, still clearing the cobwebs in her brain. He wanted her to meet him *now?*

"It's the middle of the night," she said. God, she was exhausted. The police beat was tougher than she'd ever imagined. She'd been up at the crack of dawn covering a traffic fatality in the next county. And now Juarez was interrupting her much-needed rest. "Can't it wait 'til morning?"

"Fifteen minutes," he repeated.

"I don't even think they're open this late."

"You'll be glad you came. Trust me."

He clicked off.

She entered the restaurant wearing a Texas Rangers jersey and a sullen expression. The shirt fit nice and snug, and her curls tumbled haphazardly around her face. He smiled at her, and for once it wasn't fake.

"This better be good," she said, sliding into the booth. She crossed her arms and scowled at him.

"You know, the last time I saw you looking like that, you were holding a .22," he said.

"Cut the crap, okay? I'm not in the mood."

Rosie appeared at their table and nodded at him.

"Hola, Marquito. Cómo andas?"

In rapid Spanish, he greeted Rosie and ordered some enchiladas. When Rosie left, Feenie seemed to have softened up somewhat.

"I didn't know you knew Rosie," she said.

Juarez shrugged. "Everybody knows Rosie."

"In your circles, maybe. I've been coming here for ages, and she won't give me the time of day."

"She doesn't know a lot of English," he pointed out.

"Our features editor has been trying to do a story on her for years. She won't talk to him. He even offered to interview her in Spanish."

"Yeah? What's his name?"

Feenie frowned. "Paul Gutterson."

"There's the problem."

She rolled her eyes and leaned her forearms on the table. "Get to the point, *Marquito*. Why am I here?"

"I've got something for you," he said.

She raised an eyebrow.

"Martinez is in trouble again."

Rosie returned to the table and slid the enchiladas in front of them. Two Coronas came next. Feenie looked surprised but immediately reached for the beer.

"What kind of trouble?" she asked when they were alone again.

"He's dead."

Juarez dug into his enchilada plate, savoring the greasy strands of cheese. He washed the first few bites down with a swig of beer, all the while gauging Feenie's reaction.

Total bewilderment.

"But . . . but how?" she sputtered.

"Gunshot. Turned up in a parking garage."

"When did this happen?"

Juarez leaned back in his seat and watched her.

Her skin had paled, and her usual snotty attitude had vanished. She was either an Oscar-worthy actress, or she had no prior knowledge of what he'd just told her.

The knot in his stomach loosened.

"Last night," he said.

"But I was at the police station just this afternoon. I didn't hear anything about it."

"Murder happened in Corpus, so it's not in the log. And the cops around here who know about it would never tell you."

"Well, why not?" she demanded. "I've been making inquiries about him for days."

"No one likes you."

She jerked her head back, apparently shocked by this revelation. "No one *likes* me? Why the heck not?"

"They think you're a lightweight. They don't want to deal with you."

"What, just because I have breasts, no one takes me seriously? I'm not John freaking McAllister, so they decide to freeze me out? I'm trying to do a job here, dammit!"

Her cheeks were flushed now, and he tried not to smile. He liked her when she was fired up like this, but he wasn't buying the diligent reporter act for a minute. He was ninety-nine-percent certain her questions about Martinez went beyond journalistic curiosity. She had some other agenda, and he needed to know what it was.

"It's not the breasts," he said, eyeing them appreciatively. "If anything, they should help. It's this attitude you've got going, like you're better than everyone. You're going to have to bring it down a notch. And you're going to have to prove yourself to these people."

She glared at him. "How am I supposed to do that if everyone's keeping things from me?"

"I'm here, aren't I? Keeping you in the loop, just like I promised."

She seemed placated by this, and she leaned back against the booth. "Okay, so what's the rest of it? Do you know who killed him?"

"I've got a hunch."

"And?"

"And I want some answers first." He leaned forward now and pinned her with a look. "I want to know why a nice woman like you is so interested in a piece of garbage like Martinez."

Her chest heaved up and down, and he could tell she was rattled. Her gaze darted around the room, which was nearly empty, and settled on him again. She bit her lip.

"Don't even think about lying to me," he said, forking another bite of enchilada. "I can tell when you're doing it."

"How do I know I can trust you?"

He looked her in the eye, ignoring the nagging voice in his head telling him he was a manipulative bastard. "You just can."

She took a deep breath. "Okay. But I don't have

any proof of anything, really. Just some ideas. So I don't want all this getting back to me if it turns out not to be true."

"If what turns out not to be true?"

She hesitated, and he did his best to look trustworthy.

"Rico Martinez," she said. "The guy they call Rico Suave, right?"

He nodded.

"Well, I think he might have been involved with my ex-husband. I think they might have had some sort of business together."

He waited for the rest.

"You see, I went to visit Josh." She paused and bit her lip. "It was a social call, really. Nothing important. Anyway, when I got to his house—he lives at the guesthouse on his parents' estate—when I got there, he had company. I sort of got a glimpse of one of the guys, and I think it was Martinez."

"So what makes you think they were in business together? Maybe they were friends."

Feenie rolled her eyes. "Yeah, right. Josh Garland doesn't befriend people like Martinez. He won't even own a dog that doesn't have a pedigree."

"Do you have a pedigree?"

Her lips pressed together, and he could tell he'd struck a nerve. "No. He made an exception for me. Don't ask me why."

"I think I can guess."

"Hey, screw you! It's not like I was his whore, for

God's sake! We were *married* for five years. And I had no idea what a sleazebag he was until recently."

Juarez highly doubted that. In his experience, a wife was usually the world's best expert on her husband's shortcomings. But he let it slide.

So far, Feenie was coming off nice and innocent. He felt extremely relieved, and that bothered him. He'd never developed a soft spot for a woman he was investigating before, and he didn't want to start with a *gringa* who had ties to the people who killed Paloma.

Juarez returned to the subject at hand. "So what makes you think this business was something illegal?"

Feenie looked down at her plate. "Because they went out on a boat together that night in a driving rainstorm. Two boats, actually. And the only reason I can come up with is some sort of smuggling operation." She looked up at him, all wide blue eyes again. "What would you think?"

Juarez didn't answer right away. He didn't want to tell her too much, but she obviously expected him to share an opinion.

"I'd think something was up," he said finally. "Maybe smuggling, like you said."

She shook her head. "And now with Martinez dead, I don't know what to think."

"I do," Juarez said. "I think you need to watch your back."

Feenie stopped by the newsroom on her way home to retrieve the police scanner she'd left on her desk.

Maybe if she'd had it with her earlier, she would have picked up on some of the chatter about Martinez. She wouldn't make the same mistake again. If the Mayfield cops were going to shut her out, she'd just have to work twice as hard to gather information.

She drove home, listening to the scanner at low volume. Even without knowing all the radio codes, she could tell just by the relaxed tones of the voices that not much was going on.

Another idyllic spring night on the Gulf Coast. No murder. No mayhem. No gang wars.

At least, not yet.

Despite the warm breeze, Feenie felt a chill as she walked up her sidewalk, mentally replaying her conversation with Juarez.

Martinez was dead. Possibly a professional hit. Who had wanted to get rid of him? And why? If he really was involved in the drug trade—and all evidence pointed to that—then the possibilities were endless. But the timing bothered her. He'd been associating with low lifes and criminals for years now, but he'd been murdered just days after she'd started asking questions about him.

Had *she* had gotten him killed? It seemed like a remote possibility, but if that's what had happened, she was in trouble. It would mean her questions were hitting too close to home, making someone really edgy.

And that someone must have contacts within the

police department who had told him Martinez was the subject of a reporter's questions.

Feenie mounted her front steps and noticed her porch light was out. She fumbled with her keychain in the dark until she located her house key. She tried to shove it into the lock, and the door swung open.

It hadn't been closed.

The back of Feenie's neck prickled. Had she forgotten to lock up? She'd been half-asleep when she'd left, and she couldn't remember for sure. She hesitated at the threshold, trying to decide what to do. Maybe she should call the police.

But maybe this was nothing. Her weather stripping was loose, so maybe she'd simply forgotten to lock up, and the wind had blown open her door. She glanced at the purse in her hand, where she'd stuffed the scanner. Nothing about her neighborhood had come over the police radio.

Feenie stepped into the house and darted her gaze around the foyer. The wall sconces flanking her doorway filled the room with a warm glow. Her Nikes sat at the base of the staircase, just where she'd left them.

Thud.

She glanced at the ceiling and dropped her purse. Someone was upstairs!

Shrieking, she dashed out the door.

Someone grabbed her arm. She screamed and clawed at the person until she got a look at his face.

"What's going on?" Juarez demanded.

"Someone's upstairs!"

He seized her shoulders and pushed her against the siding.

"Stay here," he said. "Keep your back against the wall, and don't move until I get back."

"But what—"

"Shut *up!*" He pulled a gun from the back of his jeans. "And stay right here."

He rushed into the house, leaving her terrified and confused.

Who was inside? And what was Juarez doing here? He'd just appeared out of nowhere, as if . . . as if he'd already been here when she arrived. But why would he be at her house?

She couldn't think straight. Her body quivered, and her heart raced. Keeping her back to the wall, she shuffled sideways along the front porch until she was near the window just beneath her bedroom. The thud had sounded as if it came from that direction. Someone had been in her bedroom. What if she'd come home and gone upstairs and—

"I told you to stay put."

Feenie jumped back, startled, as Juarez rounded the corner of the house. "Where did you come from? I thought you were inside!"

"I was checking the perimeter," he said, climbing the front steps. He stopped beside her front door, still holding his gun at his side. "House is clear."

"But I heard someone upstairs!"

"No one's there now. Did you leave a window open in your guest room?"

"No."

"Then that's how they left."

He motioned for her to follow him inside, and she did. Her gaze immediately veered up toward the ceiling. "Are you sure there's no one—"

"Yes." He took her wrist and pulled her through the dining area, into the brightly lit living room. Her stomach plummeted.

"Oh, my God," she murmured, looking around. The sofa had been slashed to ribbons, stuffing thrown everywhere. Her TV was smashed. The coffee table lay on its side, its little drawers yanked out. Coasters and magazines littered the floor.

"Look carefully," he ordered. "Do you notice anything missing?"

"Missing?"

"Whoever was here was obviously looking for something. Do you have any idea what it was?"

"No." She covered her mouth with her hand. Her couch was destroyed, her TV ruined. She righted the coffee table and was relieved to see the legs still intact. Amid the debris carpeting the floor, she recognized the shards from the coffee mug she'd been using earlier.

She reached out and gripped Juarez's arm. "What if someone's still here?"

"I told you, I checked everything. Your house is practically empty, so there aren't many places to hide. Was anything taken that you can tell?"

"Nothing's missing in here," she said. "At least, nothing I can see."

He led her into the kitchen. It had been given the same ruthless treatment—drawers and cabinets emptied, boxes and bottles from her pantry dumped on the floor. They'd even poured out her canisters.

Feenie knelt beside a heap of sugar and ran her finger through it. "What on earth were they looking for?"

Juarez watched her, his eyes bright with interest.

"Think, Feenie. Do you have anything here that relates to the story you're writing? Notes? Tapes? Photographs, maybe?"

All her notes on Martinez, plus the photographs she'd taken, were in a locked drawer at work. "I don't keep that stuff here," she said. "I have personal files in a box upstairs—"

She heard a noise outside.

"Did you hear that?" she asked. She stood up and peered out the breakfast-room window. A shadow moved across the back patio. "Someone's out there."

"Get away from the window," Juarez said, flipping off the light.

Moonlight illuminated the backyard. Feenie's gaze swept over the pool, the patio, and the patch of grass near the back fence. Something moved by the deck chair.

"Over there!" she said, pointing.

"Where? I don't see anything."

"There! By the chair!" She stepped toward the back door, but Juarez yanked her back.

"Don't fucking move." He shoved her against the wall. "I'll check it out."

His words reverberated through her brain as she watched him reach for the doorknob. That voice, those arms . . .

Don't fucking move.

CHAPTER
6

Feenie watched him, stunned, as he stepped outside with his gun poised. A figure moved toward him.

"Mrs. Hanak!" Feenie rushed forward. Her tenant stood at the base of the back steps in her bathrobe. "What are you doing here?"

Mrs. Hanak frowned, and Juarez lowered his weapon.

"I heard someone holler, and I came to see what was going on," she said.

Feenie turned on the porch light and noticed the pearl-handled grip sticking out of Mrs. Hanak's pocket.

"I didn't know you had a gun!" Feenie exclaimed.

Mrs. Hanak's frown deepened. "Well, of course I

do. Old lady like me livin' alone? I've gotta protect myself, don't I?"

"Tell me what you heard, ma'am," Juarez said in his cop voice.

Mrs. Hanak paused for a moment, dutifully considering her answer. "Well, at first it was just your typical racket. Like a possum in the trash can or some such. I didn't think much of it until I heard the scream. That's when I got out my pistol here." She patted the pocket of her robe. "I looked out the window and saw Feenie's car, so I thought she might be in trouble."

So you came to rescue me? Are you insane? Feenie gaped at her elderly tenant. The woman had cataracts and probably weighed less than a hundred pounds.

"Did you see anyone in the yard? Or the house?" Juarez asked.

"Not besides y'all." She turned to Feenie. "What was all the noise? Should I call the police?"

Feenie started to say something, but Juarez cut her off.

"No need, ma'am. It was just some raccoons in Feenie's kitchen. Looks like they got through the tarp and helped themselves to some food from her pantry."

Mrs. Hanak wagged a bony finger at Feenie. "Now, didn't I tell you about getting this roof fixed? No tellin' what kinda vermin you'll have in your house next."

Feenie bit her tongue to keep from screaming.

"Thanks for your concern, Mrs. Hanak," Juarez said, all charm. "We'll take care of it from here. You can go back to bed now."

When she was gone, Feenie unleashed.

"You!" She jabbed a finger at his chest. "*You're* the son of a bitch who attacked me! I still have bruises on my back because of you!"

Juarez took her elbow and steered her toward the house.

"Keep your voice down, would you? She's gonna hear you."

He pushed her into the kitchen and pulled the door shut. Feenie shook his hand off and stepped backward.

"Don't touch me! You lied to me!"

Juarez crossed his arms over his chest. "How's that?"

"*How's that?* How about telling me you wanted to help me because you felt sorry for me?" A disturbing thought occurred to her, and she backed up against the counter. "God, you're *involved* in this, aren't you? You were with them that night. What, did you get me to meet you at Rosie's so someone could ransack my house?"

"What? No—"

"Or did *you* do it? While I was at the office? I'm calling the police!" Feenie scrambled for the living room, but Juarez clamped a hand around her arm.

"Wait a minute," he growled.

She stared up at his black eyes. His grip was like iron, and she remembered the way he'd pinned her under his knee at the boathouse. She was no match for him.

"Looks like I don't have a choice," she said icily. Her heart hammered in her chest, but she didn't want him to know she was terrified.

Juarez looked down and seemed to realize he was hurting her. He let go of her arm and stepped back, shoving his hands into his pockets as if he couldn't trust himself not to manhandle her. "Calm down, okay? I didn't do this to your house."

"Then where did you come from just now?" she demanded. "You've been following me, haven't you?"

"Yes, and you should be thanking me. Someone needs to look out for you, babe. You're in a world of trouble, and you don't even know it."

"Ha! You think I'd trust *you* after you attacked me? I don't want you near me. Get out of my house!"

He rolled his eyes. "I'm not going to hurt you. Shit. I just need to explain some things."

Feenie glanced at her watch. "You have exactly two minutes to explain why you brutalized me the other night and lied to me the very next day. If I don't like what I hear, I'm calling the chief of police. I'm sure he'll be happy to know that one of his officers beats up civilians and hangs out with drug dealers in his spare time."

Juarez sneered. "You still don't have a clue, do you? You know, for a reporter, you're not very thorough."

"What?"

"I'm not a cop anymore, Feenie. I'm a PI."

Her mouth fell open. "You're what?"

"A private investigator. I've been looking into Rico Martinez for nearly two years now, and what I've learned isn't good. It involves dope smuggling and crooked cops and your pretty-boy ex-husband."

Her stomach clenched, and she tried to get her mind around everything he'd just said.

"But why didn't you tell me? And why did you attack me at the boathouse?"

"Christ!" His gaze shot up to the ceiling. "That was an accident, okay? I had no idea you'd be there. And then there you were, taking pictures and making a scene. You could have gotten yourself killed, do you realize that? I had to shut you up."

"So you threw me in the bay? Gee, thanks."

He smirked. "You said you could swim."

She stepped toward him and jabbed a finger at his chest again. "You think this is funny? I've been having nightmares about rapists and murderers. I thought you wanted to kill me!"

He sighed heavily and closed his hand around hers, neutralizing the next jab. "It's occurred to me. You're a pain in the ass, you know that?"

She sucked in a breath, outraged. A dozen retorts tumbled into her mind, but none of them seemed scathing enough.

"Come here," he said irritably, and jerked her closer. Then he kissed her.

She wanted to kick him, or punch him, or send his testicles into his throat.

But instead she kissed him right back.

Big mistake. He backed her up against the counter and went after her with a vengeance. Heat spread through her, and she was plastered there, feeling every ridge of his body as he kissed her until she was dizzy.

She couldn't let go. She knew she needed to, but everything about him felt good and strong and male, and she whimpered at the pleasure of it. *God,* he tasted good. He smelled good. If she ever got into bed with him, she was going to explode. She slipped her hands into the pockets of his jeans and pulled him even closer.

"Your neighbor was right about you," he muttered against her throat.

Her neighbor . . . what?

"You're a little firecracker ready to go off."

She kissed him to shut him up and felt his stubble against her chin. She was going to have chafed skin tomorrow, and she was looking forward to it. He lifted her arms, and soon her Rangers jersey was over her head and drifting to the floor. His gaze dropped to her lacy white bra, and then his mouth was on her, hot and wet through the lace, and it was all she could do just to breathe. She slid her hands down his back and felt something . . . cold and steely?

His gun.

She jerked away and looked at him. Really looked at him. His eyes were black with desire. And something else.

"We can't do this," she said breathlessly.

His eyes narrowed. "Why not?"

Because she didn't even know him. He wasn't a cop. Or a boyfriend. Or even a friend she could trust. He was just some random guy who claimed to be a private investigator and who had misled her. And for what, exactly? She still didn't really understand it.

"Because I don't want to," she said.

His brows arched, and she realized how transparent she was.

"This isn't *right!* I don't even know you. You lied to me." Her words came out jumbled, but it was the best she could do under the circumstances.

He stepped back and crossed his arms, giving her another heated look. But it wasn't passionate heat anymore—more like a mixture of frustration and anger. "You're one to talk about honesty, you know that? An hour ago, you told me you were visiting Garland's boathouse on a 'social call.' But I was there, remember? You were sneaking around dressed like a ninja. Want to explain that?"

Feenie chewed her lip. It was painfully obvious that neither one of them knew squat about the other. Yet they were about to get naked in her kitchen! She needed to put some space between them before she lost her head again. Brushing past him, she scooped her shirt off the floor and slipped it over her head. That helped, but only until she saw that it was inside-out. She was too embarrassed to take it off again, so she pretended not to notice.

She stepped across the room and retrieved a plastic

water bottle that had rolled under the breakfast table. She twisted the top off and took a swig, then held it out. "Want some?"

"No." He eyed her inside-out shirt and looked annoyed. "I want an explanation. What were you *really* doing the other night?"

She took a deep breath to steady her nerves. "Okay. It's a long story."

"Fine. Let's hear it."

"See, it all goes back to this anniversary present. For our first anniversary, Josh gave me a thirty-six-foot Grady-White with twin Yamaha engines."

His eyes widened. "Shit, do you know how much a boat like that costs?"

"Yes, as a matter of fact. That's why this is important. If you'd just listen—"

"You have my undivided attention."

"Good. The boat was called *Feenie's Dream*. We used to take her out into the Gulf for day trips, spend the night in Las Brisas occasionally. I loved that boat. Josh told me he lost her in a poker game right before our divorce. I was naive enough to believe him."

Juarez looked skeptical, but he didn't say anything.

"Anyway, last week, I was out covering a story over near Fisherman's Grill, when Josh pulled up with some girl in the Grady-White. When I confronted him about it, he acted like I was crazy, like it wasn't the same boat. So I went to get proof."

"You went to Garland's to see a boat." He didn't

sound convinced. "You mean you never got a tip from Martinez?"

Feenie frowned. "I never knew anything about Martinez until the other day."

He watched her for a few moments, and she tried not to squirm. She knew he was trying to figure out if she was lying.

"A couple weeks ago, I got information that Martinez and Garland weren't getting along," he told her. "They were arguing about money. Martinez wanted more, and Garland didn't want to give it to him. Martinez threatened to tip off the media about his illegal import/export business if he didn't pay up. I figured Martinez picked you because you work for the *Gazette*, and you'd also have an axe to grind with your ex-husband."

"Why go to the media?" she asked. "Why wouldn't he tip off the police?"

She saw his jaw tighten and remembered what he'd said earlier about crooked cops.

"So," she said, putting it together, "Martinez threatened to expose Josh to the press—which he would hate because he's been running for mayor of this town practically since he was born—and Josh didn't like being bullied."

The only thing Josh hated more than bad publicity was ultimatums.

"Where'd you get this tip?" she asked.

"I let myself into Martinez's apartment and

planted a bug. He was stupid enough to brag about blackmailing Garland to one of his buddies."

She was pretty sure private investigators weren't allowed to just break into people's homes and hide listening devices, but she didn't comment. "Who do you work for, anyway?" she asked instead.

"Gulf Shores Investigations."

"No, I mean who hired you?"

She watched his eyes, and there it was again—that flicker of evasiveness that had been bothering her since he'd approached her at Rosie's.

"Garland's made some enemies over the years," he said. "Probably even killed a few. I work for one of the victims' family."

She couldn't stand to think of Josh tearing families apart. Feenie knew what grief felt like, and she didn't wish it on anyone, no matter what their loved one might have done.

"So, you think Josh had Martinez killed?"

Juarez cocked his head to the side. "Either that, or he did it himself."

"That doesn't sound like Josh to me." Feenie surveyed the ransacked kitchen. "Trashing my house isn't his style, either. He doesn't like to get his hands dirty. And he wouldn't have wanted to risk getting caught."

Juarez shrugged. "You'd be surprised what people will do when they're cornered. Or maybe he just did this to scare you."

Now, *that* sounded like Josh. Terrorizing her definitely would have appealed to him. He liked to play games with people.

But what if this wasn't just a scare tactic, and Josh had someone dangerous on his payroll?

"You think maybe whoever killed Martinez is after me now?" she asked. "Maybe he wants to see if I know anything?"

The grave expression on Juarez's face was a yes.

She was beginning to feel sick, like a giant hand was squeezing her stomach. She put the water bottle on the counter and closed her eyes to think.

"You shouldn't stay here tonight," Juarez said, voicing her thoughts.

"I know. I'm just trying to decide where to go." Why did he have to sound concerned? And why did she want to believe it was genuine?

"Crash at my place, if you want. It's small, but I promise not to hog the covers."

She glared at him. "I don't think that's a good idea, do you?"

He gave her a slow, penetrating look, and she felt her hormones kicking in again. She needed to get away from him before her brain shut down completely.

"I'd better stay with Celie."

Sunday afternoon, Feenie was kneeling on her bathroom floor, cleaning up broken glass, when the front door creaked open. She dropped her hand broom and reached for her cell phone.

"Yoo-hoo!" Cecelia's voice floated up from the foyer. "Special delivery!"

Feenie tucked the phone back into her pocket, alongside the vial of Mace she'd been carrying around nonstop for the past two days. Moments later, Cecelia breezed into the bathroom, loaded down with shopping bags.

"Hey there," Feenie said, sinking down onto the side of the tub for a break. She felt whipped. She'd been cleaning all weekend, stopping only for a few fitful nights of sleep in Cecelia's guest room. "I thought you had a party to go to."

Cecelia rolled her eyes. "Just some business thing of Robert's. We called in sick. Whew, it smells like a perfume counter in here!"

"Tell me about it." Feenie's head was pounding from being surrounded by Bijan fumes for the past hour.

Feenie had tackled her bedroom and bathroom last, because merely standing in the doorway made her feel violated. Her sheets and mattress had been slashed, her closet torn apart, and the contents of her dresser drawers strewn everywhere. She'd rehung and refolded everything she could salvage, with the exception of her underwear. The idea of some stranger combing through it gave her the willies, so she'd pitched it all in the trash and decided to treat herself to a trip to the mall. At least one of her credit cards wasn't maxed out.

Her bathroom had been left in shambles, too—

cabinets rifled, drawers emptied, glass bottles shattered on the floor.

Feenie eyed the shards, wondering if she'd ever walk barefoot again in her own house.

"What's that?" she asked Cecelia, nodding at the shopping bags.

Cecelia smiled brightly. "Oh, you know. Just some odds and ends." She pulled out a brand-new set of sheets, butter-cream yellow, the same color as Feenie's bedroom.

"You didn't need to do that, Celie."

"I know. But I wanted to. I've got a comforter over there by the door."

"Hey." Robert appeared in the doorway in his typical weekend attire of Dockers and a golf shirt. "You guys wanna give me a hand with the mattress?"

"What mattress?" Feenie asked.

"We got you a mattress," Cecelia said. "You said your box springs were okay, so we didn't bother with that."

Feenie's eyes started to sting as she picked her way across the floor. "Y'all shouldn't have done that. I can't pay you back right now—"

"Hush!" Cecelia said, enveloping her in a hug. "What are friends for? I can't have you in my guest room forever, can I? We're trying to make a baby. We need privacy for our wild and crazy sex life!"

Feenie rubbed her runny nose on the back of her hand and smiled as Robert blushed.

"God, Celie," he muttered, sending her a look.

"Well, it's true!"

He adjusted his wire-rimmed glasses and cleared his throat. "So, anyway, about that mattress?"

"Thanks," Feenie managed. "I really appreciate it."

"Forget about it," Cecelia said. "It's no big deal."

Together they muscled the queen-size mattress up the stairs and move the ruined one into the spare bedroom. Feenie's television and the sofa were beyond repair, and she asked Robert to carry the TV out to her garbage can. The next big trash pickup was six weeks away, so Feenie and Cecelia simply shoved the tattered sofa against the wall. It would have to wait.

Then Cecelia unpacked the new linens and helped Feenie make the bed. The fluffy cotton comforter was printed with a soothing pattern of pale yellow roses. As Feenie tucked in the edges of the top sheet, her gaze landed on something peeking out from under the bed. It was her favorite photograph, a picture of her mother and Rachel taken the year before they died. The snapshot was bent at the corner from where someone had stepped on it.

A lump lodged in Feenie's throat. She picked up the picture from the floor and gingerly wiped it with the tail of her shirt before sliding it into the drawer of her nightstand.

"I'm so sorry this happened," Cecelia said quietly.

Feenie swallowed her anger. "Thanks for coming over. You and Robert have been a big help."

"What did the police say?"

"I still haven't made it over there. I'll go right after y'all leave." This was a fib, but she couldn't tell Cecelia what was really going on. In reality, Feenie had no plans to go to the cops, because Juarez had told her they might somehow be involved. Instead of bringing in official police, Juarez had stopped by Saturday morning with a fingerprinting kit. He'd lifted some latent prints from her doors and windowsills—prints that most likely belonged to Feenie—and he'd also carefully photographed a shoeprint from one of her back flower beds. He'd been very diligent about collecting evidence, but he didn't seem at all optimistic it would lead anywhere. Feenie wasn't optimistic either.

Late that night, Feenie lay beneath her new bedspread and color-coordinated sheets. She was tired to her bones, but still she couldn't sleep. Every sound outside had her sitting up in bed and reaching for her .22. It wasn't much in terms of firepower, but her aim was dead-on, thanks to a father who was a card-carrying member of the NRA. She couldn't stop feeling jumpy, though. When she wasn't thinking about her home being invaded again, she was thinking about the mess she'd gotten herself into.

Juarez was right: she was in a world of trouble, and it wasn't going away. And although Juarez had offered to help, Feenie wasn't sure about his motives. Looking back on it, he'd been pumping her for information all along. Despite whatever attraction they had between them, she was just a piece of the puzzle to him. His client must be paying big bucks, because he seemed willing to go to great lengths to solve the case. She couldn't trust him.

As much as she wanted to.

Why was she so gullible when it came to attractive men? They always used her for their own ends, and she always fell for it. Josh had used her to keep his house and to be his arm candy at social events throughout their marriage. Juarez had used her to further his investigation. Feenie was tired of being used.

She wouldn't let it happen again. In fact, it was time to turn the tables. She needed to come up with a strategy.

The doorbell rang, and Feenie bolted upright. She reached for her gun and glanced at the clock. It was after ten. She kicked back the covers and tiptoed to the window, clutching her .22 in both hands. She peered through a narrow gap in the curtains and saw a black pickup parked in front of her house.

"Goddamn him," she muttered, grabbing her terry robe off the end of the bed. Ten seconds later, she was staring through her peephole at a surly looking man in a black bomber jacket.

Feenie swung open the door. "Kind of late for a visit, don't you think?"

Juarez looked her up and down, his gaze pausing briefly on the front of her robe. Then he glanced behind her and frowned. "That thing loaded?" he asked, brushing past her into the house.

"Yes." She closed the door, turned her back on it, and crossed her arms.

She'd leaned her gun against the corner by the stairs. Juarez picked it up, pointed it toward the floor, and checked the chamber.

She blew out an annoyed sigh. "I hope you have a good reason for waking me up."

He replaced the .22 against the wall and shrugged. "Didn't expect to see your car here. I thought you were staying at Cecelia's."

His gaze dropped to her chest again, and she glanced down. A scrap of pink lace was peeking up from the terry cloth. She adjusted the robe and shook her curls out of her face. "I came home to get my house back in order."

He shoved his hands into his pockets. "You really think that's a good idea?"

Instead of answering, she tipped her head to the side. "Don't you have some fleabag motels to stake out or something?"

"No."

"Hmm. Well, it's been a long day, and I'd really like to get back to bed, if you don't mind."

He raised an eyebrow suggestively, and a tingle ran down her spine.

"Please? I've been cleaning all weekend, and I'm wiped out."

He strolled casually into the darkened dining room, as if she hadn't just asked him to leave. "Buddy of mine ran those prints through AFIS. No hits."

He peered into the living area, where she'd left the overhead light on, and frowned at the mutilated sofa. "You need some new furniture."

"I'll get right on that." She trailed him into the dining room. "What's AFIS?"

He turned around, and she realized she'd made a tactical error.

"Fingerprint database," he said, closing in on her.

She backed up a step, bumping into the wall beside the doorjamb. His face was shadowy, but for once she knew exactly what he was thinking.

He slid his finger down the collar of her robe. "Why're you so anxious to get rid of me?" His voice sounded eerily quiet. His knuckle brushed her skin, and an electrical current charged through her body. "You got company?"

"No."

His finger trailed lower, exposing more of that damned pink nightgown she'd bought that afternoon at the mall. She should have stuck to plain, practical underwear, but she'd been feeling sorry for herself so she'd gone a wee bit overboard on a few things.

He edged closer still. "You *want* company?" He smelled like summer air and leather, and his breath was warm against her temple.

She wondered if he could hear her heart pounding as she tried to dream up something reasonable to say. She couldn't think of a thing, and her back was pressed firmly against the wall as he stared down at her with that gleam in his eyes.

This could not happen. What about turning the tables on the men who were using her? She was just as vulnerable now as she had been after their first kiss on the driveway. Only now, it was the middle of the night and they were in a darkened room alone together.

She eased sideways, half expecting him to take her arm, but he didn't. She wandered back into the foyer and did a huge fake yawn-and-stretch.

"I am *so* beat," she said, turning back around to see him now slouched against the doorway. "It's been a long, tiring weekend." She put her hand on the doorknob in a gesture of non-Southern inhospitality. She didn't care if she was being rude; she needed him out before he talked his way upstairs under the pretense of checking her security.

He eyed the doorknob irritably, and then finally stepped close and gazed down at her.

"Keep your gun close," he said. His hand covered hers on the knob. "And don't open the door for any more strangers."

CHAPTER

7

Teresa Muñoz swiveled around in her desk chair when Juarez stepped through the door of Gulf Shores Investigations. She put the caller she was talking to on hold and gave him a smile.

"Didn't know you'd be in today," she said. "Your mother just called, and there's a pile of messages on your desk."

"Who's that?" Juarez asked, nodding toward the phone.

She rolled her eyes. "George Wainwright. He's called twice for an update on the Masterson case. Want me to put him through?"

Juarez recalled the file sitting on his desk. It contained information on a workers comp claim. Juarez was fairly certain the claim was bogus, but he hadn't found time to gather the evidence yet.

"Tell him I should be checking in later and I'll get back to him by close of business."

Teresa glanced at her watch. "That's in half an hour."

Damn. Where had the day gone? "Tell him I'll call him in the morning," he said. "First thing."

Juarez hated insurance work, but it kept the agency afloat. Between his insurance work, skip traces, and a steady stream of suspicious spouses, he cobbled together enough income to subsidize the investigation of Paloma's disappearance. Ever since the San Antonio police had closed her case file, Juarez had been on his own.

Juarez entered his sparsely furnished office and rummaged through the messages Teresa had stacked neatly on his desk, separating out the few that needed responses. He didn't want to get sidetracked, but he couldn't afford to ignore his paying clients. After returning a few calls, he unlocked his safe and pulled out the folder that had brought him into the office today.

The Paloma file.

It was pretty thin given that he'd been working on it for two years, but Juarez wasn't big on writing things down. He knew what he knew. Still, he appreciated the value of hard evidence, so he'd slid a few photographs and relevant documents into the folder with his sister's notes, hoping that someday everything he'd compiled might see the inside of a courtroom.

When—not if—it all came together, Josh Garland and his cronies were going down. They'd spend the rest of their days locked up, and Juarez could finally give his mother some peace.

Not everyone would make it to trial. Juarez had other plans for the person who had last seen his sister. After twenty-three months of investigating, Juarez had narrowed it down to two suspects. Both were hired guns operating along the border. Both had reputations for being lethal and extremely discreet. They were expensive, too, which was why they typically only worked for drug lords or other scumbags wealthy enough to shell out big bucks to eliminate their enemies. Plenty of guys were known for doing nickel-and-dime shit, but that hadn't been the case with Paloma. Whoever had abducted her and her partner—both trained law-enforcement officers—had been clever enough to do it without leaving a trail. So Juarez had quickly dismissed the typical lineup of street hoods and zeroed in on more professional candidates. After crossing several off his list for logistical reasons, he'd been left with two names: Todd Brassler and Vince Rawls. When he found out which one of them had ended his sister's life, he planned to take care of the fucker himself.

Juarez rifled through the file until he found what he was after. The tattered notepad contained only a half-dozen pages filled with his sister's cryptic scrawl, but it was the best evidence he had that her disappearance hadn't been voluntary, that she hadn't abandoned her daughter and the job she loved to run off with her rookie partner, as the San Antonio police would have everyone believe. Anyone who knew Paloma thought it was absurd. But the SAPD had insisted there was no evidence of foul play, and eventually the furor over the pair's disappearance had died down.

But Juarez refused to accept it. Not only did he feel partly responsible for his sister's fate, but he was in a unique position to investigate what had happened. Juarez had taken ownership of the case from the very beginning.

At the time of her disappearance, Paloma was on the SAPD vice squad. He knew she'd been working on a big case and that she'd been under a lot of stress. Looking back, Juarez wished like hell he'd paid closer attention to the details. Their last phone conversation, for example. After twenty minutes of casual chitchat—a Paloma record—she'd mentioned that her case had turned up a Mayfield connection, and had he heard of anyone named Garland? The name had come up during some kind of audio surveillance they were running. She'd also casually mentioned that her apartment had been broken into and that she'd moved her important papers to the gym.

And what had big brother Marco done in response to this strange conversation? Had he immediately checked out this guy Garland? Had he suggested his sister find another place to stay for a while? Had he driven his ass to San Antonio and offered to help her in any way? No, no, and no. Instead, he'd barely given the conversation a second thought until Paloma turned up missing a few days later.

By the time he actually did get to San Antonio, Paloma and her partner had been MIA for nearly nine hours.

After speaking with the neighbor who was taking care of Paloma's daughter, Kaitlin, Juarez had paid a visit to his sister's fitness club and talked his way into the ladies' locker room. Sure enough, Paloma's locker had been jammed with files. Personal stuff, mostly, like her passport and Kaitlin's birth certificate. The notebook had been tucked underneath a pair of worn cross trainers.

Now Juarez flipped through its pages for the hundredth time and failed to spot any new clues. He scoured the notes for any mention of Las Brisas, where Feenie and Garland had traveled on their boat. There was no reference to it—or any other Mexican coastal city, for that matter. None of her notes mentioned places across the border, at least as far as he could tell. Another fucking dead end.

"I almost forgot to tell you," Teresa said from the doorway. "We had a visitor this morning. I think it might be a new client."

"Who was it?"

"She didn't give a name." Teresa walked over and

dropped a sealed envelope on his desk. "She was short. Blond. Nosy, too. She poked around for a few minutes and asked questions, like she was trying to figure out if your business was legit."

"Oh, yeah? What'd you tell her?"

Teresa smiled. "You know me. The soul of discretion. I didn't tell her a thing except that I'd give you the letter."

Juarez picked up the envelope, which had his name across it in loopy handwriting.

"She looked like she was on a mission," Teresa said. "No wedding ring, so I think maybe she's someone's jealous mistress."

Juarez chuckled at the idea as he tore open the envelope. "Thanks, Teresa. Hold my calls for a few minutes, would you?"

"No problem."

He pulled out a stapled set of papers. It was a typed, five-page list of names, addresses, and phone numbers. Nearly half the entries had been blacked out with a thick marker. What the hell?

Juarez picked up the phone and dialed Feenie. She answered after the first ring.

"You wanna tell me what this is?" he asked.

"I thought you were an investigator. You tell me."

He scanned the entries that hadn't been blacked out. The names read like a Who's Who of Rio Grande Valley politics, with a few law-enforcement bigwigs thrown in. A handful of entries simply consisted of phone numbers without names beside them.

"Okay, I'm guessing it's a list of everyone Garland's bribing."

"Could be."

He gritted his teeth. "Don't be cute, Feenie. What the fuck is this?"

"It's my old Christmas card list."

"Your old Christmas card list."

"Yep. I found it folded up inside my Christmas card file when I was cleaning my house Saturday."

"You save all your Christmas cards? Like, from years past?" This woman was unbelievable.

"Just the envelopes with return addresses. And just for one year. That way, I know who to add to my mailing list every season. But then I keep all my master lists from year to year. That's important. See, if you lose track—"

"You wanna tell me how this relates to Garland?" He tapped his pen on the desk and glanced at his watch.

"You know, for an *investigator*, you're not very thorough."

"Ha-ha. Can we cut to the chase? I've got things to do today."

"Okay, fine. That's my *old* Christmas card list. From the last year Josh and I were married. All the names that aren't blacked out are Josh's contacts, downloaded directly from his BlackBerry. I did it without his permission one day, and he went totally ballistic when he found out. That's what made me think it might be something sensitive."

Juarez's irritation vanished as he scanned the list with renewed appreciation. "Did you actually send cards to all these people?"

"Just the ones with asterisks. There are a couple of numbers with no names next to them. Is there something you can do to look up where these numbers go?"

"Yeah, it's called a telephone break."

"Some of the numbers are twelve digits long, so they're foreign. I thought you might be interested in them since they came off Josh's BlackBerry."

She was right. He was very interested. He was already getting on the Internet so he could look up the numbers using a reverse directory. He started with a local number first, because his subscription service only did domestic listings.

"This is really helpful, Feenie. I need you to get me another copy of this without all the blackouts."

"No can do," she said. "You get the redacted version."

"What?"

"The redacted version. It's a little term we journalists use for all the reports we get where potentially critical information is carefully marked out. Kinda sucks, huh?"

She was definitely fucking with him. He should have known better than to insult her reporting skills the other night.

"Who's Sam de Palma?" Juarez asked after the first hit came back.

"Who?"

"Sam de Palma. Two-sixty-two Crescent Lane."

Silence.

"Feenie? Who is he?"

"It's a *she*. She used to be a member of our country club. I didn't know her very well . . ."

Feenie's voice trailed off and Juarez got the picture. Sounded like Garland probably knew her a little *too* well.

Juarez moved on to the international numbers.

"Seriously, I need the whole list here, Feenie." Juarez checked a Web site for country calling codes. Three of the unidentified numbers had area codes for the Mexican state of Nuevo Léon. Very interesting. Todd Brassler's operation was rumored to be head-quartered in Monterrey, the state's capital.

"Seriously, that's all you're getting," Feenie said. "The rest of the names are close relatives and personal friends, and I don't want them involved in any way. You'll just have to trust me when I tell you they're not worth looking into."

A few clicks, and Juarez was on Google.

"Don't I even get a thank you?"

"Thank you," he said, entering the first unidenti-fied number. "Really. This is a big help."

"You're welcome."

Holy shit, the number belonged to a Monterrey hotel, the Presidente InterContinental.

The InterCon. Brassler had once cut a deal in that very location. Juarez had heard about it from an FBI pal of his, a guy out of Houston whose task force was investigating the money-laundering operations of a major Mexican drug cartel. Investigators suspected Brassler of offing one of their key witnesses, some drug kingpin's cousin who was working as an informant. Juarez's pulse pounded. This was the most concrete evidence he'd had so far linking Brassler to Garland. Juarez scanned the list again. He still had six unidentified numbers to go, all with Mexican area codes. Maybe one of the numbers was the fucker's cell phone.

"Juarez? Are you listening?"

"What?"

"I *said*, now that I've done you this favor, I'm gonna want something in return. Information is a two-way street, you know."

Shit. It was the second time today she'd thrown his words right back at him. He'd underestimated her ability to play games. "What is it you need?"

"I don't know yet," she said, suddenly cheerful. "But I'm sure I'll think of something. Ba-bye now!"

She clicked off. Juarez entered the remaining numbers but didn't come up with any matches. He shuffled through his desk drawer, looking for a disk. Somewhere he had a software program that allowed the user to do a reverse look-up of foreign telephone numbers. He located the disk, popped it into his computer, and waited for software updates to download. When the program was ready, he entered the first number. No match. He entered another and got the same result. On the third try, he stared at his computer, hardly able to believe his luck. One of the numbers actually tied to a private residence in Monterrey, owner unlisted. Was it possible? Could that be the actual location of Todd Brassler? Juarez had been looking for the guy for a good eighteen months now, but he was elusive. Juarez had been back and forth over the border searching for him, but no one had seen or heard of him in more than a year. Maybe Feenie's list was a break in the case. It was two and a half years old, but it was the best lead Juarez had had in months.

Teresa's voice came over the intercom. "Phone call holding on line one."

"Take a message."

"It's Peterson. He said to tell you he knows you're in and you'd better pick up."

Juarez picked up the phone. "Yo."

"Marco, man, you got to get down here." His ex-partner's voice sounded muffled, as if he was whispering into his cell phone.

"Get down where why?"

"The park by Laguna Bonita. Near the boat ramp. We got a DOA, and you're not gonna believe who it is."

Finding McAllister amid the evening crowd at Eddie's Pool Hall wasn't difficult. Feenie simply scanned the bar for halos of smoke and then looked beneath each one until she spotted a golden-haired beach bum surrounded by women in painted-on jeans.

She approached him, ignoring the irritated stares from his fan club. They'd probably been vying for position for hours and didn't welcome any new competition.

Feenie cleared her throat and waited for McAllister to tear his eyes away from a young brunette who was spilling out of her tube top.

"Feenie!" he said, finally noticing her. "How's it going, gorgeous?"

If he'd intended to endear her to his admirers, he couldn't have picked a worse tactic. Three pairs of heavily made-up eyes bored into her.

"Hi," she said. "Do you have a minute?"

"Sure. Pull up a stool. We just ordered some wings."

"Thanks, but we need to talk," she said, eyeing the women. She had at least five years and twenty pounds on every one of them. "It's important, and it's private. Do you mind?"

"Sure, no problem." McAllister looked amused, while his companions looked anything but. The brunette actually mouthed "bitch" as she got up from her bar stool. Feenie slid onto the stool without comment. She stowed her purse on the floor and turned to face the bar.

"So, what's up? I hear you've been covering for me. Guess I owe you a drink." He waved over the bartender and ordered her a Cuba libre. Feenie hadn't had one since the Gazette Christmas party, and McAllister had bought that one, too.

"Thanks," she said, wondering if he'd remembered her drink or made a lucky guess.

When the drink came, McAllister lifted his Shiner Bock and clinked it against her glass.

"To my favorite cub reporter," he said, smiling. "The one who'll probably have my job by tomorrow morning."

Feenie snorted. "Yeah, right. Grimes adores you."

"I don't know about that." He swilled his beer. "He nearly canned me when I came in this morning. I think I may have pushed my luck with that extended vacation."

"Yeah, how did that go?" she asked. He looked rested, and his usually bronze skin had darkened a few shades. "You were down there with your girlfriend, weren't you? Someone serious?" Feenie thought of the women she'd just dethroned.

He winced. "Ah, not really. Things didn't exactly end on a good note."

Feenie sipped her drink and decided she didn't want details. McAllister was the ultimate playboy, and she felt obligated to disapprove, but somehow she couldn't muster the indignation.

He lit a cigarette and gave her his beach-boy smile. "So, what's up, Feenie? I know for a fact I haven't gotten you pregnant."

She smiled slightly and looked over her shoulder. His fan club had taken over a booth near the jukebox and appeared about ready to claw her eyes out. "Yeah, I didn't mean to start the rumor mill."

"Forget about it," he said. "What's on your mind?"

"I have a scoop for you."

He raised his eyebrows, and she couldn't tell whether he doubted the scoop or doubted that she would really give it to him if she had one. He took a drag of his cigarette. "I'm listening."

She cleared her throat. "You know Rico Martinez?"

"Drug dealer out of Corpus. Turned up dead a few days ago. ME recovered two slugs during the autopsy this morning."

Feenie rolled her eyes. He'd been in town less than forty-eight hours, and already he knew more than she did. McAllister smiled, seeming to read her thoughts.

"Okay, but here's something you might not know," she said. "There's a local connection."

"What kind of connection?"

"I think the guy who killed him—or had him killed—is a prominent citizen around here."

He exhaled smoke and looked skeptical. "What makes you think that?"

This was the part she wasn't sure of. How could she make herself sound credible without revealing Juarez's involvement?

"I have a contact," she said. "A law-enforcement type. His information is solid, but he wants to remain anonymous."

McAllister looked serious now. He tapped his

cigarette and took another drag. "Okay. So if this lead's so great, why don't you follow it up? Show Grimes he's wasting your talents on all that wedding and funeral shit."

"I can't write it," Feenie said.

"Sure you can. You're better than you think. I'll even help you—"

"No, I mean I *can't* write it. I want to, but I can't."

She pulled the manila envelope from her purse and glanced around. No one was watching, but she put her purse on the bar as a shield, just in case. She pulled out the photograph of Josh and Martinez.

McAllister studied the photo, not saying anything for a minute. "Shit," he muttered finally.

She nodded. "See my problem?"

"Yep." He stubbed out his cigarette and studied the picture some more. "Where was this taken?"

"A boat dock." She tapped a fingernail on Josh. "*His* boat dock. Late at night. Right before they went out together in a driving rainstorm. My source tells me they were arguing about money in the days before Martinez got shot."

A waitress came up to them with a heaping platter of buffalo wings and ranch dip. Feenie quickly slid the photograph back in its envelope. McAllister doused the wings in Tabasco sauce, and for a while they ate without talking.

"So what's the catch, Feenie? You dump this gem in my lap. You've got to want something in return."

Feenie sipped her drink and summoned her courage. "You're right, I do. I want a full-time job. On the *news* desk, not writing fluff pieces."

McAllister laughed. "I'd love to help you out, sweetheart, but until they crown me editor-in-chief—"

"I want you to throw me a bone, okay? Give me a tip on something good so I can prove myself to Grimes. I'm within inches of losing my house, and I need to get on salary. But now that you're back, Grimes is putting me off again. He just assigned me to cover a spelling bee, for crying out loud."

He grinned at her.

"It's not funny! I need a break. Otherwise, I have to start looking for a new job. I can't afford to wait around forever making next to nothing."

"Okay, I get your point. I'll find something and send it your way, all right?"

Infinitely relieved, Feenie tucked the envelope back into her purse and helped herself to another wing. "Just one more thing. I need you to sit on the Martinez thing for a little while. I think I can get you some more information, but I promised my source I would try to keep a lid on the story until he gets a few things nailed down. He's sort of involved in the investigation."

"Waiting isn't my strong suit." He took the last swig of his beer. "This source of yours. What's his rank?"

Feenie licked some spice off her fingers and fanned her mouth. "Well . . . he's kind of *ex*-law enforcement."

McAllister gave her a sharp look. "It's not Marco Juarez, is it?"

She stopped chewing. "Why?"

"Shit, Feenie," he said, pushing the plate away. "You know who that is, don't you?"

She shook her head.

"He got fired last summer for drug possession. They found marijuana in his car. It wasn't enough to land him in jail, but it got his ass kicked off the police force. I wrote a story about it."

Feenie's chest tightened. Juarez hadn't told her any of that. Why hadn't he told her that?

"It may have been a plant, though," McAllister said. "One of the cops—I think it may have been the guy's partner—he didn't like the bust. Guy called me up and gave me a big earful. Said Juarez wasn't into drugs. Said the whole thing stank, but he didn't have proof."

She hoped to hell the partner was right. Then she wondered why it mattered to her so much.

"The partner told me something else that was interesting," he continued. "This guy said the police chief had had it in for Juarez for months before the bust. Said he'd been looking for a way to get rid of him because he was a loose canon."

"Why'd they think that?" Feenie asked, although given her experience with Juarez, it didn't seem like much of a stretch.

He shrugged. "I don't know. Think he had a history of insubordination or something. Hey, you're not sleeping with him, are you?"

"What?" Feenie felt her cheeks flame. Where had *that* come from?

"Shit, you are, aren't you?" McAllister sighed and shook his head.

"No!"

"Well, you should know, the guy hates reporters. Take it from me. I tried to follow up with him after my original story, but he wouldn't give me the time of day. I dug around for a while on the phony-bust thing, but then the partner stopped talking and I couldn't get anywhere with it. So if Juarez is talking to media all of a sudden, he has an agenda. You better find out what it is before you get involved with him."

Feenie got a sinking feeling in her stomach. She'd known Juarez had been using her, but hearing it from someone else stung.

Something chirped, and McAllister reached for his cell phone.

"McAllister," he said, then fell silent for a few moments. "No kidding? Where?" He pulled a notepad from his pocket and began scribbling. "Boat ramp, right. I'll be right there. Thanks for the call."

Lieutenant Brian Doring had been an all-state running back, a keen marksman, and a classmate of Juarez's at the police academy.

At the moment, he was crab food.

Juarez watched the crime-scene technicians hover near the waterlogged body that had been found on the marshy shoreline of Laguna Bonita Park. Doring wore civilian clothes, down to a pair of brown cowboy boots. His shirt hung open, a crab clinging stubbornly to the fabric as a body removal team lifted the corpse from the salt grass and placed it on an unzipped black bag. In recent years, Doring had put on a few extra pounds, but now he looked especially bloated, his belly spilling over the waist of his jeans like a soggy doughnut. One of his eyes was missing, probably thanks to the crabs. Two workers in blue jumpsuits zipped him in for transport to the morgue as the bald-headed medical examiner looked on.

"Shit. What a waste," Juarez said.

Peterson glanced over his shoulder and nodded. "He was a good cop."

He was a talented cop, yes. Calm in a crisis, best shooter on the force. But good? The jury was still out on that one. Getting gunned down while *off* duty wasn't doing much for his reputation. Especially since it looked as if he'd taken two bullets to the chest, just like Martinez.

"Damn, he's a mess. Any guess on the caliber of the weapon?" Juarez asked.

"Nah, not yet. But there's a rush on this thing. Chief's already shitting bricks over the potential bad publicity. He wants the autopsy done ASAP so they can send any slugs to the lab."

Juarez would bet his Chevy Silverado that ballistics would come back with the same caliber used to kill Martinez. If the bullets weren't too misshapen, the lab might even be able to link the murders to the same gun. Juarez glanced around at the officers combing the vicinity for clues. On the far side of the park was a tricolored playscape surrounded by a wrought-iron fence. An officer was hunched next to the gate there, sifting through some dirt.

"Strange place for a shooting," Peterson said, reading Juarez's mind. Laguna Bonita was a well-maintained park in a nice section of town. Kaitlin loved the swing set, and Juarez brought her to play here almost every weekend.

That was about to change.

A white news van pulled into the parking lot next to the boat ramp. It was followed by a black Jeep Wrangler. John McAllister hopped out and sauntered over to a pair of uniforms milling around near a cruiser.

"Fuckin' media," Peterson said, shooting Juarez a dirty look.

Juarez held up his hands. "Hey, man. I didn't call them. I hate 'em more than you do." He reached for his car keys and nodded at Peterson. "Keep me posted, okay?"

"You got it."

Juarez took a last look at the scene, which had already been roped off with yellow tape, and headed for his truck. Peterson had done him a favor by giving him the heads up about Doring, but he didn't want to make his friend's job tougher than it already was. The chief wouldn't like Peterson talking to Juarez at a crime scene.

He hitched himself behind the wheel and noticed McAllister watching him. Juarez scowled and drove away.

Feenie cut through the water, enjoying the chill on her skin and the burn in her muscles. She tapped the side, counted off another lap, and switched to backstroke. The sun had disappeared an hour ago, and stars were beginning to wink through the lacy canopy of leaves. With Mrs. Hanak out of town visiting her daughter, Feenie had the whole backyard to herself. She'd turned her radio up louder than usual and even considered swimming naked in the moonlight. Practicality had won out, however, and she'd donned her old blue Speedo. She was almost finished with her laps, and her body felt nice and tingly. She closed her eyes and let herself glide.

She loved her pool. It had been one of the first things to draw her to the house on Pecan Street. The old-fashioned architecture had been a major selling point, but the pool had been the clincher. She'd liked the thought of taking a dip whenever she wanted or doing laps in the heat of the summer. But most of all, she'd envisioned the pool filled with kids. Growing up, she'd never had such luxuries, which made her even more determined to provide them for her own children.

She'd expected to have a houseful of children by now. Or at least a couple. She'd planned on being a stay-home mom, happily filling her time with her kids' activities, involved in their lives—but not overly so—showering them with hugs and kisses when they came home from school. She and Josh would be the perfect parents, sharing a perfect house, a perfect marriage, a perfect family.

That was Plan A, and it had been an abysmal failure. Not only was her house devoid of family, but it was about to be repossessed. And now there was that hole in the kitchen . . .

Plan A was history.

Plan B had been to meet an eligible bachelor and get remarried without missing a beat. After a few disastrous setups with friends of friends, she had dumped that plan, too.

She was on Plan C now. According to Plan C, she would continue to live in the house she loved, but she was no longer waiting for Mr. Right to come along. She'd realized such a creature didn't exist, at least not for her. Under Plan C, she would develop her career, take charge of her financial well-being, and stand on her own two feet. Practically speaking, this meant she'd learned to use the red Toro mower that lived in her storage shed, and she'd learned to go to movies by herself without feeling like a social reject. So far, Plan C was working. Its main appeal was that it didn't require a man.

As for the children, Feenie still intended to have

them, but she wasn't convinced she needed a man for that, either. Maybe she'd adopt. She knew foreign adoptions were becoming more and more common, but she hadn't really looked into it.

So that was Plan C. The main drawback was not having anyone to share the parenting. Still, it could be done. Her father had managed fine as a single parent.

The plan wasn't perfect, but Feenie didn't believe in perfection anymore. Not when it came to her love life, anyway. Her house was another matter. Despite the hole in the kitchen, she still thought her house was about as close to perfection as she could get.

Feenie counted off lap number fifty and hitched herself out of the water. Her heart thudded, and her muscles felt rubbery. But it was a good feeling. Time to go into her perfect house and sink into a perfectly relaxing bubble bath.

She'd worry about the repo man later.

She stood up and squeezed the water from her hair. It was another warm night, and pleasant. The hum of cicadas filled the air, singing backup for Willie Nelson's easygoing twang on the radio. Fireflies blinked near the hibiscus bushes lining the back fence, and Feenie paused to watch, remembering how she and Rachel used to love chasing glitter bugs together when they were kids.

She glanced around now, suddenly realizing just how dark it had become. She should have thought to turn on the patio lights before her swim. Come to think of it, she should have kept her Mace handy.

Or maybe she shouldn't even be out here in the first place. It would be smart to get inside. Shivering now, Feenie searched around for the towel she'd left on a lawn chair.

A lawn chair now occupied by a man, watching her from the shadows.

CHAPTER
8

S he gasped, stepped backward, and fell into the
pool.

When she came up for air, Juarez crouched at the
water's edge and laughed at her. It was dark, but there
was no mistaking the white flash of teeth. He held
out her towel.

"What are you doing?" she sputtered. She paddled
to the side and rested her arms on the concrete apron.
It still felt warm from the day's sunshine.

"Watching you."

"I can see *that*." She tried to lever herself out, but
a sudden onslaught of nerves had her arms quivering
as she slid back into the water. Juarez tossed away the

towel, reached down, and lifted her from the pool. He set her lightly on her feet in front of him.

"Why are you here? You scared the hell outta me!"

Her pulse was racing now, from the scare, and the exercise, and the realization that Juarez was standing between her and her beach towel. And she had on nothing but a tissue-thin swimsuit that did little to hide her postdivorce cellulite. Goose bumps sprang up all over her skin, and she folded her arms strategically over her breasts.

"Cold?" he asked.

She pressed her lips together and tried not to throttle him. "Could you hand me my towel, please?"

"I could." He smiled and stepped closer. She was trapped next to him unless she wanted to take another dip.

Fine. She could get over her vanity. After all, just the other night, he'd seen her half-undressed and hadn't run away screaming. In fact, he'd done the opposite. Bolstered by the memory, she planted her hands on her hips and tipped her chin up.

"What do you want, Juarez?"

His smile faded. "You didn't answer your phone. I was worried."

"I don't usually take calls from the pool."

He frowned down at her for a moment. Then he snagged her towel off the ground and handed it to her. "Why isn't your kitchen fixed? I told you my friend would do it for cheap."

She wrapped the towel around herself and tucked the corner into her cleavage. "Yeah, well, cheap isn't the same as free. I don't have the money right now."

"You don't have the money," he stated.

"That's what I just said, isn't it? You see a money tree growing in my yard?" She breezed past him and headed for the back door. He followed her inside without an invitation.

"I thought you were loaded."

She felt her patience draining away. Why did everyone assume she was some spoiled airhead? She drove a heap, she barely had a stick of furniture, and she hadn't been shopping for anything besides underwear in more than a year. Yet many people still thought she was leading the pampered life she'd had with Josh.

"You thought wrong." She opened the refrigerator and reached for her water bottle. She slammed the door shut without offering him a drink.

He smiled indulgently, as if he knew she was lying but didn't want to pursue it. He was so damned arrogant.

"You want details? Fine," she said. "I hardly got a dime in my divorce, I've exhausted the money I got from selling my Mustang, and I'm not exactly setting the world on fire careerwise, in case you hadn't noticed. I've got bills stacked up to the ceiling, and somehow I haven't been able to get my hands on the twenty-five hundred dollars I need to get my roof fixed."

He watched her, his face neutral. "When's your next paycheck?"

What the hell? That was none of his business. "Friday," she snapped.

He nodded. "I'll give Carlos a call. Put down whatever deposit you can, and I'll tell him to get started this weekend. In the meantime, you can stay at my place."

Feenie stared at him, speechless.

"Go get packed," he ordered.

"Why would I want to stay at your place?"

His jaw tightened, as if she'd wounded his pride. Was his ego really that inflated? Evidently so.

He stepped closer and gripped her shoulders. "You want details? Fine," he said, mocking her. "There's been another murder. Probably the same gunman who killed Martinez. I'm pretty sure you're on his hit list, your house is wide open, you can't afford a hotel room, and I want you somewhere I can keep an eye on you. So you're coming to my place."

Despite the warmth of the towel, her goose bumps were back. What had happened to her boring, run-of-the-mill life? Tonight she'd sleep with her gun *and* her pepper spray. And her cell phone.

"I can protect myself just fine, thank you. I don't need a bodyguard."

His eyes narrowed. "You have no idea what you need. And your little pop gun is no match for this guy. He took out a cop and a drug dealer, and both of them had a hell of a lot more street smarts than you, babe. So get your stuff together. We're leaving."

Feenie despised being called "babe." Josh used to do it all the time, usually in front of his jackass friends.

She plucked Juarez's fingers from her shoulders. "I'm not leaving. This is *my* house. Josh tried to boot me out of here once before, and I fought him tooth and nail. I'll be damned if I'll let him win now. I'm not going anywhere."

Juarez stared down at her, clearly exasperated. "You're gonna get yourself killed, you know. Over what? A house? Don't be stupid."

"It's more than a house, and I'm not stupid. I know how to handle a gun, and I can protect myself."

He arched his eyebrows, and Feenie remembered how he'd taken her down at the boathouse without breaking a sweat. Okay, so she might not be the best at hand-to-hand combat, but she could hold her own with a gun.

"Fine," he snarled. "It's your neck. What do I care what you do with it?"

He stormed out the back door, muttering something in Spanish. Feenie felt sure it wasn't complimentary.

Despite her bravado, she couldn't relax for the rest of the evening. She decided to put her nervous energy to good use by beefing up her security. She closed the door between her kitchen and living room and dragged her mangled sofa in front of it. The thing weighed a ton. No way could someone push it aside from behind the door, at least not without making a racket. Then she dead-bolted the front door, checked the window locks, and turned on all the downstairs lights. She was thankful, her electric bill was one of the few she'd paid on time. With Mrs. Hanak living in the garage apartment, Feenie couldn't afford to let the electricity and water get cut off. She'd let her phone and cable go instead. She didn't miss the cable, especially since her TV was out of commission anyway, but it would have provided a nice distraction. As it was, she had nothing to keep her mind occupied except Juarez's dire predictions.

Would someone really try to attack her in her own house? The more she thought about it, the more she felt like a sitting duck. She considered calling Juarez back and telling him she'd changed her mind, but she'd feel like an idiot. Plus, she hadn't been lying to him about her shooting skills. If the need arose, she could protect herself.

At least, she hoped so.

After a thorough tour of the house and a brief shower, she threw on a T-shirt and climbed into bed. She had just settled under the covers when she heard a noise downstairs.

She sat up and reached for her gun. She waited, breathless, hoping it was merely her imagination.

Snap. She held her breath. *Snap. Snap.*

It wasn't her imagination. Someone was making noise in her kitchen.

Feenie wrapped herself in her fuzzy robe and shoved her cell phone into the pocket. Gun in arms, she tiptoed toward the stairs. If someone intended to get to her from the kitchen, they'd have to move the sofa first. Feenie crept halfway down the stairs and waited for the telltale noise that someone was trying to do just that.

Snap. Whip.

It was the *tarp* flapping! Feenie tipped back her head and sighed with relief. Still armed, she hurried toward the kitchen, just to make sure. She shoved the sofa over a few inches and cracked the kitchen door so she could peer inside and make sure.

No bogeymen. Just a flapping piece of plastic. Tomorrow she'd take Juarez's advice and give his builder friend a call.

Two minutes later, Feenie was back in bed with her gun positioned beside her. As she reached for the lamp, her gaze landed on her cell phone. She grabbed it impulsively and dialed.

He picked up right away. "Frank Malone."

The familiar drawl immediately made her feel safe. "Hi, Dad. It's me. How've you been?"

"What's wrong?"

"Nothing. I just hadn't talked to you in a while, and I thought I'd call to chat."

"You never call to chat. What's going on?"

God. Why couldn't they ever have just a normal conversation? "Nothing, Dad. Really. I was just, I don't know, lonesome for the sound of your voice."

Her father was totally unaccustomed to such emotionally loaded statements.

"Dad?"

"You sure you're okay? You didn't get fired, did you?"

She squeezed her eyes shut. Why did she even bother? Everything was about accomplishments with him. They could never just talk.

"No, Dad, I didn't get fired." Although she still hadn't actually been *hired*. At least, not full-time. Of course, she'd led her father to believe she had more of a real job. She hadn't wanted him to worry, and he'd done nothing *but* worry about her ever since her divorce.

She'd been crazy to think she could tell him what was really going on in her life. Break-ins and hit men. He'd worry himself to death over it.

She fell back on her usual tactics. "Everything's good, Dad. Wonderful, in fact. I may even be getting a promotion."

"That's great news. Is this an editor's job?"

Damn. Why did she back herself into these corners? She'd told him she was a staff writer, so naturally he'd assume the next step up was editor. If he only knew. "No, nothing like that. Just a more important job on the news desk."

"Well, that sounds fine," he said. "I'm real proud of you."

After wrapping up their conversation, she felt better. And sleepier. She replaced the phone on her nightstand, killed the light, and tried to get some sleep.

She dreamed about fire.

It started the usual way—the crash of metal, the dizzying spin as the car rolled over, a stinging sensation traveled up her side. When she looked out the window, everything was upside down. Her father's voice came to her, faintly at first but then stronger. Then she was lying on her back next to a ditch. Everything was upside down still. She couldn't see her dad, but she could hear his voice. She turned her head to look for him, but all she saw were flames licking up from a twisted pile of metal that had once been their family sedan.

Her cheeks burned from the heat of the blaze, and she looked away. Her mother and Rachel stood on the side of the highway, watching the flaming wreckage with curious expressions. She called out to them, but they didn't hear her. They never did.

Feenie stared at the ceiling, trying to regulate her breathing. It was a dream. She'd had it countless times before. She hated the dream, but she loved it, too. For a brief moment, everything was all right again. Her mother and sister stood near her. Alive. Unbroken. Unburned.

She sat up and reached for the glass of water she always kept by her bed. She tried to throw off the covers, but they were clingy and damp.

After a few sips of water, she stopped shaking.

Would Josh really send someone to kill her? Obviously, she thought so, or she wouldn't have had the dream. It came to her during times of stress. She'd had variations of it almost every night in the months following the accident, but over the years it had become less frequent, vaguer. Sometimes she wouldn't dream about the accident at all but simply fire. Kitchen fires, forest fires, brush fires.

Feenie glanced at the smoke detector perched above her door. The red light blinked down at her reassuringly. She was safe. She just needed to get some rest before work. She eyed the gun beside her on the bed. It was loaded and ready. She sank back against the mattress and tried to will herself to sleep.

Which, of course, wasn't possible. Maybe yoga breathing would help. She closed her eyes and tried deep, even breaths. Slow . . . and rhythmic. Slow . . . and rhythmic. Slow . . . and rhythmic. But something about slow and rhythmic reminded her of Juarez, and before she knew it, her heart was racing again.

Damn Juarez. Damn him for leaving her alone like this.

Forget that she'd insisted. Forget that she'd practically kicked him out. If he really cared about her, he wouldn't have left her alone tonight. He would have stayed, if not to protect her, then at least for the sex.

Unless he didn't find her attractive.

No, that wasn't right. She knew he was attracted to her. She'd felt it.

But if he really was attracted to her, and if he really did care about her, why wasn't he here?

Because he's just using you! a voice told her.

There it was. The unvarnished truth. In fact, he'd probably only stopped by tonight to see if she had any new leads for him—

Feenie bolted upright and reached for her .22. She could have sworn she'd heard a noise. Not the tarp but a high-pitched, rattling sound.

There it was again. She eased the gun down as she eyed the glowing cell phone on her nightstand. She'd set the damn thing to vibrate during an interview this afternoon.

She snatched up the phone. "What?"

"Malone! Are you asleep?" It was Grimes, and he sounded much too awake for eleven fifty-five.

"Um . . . no?"

"We've got a fire, goddamn it! What the hell's wrong with your home phone? And why didn't you answer your pager?"

Feenie fumbled with the lamp switch. The device in question was clipped to the crumpled jeans on her bedroom floor. It, too, was set to vibrate. Great. She was surrounded by vibrators.

"Malone?"

"Yeah, I'm here. Sorry. Did you say there was a fire?"

"At Northside High School. Get there ASAP. McAllister's tied up, so I need you to take this. Interview the fire chief and some witnesses on the scene. This is tomorrow's top story."

Feenie glanced at her clock. She had two hours to get herself to the high school, interview sources, and file a front-page story before the presses started at two a.m.

"No problem," she said, and hung up.

McAllister had come through for her, and now it was up to her to prove herself. She threw on her jeans and gathered her unruly hair into a ponytail. Shoes and purse in hand, she stumbled out of her house and made her way to the scene.

It seemed strange that she'd been called out to cover a fire the same night of her dream. Or maybe it wasn't strange at all. Maybe the dream hadn't resulted from stress but from her brain picking up the sound of sirens while she'd slept. She wasn't a psychologist, but it seemed plausible. As she sped toward the high school, she tried not to focus on her phobia. It was her first breaking news story; she had to nail it.

Her alma mater was surrounded by fire trucks, police cruisers, and several ambulances. Nearby residents—awakened by the noise, no doubt—stood in the school parking lot, gawking at the spectacle. Smoke billowed out from the school gym.

She watched the play of flames behind a row of windows on the bottom floor. She shuddered, remembering how she'd struggled through advanced algebra in that very classroom.

But she couldn't let this become personal. Every news reporter covered a fire eventually. She just wished this one hadn't happened so soon after her dream. Her fear was fresh, palpable. She took a deep breath and trudged into the fray.

She spotted Drew standing atop his Tercel, trying to get a good shot with his zoom lens. Fires were invariably dramatic, and whatever he ended up with would be splashed across page one in the morning.

Feenie skirted the crowd and tried to identify the people in charge. The fire chief stood near a red Suburban, barking orders and pointing at the building. She took a step toward him, but a burly police officer immediately blocked her path.

"This is a secured area," he told her. "Emergency workers only."

Feenie dug her media pass out of her purse and waved it in front of him, to no effect. Rolling her eyes, she darted to the other side of the crowd and tried to locate an opening. Barricades surrounded the main entrance to the building, and a row of emergency vehicles made access to the side entrance nearly impossible.

Nearly.

Feenie recalled the back entrance to the girls' locker room. The doorway was hidden from the street by a tall hedge, making it the perfect place for sneaking cigarettes when the cheerleading coach wasn't watching. Feenie had used it on many occasions during her four-year career at Northside. She walked around the side of the building until she saw the familiar hedge. The door had been propped open, and firefighters streamed in and out.

She stood off in the shadows for a few moments, watching and listening and trying not to let the acrid smell of smoke bother her. The emergency workers filed back and forth, dragging hoses and communicating with clipped phrases and hand gestures. After a few minutes, she concluded that the worst of the fire was concentrated in the boys' locker room and that someone was trapped inside. Feenie took out her cell and called Drew. He arrived at the doorway just in time to snap a photo of two firefighters hauling a pair of unconscious teenagers out of the smoke-filled gymnasium.

Fifty minutes later, Feenie put the final touches on her first breaking news story. No one had been seriously injured, although Feenie had sustained her first war wound when she'd jumped between two teenage girls who were fighting over whose boyfriend was to blame for the fire. Was it the varsity football captain, who had organized a hazing event for freshmen ball players in the school gym tonight? Or was it Northside's biggest offensive tackle, who had provided beer and pizza for the athletes and then "suggested" the freshmen torch a pile of pizza boxes? After interviewing teens in the parking lot, as well as the fire chief and the school principal, Feenie felt confident all sides of the story were represented.

Her article would be widely read tomorrow. Even

without injuries, a fire at one of Mayfield's three high schools was big news. The gym was destroyed, and the campus had been shut down indefinitely. Parents were going to want to know if and when their children could safely return to school.

Despite the fire chief's official statements about "unknown causation" and "pending further investigation," Feenie's article provided details and quotes that would give people an idea of what really happened. That was her job, wasn't it? To cut through all the official mumbo-jumbo and tell the public the truth? For the first time since joining the *Gazette,* she felt she was performing a public service. Her hands flew over the keyboard, and her chest swelled with pride.

Grimes stood behind her, reading every word as it appeared on the screen. She heard him mumbling at various points in the story and tried not to flinch when he reached over her to delete her last three paragraphs and change the lead. Finally, he stood back and nodded.

"Not bad, Malone. Go rest up, and I'll see you at eight."

Juarez woke up with a pounding headache made worse by the seagulls screeching outside his window. He'd spent most of the night drinking bourbon, watching reality TV, and battling insomnia, only to doze off sometime before dawn. Now it was after eight, and he felt like shit.

He pulled on some jeans and went up on deck.

The day's first shrimp boat was cruising into the marina, trailed by a whining flock of scavengers. Juarez stood at the helm, rubbing the kink in his neck and cursing every last one of the noisy little fuckers. He looked up and winced at the sunlight.

A large brown pelican perched on the dock. Juarez didn't mind the birds usually. In the sixth months since he'd started living on his boat, he'd actually come to like them, but this morning they grated on his nerves.

His stomach growled, reminding him that he'd skipped dinner the night before. His desk was piled with work, but he'd be useless without fuel. He ducked back into his cramped living quarters, grabbed a shirt and shoes, and drove to Rosie's.

The place was crowded with morning regulars. On his way in the door, Juarez stopped and bought a newspaper. He took an empty seat at the counter and plunged into the Doring story.

"Hola, Marquito," Rosie said, wiping down the counter in front of him with a damp rag.

He ordered coffee and *migas* and then put his crankiness on hold for a minute so he could answer Rosie's inquiries about his family. People who knew about Paloma always made a point to ask about his mother. How was she holding up? When would they see her back at mass? Was she still taking care of that beautiful granddaughter? After satisfying Rosie's curiosity, Juarez turned his attention back to his paper and finished the Doring article.

John McAllister had been thorough, but he hadn't made the Martinez connection. Not yet, at least. When the ballistics report came out, it wouldn't take him long. Typically, those reports could take weeks, but someone at the FBI had a bug up his ass about this shooting, and the bureau had generously "offered" to analyze the slugs at their own lab, or at least that's what Juarez had heard. Peterson had told him the chief was in a hurry for the ballistics, too. What a co-incidence. Juarez wondered whether the FBI was just being helpful or was horning in on the investigation for other reasons.

Juarez knew for a fact that Mayfield's chief of police was on someone's payroll, which was why Juarez had lost his job over a bogus drug charge. He was fairly sure that members of the San Antonio PD were on the take as well. His theory was that Paloma and her partner had learned of the corruption through their investigation, but one of their suspects ratted them out before they could take it very far. The two detectives—Paloma and her partner—prob-ably had been set up by someone they knew. How else to explain two trained investigators showing up for work one morning and then disappearing without a trace? Juarez would probably never know for sure, but he did know he didn't trust the local cops. In Mayfield or San Antonio. At least his FBI contact and Peterson were reliable.

"So what do you think?"

Juarez turned and raked his gaze over the curly

haired blonde standing at his elbow. "Hey, Feenie," he said, wondering why he should be glad to see the person responsible for his crappy mood. "Shoot any prowlers last night?"

She grinned. "Obviously, you haven't read your paper. I was barely home last night. I covered the school fire."

Juarez scanned the front page. Her story was right below the photo of a firefighter carrying a kid through a doorway.

"Congratulations," he said. "You finally made the front page."

She gave a little toss of her head, and her curls bobbed. "Yeah, well, it's about time."

He noticed three parallel scratch marks on the side of her chin. "Get in a cat fight?"

She lifted her hand to her face. "Stopped one, actually. You can still tell?"

"Yeah."

Sighing, she pulled a compact from her pink handbag and began powdering.

Rosie slid a plate in front of him and watched Feenie with a raised brow. Juarez pretended not to notice the look, and Feenie was oblivious, as usual.

"So I went by your office," Feenie said, stuffing the compact back into her purse. Today she had on jeans and a plain white button-down, but somehow she still managed to look like a debutante. He chalked it up to the girlie-looking pink sandals she wore. They matched her purse and her fingernails.

He glanced at her feet again. And her toenails, dammit.

She leaned an elbow on the counter. "Teresa said I might find you here. Do you ever eat anything besides Mexican food?"

He filled a tortilla with scrambled eggs, potatoes, and sausage. "Not really. Why'd you go by my office?"

Her perky expression faded, and she glanced over her shoulder. Juarez paused with the taco halfway to his mouth. "What happened?"

She shrugged, obviously trying to look nonchalant but failing. "Nothing, really. I just need a favor."

"Let's hear it."

She dug into her front pocket and produced a scrap of paper. "Could you check this license plate for me? I think someone's been following me."

He examined the paper: *tan Chevy Blazer UT3???.* "You don't have the full tag?"

"That's all I could get. It was a Texas plate, though."

"When was this?"

She glanced over her shoulder again. "This morning, when I was headed to work. So I pulled into a gas station and bought some coffee. I think he noticed me watching him, because he slowed a little, but he didn't stop. He went right through the intersection."

She was smarter than she looked, apparently. He would have expected her to do something more obvious, like turn around and gawk at the car.

"You get a look at him?"

She shook her head. "Tinted windows."

"What makes you so sure he's following you?"

A worry line appeared between her brows. "Just a hunch, really. The car looks familiar, but I don't really know why. Maybe I've seen it around before."

His stomach tightened. "You need to be careful, Feenie. This isn't a game."

Her anxious look was replaced by the familiar flash of temper.

"I know it's not a game! That's why I'm *here*, asking you for a favor and making myself late for work. Now, are you going to help me or not?"

He shoved the piece of paper into his back pocket. "I'll see what I can do. Meantime, I'll drive you to work. Stay at your office today."

"But what about my car?"

"Leave it here for now. You can call me when you need a ride home." He had no intention of taking her home, but he didn't tell her that. She'd just throw a fit, and that was something he didn't need. His day was growing more complicated by the minute, and he'd probably never get any real work done. Feenie Malone had a way of screwing up his productivity.

She stuck her chin out. "I don't like this plan."

"Yeah? Well, tough toenails, babe. It's the best I can do right now, so you'll have to live with it."

Feenie sailed into the newsroom, trying not to let fear overshadow her excitement. Everybody in town was waking up to her front-page story this morning, and as much as she wanted to pretend she didn't care about such things, she couldn't help but feel a little proud. *Her* name. *Her* byline. If she accumulated enough of them, maybe other people would start seeing her as a real reporter, not just some bubblehead with D-cups.

She stopped by McAllister's desk on the way to her cubicle.

"Thanks for last night," she said.

He looked up from his computer. "Hey, nice story. You really got the goods, didn't you?"

"Yep. Think Grimes liked it?"

"No doubt. You scooped everybody with that hazing angle. The radio guys were quoting your story this morning."

"Really?" She beamed at him. "Well, thank you for sending it my way."

"Malone!"

Feenie jerked her head up and saw Grimes standing in the doorway to his office. He didn't look happy. "Get in here!"

What now? She glanced at Darla, but she was distracted on a phone call. Feenie dropped her purse off at her desk and straightened her shoulders before walking in.

"Yes?" She perched on the edge of a chair and crossed her legs. Her editor's desk was drowning under files and newspapers.

"I just got off the phone with the father of one of your high school kids." He rounded his desk and stopped in front of her. "He's threatening to sue us if we don't print a full retraction. The dad says your article was complete fiction."

Feenie's spine stiffened. "Everything I wrote was corroborated by the cops. Why should we print a retraction?"

"According to this guy, because we've ruined his kid's life. He and several others were suspended this morning and kicked off the football team. The dad says it's our fault his son lost his shot at a football scholarship."

"That's crazy," Feenie said. "It was the players who set their school on fire. It's not my fault they're morons. Why should we retract?"

"We shouldn't," Grimes said. "We didn't use the students' names because they're minors, and everything you put in the story is documented in the police report, right?"

"Right," she answered, feeling immensely relieved that she'd been thorough about her fact checking last night.

"Then we have nothing to worry about. The dad's just looking for someone to blame because his kid screwed up. Don't worry about it."

Feenie let out the breath she'd been holding. "Okay . . . so why are you so upset?"

He frowned. "It's this cop shooting. It stinks to high heaven. You didn't hear anything funny about Doring while you were covering the police beat, did you? Any chatter among the uniforms or anything?"

She shook her head. "I didn't get much in the way of gossip."

Grimes sighed. "That's what I was afraid of. The official line is that some guy Doring put away must have come back for revenge, but McAllister isn't buying it. He thinks Doring was accepting bribes."

"Was he?"

Grimes shrugged. "Possibly. But we can't run that without a mountain of evidence, unless we want to burn every bridge we have with the police department. Hell, everybody over there's wearing black armbands and collecting money for the guy's widow. If we run a dirty-cop story, they're gonna go nuts."

Her heart sank. She'd never thought Grimes would bow to this kind of pressure. "So we're backing off?"

"I didn't say that." His gaze sharpened. "I've never backed off a news story in my life. I just said we need a mountain of evidence. So if you hear anything helpful—and I mean *anything*—pass it on to McAllister. And get busy on your fire story, too. We need a follow-up for tomorrow. Community reaction, plans to rebuild, the full rundown. Can you handle it?"

"Absolutely."

"And make it good, Malone. We've got you on the front page again."

Juarez saw her that afternoon at the intersection of Main Street and San Angelo. She was driving someone else's car—a green Tercel—and wearing sunglasses, but there was no mistaking the mop of blond curls. Cursing, he made an illegal left turn and fell in behind her.

He stayed fairly close, but she didn't seem to notice him. She was too busy yacking away on her cell phone. At the next stoplight, she put the phone away and craned her neck to look in her rearview mirror. He thought she'd spotted the tail, but then she started fiddling with something else. What was she doing? He squinted and leaned forward.

Fucking unbelievable. The woman was being shadowed by a hit man, and she was driving around town in broad daylight putting on lipstick.

She pulled into the lot of a fire station and parked. Without so much as a glance over her shoulder, she jumped out of the car and walked across the parking lot to the front entrance.

Juarez sat there, fuming. Whenever he started to think she had a brain, she pulled something like this. He clenched his hands on the steering wheel and counted to ten. It didn't help. This woman was making him crazy, and he needed to get a grip. If she was hell bent on making a target of herself, there was nothing he could do about it. When she turned up dead, it wouldn't be his fault. He didn't want, or need, to protect her.

Except that he did. He wanted to protect her in the worst way. And for the worst reason.

She reminded him of Paloma.

It wasn't her looks; it was her attitude. That stubborn, go-to-hell attitude that had been his sister's trademark. It had gotten her through the academy. It had helped her make a name for herself as a balls-out cop, despite being a woman. It had helped her rise quickly through the ranks of the SAPD and land a job on their elite vice squad.

It had probably gotten her killed.

Paloma had been determined, confident, even cocky. And it had probably cost her her life.

If Feenie wasn't careful, it would cost her hers, too.

Juarez stared out the window and worked on not grinding his teeth. How long was he going to sit out here waiting for her? He had real work to do, but instead he was stuck in a sweltering truck staking out a fucking prom queen who was too clueless to take care of herself.

Why was he getting so worked up over this? He took a deep breath. Maybe he was just pissed off because an asset to his investigation was being threatened.

Yeah, right. He was pissed off because he liked her. She was careless and irritating as hell and probably untrustworthy, but he liked her anyway. What he needed to do was sleep with her and get it out of his system. Sex was the best cure he knew for emotional attachment. No matter how much he liked a woman, the feelings faded soon after he slept with her. She'd become clingy and possessive, and then he'd cut her loose. Always. Without exception. No matter how hot she was, he'd leave without looking back. Feenie would be no different. He needed to nail her.

His phone rang, and the caller ID told him it was his contact at the DMV.

"Juarez."

"Hey, Marco," a female voice crooned. "I ran that tag you asked about."

"Come up with anything?" He wasn't expecting much. An incomplete license number was a long shot at best.

"You're in luck," she said. "You said 'UT3,' right?"

"That's right."

"Well, a license with 'UT' in it is most likely a vanity plate. Longhorn fans pay big money every year to drive around with those letters on their cars."

"Okay," he said, liking where this was going. "Do you have a name for me?"

"I'm not a miracle worker, honey buns. But like I said, you're in luck. It just so happens that there are only a dozen or so vanity plates with the characters 'UT3' in them in that order. I'll email you the list."

Feenie breezed out the door of the fire station and made her way back across the parking lot, barely noticing her surroundings as she went.

"Thanks," Juarez said, putting his truck in gear. "I owe you one."

"Humph. That's what you said last time. I've started you a tab."

As he hung up, Feenie slid behind the wheel. Juarez followed her back to the office where he'd dropped her off just hours before. Looking slightly more alert now, she passed the newspaper building and swerved into a lot next to a nearby bank. She parked and got out. She locked the car and glanced around briefly before ducking into the alley between the bank and the *Gazette* building.

Juarez made a U-turn, parked, and caught up to her in a few brisk strides. She never even heard him. When he was inches away from her, he grabbed her from behind and shoved her against a Dumpster. She let out a high-pitched squeal, but he silenced it by clamping a hand over her mouth. She squirmed and tried—unsuccessfully—to bite his fingers.

"Shit!"

She'd jabbed him in the thigh with the goddamn heel of her sandal. He used his other leg to sweep her feet out from under her and then twisted his body to catch her weight as they both tumbled to the pavement.

She sprawled on top of him, her eyes wide with fear that instantly turned to anger.

"Juarez!" she yelped, pounding his chest. "What the hell?"

She tried to wriggle away from him, but he tightened his grip on her hips. She wriggled again, and he felt a warm surge of lust.

"I thought I told you to stay put," he said through clenched teeth.

"Let me go! God, you scared me to death!"

He loosened his grip, and she scrambled to her feet. He got up, too, and scowled down at her. The smell of sun-baked garbage surrounded them.

"What are you *doing?*" she demanded, brushing dirt off her jeans.

He crossed his arms. "Just proving what I told you earlier, that you're about to get yourself killed."

"That hurt, you idiot!" She twisted her arm to examine a scrape on her wrist.

"Yeah? Well, a bullet hurts more. I don't know where you got the idea you could protect yourself, but you can't. I've been tailing your ass for nearly an hour now, and I had you trapped in an alley before you even noticed me."

Her chest heaved up and down as she balled her hands at her sides. "If you've been following me, then you know I took a friend's car. To be less conspicuous."

"That worked great."

She frowned, and he braced for a stream of insults. Instead, she burst into tears.

*S*hit. He hated tears. Growing up, they'd always been Paloma's trump card.

"Hey." He put his hand on her shoulder, and she turned away. He eased her around and saw that she looked . . . embarrassed?

"Don't you know I'm a nervous wreck? I *know* my life's in danger! I don't need you reminding me all the time!"

Yes, she did, but he didn't think it was a great moment to mention it. Instead, he pulled her against him and let her cry all over his T-shirt. Her breasts pressed against his rib cage, and the fruity scent of her shampoo drowned out the garbage smell.

Finally, she quieted.

"Babe, I'm trying to help you, but you're making it very hard." In more ways than one. He stepped back.

She sniffled. "You have a real funny way of helping."

She looked up at him, her nose and eyes all pink from crying. He felt a tug of guilt, then dismissed it. Maybe he'd finally gotten through to her.

"Listen," he said. "You've got to protect yourself, but you don't know how. Quit being so stubborn, and admit you need my help."

She drew away and swiped at her cheeks. After straightening her blouse, she tucked her hair behind her ears.

"Fine, you win." She sounded composed again. "What do you want me to do?"

He stared at her a moment, knowing he'd be stupid to answer that question honestly. "Go wrap things up for the day," he told her. "I'll pick you up at the back entrance in twenty minutes."

When Feenie exited the newspaper building fifty minutes later, she saw a black Silverado parked in the alley. A hot guy leaned against it, doing a masterful imitation of a pissed-off boyfriend.

"You're late," Juarez said, taking her elbow and steering her around to the passenger side.

"I've got a job, you know. I can't just vanish into thin air."

"I don't like waiting."

He opened the door and pushed her in before she could think of a witty retort.

"So, where to?" she asked when the engine started.

He backed out of the alley onto Main Street. He glanced at all the mirrors and made a series of turns down random streets until he seemed certain they weren't being followed. Feenie took mental notes on the technique and resolved to try it next time she had to drive anywhere.

"Hello?" she said. "I want to know where we're going."

He spared her a brief glance. He looked irritated, and she didn't know if it was because she'd been late meeting him or if there was something more. His temper seemed constantly set to simmer.

She stared through the windshield and crossed her arms. "Fine. If you're not going to talk to me—"

"Firing range," he said.

"You mean, like, target shooting?"

He looked at her. "You want to protect yourself, you need to know how to use a weapon."

"I do. I'm trained in riflery."

"You're trained."

"Yes."

"And where did you get this training?"

"My dad taught me the basics, and then, before my senior year of college, I worked as a riflery instructor at a summer camp. I had to learn to shoot in prone, sitting, kneeling, and standing positions." She ticked off the four positions on her fingers.

He smirked. "And this was what? Ten years ago?"

"Eight! And besides, I practice. Sometimes when I visit my dad, we shoot skeet together."

"That's great for bird hunting, but when was the last time you fired a handgun?"

It had been at least a decade, but damned if she'd tell him that. "It's probably been a while."

"Then you need to brush up. You can use mine for starters until I can get you something more your speed."

"What's that supposed to mean?"

He smiled. "Trust me. My gun's much too big for you."

She narrowed her eyes at him. Was he teasing her now, or was she just imagining it? She looked out the window. "Yeah, I just bet."

But he wasn't kidding. His gun was all wrong for her. By the fourth clip, Feenie's arms felt as if they were going to fall off. She lowered the Glock and plucked out the earplugs he'd given her.

"How much longer do you want to do this?" she asked.

"Tired already?"

"It's just that it's getting late, and I skipped lunch."

"One more," he said, handing her another clip. She loaded it the way he'd shown her and pointed her arms toward the target again.

"Try it with your left hand," he said.

"But I'm right-handed."

"All the more reason to practice with your left." He eased up behind her and settled his hands on her hips, then nudged her feet apart with the toe of his boot. "Wider stance."

She followed his directions, but he continued to stand right behind her, so close she could feel his body heat. The muscles in her neck tensed. It was impossible to concentrate with him standing there.

"Don't lock your knees."

"Do you mind?" she snapped. "You're crowding me."

He backed away and leaned against the divider separating them from the neighboring shooter.

"Thank you." She adjusted her stance and lifted the gun. Her arm started quivering. She fired but didn't even hit the target, much less the silhouette.

"Whoa, there," he said. "Why don't we call it a day? We can come back tomorrow."

Feenie shrugged and carefully passed him the gun. "Whatever you say."

He took the Glock, put on the safety, and tucked it into his holster. She suddenly understood why he wore a leather jacket everywhere, despite the warm South Texas climate.

"Don't you have to have a permit to carry a concealed weapon?" she asked.

"I've got one. You will, too."

She scoffed. "I don't think I'll need it. I don't own a purse big enough to conceal a thing like that."

"It's kind of clunky, I know. But old habits die hard. These things are pretty standard for law enforcement."

Feenie watched him, debating whether this was a good opening to ask him why he'd left his police job. She'd been curious about that drug bust ever since her chat with McAllister.

"So, I was wondering—"

"Don't worry," he said. "We'll get you something more your size. Good news is, your aim's not bad. You need to get in shape, though." He shrugged into his jacket and pocketed the earplugs they'd been using.

"What's wrong with my shape?"

"You have no upper-body strength. You need to get some. You won't be able to hit crap if your arms turn to Jell-O every time you pick up a gun."

Jell-O arms. How nice. Sure, she'd put on a few pounds since her divorce, but she didn't look *that* bad.

Or did she?

"Hey, relax," he said, finally noticing he'd offended her. "We'll work on it. You've got a pretty good start—probably from the swimming."

He punched the button to bring their target back in. She removed her safety glasses and took a long look at the paper. Several shots—his—had hit the center of the silhouette, while the rest had peppered the area around the black form. Those were her shots, along with some that had missed the target completely. He was right. Her body and her marksmanship both needed work.

"Fine," she said, swallowing her pride. "Just tell me what I need to do."

He chucked her under the chin. "We need to hit the gym. But we'll get something to eat first."

They stopped by her house to change clothes—he kept his gym bag in his truck—and then he took her to a drive-through burger joint in a shady section of town. Feenie had never been there before, but she took the line of cars as a positive sign.

"What's good here?" she asked when they pulled up to the menu board.

"Everything."

"That's helpful."

"Try the onion rings. Guaranteed to clog your arteries, but they're worth it." He turned to the window and ordered two cheeseburgers and a side of onion rings.

Just hearing the words made her mouth water, but she remembered the Jell-O comment. "I'll have a strawberry milkshake. Kiddie-size."

He arched his eyebrows.

"What? I don't want to fill up too much before we work out."

"Suit yourself." He called in her order and waited, window down, as the line of cars crept forward. The smell of deep-fried onions wafted into the pickup, and Feenie's stomach growled.

"So this case you're working on," she said, more to cover the noise than anything else. "Is it typical for you? I thought PIs mainly did I-think-my-wife's-cheating-on-me kind of stuff."

"I get some of that. But workers comp cases are

my bread and butter. Factories in the valley are always getting hit with claims. The insurance companies hire me to look into things and see whether they're legit."

"Are they?"

He checked all the mirrors and scanned the horizon with an eagle eye. He always seemed on high alert. "Sometimes. But sometimes they're phony. It's all pretty boring, really, but it pays the bills."

He didn't strike her as the type of guy to stick with a job he thought was boring. But then again, she wrote obits for a living, so who was she to criticize? Maybe he liked other aspects of his work.

"I guess the clandestine-affair stuff's a little more exciting?"

He pulled up to the pickup window and took out his wallet.

"Not really," he said. She tried to hand him some money, but he waved it away. "My favorite cases are deadbeat dads. I like tracking down those guys, making 'em pay up. The suspicious spouse stuff's depressing."

"Why?"

He shrugged. "Most times when people think their spouse is cheating, they're right. But when they come to me—especially the women—they're hoping I'll prove them wrong. It's pretty rare I get to do that. Ninety-nine percent of the time, I nail the guy. Or girl, whichever it is."

"Woman," Feenie said, stuffing the bills back into her purse.

"What?"

"You nail the *woman*. Calling someone's fifty-year-old wife a girl is a little demeaning, don't you think?"

The corner of his mouth curled up. "I didn't realize you were a feminist."

"I'm not." Maybe if she had been, she would have had sense enough not to quit her job after she married Josh. Then she wouldn't have had to start over careerwise after their divorce. "I'm just making an observation. People are always saying stuff like 'How come a pretty girl like you's not married?' It gets annoying."

He laughed. "Okay, didn't mean to annoy you. Next time, you can pay for dinner."

Whoops. He had here there. She was about to get her money back out, but he seemed to enjoy watching her squirm, so she changed the subject instead.

"I wish I'd known someone like you when I was married to Josh. Of course, I had no idea he was cheating, so I guess I wouldn't have hired you anyway."

Juarez paid for the food and passed Feenie a cold paper cup and a warm sack. She put the cup between her legs and peeked inside the bag. It smelled heavenly, and again she wished she'd ordered the rings.

Juarez pulled out of the parking lot. "Mind handing me one of those burgers? I'm starving."

She unwrapped the sandwich and gave it to him before settling in with her shake. The bag sat on her lap, all warm and aromatic. Juarez reached in a pulled out an onion ring.

"You really never knew your husband was cheating on you?"

She sucked on her straw, which immediately became clogged with ice cream. She removed the lid and stirred the shake around. "Nope. Not a clue."

He sneered.

"What? You don't believe me?"

"There's always a clue. You probably weren't paying attention."

She bristled at that, mainly because she'd told herself the same thing repeatedly in the months following her divorce. But she really hadn't known. She'd been the quintessential clueless wife, which was part of the reason her divorce was so humiliating. She sighed and scooped up a glob of milkshake. "Guess that about describes it. Dumb blonde. Last to know."

He pulled up to a stoplight and reached over for another onion ring. She held her breath and looked away while his hand delved into the sack.

"You're not dumb," he said. "I bet you'd picked up on a lot of clues, you just weren't ready to face facts. Where'd you two meet, anyway?"

She stirred her shake. It was good, but his food smelled much better. "At a soup kitchen."

"A soup kitchen?"

"Yeah. I'd just moved back here after college, but I didn't have a job yet, so I was volunteering at the food pantry. They used to run a soup kitchen there before the funding dried up. Now they just deliver groceries to people who are homebound. Kind of like Meals on Wheels."

"You're telling me Garland was busy feeding the poor when you met?"

"Yep. Pretty heartwarming, I know. I totally fell for his act." Screw it. She reached into the bag and pulled out a warm, greasy onion ring. It tasted even better than she'd imagined. "Wow."

"Told you."

She shot him a peevish look as she ate another ring. "Anyway, we met at the soup kitchen on Thanksgiving Day. After we'd dated a few weeks, he told me about this job opening at his law firm. His father's firm, actually. It was a receptionist job with 'potential for advancement,' or at least that's what he said."

"You don't need a college degree to answer phones."

"Thank you, I'm aware of that. But my degree was in English lit, so it didn't exactly open a lot of doors. The job paid better than volunteer work, so I jumped on it. At the time, my dad was on my case about being unemployed after he'd spent hard-earned money on my education."

"What'd you think of Garland's law firm?"

"It was okay, I guess." She frowned at the memory. "The lawyers were kind of stuffy, though. And they treated the support staff like crap." She remembered Juarez's assistant. Feenie had met her twice now, and both times she'd gotten the impression the woman was intelligent, capable, and bored out of her mind.

"Most people do, you know, which is really poor strategy. If I had my own business, I'd make sure to keep my support staff happy."

Juarez shot her a sideways look. "You have something to say, spit it out."

Feenie shrugged. "I think Teresa's underutilized. She seems too smart for what she's doing. Why don't you let her help you with clients? Maybe some of the insurance work you don't enjoy."

Juarez took a few turns, winding his way through a part of town Feenie had definitely never been in before. "I wasn't aware you two were close," he said.

"I talked to her when I came to your office, and I recognize boredom when I see it. If you don't give her something interesting to do, you're going to lose her. But what do I know? I'm not a PI."

He mumbled something that sounded like agreement.

"Where are we going?" she asked, changing the subject. Juarez clearly didn't welcome her business advice.

"The gym. We're almost there." He reached into the sack for the second burger. "What did you mean when you said you totally fell for Garland's act?"

She put her shake in the cup holder and devoted herself to the rings. Maybe if she ate enough onions, she'd make sure to avoid kissing him. As it was, she'd been thinking about little else since he'd stood behind her at the firing range.

"Everything Josh does is for show," she said.

"That's how he is. He volunteered at the soup kitchen, but I realized later he only did it on holidays when the media was likely to show up. He did pro bono work for his dad's firm, but only when it was an easy case or something with a publicity angle. It's all about image. And everything's a part of his five-year plan."

Juarez pulled into a lot and parked next to what looked like an old warehouse.

"Are we here?" she asked.

"Yeah. But I want to hear about the five-year plan."

She slurped up the last of her shake. She hated talking about Josh, but she supposed it was better to get it out of the way. Juarez would just keep prodding until he got the answers he wanted.

"He had these five-year plans," she said. "He just finished up the first phase, which was getting married and making partner by age thirty-five. Next five years, he'll be building rapport with business leaders around town and running for city council. He never talked more than two plans ahead, but I'm pretty sure he has his sights set on mayor."

Juarez watched her, clearly hanging on every word. He seemed to have boundless curiosity where Josh was concerned. Once again, she wondered if he was merely using her for his investigation. His concern seemed so genuine at times, but then whenever she let her guard down, he started fishing for information.

"I take it divorce wasn't part of the plan?" he asked.

She scoffed. "Wasn't part of mine. But if he didn't want me to throw off his schedule, he should have kept his pants zipped. My guess is, he'll be remarried in the next year or two. Probably to someone well connected and wealthy."

"Interesting. And I guess his father's contacts help pave the way for all this?"

"You bet. Look, let's not talk about Josh anymore, okay? I'm sick of thinking about him." Feenie reached into the sack and was surprised to find only one onion ring left. She looked up, and Juarez was grinning at her.

"Sorry," she muttered, offering him the last one.

"You take it."

"No, you. Then at least I know you won't try and kiss me."

Her cheeks warmed as she realized she'd said that out loud. She hadn't meant to. Except that she had. She was baiting him, and they both knew it.

He leaned closer. "You really think an onion ring is gonna get in my way if I want to kiss you?" His voice was low and sultry.

She gulped. "Yes."

He dipped his head down and kissed her, and she felt a surge of heat in her lap. She wished she could blame the fast-food bag, but it was empty now.

He was smiling when he pulled back. "See? Onions not a problem."

"Not for you, maybe. I hate onion breath." She tried to sound annoyed, but it came out more like flustered.

He grinned, clearly seeing right through her. "Let's go inside," he said. "We'll finish this conversation later."

In her former life, Feenie had worked out in the posh fitness center attached to the Mayfield Country Club. Decked out in stylish workout clothes, she had sweated and pumped iron surrounded by peppy music, surgically enhanced bodies, and all the latest fitness equipment.

Chico's Gym was the opposite of posh.

Feenie looked around in wonder as Juarez led her through the door. The place was a converted warehouse with a concrete floor and fluorescent lighting. Weight machines and punching bags were scattered about, and the focal point of the room was an elevated boxing ring. No one was sparring at the moment, but Feenie got the impression the ring had been well used.

A heavily tattooed behemoth stood guard just inside the entrance. Juarez nodded at him and said something in Spanish as they walked by. The guy looked Feenie up and down, then nodded his head a fraction.

"Was that Chico?" she asked when they were out of earshot.

"His brother, Eduardo," Juarez said.

"No wonder. He doesn't look very *chico* to me."

"Neither does Chico. They're pretty hard-core. Chico runs a weightlifting clinic called House of Pain."

"Yikes. And what's Eduardo do?"

Juarez shrugged. "Dunno. Keeps out the riffraff?"

Yeah, sure. Most of the gym's inhabitants looked pretty rough around the edges. All had tattoos. Few were female. She felt dozens of pairs of eyes on her as she crossed the room, silently cursing her choice in workout gear. In a sleeveless yellow tank top and pink shorts, she felt like an Easter egg. Juarez's hand pressed against the small of her back, ostensibly to steer her in the right direction but in reality to announce to everyone in the place that she was with him. The underlying threat was clear. The fledgling feminist in her wanted to be offended, but her inner wimp felt absurdly grateful.

Instead of peppy music, Feenie heard clanging metal and moans of pain as they made their way to an empty corner. Juarez put her duffle bag on the floor and picked up a big black ball.

"Let's start with the medicine ball," he said, holding it out to her. He wore a black T-shirt and shorts, and she tried not to dwell on the way his pecs looked pressed against the cotton. She didn't see any tattoos, but that didn't mean—

"Here," he said, cutting off her thoughts.

She took the ball from him and immediately dropped it on her foot. "Ouch! You didn't tell me it was heavy!"

"It's a medicine ball. What'd you expect?"

She took a deep breath and picked it up. "This weighs a thousand pounds. What do you want me to do with it?"

He stepped back. "Twelve pounds. And we'll start by passing it back and forth."

Twenty minutes later, her arms were shaking again.

She'd passed the medicine ball. She'd thrown the medicine ball. She'd done squats and crunches with it held high above her head. They moved on to barbells and a few machines before ending up on the mat again. Feenie managed three push-ups before collapsing.

"Okay, that's enough," he finally said. "Let's move on to some footwork."

"Footwork," she repeated, gasping for air. They'd been at it for nearly an hour, and Juarez had barely broken a sweat.

"I'm going to show you some basic self-defense. Now, just stand there while I grab you from behind."

"That sounds familiar."

Seconds later, he'd hooked his arm around her neck. She pulled against it, but it didn't budge.

"You're wasting your effort," he said. "You're gonna be smaller than your attacker, so don't make it about strength."

He showed her how to stomp on her assailant's foot and slip out of the neck hold. He demonstrated how to go for all the vulnerable body parts: eyes, ears, throat, and—of course—groin. They practiced several kinds of holds, and Feenie managed to slip out of a few of them. At one point, she swept her leg around and tripped him. He dropped to his knees and popped up again.

"Not bad," he said, smiling. "Your agility's good."

His breathing matched hers for the first time since they'd started, and Feenie felt incredibly happy with herself.

"Agility's my specialty. Four years of cheerleading'll do that for you."

"Cheerleading, huh? I should have known."

"Hey." She picked up a towel and blotted the sweat off her neck. "Don't knock it. If I have any coordination at all, it's from all those dance routines."

"I'm not knocking it." He slipped the towel out of her hand and draped it around her neck. "Anything that makes you safer works for me."

Her throat tightened. Did he really care about her, or was this all part of the act? She watched him for a moment, wishing she could read his mind. But he was good at concealing his thoughts.

The lights blinked. She looked around and suddenly noticed they were the last two people in the gym. The clock on the wall said ten twenty-five.

"I think I'd better get home," she said, reaching for her duffle bag. "I've got some stuff to do, and if

I'm not in bed by midnight, I turn into a pumpkin."

Juarez took the duffle bag from her and shouldered it. It wasn't heavy, but he'd stashed his gun in it and seemed intent on having it nearby at all times.

"I'll have you in bed by midnight, but I'm not taking you home," he said. "You're spending the night with me."

CHAPTER

10

W hat?" she said, scurrying after him. He was
halfway to the door when she grabbed his arm.
"Juarez, wait!"

He halted and looked back at her.

"I'm not spending the night with you!"

No way. No how. She never should have baited
him into kissing her back in the pickup.

"Yes, you are." He turned around and continued
walking.

She followed him to the gym entrance, where
Eduardo stood with a ring of keys. He and Juarez exchanged a few words as they stepped outside. Juarez
hustled Feenie into his truck and slid behind the
wheel.

"Look, Juarez—"

"Save the arguments." He started up the engine and checked all the mirrors. He wove through downtown Mayfield, making random turns until she was utterly lost. Were they heading to Pecan Street or his place? She had no idea. Then she caught a glimpse of the water, which meant they were nowhere near her house.

"Juarez, I don't think—"

"You got that right."

"Hey, I'm talking here! I said I'm not spending the night with you, and I meant it!"

He pulled into a gravel lot, where a hand-painted sign advertised live shrimp and mackerel. He backed the Silverado into a parking space facing out.

"Where are we?" she asked.

"Bayside Marina. You were saying?"

She glanced around. Several long piers stretched out into the water, and dozens of sailboat masts thrust up into the night sky. Moonlight shimmered off the water, and the place looked deserted.

"Are we . . . parking, for God's sake?"

He chuckled softly. "I hadn't thought of that. But we are parked." He leaned over and slid his hand behind her neck.

"Juarez—"

"Look, you're here so I can protect you. That's it."

She shook off his hand and looked around. "You mean to tell me you live here? At a marina?"

"Yep."

"Like, on a boat?"

"Yep."

"And you want me to stay on your boat with you?"

"You're catching on."

He unzipped the duffle at her feet, pulled out his Glock, and checked to make sure it was loaded. Then he surveyed the area around the truck. After a moment, his gaze landed back on her.

"No come-ons, I promise," he said. "I just want to keep an eye on you."

She watched him and felt her resolve waning. In all honesty, she'd felt safer for the past six hours than she had for the past several weeks. Her body was screaming for a good night's sleep, and with Juarez on guard, she could get one.

At least, she hoped she could. He'd said no come-ons, and she was tempted to take him at his word. Although *his* good intentions might not be the real problem here. It was entirely possible he had more willpower than she did.

"Does your boat have a smoke detector?" she asked.

He looked puzzled, and she could hardly blame him. Her obsession with smoke detectors was a little odd.

"Sorry, no smoke detector. But I've got a fire extinguisher under the sink."

A sink. So it had plumbing. "Does your boat have a shower?"

He smiled. "All the comforts of home. Hell, you can even have the bed."

"If it has you in it, I'm taking the floor."

"Not necessary. I'll sleep on the sofa."

"Your boat has a sofa?"

"It's more of a bench seat." He shrugged. "I'll be fine."

She followed him down the pier, past ski boats and sloops and a few yachts. He stopped in front of a white fiberglass fishing rig and offered a hand to help her aboard. The boat was spacious but kind of old, judging by the shape. Feenie couldn't tell much else in the dimness. He led her down a short ladder into the cabin and showed her the galley and the head. He flipped on a light. As promised, there was a cramped shower. He opened a cabinet and gave her a towel.

"I can probably dig up a spare toothbrush somewhere, too. And the bed's just in there." He nodded toward a dark little space that occupied the hull. "Make yourself at home." He left her alone in the tiny bathroom and closed the door.

Feenie immediately noticed the faint scent of shaving cream. It was such a masculine smell, and it reminded her just how long it had been since she'd shared quarters with a man. Josh had always been big on expensive colognes, which Feenie couldn't stand, especially after she'd realized he'd probably been using them all the time to cover up other kinds of scents from his nights "working late." She hadn't hated the colognes at the time, but she hated them retroactively.

Kind of like Josh.

On a hunch, Feenie opened Juarez's medicine cabinet. Horrible etiquette, yes, but she was besieged by curiosity. Ha! She'd been right. Not a bottle of cologne in sight. Just a few blue disposable razors, a tube of toothpaste, some sun block, and a can of Gillette shaving cream. For some reason, she felt relieved.

But then her eyes veered back to the sun block. It was that pricey Bain de Soleil made especially for faces. Definitely something a female would buy. Clearly, Feenie was not the first woman to spend time on Juarez's boat.

She stared at the bottle, biting her lip. *Curiosity killed the cat.* That's what Feenie's mother used to say when she would find Feenie and Rachel snooping around for hidden Christmas presents. Except in this case, maybe curiosity was *warning* the cat. Feenie shut the cabinet, took off her clothes, and got into the shower.

Afterward, she went into the sleeping cabin and found a T-shirt folded neatly on the bed. She slipped into it, switched off the light by the door, and crawled under the blankets to try to get some sleep.

Given how exhausted she was, she thought she'd be out instantly. She heard the shower running and some rustling around in the galley and then Juarez's footsteps on deck. He was as far away from her as he could get and still be on the boat. Good. She should really sleep. But she couldn't relax. It was probably adrenaline or nerves or . . . something. Finally, she tossed back the covers and went into the galley. She opened the mini-fridge and found a few cans of Tecate. She grabbed a beer and was about to take it up on deck when she heard voices.

"That's the part that doesn't make sense," someone was saying. "Why not two to the back? And doesn't your guy have military training?"

"Yeah, sharpshooter." She recognized Juarez's voice and crept toward the ladder so she could hear better.

"Okay, so you'd expect him to do something subtle, right? Like hide at a distance and use a scope."

"But instead we've got a close-range handgun," Juarez said.

"A .45, both jobs. Which—"

The floor creaked under Feenie's feet, and they stopped talking. They'd obviously heard her, so she might as well come clean.

"Hi," she said, going up the ladder. The guy talking to Juarez was tall and beefy, but she couldn't see much more in the moonlight.

"I thought you were asleep." Juarez's gaze swept over her, and she didn't know whether the heated look was because he liked or *didn't* like her modeling his San Antonio Spurs T-shirt in front of his friend. "Meet Rick Peterson, my former partner."

The man looked at Feenie and then back at Juarez. "Sorry, man. I didn't know you had company."

"He doesn't," she said. "I mean, I'm just visiting." That didn't help, either. Juarez just stood there smirking. "I'm not *that* kind of company."

"This is Feenie Malone," Juarez finally said.

"Ma'am." Peterson nodded and shook her hand, which felt pretty strange considering she had barely anything on and her hair was still damp from the shower. Anyone with two brain cells would assume she and Juarez were sleeping together, and Juarez didn't seem at all eager to correct the impression.

"Peterson was just filling me in on the ballistics reports from the Martinez and Doring murders."

"Oh." As if she hadn't already gathered that.

"Feenie's a reporter," Juarez said. "She likes to eavesdrop."

She crossed her arms and turned to Peterson. "So you were saying? About the .45?"

Peterson looked at Juarez, clearly not sure whether to continue.

"It's okay. She's in the loop."

He cleared his throat. "I was just telling Marco, both victims were shot with a .45 at close range. Which is kind of surprising."

"Surprising because?" Feenie asked.

"Well, ma'am, they were shot in the chest. Which means—"

"Which means the victims probably knew their assailant because they let him get close." It was a guess, but she thought it sounded logical.

Peterson's eyebrows went up, and she glanced at Juarez. "Am I right?"

He cocked his head to the side. "It's possible. It's also possible they *didn't* know the shooter, but he didn't seem threatening. Otherwise, they wouldn't have let him pull a weapon."

"Because cops and drug dealers are so street-smart," Feenie said. "There's no way they'd get taken by surprise like that. Is that what you're saying?"

"That about sums it up," Juarez said.

Peterson glanced at his watch. "Look, Marco, I need to get home. I just wanted to fill you in." He turned to Feenie. "It was nice meeting you. I'd appreciate not reading about this conversation, you know, in the newspaper or anything."

Feenie smiled. "It's off the record. If you see anything about this in the paper, it didn't come from me."

"Thanks." He nodded at Juarez. "Sorry for interrupting."

After he left, Juarez seated himself on the port side of the boat and hung his legs over the edge. He'd changed into jeans and a white T-shirt after his shower. Feenie sat down beside him.

"Thanks for letting him think I'm your playmate," she said.

"Hey, I didn't tell you to come up here dressed like that. What was he supposed to think?"

"I don't know. I guess I didn't really consider it until it was too late."

"You mean until we caught you eavesdropping?"

She rolled her eyes.

He knocked his knee against hers playfully. "What happened down there? Couldn't sleep?"

"Nope." She took a sip of beer. They had a nice

view of the marina and the seemingly endless line of boats. She loved boats, but not enough to live on one. "How long have you lived here?"

"About six months, I guess. I used to have an apartment, but living here's cheaper. And it's closer to downtown, so it cuts down on my commute." He smiled. Mayfield wasn't big enough for anyone to have much of a commute, so it had to be purely economics that kept him here.

"So, you've had this thing how long, then?" she asked. His boat looked sturdy but aging. It was big, though, at least thirty-two feet.

"Used to belong to my dad." He took a swig. "After he died, my three brothers and I used her for fishing. But they don't live in town, so it was really mostly me. Finally, I just bought their shares and moved in."

"Wow. Three brothers. That's a big family."

"Yeah."

Bit by bit, she was getting a picture of his personal life. She'd have to be patient, though. He didn't seem like someone to open up all at once.

"What did your dad do?" she asked.

"He was a cop."

Interesting. He'd followed in his father's footsteps. Also interesting that he didn't elaborate.

"And your mom?"

"She used to work at a preschool, in the nursery. But she quit a while ago. Started having back problems, probably from picking up babies all the time." He looked at her. "What about your family?"

Very crafty. The question steered the conversation back to her without making it seem as if he wanted to shut her out. If there was one thing she recognized, it was interview techniques. Make the subject comfortable. Give them just enough information to put them at ease, then let them talk.

"Well, it's just my dad and me, really. My mom and sister died in a car wreck when I was a kid." She watched him but couldn't read his face. It wasn't just the darkness—he was good at masking his emotions. He hadn't so much as flinched when she'd said the word *died*. Most people did. "My dad's retired now. Used to be a manager at one of the oil refineries here, but now he lives in Port Aransas. He spends most of his time fishing and hunting and stuff like that."

"Tell me about your mom."

She looked away. "You know, for someone who doesn't say much, you really get to the point, don't you?"

He shrugged. "I'm curious."

She sighed. "I don't know. Like what?"

"Like, what was she like? Career woman? Stay-at-home mom? Nut case?"

She laughed softly. "None of those things, really. She was just, I don't know, a *mom*, I guess. She worked as a librarian at an elementary school. She loved to read. She loved . . ." Her voice trailed off as she pictured her mother singing and moving her hips back and forth as she washed up the dinner dishes.

"She loved . . . ?"

Feenie smiled. "This is gonna make her sound like a total dork, and she wasn't, but she loved the Statler Brothers."

"The Statler Brothers."

"You've probably never heard of them, I know. They're this kind of barber shop quartet out of . . . I don't know, Tennessee, I think? Anyway, my mom loved them. I always think of her when I hear their music, which is pretty rare, really, because it's not like it's Top Forty or anything. I pretty much only hear it at my dad's. He has all her old albums."

"The Statler Brothers, huh? *Flowers on the Wall,* that kind of thing?"

He could have started speaking Chinese and she wouldn't have been more shocked. "You've heard of them?"

"Sure."

"No way. I can't believe—"

"I'm a Quentin Tarantino fan."

"Okay." She wasn't following.

"That song's on the soundtrack for *Pulp Fiction,* one of my favorite movies."

The fact that he knew it from a movie made it only a little less astonishing. "Okay, I'm officially impressed," she said.

He smiled at her in the moonlight, and she felt a warm glow. But then her thoughts turned serious.

"There's something I'm confused about," she said. "It's about your conversation with Peterson."

"I knew you were eavesdropping."

"That's right," she said, watching the smile leave his face. He probably knew what she was about to ask. "This guy you think might be trying to kill me, if he's a sharpshooter, how come I'm not dead?"

He didn't say anything for a moment. "I don't know."

Not the response she'd been hoping for.

"So why are you bothering with all this self-defense stuff? If you're right about this guy, I don't really stand a chance."

"Great attitude," he said. "I didn't know you were such a cynic."

"I'm just trying to be realistic here." She tried to sound tough, but he must have heard the fear in her voice, because he reached over and took her hand, surprising her. The concerned look on his face surprised her even more.

"First of all, I don't know who's after you. Not for certain. But my two primary suspects have military training, so I'm worried. I want you to be able to protect yourself in case this thing gets up close and personal. I know you think I've been following you around because I'm paranoid or I just want to get you into bed, but that's not it. I think this guy might try and grab you. Sometime when I'm not around."

"Wow," she said. His words were giving her chills.

"If you *are* being targeted," he continued, "it's be-cause you have information or might get information someone doesn't want you to have. If that's the case, that person probably wants a chance to find out exactly what you know."

Her stomach did a flip-flop. "You mean before he kills me?"

"I don't know." He squeezed her hand. "It's just something I'm worried about."

Her heart was thudding so loudly she was sure he could hear it. She felt scared and confused. And on top of it all, she felt an unexpected wave of tenderness toward Juarez. Where did he get this fierce desire to protect her? If he loved her, that would be one thing, but she wasn't even his girlfriend. She looked down at their intertwined hands. His was big and brown and roughened by calluses. Hers was small and smooth and lily-white by comparison. They were from two totally different backgrounds, but that fact seemed insignificant at the moment.

She looked up at him, and his eyes were dark and warm. She held his gaze, trying to read what was in his mind.

Then his cell phone buzzed, shattering the moment.

He pulled his hand loose and dug the phone out of his pocket. Looking away, he flipped it open. "Juarez." A long pause. "Who the fuck is this?"

He jerked the phone from his ear and checked the caller ID.

"Listen, you sick fuck—"

He stopped talking and went very still. "Where?" Another long pause. "I'll be there. And you'd better be, too."

He snapped the phone shut and jumped to his feet.

"What was that?" Feenie said, jumping up, too.

"Come on."

"Come where? Who was on the phone?"

He grabbed her hand and pulled her toward the cabin door. "Put some clothes on. And get your purse." He glanced at his watch. "We don't have much time."

"Time for what?"

He looked at her, his mouth set in a grim line. "We're going on a field trip."

Juarez spotted the sign for Luv's Truck Stop and careened across two lanes of traffic to make the turnoff. He sped across the pavement, ignoring speed bumps and stop signs as he searched the area for a black Ford Bronco. It wasn't here. Juarez checked his watch. He was twenty minutes late, and the caller might have already left. Or maybe he'd never shown up in the first place. It would be just his shitty luck.

Luv's was bustling with late-night customers— truckers, mostly, by the look of the lot. Juarez slowed his pickup as he passed the restaurant entrance. There were dozens of people milling around smoking and talking. He let his gaze skim over the faces illuminated by floodlights and neon beer signs, looking for anyone who seemed to be watching him too closely. He saw a few working girls and a lot of middle-aged men wearing cowboy hats and shit-kickers. None of them looked like an ex-con out on a scam.

A pretty blonde in low-rise jeans stood next to the front door, talking on her cell phone. She was short and stacked, and she made Juarez think of another pretty blonde, the one he'd dumped at Peterson's apartment on his way out of town. Feenie had pro-tested wildly and called Juarez every foul name she could think of—which had been comical, really—before finally realizing nothing she could say would make him explain what was happening or bring her along. If this meeting took place at all, Juarez ex-pected it to be brief. Still, he owed Peterson big-time. Babysitting a spitting-mad female definitely merited at least a case of beer.

Juarez pulled the Silverado into a space and took a moment to look around. The far side of the lot was occupied by eighteen-wheelers and a few RVs. Beside the diesel pumps, underneath the garish light of the gas station, he spotted a black Ford Bronco.

The caller was here.

Juarez pulled out his Glock and checked it. He returned it to his holster before driving over to the pumping station and pulling up alongside the beat-up SUV.

The kid slouching against it couldn't have been

more than twenty. He was hairless except for a soul patch under his bottom lip, and he wore olive-green cargo pants and an SS Bootboys T-shirt. Juarez noted the swastika tattoo on his right forearm, which confirmed his suspicions that the guy was a skinhead. Tonight's phone call was no joke. Whoever this guy was, he knew details about Paloma that hadn't been released to the media.

The piece of shit had talked about her tattoo, the naked angel that Paloma had had inked just above her left hip bone on her eighteenth birthday. Few had seen it. Juarez himself wouldn't even know of it except that he'd been at his parents' house visiting one Sunday when Paloma had walked through the kitchen in a bikini, and his father had nearly had a stroke. He hadn't cared so much that his daughter had a tattoo, but he'd thought the design she'd chosen was a sacrilege.

The skinhead looked on sullenly as Juarez got out of his truck. He was tall but bony. He'd probably joined a white supremacist group in prison for protection. "You bring the money?" he asked.

Juarez did a visual inventory of the guy's silhouette. He wasn't packing a gun, unless he had something small stashed in his combat boot. But that didn't mean he didn't have an armed buddy lurking around somewhere, possibly in the SUV.

"Hey, fuckhead! *Habla inglés?*"

Juarez stopped in front of him and crossed his arms. "Yes."

"I said, did you bring my money?"

"We'll get to that. First I want to hear about your cell mate."

The kid stepped away from the car and glowered down at him. He was taller than Juarez by several inches, so he'd mistakenly assumed he could take him on.

"Money first. We agreed on a thousand."

Juarez pulled a roll of bills out of his pocket. He peeled off a hundred and held it up. "Here's a down payment. You'll get the rest when I get information."

"I'll get it when I fucking want it, wetback."

In two swift motions, Juarez jabbed the kid's throat and swept his feet out from under him. He landed flat on his back, and Juarez pinned him there, pressing the heel of his boot against his sternum. Something moved inside the Bronco.

"Here's how this is gonna work," Juarez told him. "First, you tell your friend to aim that gun someplace else. Second, I let you stand up so you can tell me about your cell mate without attracting attention. Third, I give you the money. *Comprende,* fuckhead?"

The punk was wide-eyed now and struggling for air. Juarez leaned on his boot and pulled his jacket back so the guy could see his Glock.

The kid glanced at the Bronco and gave a slight shake of his head. Juarez stepped back and watched him struggle to his feet. His attention was focused on Juarez's roll of bills.

"About six months ago, I was doing a stint in

Sugar Land," he said hoarsely. "They put me in with this guy Ruiz."

"First name," Juarez said.

"I dunno, man. We were only together a few days. He just went by Ruiz. He was in for drugs."

"Okay. What'd he tell you?"

He eyed the money again. Juarez got the impression he and his friend needed a fix.

"He was always bragging about his hot-shit connections. Said he wouldn't be in for long because someone was taking care of him."

"Taking care of him how?"

"I dunno. But he was untouchable. Not like he was big or nothin', but no one ever bothered him. He said he was related to Manny Saledo, and shit, maybe he was."

The kid's story had a ring of truth to it. Manny Saledo was a notorious drug kingpin who controlled a large part of the Mexican marijuana market. Juarez wanted to hear more. "And?"

"And he was transferred outta there a few days later. The day before he left, he started bragging about how a few years back, he helped some guy kidnap and torture a coupla cops. Said he watched the guy cap 'em and helped bury the bodies."

Torture. God*damn* it.

Juarez swallowed the bile in his throat and stared into the kid's gray eyes. Was it possible he was looking at Paloma's killer?

An eighteen-wheeler rumbled up and hissed to a

halt next to one of the gas pumps. Juarez sensed the driver climbing out of the cab, but he couldn't tear his gaze away from this skinny punk who might have murdered his sister. Juarez's chest constricted, and he could hardly breathe. His rage was choking him.

He searched the kid's eyes, looking for something, some flicker of evil. Or even intelligence. But it wasn't there. This kid didn't seem capable of covertly kidnapping and murdering two cops. He barely seemed capable of holding up a liquor store.

"Where?" Juarez asked over the noise of another approaching truck.

"Where what?" the kid shouted back.

"Where'd he bury the bodies?"

He rolled his eyes. "Fuck if I know. That's all he told me."

Juarez fought for control. "What's your name?"

"No dice, man. You think I want trouble with Manny Saledo?"

Juarez started to pocket his money, and the guy panicked.

"Okay, okay! My name's . . . Dave Johnson. But this isn't about me. I didn't have nothin' to do with Ruiz except for those three days in the joint. I told you everything I know."

"Oh, yeah? Then how'd you find me? How'd you know my sister's a missing police officer?"

The corner of the kid's mouth lifted, and Juarez struggled not to bash his teeth in. *Dave Johnson.* What a load of bullshit.

"Internet, man," he said.

"Internet?"

"Yeah, I checked on the Web after Ruiz left. Read some news stories about two cops in San Antonio who disappeared. Article said your hometown, so I tracked you down."

That sounded like bullshit, too. There had to be dozens of Juarezes in Mayfield alone. What, had he taken out the phone book and dialed them all? If so, had he freaking called Juarez's *mother* and asked her if her daughter was missing? Juarez wanted to kill the guy.

"Hey, I ain't got all night. Where's the money?"

Juarez held out the roll. When the kid reached for it, Juarez yanked it away.

"Hey!" This time, he lunged.

Juarez body-slammed him into the Bronco and pressed his cheek against the glass. Through the tinted windows, Juarez saw a chubby girl cowering in the backseat, clutching a pistol. She looked bug-eyed and terrified, and she was pointing the gun straight toward the ceiling. What a couple of posers. Juarez needed to end this.

"How did you *really* find me?" Juarez growled in his ear. The kid smelled like BO and desperation.

"Really, man. It was the Internet. I swear. You have a Web site! Gulf Shores Investigators. That's how I found you."

The trucker fueling up his rig was starting to stare,

and Juarez loosened his grip. "Dave" slumped back against the car and looked at Juarez's hand.

"Come on, man," he pleaded. "I really need the money."

Juarez grabbed a fistful of his T-shirt and leaned in close. "If you ever call, or touch, or even *look* at anyone named Juarez ever again, I will make you sorry you were born."

Juarez tossed a hundred on the ground and went back to his truck.

What a fucking night. And it wasn't over yet, either. Now he had to drive forty miles back to Mayfield and face the wrath of Feenie.

CHAPTER

11

Feenie woke the next morning to the squawking of birds. She tried to sit up, but her body felt as if it was covered in sandbags. She remembered the medicine ball. Then she remembered Juarez.

He'd collected her at Peterson's apartment shortly after one a.m. Collected her, like she was a child out on a play date or something. Furious beyond words, she'd given him the silent treatment all the way back to his boat. Then she'd stalked into his bedroom and slammed the pathetically thin door, hoping the bench seat was every bit as uncomfortable as it looked. Soothed by the prospect of his misery, she'd curled up under his blankets and slept like the dead. Now her muscles ached, and she felt very much alive.

Damn that medicine ball.

She buried her face in the pillow and thought about going back to sleep. The sheets were soft and cozy and smelled like fabric softener. She opened her eyes. Gray sheets and a navy bedspread. Not fancy but comfortable. Was that the real Juarez? He was so secretive she really didn't know.

Feenie propped herself on her elbows and looked around. Sunlight streamed through the portholes, and she got her first good look at the place. The bed, such as it was, occupied the V-shape of the hull. The walls were lined with shelves, which overflowed with paperbacks. She surveyed the titles. He liked true crime and military history, apparently. Next to the books were a portable TV and some personal items: a sports watch, a framed photograph, a chipped mug.

Feenie studied the picture. A dark-haired woman pushed a toddler on a swing. The woman looked to be sixty or so. His mother? And who was the child? A kid from a previous marriage, maybe? That was definitely something she needed to find out about. She reached for the watch. One look at it had her catapulting out of bed.

"Juarez!" she yelled, yanking open the door. She scampered up the ladder and found him lounging in the captain's chair with a newspaper.

He glanced up. "Morning," he said, and reached for his cup.

Morning? Had he forgotten she'd gone to bed furious with him? And was this how he tried to make nice? By letting her oversleep? "It's ten o'clock!"

He checked his watch. "Nine fifty-five."

"I'm late for work! My boss is gonna freak!"

He lifted his paper. "Looks like you're doing fine to me."

She dropped her gaze and spotted her byline on the front page. It was the third time that week she'd made A-one. She started to smile and then remembered her outrage.

"I'm supposed to be in a staff meeting in five minutes. Why'd you let me sleep so late?"

"You needed the rest." He tossed the paper aside and sauntered over. He put his hands on her shoulders and began kneading. Her anger seemed to evaporate right off her body.

"You sore?"

His hands felt heavenly, and she wanted to melt against him. She didn't, but she couldn't bring herself to ask him to stop. He turned her around so that her back faced him and kneaded deeper.

"That feels good," she murmured, hoping her knees didn't give out. He had amazing hands.

"We'll lay off the weights today. Maybe do some cardio."

The mere thought of more exercise had her moaning.

"Sorry, babe. Gotta whip you into shape. I've cleared my evening for target practice and another self-defense lesson."

"I can hardly wait. Hey, are you sure Chico's is such a good idea? The guys in there look like the reason most women *take* self-defense lessons."

He brushed her hair aside so the warm pads of his thumbs could work on the knots in her neck.

"I've been working out there for years, and I know most of those guys pretty well. After seeing us last night, they'll think we're together, which means they'll be watching your back. It's not a bad thing."

His hands felt wonderful, and she started to rethink her decision to sleep alone. She needed a man. Badly. Ever since her divorce, Cecelia had been telling Feenie to go have a fling. She was convinced a male distraction would help her get over Josh. Feenie didn't know because she'd never tried it. Maybe that was her problem.

No, her problem wasn't about sex. Her problem was that her ex-husband had sent a hit man after her.

Still . . . For the first time in her life, a fling sounded good. Especially with Juarez. He was extremely attractive, pure hormone overload. Of course, that was only when he wasn't acting like an infuriating pig. Or when he wasn't freezing her out. He was extremely attractive when he bothered to be nice.

Right now, for example.

His hands moved to the small of her back, and her breath caught. His thumbs worked on the tension at the base of her spine, and she released an unsteady breath.

"I need something from you," he said in her ear.

Of course. Why else would he be showering her with kindness? She cleared her throat. "What?"

"I need you to do some checking on the Garlands. We're running out of time here, and we don't have enough information to take to the authorities."

She eased away from his hands and turned around. She'd never admit it, but these constant inquiries about Josh were starting to hurt her feelings. She wanted to believe Juarez would be spending time with her even if she *weren't* connected to the Garlands.

But, of course, he wouldn't.

"You said the police were crooked," she reminded him. "I thought that was why I've been avoiding them."

"They are," he said. "Or at least some of them are. And those happen to be well placed within the department. I'm talking about the feds."

"You want to go to the FBI?" She'd known Josh was in trouble, but the extent of it was just starting to sink in.

"I've got a friend in the Houston field office. I'm keeping him in the loop on my investigation in case something goes wrong."

Her blood chilled. "You mean in case you get killed."

His eyes remained flat. "My contact wants to help me, but he needs more information to take up the chain. So far, I've just got a couple of unexplained murders and some flimsy circumstantial evidence."

"Okay. So what do you want me to get?"

"Records, bank statements, anything that could tie the Garland family to money laundering. If they're running the amount of dope I think they are, we're talking about serious funds."

"You think Josh's parents are involved? That seems pretty far-fetched to me."

Juarez shrugged. "I don't know for sure, but that law firm Josh and his dad work at might be a good front for moving money around. Isn't Bert Garland the senior partner?"

Feenie swallowed. "Yes."

"So he's bound to know if his son is moving money through it. Or maybe he's helping."

This was getting much too weird. Her former father-in-law helping dope smugglers? It didn't compute. Feenie had never warmed up to the man, but she had a hard time imagining him laundering money for a drug cartel. She had an even harder time imagining him serving time in a federal prison.

"Why do you think the Garlands are laundering the money?"

"I have my reasons."

"Which are?"

"How much time you got?"

Shoot. Not much. Still, she needed to understand what was going on. "Give me the nutshell version," she said.

"Okay. You remember about four years back a story about the DEA and Operation Money Trace?"

Four years seemed like ages ago, and she'd been more interested in decorating magazines than newspapers back then.

"I must have missed the story."

"It started with a traffic stop in Kimble County," he said, "where they netted over two million in cash. It led to this major multiagency operation where authorities found a shitload of product and identified over two hundred mil in laundered drug money."

"This is the nutshell version?"

"Just listen. It was a major bust. The head of the Saledo cartel went to prison over it. You ever heard of Jorge Saledo?"

"No."

"What about Manuel Saledo? Goes by Manny. He took over for his brother a few years back."

"Neither of those names means anything to me," she said.

Juarez looked disappointed.

"What, did you think I might've had them over for a dinner? Beer and burgers by the pool?"

He sighed. "Could you hold the sarcasm and just listen for a change? Jorge Saledo going to prison was a big deal. But it didn't slow down the traffickers for long. They started experimenting with new ways to get their product into the U.S. and their money south of the border. Lots of businesses with Mexican ties were targeted in the investigation, so the cartels started looking for less conspicuous ways to wash the money. They began expanding their contacts with non-Mexicans so they'd attract less attention."

"Non-Mexicans," she said. "You mean like Josh."

"He fits the profile. He's white, well connected, never been in trouble with the law. It's a great cover."

"And you think Josh is using his firm?" It seemed pretty improbable.

"Maybe," he said. "I need access to the financial records so I can get an accountant to look at them and see if anything looks suspicious."

"What if nothing does?"

"Then we keep looking. The law firm isn't the only possibility. Your ex has other investments, right?"

"Yeah. There's some real estate stuff, but I don't know much about it."

"Anything else?"

"Not that I can think of. Except maybe . . ."

"What?"

She was way out on a limb here, but so was Juarez's whole idea. "His uncle owns a small chain of grocery stores in the valley, and Josh's father's a silent partner. There was talk at one point of letting Josh buy in, but I don't know whether he ever followed up."

"That's good. That could be something. Maybe Garland's using one of those investments—or some combination—as a front. I need some financial records to see if anything looks weird."

Feenie blew out a breath. Her mission was becoming more problematic by the minute. "You seem to forget that I haven't been part of the Garland family in two years. What do you think they're going to do? Invite me into their house to look at their bank records?"

"No."

"How do you expect me to get my hands on all this evidence? I don't even know where to look!"

"Use your feminine intuition. You lived with the guy for five years. Where do *you* think he'd hide something?"

She watched his expression. Unyielding. Determined. She'd never realized before just how tenacious he could be when he wanted something. Lord help her if he ever applied that same tenacity to her.

"Okay," she said. "I'll give it some thought. But in the meantime, I've got a job to do, I've got bills to pay, and your friend is coming by my house this weekend to get started on my repairs. He's expecting a deposit. I need to go into the office today to do some work and pick up my paycheck."

He didn't look entirely satisfied, but at least he let it go. "Sounds good. I'll drop you off. But no leaving the building. For any reason. When you finish up, I'll come by and get you."

"This bodyguard thing is going to get old real fast. How am I supposed to be a reporter if I never leave the building? There are only so many stories I can cover over the phone."

He stepped closer and put his hands on her shoulders, and she realized physical contact was one of the many techniques he used to get what he wanted.

"Not too much longer, I hope," he said. "I've got some new leads I'm working on today. If I can nail down the identity of this contract killer, it shouldn't take me too long to get the situation under control."

What exactly did *that* mean? "Why do I get the feeling you're not telling me everything?"

He shrugged. "Some things you don't want to know. Trust me."

Sure. She should just trust him.

He stroked his hands down her arms. "So what's this hang-up you have about smoke detectors?"

She saw concern in his eyes and wondered again whether it was genuine. "You're changing the subject," she said.

"Does it have something to do with Garland?"

She sighed. "No. It has to do with my mom and sister."

"I thought they died in a car wreck."

God, he was persistent. "They did." She cleared her throat. "But the car caught fire and—"

"Understood."

"I just feel better, you know, when there's a smoke detector—"

"Got it. You don't have to explain."

She eyed him warily. "You don't think I'm weird?"

"What does it matter what I think? You feel better with a smoke detector, I'll get you one."

"You don't need to—"

"Forget it, okay? I'll get you one. It's no big deal."

John McAllister mounted the steps to Feenie's front porch and rang the bell. Where the hell was she? She hadn't been at that morning's staff meeting, and she wasn't answering her cell or her pager. He'd tried her home phone, but it had been disconnected, apparently.

He didn't have time for this shit. He needed to talk to her. He reached for the bell again just as the door swung open.

But it wasn't Feenie who'd opened it.

"Hi there." Cecelia Wells stood before him with her trademark thousand-watt smile. She wore one of those white tennis outfits that clung to everything and barely reached the tops of her thighs. *Fuck.*

For once, he was at a complete loss for words.

"You're probably looking for Feenie," she said cheerfully. "She's not home right now. And you are . . . ?"

"Uh . . ." Christ, she had no idea who he was. Of course she didn't. Why would she? "John McAllister," he finally managed.

She stuck out her hand. "Cecelia Strickland. I'm a friend of Feenie's."

Strickland. Right. She was married now. He knew that. He belatedly shook hands and hoped she didn't notice he was a complete moron.

"I'm just leaving her a note right now," Cecelia

said, opening the door wider. "She hasn't been answering her phone."

Apparently, she hadn't noticed, or maybe she was just too polite to say something like "Who the hell are you, and what are you doing on my friend's porch in the middle of the morning?"

"You need to leave her a message, too?" she asked instead.

"Um, sure."

She'd turned her back on him and headed into the house. He followed her inside, trying not to stare at her legs in that skirt.

"You're with the *Gazette*, right?" she asked as they entered the living room. "Feenie mentioned you guys were working together on a story."

The place was nearly empty of furniture except for a coffee table and a sofa shoved up against a wall. The couch didn't have any cushions, and the armrests had been shredded. *What the fuck?*

"I just left a note on her table," Cecelia said. "Here's some paper if you want to write something." She passed him a pen and a sticky note, brushing his hand with hers as she gave it to him.

Now what? He'd followed her in here, and now she expected him to leave a message. But no way was he writing down the rumor he'd heard at the police station and leaving it sitting in the middle of Feenie's house. He needed to talk to her in person. Now. He stared down at the paper. Then he looked up, and Cecelia was smiling at him.

"It's okay," she said. "I know all about the Josh thing. But even if I didn't, I'm not a snoop, so you don't need to worry."

"You always let yourself into your friends' houses?" he asked.

Her smile widened. "Just my best friend's. I've got a key. She leaves the place open half the time, anyway. It's not like she has much to steal."

He looked around. Feenie hadn't been kidding, apparently, when she'd said money was tight.

He returned his attention to the paper he was holding and scribbled something meaningless.

" 'Course these days, she's trying to be more careful," Cecelia continued. She dangled a key ring from her finger. He'd never noticed her hands before. They looked feminine and soft. Like the rest of her.

She's trying to be more careful. He remembered the reason he'd come. Feenie was mixed up in something dangerous, and he needed to warn her. He put the worthless note on Feenie's table and turned to Cecelia.

"Any idea where I can find Feenie? It's really important."

A little line appeared between her eyebrows. "Is there something wrong?"

"No. Well, I mean, probably not. It's just—" She looked outright worried now. "It's work-related," he finished lamely.

"Well, you could try Rosie's. She might have gone

there for a bite. Or maybe she's back at the news-room?"

"I've been there already." He checked his watch and moved for the door. "Look, I've got to go. If you see her, tell her to call me."

She smiled. "Sure thing. Nice meeting you, McAllister."

He stared at her.

"That's what they call you, right?" She looked worried again. "Feenie always said—"

"No, that's fine. You can call me—whatever." *Shit.* He reached for the doorknob. "I've really gotta go."

Feenie sat in Dottie Garland's sunroom, fidgeting with an earring and trying to ignore the knot in her stomach. She hadn't been to Josh's parents' house in nearly two years, and despite the fact that she maintained a cordial relationship with her former mother-in-law, being in the woman's house was just a tad too uncomfortable. Feenie glanced at her watch. The maid had gone to fetch Dottie nearly ten minutes ago, and she still hadn't appeared. What if Dottie called Josh? But why would she if she had no idea what her son was up to?

Maybe Dottie had been on the phone with Josh when the maid told her Feenie was waiting down-stairs. What if Josh had told her to stall so he'd have time to—

"Feenie!" Dottie breezed through the doorway

with a smile on her face and reached for Feenie's hands. She wore a yellow linen suit and matching pumps with little bows on the toes. "What a pleasant surprise! What brings you here?"

After exchanging air kisses, Feenie gathered up the stack of newspapers she'd brought and fixed a smile on her face. "I was in the neighborhood, and I wanted to drop these off. I thought you might want extra copies."

The Garland estate had been the focal point of this spring's Home and Garden Tour, and the *Gazette* had run a feature article in last Sunday's paper.

"Well, aren't you sweet?" Dottie said.

Yeah, that's right. Sweet as pie.

"The photographs of your house turned out so pretty," Feenie added, feeling like a liar *and* a kiss-up now.

Dottie beamed. "They did, didn't they? Bert and I were very pleased with how everything looked. And Mary Beth's article was lovely."

"So, the Home and Garden Tour was successful?"

"Oh, yes," Dottie said. "Nearly double last year's turnout. And we raised five thousand dollars for park beautification. We'll be putting in a hike-and-bike trail at Laguna Bonita this summer."

"Sounds like someone needs to write a follow-up." Feenie passed her the stack of papers. "Mary Beth's pretty swamped right now, but I'd be happy to cover it. Would you and Bert be available for an interview soon? I'd love to get his perspective on all your philanthropy work. Maybe we could do it at his law office, so he wouldn't be inconvenienced."

Dottie looked uncertain. "I don't know. Bert doesn't like his picture in the paper. He's not photogenic like Josh."

"Well, we don't have to do pictures this time. I'll keep it brief. Just a few quotes." Feenie had been racking her brain for a way to get into Josh's law firm, and interviewing his father during business hours seemed like the best bet. "Maybe you can plug the hike-and-bike trail and drum up some local sponsors."

"Now, that's an idea. I hadn't thought of involving local businesses." Dottie clasped her hands together and her rings sparked in the sunlight. "I'll work on Bert. But it'll have to be next week. He's got a closing tomorrow afternoon, and then he's going deep-sea fishing with Josh. They'll be gone for the weekend. How does Monday sound? I'll check with Bert's secretary."

Feenie tried to keep her face neutral. "Monday's fine if this week looks too hectic.... I didn't know Josh liked deep-sea fishing."

Dottie waved a hand. "He didn't used to, but you know how he likes the water. He and Bert have been out all the time lately."

No kidding? "Are they having any luck?"

"Guess so." Dottie smiled. "I've got a freezer full of fish, and we're running out of ways to cook them."

• • •

Juarez had spent two solid hours on the phone when Teresa stuck her head into his office.

"I'm going to lunch," she said. "Can I pick you up a sandwich or something?"

He glanced at his watch. Nearly one o'clock already, and he was still running down a background check on this Ruiz, who'd supposedly done time in Sugar Land. He hoped like hell he wasn't going to have to drive up to the prison. He needed to stick around and keep tabs on Feenie.

"No, thanks," he said. "Hey, my friend at the FBI didn't call, did he?"

"You were on the phone. I put the message right there on your desk."

The pink message slip was under his coffee cup. "Shit, I knew it," he muttered, reading it. NIBIN, the nationwide forensic firearms identification database, had linked the bullets from the Martinez and the Doring shootings. The murders were committed with the same weapon, which meant most likely the same killer.

"Did you ever call Wainwright back?" Teresa asked. "He's getting really impatient about that workers comp case. And that insurance company in Corpus called again this morning. They need an update from you by five."

"Huh?" Juarez looked up. Teresa was wearing a worried frown, her default expression these days. He knew she was anxious about the chaotic state of the business, but there wasn't much he could do about it at the moment. Lately, everything non-Paloma-related had taken a backseat. Sometime in the last week, he'd passed the point of caring about his other clients.

"Wainwright. And the insurance company. They both need to talk to you."

"I'll take care of it," he said. "Hey, and I'm still waiting on the hot list from Corpus." Juarez was having trouble tracking down that Blazer, so he'd asked Teresa to call Corpus PD for a list of recently stolen cars. He'd already checked San Antonio and Austin.

"I put it in your in box."

"Right. Thanks." He snatched it up and took a moment to give Teresa a reassuring smile. She was a good assistant. He'd been through two others before he'd managed to recruit her away from the Mayfield PD dispatch desk. He wondered if Feenie was right when she'd said Teresa was bored.

He looked down at his stack of neglected files. "Hey, you interested in taking the lead on this workers comp case for Wainwright?"

Her eyebrows shot up. "Me?"

"Yeah, I'm pretty buried. You could go through the paperwork, make a list of anything that raises a red flag, any inconsistencies you see." He passed her the file. "If you think the claim's fraudulent, we'll come up with a game plan for getting proof."

"Really?" She smiled broadly and took the folder. "I'd love to handle it. Actually, I've already skimmed through the file, so it shouldn't take me long to come up to speed."

"Great," he said. "We'll touch base later. Have a nice lunch."

Teresa already had her nose in the file. She glanced up. "What? Oh. I think I'll get started on this instead."

Feenie had been right, apparently. The woman had good instincts about people, he had to admit.

Except when it came to her ex. Of course, Josh Garland had that all-American jock look about him that women drooled over. She'd probably been toast the minute he decided he wanted her.

Juarez skimmed through the list. A light brown GMC Jimmy had been reported stolen last week in Corpus. Its tag began with UT8.

Could Feenie have mistaken the Jimmy for a Blazer? Very possible. He'd ask her about it again.

And here was a gem: Corpus was the site of the last known permanent address for Vince Rawls, one of his two chief suspects. Juarez had worked up a thorough profile of the guy and knew that the former Marine lieutenant had a brother who operated a chop shop in Corpus Christi. Coincidence? Probably not.

Shit. Ever since Feenie had given him that list of Garland's contacts, he'd been so sure Brassler was his man. Now it looked like Rawls might be the guy.

Maybe Garland used more than one contract killer. Maybe Brassler had murdered Paloma and her partner, and now Rawls was gunning for Feenie.

Juarez needed to be certain. He needed to get more on this Ruiz in Sugar Land and find out if he was affiliated with anyone in particular. And then Juarez could pay him a little visit behind bars. Maybe he'd be willing to use his knowledge of the crimes as a bargaining chip to shorten his sentence. It would be a tough sell, though. In Texas, admitting involvement in a cop killing was a good way to end up on Death Row.

This was getting complicated. It would be so much easier if the feds could get enough dirt on Garland to bring him in for questioning. Garland was obviously the one who had orchestrated all this shit, and he was the one who had all the answers. Juarez would trade his right arm for the chance to see Josh Garland rotting behind bars for the rest of his life. The pretentious prick deserved hard time, and Juarez intended to make sure he got it.

Feenie would help him. Juarez felt confident she had insider information, like the BlackBerry thing, that she hadn't even tapped yet. And her best friend being married to Garland's former accountant was a stroke of luck. Juarez was pretty sure Feenie would go nuts if he suggested she go sniffing around Robert Strickland, but there might be a subtler way to find out if the accountant knew anything. Juarez had investigated the guy, and he'd come out clean—squeaky, in fact—but that didn't mean he was in the clear. He could just be covering his tracks.

Again, Feenie could help him find out.

He was counting on her for a lot. More than he felt comfortable with, actually. But he didn't have a choice. Bringing his sister's killers to justice was his most important objective. And he'd do whatever he had to do to get the job done. If Feenie was reluctant to help him, then he'd just have to find a way to persuade her.

Feenie turned on her cell phone as she left Dottie's house. Four new messages. One from Cecelia and three from McAllister. Now, *that* was weird. She punched in his number.

"Shit, Feenie. Where have you been?"

"Nice greeting," she said.

"Don't you keep your phone on? Jesus, I've been looking for you all—"

"What's wrong?" It wasn't like McAllister to sound worried. He never worried about anything. Ever. Except maybe getting laid.

"The ballistics report just came back on Doring," he said. "Bullets recovered match the ones from Corpus Christi. Remember Rico Suave? Same gun."

"Okay."

"Same gun, same shooter," he said. "At least, that's what the cops think."

"I already knew that. Juarez told me."

Silence on the end of the line.

"McAllister?"

"Well, did your *source* tell you there's a rumor

someone's working a hit list? And that your name is on it?"

Her stomach lurched. "Where'd you get that?"

"One of the CIs called it in. A friend of mine at the department passed it on."

"What's a CI?" she asked.

"A confidential informant. Did you know about this?"

She closed her eyes but opened them quickly as she steered Drew's Tercel toward the *Gazette* office. She checked her rearview mirror for the phantom Chevy Blazer, but she didn't see it. "Juarez kind of indicated—"

"Are you fucking crazy? Drop the story, Feenie!"

"But—"

"You're in way over your head."

Her temper flared. "At the pool hall, you said you wanted my help! God, you sound just like Juarez."

"What?"

"You want my help, but then you want to shut me out!"

"Look, Feenie, I understand your ambition. I really do. But you can get promoted without getting near this story. So drop it before you get hurt. I'm telling you—"

"You can skip the lecture. I don't need any more men telling me what to do."

"Oh, great, here we go with the feminist shit. I'm serious, Feenie. Stay away from this. And keep your friends away, too. I just saw Cecelia Wells and she seemed to know all about this research you're doing. That puts her at risk, too. Did you ever stop to think of that?"

When had McAllister met Celie? And how did he know her maiden name? "Her name is Cecelia *Strickland*," Feenie said, "and I *am* trying to keep her out of it. But it's kind of hard when she's not a total idiot, and she knows Josh and she knows me, and she can put two and two together." Plus, she'd been with Feenie that night at Josh's boathouse, which made it next to impossible to keep her from figuring out something was up.

McAllister had gotten quiet all of a sudden.

"McAllister?"

"Just be careful, Feenie. I mean it." And he clicked off.

Feenie steadied her arms and took aim at the target. She squeezed the trigger and watched a hole appear in the silhouette.

"Not bad," Juarez said.

She dropped her arms and smiled. Practice was going much better today. "Thanks. I like this gun better."

Juarez smirked. "Thought you would. It's light as a feather."

Feenie turned over the Smith & Wesson revolver and examined the textured black grip. It felt comfortable in her hand. The .38 was very compact, and although it wasn't light as a feather, it certainly weighed less than Juarez's Glock.

"Where'd you get this, anyway?"

"It's my mom's."

"Your *mom's?*"

"I got it for her after my dad passed away," he said. "Someone broke into her house."

"Was she hurt?"

His jaw tightened. "No. She wasn't home, but it scared her pretty good. I thought the gun might help her feel safer."

"Does it?"

"Nah, she won't touch it. It just sits on the top shelf of her closet. She threw the ammo away, so I gave up and got her a dog."

"Must be hard being a widow," she said, hoping he'd tell her more about his family. But of course he didn't. He just handed her some more bullets. Feenie watched him, wishing he'd open up to her but doubting he would.

Feenie loaded the gun again and squeezed off another round. Again, her aim was dead-on.

He eased up next to her and squinted at the target. "You're really coming along. Sure you haven't fired a handgun lately?"

"Just yesterday with you."

"You're a natural, then."

Feenie noticed his relaxed expression and spotted her opening. "I talked to Dottie Garland today."

Avoiding his gaze, she put the gun down and punched the button to bring the target forward. Most of her shots had hit the silhouette this time.

She glanced at Juarez and wasn't surprised to see him scowling at her.

"On the phone, I hope?"

She unclipped the target and held it up for him to see. "Pretty good, if I do say so myself."

He ignored the distraction and crossed his arms. "Don't tell me you went out there."

She didn't say anything.

"I thought I told you—"

"You asked me to help, and I'm helping. It's hard to glean information from people over the phone. Besides, Josh wasn't there. I made sure he was at work before I went over."

"Feenie—"

"I got some good information. Josh and his dad are going deep-sea fishing. They leave tomorrow. Dottie says they've been fishing a lot lately."

Juarez cocked his head to the side and looked her up and down. As she'd suspected, the value of the information outweighed his concern for her. She felt a prick of disappointment but forced herself to ignore it.

"What time do they leave?" he asked.

"Tomorrow evening, I think. You want to follow them? It'd be a good way to learn more about their operation."

"That depends."

"On?"

"On you," he said. "I'm not sure I can trust you to stay out of trouble while I'm gone. Your track record of following directions isn't good."

"Oh, yeah? Well, don't worry about me. You'll know exactly where I am, because I'm coming with you."

CHAPTER

12

Feenie spent her Friday buzzing with anticipation. She worked from her desk, casting impatient looks at the newsroom clock and counting the minutes until it was time to leave. Again and again, she mentally reviewed Juarez's plan as well as the few minor ways she intended to deviate from it.

Finally, it was three-thirty, time to go get changed and into position before the Garlands set out on their fishing trip. Even if Josh and his father didn't plan to fish, Feenie figured they'd want to depart well before sundown to maintain their cover.

She checked her email one last time, relieved to see no last-minute messages from her editor, and then shut down her computer and stood to leave.

"Getting a jump on your weekend?"

She looked up to see John McAllister towering over her.

"Not really, I've just ... got some things to do tonight." She shot a furtive glance at the clock.

"Any chance you could change your plans?" McAllister handed her a slip of paper with a name and a number scrawled across it.

"What's this?"

"Name of a buddy of mine in the police department. I told him we were training a new reporter, and he offered to take you on a ride-along tonight."

Feenie looked down at the paper and bit her lip. "Wow. I appreciate that, but—"

"If you want to cover breaking news, you need to develop some sources within the department," McAllister said firmly. "This guy's one of the nicer cops on the force, and he's happily married, so you don't have to worry about him hitting on you every time you use him as a source."

Feenie met McAllister's gaze. "I appreciate the help. Really, I do. But tonight's no good for me. I've got a date."

He eyed her coolly. "Could you bump it to tomorrow? This guy's expecting your call."

McAllister knew she was lying. She could see it in his face. She swallowed hard. "I really can't. But I'll call your friend and arrange to postpone." She smiled. "Thanks for the help."

He looked at her for a long moment, then shook

his head. "You have some kinda death wish I don't know about?"

"What? No—"

He turned and walked away, and she blew out an exasperated breath. It was none of his business what she did with her Friday evening. She shoved the paper into her purse and stalked across the newsroom, taking care to keep her gaze trained on the door as she passed McAllister's desk.

"Malone, hold up."

She stopped. *Dammit,* he was going to make her late. She whirled around. "What?"

He was standing beside his desk, shuffling through a folder. "Here," he said, holding something out to her.

She sighed and backtracked toward him. "What is it?" she asked, taking the papers.

She looked down and nearly dropped them. They were photographs. Of a corpse. An eyeless, bloated corpse with two black holes in the chest. Both repulsed and fascinated, Feenie thumbed through the stack.

"That's Brian Doring," McAllister said. "Scavengers got to him before the ME."

"How'd you get these?" she asked hotly.

He shrugged. "I've got sources."

She shoved the pictures back at him. "Well, why are you showing them to *me?*" She was angry now, and she couldn't really say why. She didn't even know Brian Doring.

Still, she knew he'd been a *person*. And the idea of his autopsy photos circulating through the newsroom enraged her.

McAllister took the pictures back and dropped them on his desk. Doring's mutilated eye socket stared up at her.

"A picture's worth a thousand words," McAllister said. "Just thought I'd make my point again before you and your *date* decide to do any more investigating."

Juarez waited in the dark, cursing her. What was taking so long? Josh and his dad should have left hours ago, and Feenie still hadn't called to tell him their boat was pulling out.

Maybe they'd spotted her. She was lousy at keeping a low profile. Fortunately, she made up for it by thinking on her feet. Still, no amount of sweet talk would convince Josh she had innocent intentions if he noticed her staking out his boathouse.

They'd been over the plan half a dozen times. He'd told her she could be the point man for this surveillance, and she'd looked extremely pleased to get the job. She was supposed to wait for the Garlands to leave, then call and give him the heads up. Juarez was waiting in his boat, lights out, near where the harbor opened up into the bay. Even if Garland killed his running lights, Juarez would be able to track him at a distance using GPS. He'd slipped into the Garlands' boathouse earlier today and placed the tracking devices, which should work great as long as the Garlands took the Grady-White or the Boston Whaler. If they took someone else's boat for some reason, Juarez was screwed.

Suddenly, the green light on the screen of his handheld computer started to move. Any second now, Feenie would call to report Garland's departure. Then she'd head to their meeting spot at the marina. But instead of Juarez picking her up in his boat, Peterson would be picking her up in his car.

She'd be mad as hell. Again. Which would be a crying shame, because Juarez would be forced to spend yet another night on that cramped little bench instead of in his own fucking bed.

With a nice warm body beside him.

But it couldn't be helped. Tonight was likely to be hazardous, and Feenie would be safer with Peterson.

The green light moved toward the mouth of the harbor, where Juarez was waiting on *Rum Runner*. As soon as the boat entered the bay, Juarez would follow. At a safe distance. Tonight's half-moon would make Garland easier to track, but it would also make *Rum Runner* easier to spot. The good news was that Juarez had the element of surprise working for him, because Garland didn't know he was being followed.

Unless he caught Feenie sneaking around on his property. Her presence might just tip him off.

Why the hell hadn't she called?

Juarez thought of the two men who might be after her: Todd Brassler and Vince Rawls. Two very well-trained and very lethal operatives, and he'd investigated them both thoroughly.

Brassler was ex-Army and had been deployed in the mountains of Afghanistan. After a year of hunting terrorists in the rugged terrain, he had developed a reputation as an excellent tracker and an even better shot.

He was also a wild card, according to his Army buddies. They all had the same feedback: when crossed, especially if he'd been drinking, Brassler was violent and unpredictable. He'd been dishonorably discharged from the Army and had since been working solo.

Rawls was also a former military guy, but he'd been in the Marines. After leaving the service, he'd built a career as a thug for hire along the Texas-Mexico border.

The local authorities knew about both men, but thanks to their military training, they were good at covering their tracks. They lived well under the radar, using aliases and moving around, avoiding the types of activities that would put their names or other vital information into electronic databases, which would flag them for investigators. Juarez's usual bag of skip-tracing tricks didn't work with these two.

To make things even tougher, Brassler had been quiet for a while. Most of his suspected crimes had taken place prior to the last eighteen months. Juarez had been back and forth across the border trying to find out what he'd been doing during that gap, but he'd come up empty. It was as if the guy had fallen off the face of the earth.

The phone numbers Feenie had given Juarez had been his best lead in months. The Mexican residential numbers had turned out to be nothing, but that listing for the Presidente InterContinental Hotel was important. A man using one of Brassler's known aliases had checked into the InterCon just three weeks before Paloma's disappearance. This supported Juarez's theory that Garland had met with Brassler in Monterrey and contracted him to kill Paloma and her partner.

But then there was the Chevy Blazer Feenie had spotted, which suggested Rawls might be Garland's hired gun. After all, he'd been working regularly, while Brassler would be coming out of retirement to take this contract.

This conflicting information was fucking frustrating. It wouldn't matter so much, except that Juarez couldn't stomach the idea of exacting his revenge on the wrong guy. When he caught up to Paloma's killer, he needed to be sure he had the right man.

Juarez thought of Feenie. It wouldn't sit well with Brassler—or Rawls—that a little powder puff like her had given him the slip for nearly two weeks now. Juarez had a hard time believing it himself. In fact, he didn't. If Brassler or Rawls had wanted her dead, she'd be dead by now. More likely, one of them wanted to draw out the game and have some fun—shadow her, tear up her house, get her good and frightened. The hit man was playing cat-and-mouse, and if Juarez was right, he had big plans for his prey when he captured it.

A motor hummed in the distance and gradually grew louder. The green light on the screen showed the boat was about fifty yards away now and approaching quickly. He'd have to get moving soon.

Finally, his phone vibrated.

"Juarez."

"They just left." Feenie's voice was muffled, but just hearing it was a relief. "They're headed to the south side of the harbor."

"Where are you?"

"On my way to the marina. Are you going to pick me up, like we planned?"

He hesitated a second.

"Juarez?"

"Looks like I won't have time."

"We had a deal! I thought you wanted to keep an eye on me!"

He smiled into the phone as he started up the engine. "I do. That's why I've asked Peterson to pick you up. He'll meet you in the parking lot at the marina. Don't get out of your car unless you're sure it's him."

She fell silent, and Juarez imagined her face as she realized she'd been duped. Her cheeks would flush, and her chest would heave up and down. She was so damn sexy when she got mad.

"You're a lying jerk, you know that?"

Juarez checked his gauges and put the boat in gear. "Sorry, babe. Safety first."

She didn't answer, and the back of Juarez's neck prickled. He looked up and saw Feenie standing in the doorway of the cabin.

"What the hell are you doing?"

She folded her arms over her chest, which wasn't heaving after all. "Coming with you. Did you think I'd fall for the same trick twice?"

Shit. "Who's staking out the boathouse?"

"Teresa. She seemed really eager to help out." Even in the near-darkness, he could tell she was smiling. She wore the same black getup she'd had on during the rainstorm at Garland's boathouse.

"This isn't a video game, Feenie. This meeting could be dangerous."

"What's more dangerous than sitting around waiting for a hit man to find me? I'd rather be here helping you. Anyway, it's too late to take me back."

As she said this, a large Grady-White zoomed past their hiding place and veered into the bay.

He watched the boat, then glanced at Feenie. She had him cold, and she knew it, too. He didn't have time to take her back to shore, and he wasn't willing to scrap the plan when they were inches away from collecting hard evidence against Garland.

And Garland would lead him to Paloma's killer.

"Fine. But stay out of the way. And when the meet happens, I want you below deck."

She tossed her head. "Oh, really? Are you planning to tie me up and gag me?"

"Don't tempt me. Now, sit down so we can get going."

The instant she was seated, he punched the throttle forward and had *Rum Runner* riding high on the water. Now he had to trail the Garlands discreetly, get close enough to gather useful evidence, and keep a lid on Feenie at the same time.

"If you get in my way, you're going overboard," he said.

"Don't worry," she crooned. "You won't even know I'm here."

After they'd been speeding through the water for nearly an hour, Feenie watched the green light on the computer screen stop moving.

"Hold up," she told Juarez. "Looks like they're stopping."

Juarez glanced down at the GPS and nodded. He abruptly slowed. Feenie looked out over the choppy black water, but she couldn't even see the Grady-White.

"Where are they?" she whispered.

He pointed over the bow, which was rising and sinking with the swells. "About eleven o'clock."

"Where?"

"There. See the white light? And you don't need to whisper. They're too far away to hear us, especially with the wind out of the south." He consulted the computer, which cast his face in a greenish glow. "We're about thirty miles southwest of South Padre Island."

"So we're in Mexico?"

Juarez clicked off the device and melted into the shadows again. "A few miles offshore."

Feenie had brought a pair of binoculars. She trained them on the Grady-White, which was illuminated only by a light at the helm. To her amazement, Josh and his father were prepping their fishing poles. Moments later, Josh cast a line into the water. His father soon did the same.

"They're *fishing?*" she said, gaping. Could she have been wrong about everything?

"Sure, why not? They've probably got some waiting to do, and it's as good a cover as any." Juarez reached into a cooler and pulled out a bottle. He twisted the top off and held it out, and icy water trickled onto her jeans.

"No, thanks. I'd like to be alert if anything happens."

She saw a flash of white teeth in the darkness. With the moon obscured by clouds, she could barely make out Juarez's silhouette just three feet away.

"It's root beer," he said.

"Hmm." She took the bottle. "You don't strike me as the root beer type."

"Yeah? You don't strike me as the type to marry a drug runner, so I guess there's a lot we don't know about each other."

She took a sip. The drink was fizzy and syrupy and tasted like childhood. "What's that supposed to mean? I told you, I had no idea about all this while I was married."

Juarez pulled another bottle out of the cooler for himself. "So you say."

"You don't believe me? After all this, you think I—"

"I'm kidding," he said before taking a swig. "But I did have my doubts at first. I thought the clueless-wife thing was all an act."

She winced. So which was better? To be clued in and guilty or innocent and oblivious? All her life, people had taken her for a dumb blonde, and she hated to think there might have been a kernel of truth in that. But how else could she explain living with a man for five years and never realizing he was a criminal? The thought irked her. It was one of the many reasons she was determined to make sure Josh got what he had coming to him.

"So when did you figure it out?" she asked him.

"What's that?"

"That it wasn't an act."

He paused a minute, and she wondered if he was making something up. "I did some digging." He swigged his drink. "Seems to me if you really were in on Garland's shit you'd have come up with the funds to bail yourself out of debt by now."

Great. He'd done some "digging." Feenie hugged her knees to her chest, resigning herself to the fact that this man probably knew a heck of a lot more about her than she would have liked.

A balmy breeze swept over her face as she turned to watch the boat. It was just a speck of light bobbing in the distance. Feenie passed Juarez her binoculars, and he looked through them.

"Looks like they're biting," he said. "Too bad we don't have lines in the water."

"I'm terrible at fishing. I never catch a thing."

"What do you use for bait?" He gave her back the binoculars, and she hung them around her neck.

"Live shrimp," she said. "That's not the problem. My dad taught me what to do and everything when I was a kid. But it doesn't matter. Even when everyone around me's reeling them in, I can't get a bite. I'm unlucky with fish."

"In that case, my dad wouldn't have liked you on his boat. He was pretty superstitious about fishing." He turned to look at her, but it was too dark to read his expression. "You see your dad much?"

"Not a lot. We haven't been on great terms the last few years. Ever since my divorce."

"You're kidding?" He scoffed. "Don't tell me he wanted you to stand by your man or some shit."

"No, nothing like that. It's just I know he was disappointed when it didn't work out. You should have seen him on my wedding day. He looked so . . . I don't know, proud, I guess."

"You don't think he's proud of you now?"

She shrugged. "Maybe. I don't know, really. I just

thought I'd have made him a grandfather by now. He's not getting any younger. And without any siblings, it's pretty much up to me." She looked out over the water. "We were close when I was growing up, but now that he's retired, we barely even talk on the phone."

"I doubt it's a grandkid thing."

"Why do you say that?"

He shrugged. "Because. Most guys don't like talking on the phone unless there's a reason. You should just go see him."

"I *have*." She knew she sounded defensive, but this was a touchy subject for her. "On his last birthday, I drove up to Port Aransas and took him out for a nice dinner, but we hardly had anything to say to each other at the table." The evening had been miserable. She'd felt guilty about not visiting, so she'd made a reservation at the nicest Italian restaurant in town, and what had he done? He'd ordered a Budweiser and a plate of spaghetti. And then he'd gotten cross with the waiter when he delivered the bill to Feenie instead of him.

"You said he likes guns, right?"

"Yeah," she said.

"So go hunting with him. Or catch a baseball game. Shit, just go somewhere he doesn't have to talk the whole time."

Juarez tipped back his drink, and she watched him in the darkness. She couldn't believe he was giving her relationship advice, but it actually wasn't bad. He'd never even met her father, and he'd accurately pegged him as a man who'd be more at ease tromping around a deer lease than being treated to a fancy dinner.

She remembered the little girl in the picture by Juarez's bed and decided it was time to voice the question that had been nagging her ever since she'd seen it.

"Do you have any kids?" she asked.

"Nope. Never been married."

Interesting response. She cleared her throat. "I saw the picture in your bedroom, and I just thought—"

"She's my niece."

"Oh." Relief flooded her. She chewed her lip, wondering why she should care one way or the other. But of course she cared. She *liked* this guy. Which meant she didn't want any ex-wives or girlfriends or kids from a previous marriage competing for his attention.

God, she was stupid. How had she let herself get hung up on someone like Juarez? He was fiercely independent. A lone wolf. The exact opposite of what she wanted in her life.

"So . . . were you close to *your* dad?" she asked.

He didn't answer, and she felt sure he was going to evade telling her anything personal again.

"Nah, not really. I didn't like him much, or even respect him, really, until after he died."

Whoa. Two whole sentences loaded with personal revelations. She was making progress. She might as well push it.

"Why didn't you like him?" she asked.

"I don't know. The usual."

Feenie's childhood had been far from usual. But maybe Juarez's had, too. He had that quiet, brooding nature that she recognized. She herself was prone to brooding sometimes. "What does 'the usual' mean?" she asked.

He didn't say anything for a few seconds. Then, "He was a real hard-ass while I was growing up. Didn't say much but had real high expectations. The strong, silent type, you know?"

Uh, *yeah.* "I can relate to that."

"Anyway, I spent most of my teenage years getting into trouble. Drugs, alcohol, ditching school, the works. I pretty much did anything I could just to piss him off, you know, because he was a cop. Every time I got in trouble, I think it embarrassed him."

"So what changed?"

He looked away. "He died of a heart attack, real suddenly. And after we buried him, I realized what a complete shit I'd been all those years. I decided I wanted to do something with my life. So I stopped smoking weed. I got a job. I put myself through two years of junior college, and then I enrolled in the police academy."

She was listening with rapt attention, afraid if she so much as blinked, he'd clam up. "That's quite a transformation."

"Yeah. Didn't really take, though."

"What do you mean?"

He looked at her. "Come on. Don't tell me you haven't checked me out. The only reason I got on the force was because some of the old brass liked my dad. But it turns out I'm still a pothead. Got busted with a stash of marijuana in my cruiser."

His tone was bitter, and Feenie knew his partner had been right about the drugs being a plant.

"Do you know why you were set up?" she asked.

His eyes locked on hers for a long moment. Then he looked away. "Who says it was a setup?"

She tipped her head to the side and waited him out.

"Nah, I don't know," he finally said. "But I'm pretty sure it had something to do with the chief. Son of a bitch never liked me, thought I was a troublemaker. Anyway, the job really wasn't that great."

She watched him shrug it off, but she seriously doubted it was that simple. He'd worked hard to get through school and the academy, and then he'd lost his job and had his reputation sullied because of a corrupt boss.

But he'd bounced back from all that and started his own company. Feenie admired his resilience.

"But it's all for the better, right?" she said. "I mean, now you run your own business. You're successful. Look at how it all worked out. I'm sure your dad would have been proud of you." *Easy there, Pollyanna. A little too perky for the likes of Juarez.*

He snorted. "Yeah, right. Look how it worked out."

"What?"

He shook his head. "You have no idea what you're talking about, Feenie. I've made some major mistakes. I have a list of fuck-ups—"

He halted mid-sentence, as if he'd suddenly realized he was actually *talking* to her, actually opening up.

"You have a list?" she prompted.

"You hear that?"

Yes, she did. It was the sound of a boat.

They listened silently as the noise grew louder. Juarez stowed his bottle back in the cooler and pulled out a black duffle bag. He unzipped it and took out some equipment.

"What's that?" Feenie whispered.

Juarez didn't look up from his task. "Listening device. It's extremely sensitive. As long as the wind doesn't pick up, I should be able to get some of what they're saying. I brought a Nightshot, too."

"What's a Nightshot?"

"Infrared camera," he said. "But it probably won't do much good at this distance."

Soon he had a black recording device hooked up to what looked like a satellite dish. The engine noise became louder, and Feenie watched through her binoculars as the Garlands stowed their fishing poles. A boat suddenly pulled up alongside the Grady-White. She hadn't seen it coming, because it wasn't using any lights.

"Okay," Juarez said, glancing over his shoulder. "Party time. Go down and wait in the cabin. Don't say anything, and don't come out. Did you bring your piece?"

It took her a moment to realize he was talking about the .38.

"Yes," she said, gulping.

"Good. *Don't* use it unless everything goes to shit. You got that? You put a bullet in me, I'll never forgive you."

She nodded, feeling a little numb. Juarez was right. This wasn't a video game. She was hiding out on a boat running surveillance on a real life smuggling operation.

Feenie crept down the ladder, took her gun out of her purse, and checked to make sure it was loaded. She wondered what was going on above deck. Maybe she should peek out and take a look. But Juarez had told her just to sit there.

So she did.

A few minutes later, she suddenly had this overwhelming urge to go see what was going on with her own two eyes. She tried to ignore it, straining to hear whatever was happening outside. She heard nothing, but she made herself wait patiently. Finally, curiosity got the best of her, so she stashed the gun on the counter in the galley and tiptoed toward the ladder. She waited there, straining to hear anything up on deck. Juarez was silent, the Grady-White was dark, and the other boat's engine had stopped.

She chewed on a thumbnail. What if someone spotted them? Surely the people aboard both boats were armed; maybe they even carried machine guns. What if Juarez got shot? What if she did? They'd end up at the bottom of the Gulf of Mexico. Feenie inched closer to the doorway and listened intently.

Faintly, she heard static, followed by some words. It sounded muffled, but she was pretty sure it was Spanish. Did Josh know Spanish? They'd traveled together in Mexico a zillion times, and he'd barely been able to order a drink. Still, given what she'd recently learned about him, nothing would shock her. He was a drug runner, for heaven's sake. Being secretly bilingual didn't seem like that big a deal.

She stepped onto the bottom rung of the ladder and peered out at the deck. Juarez kneeled next to his equipment. His gun was holstered at his waist, and he held a camera with a telephoto lens. As she eased up another rung, she watched Juarez point the camera at Josh's boat.

Feenie craned her neck and just barely managed to see over the side of *Rum Runner*. The Grady-White bobbed in the distance, but they had killed most of the lights now. She looked through the binoculars. With the moon hidden behind clouds, the two boats were nearly invisible. A faint glow came from the console, and she could discern only some shadows moving back and forth.

"Dammit," Juarez said.

Feenie jerked back, hoping he hadn't seen her. She didn't want to distract him at a critical moment, yet she couldn't bear to stay downstairs and out of sight. She wanted to *see* something.

Juarez lowered the camera, apparently giving up on getting any pictures. Maybe if the moon came out again, he'd have better luck. He pulled some binoculars out of his bag. They looked much more high-tech than her own, and she suspected they were equipped for night vision.

She peered through her binoculars again, but all she saw were shadows.

Suddenly, the clouds parted, and she had a good view of the Grady-White. About half a dozen people milled around on deck, all men. They passed duffle bags to Josh and his dad. Feenie watched as Bert took one of the bags and stowed it in the hull.

"Good Lord," she murmured.

"Get below deck, Malone."

She jerked back. Had she said that out loud? She was about to go back down the ladder, but she stole one last peek through her binoculars and saw more figures moving aboard *Feenie's Dream*. Several petite dark-haired women boarded the boat. The men helped them climb in, then shuffled them to the side. She counted five altogether, and they looked childlike compared to the brawny men surrounding them.

Childlike.

Juarez muttered something in Spanish and adjusted his binoculars. Feenie looked through hers again and watched, astonished, as Josh reached out to touch one of the girls. He fanned his hand through her hair and said something to the other men. Laughter followed, and the men began to disembark. Soon they all were back aboard the other boat, leaving the duffle bags and the girls behind.

Leaving the children behind.

Josh was smuggling *children?*

Her throat constricted, and she backed into the doorway. Her foot missed a rung, and she tumbled backward into the cabin. She flailed her arms out, catching herself on the galley counter. The sound of gunfire exploded inside the cabin.

Curses erupted on deck, and Juarez jumped down the ladder. "Are you okay?"

"I . . . I fell back and knocked my gun off the counter."

"Are you *hit?*"

"No." She stood up and looked down, somehow needing to make sure. When she looked up again, Juarez was gone.

Suddenly, the engine roared to life, and the boat lurched forward. Feenie crashed to the floor, this time *not* managing to catch herself. Her face collided with the cabin's door frame, and pain ballooned behind her cheekbone. Struggling to her feet, she grabbed the handrail of the ladder and hoisted herself above deck.

"Stay down!" he boomed. "Jesus Christ! You want to get killed?"

She looked around. He'd already put a long trail of wake between themselves and the other boats.

"Are they following us?" she yelled over the din of the engine.

"Yes! What the hell were you doing?"

"I didn't mean to—"

"Grab the equipment!" He shoved it toward her with his foot. "And *get below deck!*"

She clamped her lips shut and did as she was told. It was nearly impossible to see all the wires and camera gear in the dark, but she scrounged up everything she could. The duffle was long gone, probably having flown overboard when Juarez gunned the engine. She scrambled downstairs with the equipment, nearly tripping on the ladder yet again, and staggered through the galley into the bedroom. The boat pitched and lurched over the waves, and it took three tries before she could get a grip on a cabinet door. Finally, she got one open and shoved all the gear inside next to some life preservers. For an instant, she considered grabbing a couple. But they had armed drug smugglers chasing them. Flotation devices probably wouldn't help if they ever caught up to them. She slammed the cabinet shut and maneuvered herself to the bench seat near the galley. Gripping the walls on either side of her, she tried to remain in one place.

Where was her gun?

It had gone off in the galley, but when Juarez punched the throttle, it most likely had slid to the stern. She looked at the floor but didn't see any sign of it. She took off her binoculars and stowed them beneath her seat.

God, her timing couldn't have been worse. What was wrong with her?

A vision of the five dark-haired girls popped into her head. *Girls.* Josh was smuggling *girls.* She could think of only a few reasons to smuggle girls over the border, and none of them was good. If they were simply illegal day laborers, why had they all been female? No. They were another kind of worker, she felt sure. And they were kids.

The boat hit a wave, knocking her head against the side of the cabin. She tightened her grip on the walls and prayed. The noise behind them grew louder. Josh was catching up. *Feenie's Dream* was probably faster than *Rum Runner,* so it would boil down to who could maneuver better in the dark. Gunfire sounded outside.

Or who was the better shot.

Feenie tried to think of something to do. She needed that gun. Maybe she could get a round off while Juarez steered. But that would never work unless their pursuers got really close.

More shots rang out, from Juarez this time. Had he hit anything?

She crouched down on the floor and tried to get some traction. The carpet felt scratchy, like Astroturf, under her knees. She scooted around on all fours, desperately searching for the Smith & Wesson. Finally, her hand fell on something hard and smooth. She had it.

Gripping the revolver in her right hand, she reached for the handrail and tried to pull herself up. She made out Juarez's figure at the helm.

"Get down!" he yelled.

"Do you need help?"

The windshield exploded next to her right ear, and she jumped backward.

"Are you crazy? Get below deck!"

The boat smacked into a wave, and Feenie lost her grip on the handrail. She pitched forward, then back again, landing on her butt below deck. Miraculously, she managed to hang on to the gun this time.

She hooked her arm around the bottom rung of the ladder. Maybe she should just stay in one place so she didn't accidentally shoot anything. Like the captain.

For what seemed like hours, the boat bounced and skipped over the waves. She clutched her gun and hoped for a miracle. Two huge engines powered the Grady-White. Even with Juarez's evasive maneuvering, it would be only a matter of time before she out-paced *Rum Runner*.

The boat tipped sideways, and Feenie tightened her hold. They'd made a sharp left and then tipped left again.

Was he making a U-turn? Surely he wasn't going back for a head-on confrontation. It would be suicide. They were outnumbered and most definitely out-gunned.

They slowed abruptly, and the engine went from a roar to a low hum. With the noise suddenly gone, Feenie heard ringing in her ears. They motored along for a few minutes before the engine ceased.

Why had he stopped?

She pulled herself up and poked her head through the door. Nothing but blackness. The moon had gone behind a cloud again, and she couldn't even see Juarez. Had he abandoned the boat? Maybe he'd been shot.

"Juarez!" she whispered.

No answer. He'd definitely been shot. Or he'd jumped ship. Or both. Her stomach rolled, and she felt a wave of nausea coming on.

"Juarez?" she squeaked. "Where are you?"

"Stay down," he growled in her ear.

She jumped sideways and collided with the door-jamb.

"You scared me!" she hissed. "I thought you were gone!"

"Where the hell would I go?" he whispered. "We're surrounded by water."

"Why did you stop?"

"I ducked into an estuary. I don't think they saw me, or maybe they did but they decided to blow off the chase."

"Why would they do that?"

"Could be they thought we were some kind of law enforcement. Or maybe they decided we were doing the same thing they were and they just wanted to get the hell out of there."

Feenie looked around, but she couldn't make out anything, not even a moon. Only the relatively calm seas indicated they'd entered the maze of inlets and shallow channels along the coast. This place would prove to be either a clever hiding spot or a dead end. Literally.

"Can anyone see us here?" she whispered.

"I doubt it. I spotted a fishing cabin a few minutes ago and pulled up next to it. It should obscure our silhouette if the moon comes back out."

"Will that really work?" She gripped his arm. "What if they have night-vision goggles or something?"

"No way we can outrun them in this thing. Our only chance is to hide."

She could hear the frustration in his voice. God, she'd really screwed up. He probably wanted to throw her overboard.

She looked around but saw nothing. Even Juarez was barely a shadow. Had it not been for the warmth of his arm, she might have thought she'd been swallowed by a black hole. She tightened her grip.

The water lapped against the side of the boat. That and their breathing were the only sounds.

"You hear anything?" she whispered.

"No. You?"

"No."

"Maybe they've cut the engine, too. Maybe they'll drift right into us."

Juarez eased down the ladder, brushing the length of her body with his. He wrapped an arm around her waist. "More likely, we'll drift into a sandbar and get stuck. If that happens, I may have to get out and push us into deeper water."

"So . . . we're just going to sit here?"

He tightened his hold, and his warmth seeped into her. She realized she'd been shivering.

"No choice," he said. "If we turn on the lights or the engine, we'll blow our cover."

Her teeth started to chatter, and she clamped her jaw shut. It had to be eighty-five degrees out, yet she felt freezing.

"Where'd you stow the GPS?" he asked.

"In the cabinet in your bedroom."

"I'm going to check out their position and make sure they kept going."

He was gone for a few minutes, and by the time he came back she was shivering again.

"Looks like they're still headed north," he said,

wrapping an arm around her. "We'll wait a while longer to make sure they don't double back."

She squeezed her eyes shut and nestled closer. He felt warm and solid and safe. His hand closed over hers, and she remembered the gun.

"I think I'll take this." He slipped the revolver out of her hand, checked the chamber, and tucked the gun into his jeans.

"I'm ... I'm so sorry." Her teeth began to chatter again. "I don't know what happened. It was sitting on the counter, and it just fell—"

"I thought you were holding it."

"I was. But then I put it on the counter, and—"

"Forget it."

"But I nearly got us killed! We could *still* get killed!"

He didn't say anything. How could he be so calm?

"Juarez? Aren't you mad?"

"What's the point? What's done is done. And I think we may have gotten lucky."

"Juarez ..." She gulped. "Did you know about the girls?"

He didn't say anything, and her chest tightened. Surely he wouldn't have kept something so important from her.

"No," he said. "I wasn't expecting that."

"Do you think they're prostitutes?" Just saying it made her queasy.

"That's probably what they're headed for. I'd heard

something about Garland smuggling *muñecas*, but I didn't put it together until now."

"*Muñecas?*"

"Dolls. I thought some of the drugs were being smuggled in plastic toys. Now it looks like the dolls themselves are the contraband."

His face lit up in an orange glow as he checked his sports watch. It was bulky and digital, with lots of gadgets.

"It's been twenty minutes," he said. The orange light illuminated the hard planes of his face. Sweat beaded at his temples, but that was the only sign of stress. He appeared more or less at ease, while she quivered like a snared rabbit. "I'll check the GPS again. If they're still heading north, we'll get moving."

She squeezed her eyes shut and nodded.

"Hey," he said, lifting her chin with his finger. "We're going to be fine."

She nodded again, feeling even colder than she had before. She felt lightheaded, too, and slid down onto the floor.

"You okay?"

"I just need to sit down." She felt the scratchy waterproof carpeting under her hands and rested her head against the ladder. Her cheek throbbed, and her forehead stung. She touched the skin above her eyebrow. It felt sticky. She curled into a fetal position and hugged her knees to her chest. She couldn't get warm, and she couldn't muster the effort to sit up, either.

"Take it easy," he said, and disappeared.

Feenie closed her eyes and tried to fight off the wave of nausea. Saliva pooled in her mouth, and it took every ounce of will she had not to bolt up the ladder and get sick over the side. But she couldn't. She had to stay down. She had to keep quiet. Josh and his father might find her.

Josh and his boatload of children.

Bile rose in her throat, but she swallowed it down. She couldn't think about it. Not now. She couldn't think about how the man she'd lived with, the man she'd *slept* with, was trafficking children. All those years, she'd been eager to make a baby, and now he was exploiting babies, unfortunate little girls who'd somehow fallen into his hands.

The boat began to move, and she gratefully turned her thoughts to the immediate future. They needed to get back. If they could make it safely back to Mayfield, she could go to the police. This wasn't just about Josh anymore. Or drugs. Kids were getting hurt, and she couldn't sit back and let it happen.

The police would help. If they wouldn't, she'd try the FBI. Or the DEA. Or Immigration. Someone somewhere would listen to her. Someone somewhere would care that children were being shuttled over the border for other people's recreation.

Those poor young girls. What did he do to them?

Feenie raced up the ladder and vomited over the side. When the spasms ceased, she sank to her knees and rested her head on a vinyl seat. Out of the corner of her eye, she saw Juarez watching her from the helm.

"We're about fifteen minutes out," he said. "Think you can make it to the marina?"

She rolled her head in his direction, barely nodding. Her skin felt cold and wet. She tucked her knees into her sweatshirt and tried to make a cocoon.

After what seemed like an eternity, the boat slowed and turned into the marina. She watched, dazed, as Juarez maneuvered into the boat slip and tied up. When the ropes were securely fastened, he put the .38 on the floor next to her and hopped onto the pier.

"Don't go anywhere," he said. "I'll be right back."

She nodded. All she wanted was to curl into a ball and let reality slip away. She rested her face against the boat's hard deck. It was wet and cool from the briny spray.

She closed her eyes.

Moments later, she was pulled to her feet by a pair of strong hands. Juarez scooped her up and carried her down the ladder. He eased her through the door to his bedroom and gently deposited her on the bed.

"Drink this," he said, unscrewing the cap off a bottle of Sprite and putting it in her hands.

She drank, grateful for something wet on her throat. He flipped on the light beside his bed and produced a small first-aid kit. He tore open an antiseptic towelette and dabbed at her forehead.

"Ouch!" she said, jerking her head back.

He continued dabbing even as she tried to pull away. "Hold still. I've got to clean this."

The towelette in his hand was scarlet with blood.

"How—"

"Windshield," he said. "You caught some flying glass."

She remembered the windshield exploding like a firecracker. The bullet must have been inches from her head.

"You nearly gave me a heart attack tonight," he said gruffly.

She closed her eyes. "I'm sorry."

"Don't do it again." He dabbed her cheek. "You've got a bruise here, too. What'd you do, bang your head on the wall?"

"I guess so."

He ran a thumb over her cheekbone, and she pulled away. Shaking his head, he took out some Band-Aids and taped them to her forehead. Then he eased her back against the pillow.

"You gonna heave again?"

She shuddered. "I don't think so. I'm just cold mainly."

He lifted her legs and pulled the comforter down, then spread it over her, tucking the edge around her neck. "I'll bring a bucket, just in case."

"Are we safe now?" she asked, shuddering again. "You lost them, didn't you?"

He looked at her for a long moment. "I lost them. We're safe for now."

• • • •

Through the haze of sleep, Feenie felt the mattress move. She bolted upright.

"What—"

"You were dreaming." Juarez was sitting on the edge of the bed, holding her arms.

She glanced around. She was in the familiar cramped bedroom. The clock on the shelf said one twenty-two. Her body was soaking wet, and she still wore the heavy sweatshirt she'd put on hours ago. Her mouth tasted sour, and her head throbbed.

She'd had the fire dream again.

"I need to use your bathroom," she said, swinging her legs out of bed. Her stomach muscles contracted painfully.

"You sure you're okay?"

Her gaze flicked to the spot above the bedroom door, the place where she kept her smoke detector at home.

A red light blinked back at her.

"You got a smoke detector?" How had she not noticed it before?

He followed her gaze. "I told you I would."

"I can't believe you did that." Her voice sounded shaky, and she suddenly needed to get away from him.

But he was right there. Next to her. Looking worried and sitting so close she could feel his breath against her hair.

"Feenie . . . are you okay?"

"I'm fine." She remembered the vomiting. "Sorry about earlier."

She wobbled to the tiny bathroom and shut the door. A fluorescent fixture glowed above the mirror, giving her face a greenish pallor. Or maybe her face really was green. She pulled back several Band-Aids to reveal a labyrinth of cuts. A purple bruise decorated her cheekbone.

She turned on the faucet and brushed her teeth for an eternity. Then she undressed and stood under the showerhead, letting the hot water pour over her until she felt human again. The shampoo burned her cuts, but she needed to wash the blood from her hair.

When she finished, she wrapped a towel around her body and went back into the bedroom, which was empty now. A T-shirt from her overnight bag sat folded on the side of the bed. She felt like hell. Her head throbbed, and her cuts stung, but at least she was clean. She tiptoed to the door and saw a pair of boots propped on the bench just beyond the galley.

She crept through the tiny kitchen and stood next to him. He lay stretched out on the seat, but he wasn't sleeping as she'd expected. His eyes were open, watching her.

"Marco . . . you awake?"

"Yes."

She took a deep breath and dropped the towel.

CHAPTER

14

S he held her breath, waiting for his reaction, but he didn't move. God, what had she done? He was probably lying there laughing at her. Or worse, trying to think of something to say that wouldn't hurt her feelings.

She took a step back, and he sat up.

"Come here," he said, his voice rough from sleep or ... something. He took her wrist and pulled her closer, resting his forehead against her rib cage and his hands on her hips. She knelt down. The carpet felt scratchy under her knees as she slid her arms around his neck and looked up into his face in the near-darkness. As usual, she couldn't read his expression.

"I don't think I can go back to sleep," she said.

"Then don't."

A little rush of excitement coursed through her, and she thought he would kiss her, but he didn't. Instead, his warm hands slid up to cup her breasts, and he rubbed his thumbs gently over the tips until her entire body tingled right down to the soles of her feet. Then he eased her back and let his gaze travel over her, making her feel pretty and self-conscious and impatient all at the same time. She was grateful for the dim lighting—just a shaft of gray coming through the porthole. She wondered what he thought of her. His hands moved slowly, almost reverently, over her, like he wanted to learn all the curves, even the ones she didn't much care for. His palms felt rough against her smooth skin, and she shivered at the contrast.

Why didn't he kiss her?

She inched closer. She was naked, but he wasn't, and his jeans chafed her skin. He closed his legs against her, pinning her there while he tangled his fingers in her curls and—finally—brought his mouth down to hers.

His kiss was hot and insistent, melting her from the inside out. A heady combination of lust and nerves swirled through her body, and she couldn't believe this was finally happening. She'd dropped all her defenses. A faint voice in the back of her head told her she was going to regret it, but she shut it out so she could concentrate on just him and the way he was making her feel.

His muscles bunched as she gripped his thighs

through the denim. He eased off the bench and kneeled in front of her and his hair felt thick and coarse between her fingers as she pulled his head down to hers for another kiss. She pressed herself into him, taking in the musky taste of his mouth, the faint scrape of his chin against hers, the cool softness of his T-shirt. She reached down to tug it from his jeans, but it caught on something.

"Wait," he said, and for the first time, she noticed the holster. He removed it and laid it aside. Then he pulled his shirt over his head, and she immediately reached out to touch the chest she'd been dying to feel since that day he'd cut up her tree. She loved the hard contours of him, the way his pulse hammered against her palms. Even if he didn't say it, she could tell he wanted this just as much as she did. The pounding of his heart was proof; the rigid bulge in his jeans was proof.

He wrapped his arms around her and pulled her against him. His kisses were hungry, fierce, totally different from Josh's. She wondered what else would be different, and her pulse skittered.

Then he surprised her by standing up.

"Come on." He pulled her to her feet. "We'll get rug burn out here."

Rug burn. How romantic.

She stared at his bare back as he pulled her by the hand into the bedroom, and suddenly it was all very real. Her nerves threatened to bubble over, so she sat on the edge of the bed and tried to get a grip.

He watched her watching him take off his boots and jeans. It occurred to her that she should be doing something right now, something sensual and alluring, but her mind drew a complete blank. All she could do was stare at him and feel her blood rush.

Totally at ease with his body, he stretched out beside her and tugged her back against the cool pillows. He propped his head on an elbow and looked at her with those black eyes and he was so close she felt the heat of his skin although he wasn't even touching her. He leaned over to kiss her, and she stiffened.

He stopped. "What's wrong?"

"Nothing."

"Then relax."

"Sorry." She tried to smile. "I'm a little nervous, I guess."

She waited for him to crack a joke, but he didn't say anything. He just looked her, and the intensity in his eyes made it hard for her to breathe. She pulled his head down to kiss him, and he rolled into her, the solid weight of him pressing her into the mattress. *Oh my God.* She clenched her teeth to keep from saying anything and stroked her hands over his arms and shoulders as his mouth moved down her body.

"You're shaking," he said against her breast. His breath was hot and tickly and it made her shake even more.

"I know. I can't help it." She cleared her throat. "It's been a while for me."

His mouth trailed up to her neck. "What a waste," he said. "I've been wanting you for years."

"*Years?*"

"Yeah."

He kissed the skin under her ear, sucking a little, and she had to wrap her arms tightly around his neck to control the tremors.

"Ever since that first day on your driveway. You were wearing that sexy little skirt and shooting your .22."

She drew back to look at him. "You were attracted to me *then?*"

He smiled. "The way you handle a gun really turns me on."

Then he pressed his mouth hard against hers, and she was pretty sure he was finished talking. His kisses grew more and more feverish, his hands more urgent, and she twisted and squirmed against him to get as close as she could.

The little room started to feel like a sauna as his skin grew damp against hers. He was touching her like he couldn't get enough, like he was desperate, and she was touching him the same way, gliding her hands over his back, kissing and nipping at his salty skin. She closed her eyes and felt pleasure spreading through her body like a drug, making her lightheaded and giddy and eager. She'd never felt so desired, ever. Then he murmured her name, and she opened herself to him, and in a painful, shocking instant they were joined together.

She gasped and opened her eyes.

He was looking down at her, his face tight with controlled passion, the corded muscles in his neck straining. His struggle for control plucked a hidden, tightly strung wire inside her, and her whole body started vibrating with emotion. He gave her a questioning look, and she nodded slightly and pulled him in closer. Then she tipped her head back and gave herself up.

Cecelia slipped the negligee over her head and surveyed her reflection in the bathroom mirror. Robert liked her in black. He liked her naked better, but tonight she wanted something extra to set the mood. Sex on demand wasn't as easy as it had been when they first got married, especially now that calendars and ovulation tests were involved.

She spritzed perfume into the air and stepped into the mist. She didn't want to overpower him, just give him a hint.

As if he needed one. He knew perfectly well what day it was, and she tried not to think that was the reason he'd practically leaped out of bed this morning, claiming he was late for a meeting. He'd worked extremely late tonight, too, but that hadn't been his fault. Not much he could do about a client dropping in from out of town at the last minute. He'd had to take the guy to dinner, and dinner had turned into a few drinks at a sports bar.

At least, that's what he'd told her, and she chose

to believe him. Why would he lie, anyway? She knew, she *knew*, he wanted kids as much as she did. He talked about it all the time. He'd already teed up names, for goodness sake.

This wasn't just for her. This was for him, too.

She fluffed her hair, adjusted her nightie, and stepped into the bedroom.

Where she found Robert sound asleep under the covers. He hadn't even bothered to turn off the lamp.

Sighing, she slid in next to him. Maybe she should just let him rest. But he had another meeting early tomorrow, and today was the day.

"Robert?"

He rolled toward her, eyes shut, and draped an arm over her waist. "Hmm?"

"Honey . . . you asleep?"

"Hmm . . ."

"Honey?"

He opened his eyes now and looked at her, no doubt noticing the black lace and the perfume. He closed his eyes briefly, and her heart sank.

"It's okay," she said, turning over. How humiliating was it to have to beg her own husband? She thought of all the time she spent on aerobics and tennis and shopping at Victoria's Secret. And he couldn't even be bothered to stay awake.

"Hey." He sat up now and rolled her back toward him. "I'm just tired, Celie. It's really late. Is today . . . ?"

She nodded. "There's always the morning if you—"

"I've got an early meeting."

"Right." She closed her eyes. This was so pathetic, and to make matters worse, she felt tears welling up. *God.* It wasn't supposed to be like this.

"Hey, come on," he said, touching the hem of her nightie. "I'm not trying to hurt your feelings or anything."

Not trying to . . . So was he in or out? She still couldn't tell.

"Take this off," he said.

And she did.

Feenie lay there in the dark, her head nestled against Marco's chest. His heart beat steadily beside her ear, and she realized he'd fallen asleep. A little knife twisted inside her.

How could he be asleep? Just like that? Maybe he was so accustomed to having women in his bed that tonight wasn't much of a novelty. But for her, it was a major milestone, both physically and emotionally. It was ironic, really, that after everything they'd done tonight, she should lie next to him and feel so completely alone.

What was wrong with her that she kept expecting intimacy from people? Every time she let her guard down, it turned out the same. Marco would be no different. He liked her, maybe, but he didn't love her. Sooner or later, she was bound to get hurt.

She eased away from him and peered over the edge of the bed. Only a faint shaft of moonlight illuminated the room, but after groping around on the floor for a moment, she located the soft fabric of her sweatshirt. She sat up and pulled it over her shoulders.

"Hey." Marco's arm curled around her waist. "What are you doing?"

She turned around. He sounded surprisingly alert for someone who had been asleep just seconds before.

"I need to put something on," she said.

"No, you don't." He slid his hands under the sweatshirt, lifted it back over her head, and tossed it onto the floor. "I like you like this." He pulled her back against him and encircled her in his strong arms.

"I thought you were asleep," she said over her shoulder.

His laughter was warm against the back of her neck. "Just taking a breather."

"Really?" She turned to face him.

"Really. I'm not planning to get much sleep tonight, are you?" He stroked a hand over her breast, and she felt heat well up inside her. Then his hand stilled, and he looked at her for a long moment.

"What?"

"You're beautiful, you know that?"

She smiled. It wasn't exactly a declaration of love, but it was something. Especially the way he said it, all low and serious.

"Thank you," she whispered, trailing a finger down his chest. His body was so muscular and perfect, she couldn't believe he was really here. With her. With all her *un*muscular *im*perfection. "I think you're beautiful, too."

He winced. "Guys aren't beautiful."

"Sometimes they are."

"Ripped, maybe. Or buff. Pick a word that isn't girlie."

She kissed his bicep and watched him. "I like *beautiful.*"

He sighed. "This is why I don't do pillow talk. It's too mushy."

She smiled as he kissed her again. Maybe talking *was* overrated.

CHAPTER

15

Marco roused Feenie not long after dawn, shoved a mug of coffee into her hands, and dragged her off to the gym. Despite her most recent injuries, he didn't offer to ease up on the barbells and medicine balls, and as soon as she was awake enough to think clearly, she felt oddly grateful. If anything, the previous evening had rekindled her motivation. She felt the need to defend herself now more than ever before. She hadn't spotted the tan Blazer since Tuesday, but that didn't mean Josh's man wasn't lurking around somewhere. And if the Garlands figured out that she'd tagged along on their little fishing expedition, they'd make every effort to shut her up.

As Marco practiced holds on her, Feenie's

thoughts drifted to the various ways Josh's hired gun might try to kill her. Shooting seemed the simplest method, but Marco appeared convinced he had other plans.

She landed on her back with a thud, and he looked down at her, scowling. "You're not paying attention."

She got to her feet and bent over to catch her breath. "Sorry. I'm distracted."

He raised an eyebrow and shot her a knowing look. He'd assumed she was thinking about sex, and she decided not to crush his ego.

"How about ten more minutes and we call it quits?" he said in a low voice. "We can swing by my place before we head to the firing range."

She read the look in his eyes, and her stomach tightened. Cecelia had been right about Feenie needing a fling. Last night had been amazing. Problem was, Feenie didn't think *fling* fully described what they were doing together. Things felt serious. Much too serious to walk away from after one night together, or even two.

But maybe that was just her take on it. Maybe to him it was all just sex. Feenie needed to avoid being alone with him until she figured a few things out.

"Actually, I'm famished," she said. "Why don't we shower here and go get some breakfast? What time does Rosie's open?"

He looked stung for an instant, then covered it. "Got your appetite back, eh? That's good." He glanced at his watch. "Rosie's opened fifteen minutes ago."

Over *migas* and coffee, she decided to broach the subject that had been gnawing at her for the past eight hours.

"What do you plan to do with the evidence?" she asked.

He forked a spoonful of eggs. "Evidence?"

"The tapes, the pictures. Everything from last night."

"Pictures probably won't turn out. The tape's good, but it's not enough to really make a difference."

She dropped her fork. "What do you mean? We witnessed the handoff with our own eyes! You recorded it! What more do you need?"

He returned to his food. "The audiotape is good but not conclusive. We need more."

She leaned back in the booth and crossed her arms. "I disagree." Understatement of the year. "I say we go to the cops right now, give them everything you have. Maybe they can get a search warrant and find more."

He leaned in. "Have you forgotten what I've told you about the cops? And both Garlands have connections within the legal community, too. I'd practically need a smoking gun with Josh's fingerprints on it to get a search warrant for his place. Local law enforcement is out."

"Okay, fine. Go to the FBI. Immigration. *Somebody* who can do something. We can't just sit here."

He continued eating.

"Marco?"

"We're not sitting here. We're investigating. That means patience. It takes time to put all the pieces together. I've spent two years on this, and I have no intention of blowing it by getting sloppy at the last minute."

"Two *years,* and you don't have enough evidence? I don't buy it. Who are you working for, anyway?"

"I told you. Some people who believe Garland is responsible for their relative's death."

"Yes, but *who?*"

He set his jaw. "That's confidential."

Unbelievable. He was fine with her risking her life to get information, but he still didn't see fit to give her details.

"Yeah, well, I'd think they'd be getting impatient for results," she said. "Or maybe they're okay with you milking this thing for all it's worth. You probably get paid by the hour, right?"

His eyes hardened. "Watch it."

Her appetite had disappeared, and she pushed her plate away. "What about the girls?"

"What about them? We have no idea who they are or where they went."

"They're probably in the hands of some pimp by now. And they're kids! How can you just let that go?"

He clamped a hand over hers. "I haven't let anything go. But we're going after someone who's rich and connected as hell. He and whoever he's working with have so many people on the take, you wouldn't believe it. So we've got one chance to get this right, or it's two years down the tubes and a price on our heads. We need more evidence."

She eyed him across the table. He had a point, she supposed. Josh would do anything to discredit the evidence against him, and he'd most certainly try to punish anyone who called his reputation into question. A few weeks ago, she would have taken punishment to mean a lawsuit or a smear campaign. Now she knew he was capable of much more.

"Don't you think it's possible Josh *knows* you're investigating him?" she asked. "What if there's a hit out on *you*?"

He looked at her a moment, but as usual, she had no idea what he was thinking.

"I take precautions," he said, clearly not intending to elaborate.

She rolled her eyes. Why did he always have to be so evasive? "What kind of evidence do you need?"

He released her hand. "My biggest gap now is the money. I can make a good case that he's running some drugs, especially after last night's audiotape. But I can't prove the scope. I need financial statements, bank records. Anything showing his fingerprints on the money."

Financial statements. Bank records. The kind of information someone's accountant would have—or someone's *former* accountant.

"And if we get our hands on these records, assuming they exist, *then* we can go to the police?" she asked.

"I told you about the police."

"Okay, okay. The authorities. The DEA. The FBI. Someone who can help. You're saying if we get hold of Josh's financial records, we'll have enough to turn him in?"

"That's what I'm hoping. Why? Do you have any ideas?"

She looked down at the table, feeling guilty for the plan percolating inside her head. She'd been friends with Cecelia since middle school.

"Let me think about it some more," she said. "I'll let you know."

After they finished at the firing range, Feenie persuaded Marco to drop her off at the newspaper office by promising not to set foot outside the building. It probably helped that she lacked transportation because her car was still sitting in front of her house on Pecan Street. They had decided that was the best place to keep it, to avoid drawing attention to her new living quarters.

Marco pulled up to the front of the *Gazette* building and did a thorough scan of the area. Feenie felt sure it was safe. No one would expect her to show up at work on a Saturday, and the painfully circuitous route they'd taken across town had eliminated the possibility of a tail.

"I'll be back at four," he said. "No leaving."

She reached for the door, but he tugged her back.

"Hey," he said, and kissed her. His mouth felt hard and possessive. "I mean it. Be careful."

As she swiped her key card at the front entrance, she wondered what the heck she'd gotten herself into. Nothing about his treatment of her seemed casual, yet she knew better than to expect commitment from a guy who made his home on a fishing boat. Whatever he felt for her was intense but temporary. Just like her interest in him.

Yeah, right.

She reached the top of the stairs as Grimes was coming out of his office.

"What brings you in on a Saturday?" he asked.

She plastered a smile on her face. "I just need to polish up that story for tomorrow." The features editor had assigned her an in-depth piece about the high school, and she hadn't had time to complete it because she'd been so focused on helping Marco.

His neutral expression became a frown. "What happened to your face?"

She touched her cheekbone. She'd applied concealer over the bruise, but her cut still required a Band-Aid. "Bumped into a door."

Grimes raised an eyebrow skeptically and headed into the break room.

The newsroom was deserted except for the sports guys and the features editor, who had given her a mid-afternoon deadline. Feenie seated herself at her desk and got to work. She went over her draft, made some revisions, and then sent it over to the editor for a look. While she waited for his feedback, she typed up some wedding stuff for the next week, and her mind wandered to the scheme she had brewing.

If she were Robert Strickland, where would she keep sensitive files? She'd known the man for nearly a decade, and he rarely threw anything away. Cecelia often complained that their garage was like an orphanage for unwanted tools and gadgets. He read instruction manuals cover to cover, then kept them on file long after he'd learned to work the appliances to which they belonged.

Robert wouldn't throw away something important like a former client's financial records. But where did he keep them? Not at work, Feenie hoped. She didn't have a chance in hell of talking her way into the posh offices of Robert's accounting firm. But she doubted he'd store them there if he knew what they revealed. If the records reflected illegal activities, surely he wouldn't keep them where someone in his office could nose through them. Feenie mentally went over the floor plan to Cecelia's house. She and Robert had installed a safe years before, but Feenie had no idea where and wouldn't be able to crack a safe anyway. She was pretty sure there were some file cabinets in Robert's study, but that seemed much too obvious a hiding spot, even for a totally left-brained thinker like Robert. The attic, maybe?

Feenie's cell buzzed, interrupting her thoughts.

The caller ID told her it was Cecelia, and she felt instantly guilty.

"Hi, Celie. What's up?"

"You tell me. How'd it go last night with your cop?"

Feenie had told Cecelia she had a date with Marco last night. Unlike McAllister, Cecelia had believed her.

"He's not mine. And he's not a cop."

"Feenie . . ." Her voice livened up.

"Huh?"

"I knew it! You slept with him! How was it?"

"How was what?" she asked, stalling. She'd always been pretty open with Cecelia when it came to matters of the heart—and the bedroom—but the details felt private this time.

"The *sex*, Feenie! God! I bet it was great, wasn't it? That man is gorgeous!"

"I really don't—"

"Stop right there! I want to hear about it in person. Let's go to Rosie's for margaritas."

"I had breakfast there."

Several seconds ticked by while Cecelia digested this.

"You had *breakfast* together? That's so sweet! You have to come over, Feen. Robert has a golf game, and we can have a beer by the pool. I want to hear everything."

Her heart squeezed. It was just the opening she needed to show up at Cecelia's house and poke around. She felt horrible. But then she remembered the girls on Josh's boat and shook off her reservations. She glanced at the newsroom clock.

"I'm at the *Gazette* right now. I've got to wrap some things up first, and I don't have my car. Can you pick me up around one?" That would give her several hours to hang out with Cecelia and get back to the office before Marco showed up.

"One o'clock. I'll be there."

An hour later, Feenie sat on the edge of Cecelia's pool, feeling exhausted from the strange and taxing exercise of talking to her best friend without telling her what was really going on in her life. She gulped down the last sip of the Corona she'd been drinking and gathered her courage.

"Mind if I go get another one?" she asked.

"I'll get it," Cecelia said from her chaise. She wore sunglasses and a powder-blue bikini, and her skin was slathered in suntan oil.

"No, I'll do it. I have to use the bathroom anyway."

Cecelia shrugged and handed her an empty bottle. "Get me one, too, then. There's a lime on the counter."

Feenie took the glass bottles into the kitchen and tossed them into the recycle bin. Then she walked to the guest bathroom right next to Robert's study.

She stepped through the doorway into the study and surveyed the room, which was decorated in a masculine combination of dark wood furniture and leather upholstery. Everything looked orderly, from the meticulously arranged bookshelves to the stack of files on the corner of his mahogany desk. She pulled open one of the built-in mahogany-paneled drawers behind the desk. It was packed with files.

Her gaze skimmed the folders. They were arranged alphabetically. All the labels dealt with personal topics, though. After checking the G section, she shut the drawer and tried the one below.

The second drawer contained financial records. She thumbed through the files, but all of them related to Cecelia and Robert's personal finances. There was nothing about Josh, or any other of Robert's clients, for that matter.

Feenie shut the drawer and glanced around the room again. The credenza held a digital camcorder and Robert's extensive home movie collection—arranged chronologically, of course—and his DVDs. She scanned the shelves briefly. They proved Robert was a film buff, but this wasn't exactly news. He kept a shelf of VHS tapes, too. She read the spines. They were home movies, from vacations, mostly. Feenie recognized some of the destinations—Las Brisas, Cozumel, the Caymans. She spotted a tape labeled "Monterrey" and frowned. She didn't know Cecelia and Robert had ever been down there on vacation. She pulled the video off the shelf and took the tape out of the jacket.

Instead of a home movie, it contained a professionally produced tape with the picture of a redhead wearing only a cowboy hat on the cover. *Exxxciting*

Texxxas Vixxxens. Ick. *Not* what she'd expected from the straight-laced accountant.

She quickly reshelved the tape and glanced over her shoulder. She was definitely invading their privacy here, and it wasn't fun. She glanced at her watch. *Hell.* She'd been gone nearly ten minutes, and Cecelia was probably wondering what was keeping her. Feenie tiptoed out of Robert's office, feeling both disappointed and relieved. She hadn't found any incriminating papers, but she'd given it her best shot. If Marco wanted any more dirt on Robert, he'd have to dig it up himself.

Cecelia dropped Feenie off in front of the newspaper office. "Good luck tonight," she said, grinning.

"Luck?"

Cecelia looked at her over her shades. "Juarez. You're staying on his boat again tonight, right?"

"I guess so. We haven't really talked about it."

"Trust me, you'll be there. Sounds like he's crazy about you. He's probably already burned his little black book."

Feenie opened the car door. "I don't think so. From what I can tell, his idea of commitment is a box of condoms."

"Don't be too sure. You've practically moved in, haven't you? And he didn't even have to ask. I think he's serious about you."

"I'm staying there for safety reasons," Feenie reminded her.

"Safety reasons. Uh-huh." She winked. "Very convenient."

Sighing, Feenie watched her drive off. She was right, at least about the moving-in part. He hadn't asked. *Forced* was more like it. He'd packed her bag for her, plunging his hands into all her private dresser drawers to grab socks, underwear, and T-shirts, while she'd stood there arguing. He'd paid zero attention to her. The man wouldn't take no for an answer, particularly where she was concerned. And now they were living together.

Maybe she should put some distance between herself and Marco and cool down a little. Her overheated libido wasn't helping her make smart decisions.

She dug her key card out of her purse and strode toward the glass door to the *Gazette* building.

Pop.

The glass shattered, and Feenie dropped to the pavement. *Pop. Pop.*

Her brain identified the sound, but her body seemed slow to react. Then she heard herself screaming. She felt her hands and knees scraping across the concrete as she crawled behind a lamppost and tried to hide.

She was going to die right here in broad daylight! Where was her gun? She fumbled through her purse.

A tan SUV screeched to a halt just yards from where she hid. The Chevy Blazer. *Oh, God.*

A man jumped out, gun drawn, and ran toward her.

16

"FBI! Drop the gun!" he roared, leaping on top of her.

Her wrist hit the concrete. The .38 disappeared. She lay on her stomach, shrieking, flattened underneath the man's body.

"Don't move!" he shouted. Car doors slammed, and she heard yelling across the street.

"On the count of three, we're going to run for the car. Understand? Don't stop. Don't hesitate, no matter what you hear, okay? One, two—"

Wait! What the hell was happening?

"Three!"

He hurled her forward a few feet and pitched her into the Blazer. He shoved her down onto the floorboard as he climbed over her, into the driver's seat, and peeled away, tires screaming.

Tan Chevy Blazer. FBI. He'd taken her gun.

"Can you reach the door?" he yelled.

Should she jump out of the speeding car or yank the door shut? Who *was* this man? Had he fired the shots? But then why was she alive?

Still crouching on the floor, she reached for the door and dragged it shut.

He glanced down at her, but then his gaze darted right back to the road. He took a series of sharp turns and drove a few minutes on a straightaway before coming to an abrupt stop.

She knelt there, heart thundering, waiting for him to move. His right hand still gripped a black handgun. When he saw her eyeing it, he steadied the wheel with his knee so he could reach his free hand into the pocket of his navy windbreaker.

"Special Agent Michael Rowe, FBI." He flipped a billfold open on the seat next to her, and she looked at the photo ID. Brown hair, short, graying at the temples. He had a thick neck and a square jaw. Her gaze veered back toward the driver. Sweat streamed down his face, but other than that, he looked like the picture.

She watched the gun in his hand, still not sure whether to trust him.

"I'm not going to hurt you, okay?" he said, reading her mind. "I just needed to get you out of the line of fire."

He'd thrown himself on top of her, between her and the bullets.

"We're safe now," he said. "Will you sit up?"

Her hands shook uncontrollably as she reached for his identification. She glanced at it one more time and then held it out for him.

"Thank you," he said, tucking it back into his pocket. He still hadn't let go of the gun. "I need you to sit up now."

Her limbs felt like pudding, but she maneuvered herself into the seat and faced him, keeping a hand on the door handle. It seemed pointless, given that his gun was poised between them.

"You carrying any more weapons?" he asked.

She shook her head.

"I believe you," he told her, "but I still have to check, all right? Don't be alarmed."

The pat-down didn't take long, because all she had on were workout clothes. Her purse was abandoned on the sidewalk somewhere.

Where were they?

She glanced around and realized he'd taken her to the parking lot of a dumpy motel. She recognized the place from the night of her senior prom. It hadn't looked any better then, and she'd been in a wine-cooler-induced stupor, which felt remarkably similar to her current state. Except that now, instead of being incoherent and happy, she was incoherent and petrified.

"How did you get here?" Her voice sounded raspy. "I mean there. Back there. Just like that."

"We followed you from the Strickland residence."

She stared at him.

"You've been under surveillance for a few weeks now," he said.

She cleared her throat. "Did you . . . see the person shooting at me?" She'd wanted to say, *Did you kill him?* but couldn't get her mouth to form the words.

"Not directly, no. We were down the street when the gunfire started. Looks like the shooter was in the alley across from your office. My partner went after him."

"Thank you. For jumping on me."

He smirked.

A squawking noise made her jerk back. The agent reached for a black radio at his hip. She hadn't noticed it before, or the holster there.

"Rowe," he said into the receiver.

"Shooter bugged out," a voice said. "Purnell is on the scene now, and the local PD just arrived. Target okay?"

The agent glanced at her. "Looks like," he said.

Feenie looked down at her skinned knees and wrists. Other than that, she wasn't injured. But she was a *target*. And if it hadn't been for this FBI agent, she'd probably be a bullet-riddled target.

"Purnell wants to interview her at HQ, twenty minutes."

"Got it," the agent said, and replaced the radio.

She cleared her throat, which felt like dust all of a sudden. "HQ?"

He nodded toward the shabby hotel. "Headquarters, ma'am, such as it is."

"Headquarters for what?"

"Our task force. We've got eight agents working here round the clock. Some of them, including me, haven't had more than three hours of sleep in the last two days. So don't take it personally if fuses are short in there."

He gave her a tired smile. "You ready?"

"I doubt it."

"Well, it doesn't matter anyway, because they're ready for you."

Juarez pulled into the parking lot at Bayside Marina and noticed the guy loitering near the bait shop: dark hair, sunglasses, beer gut zipped into a freebie windbreaker from some charter fishing company. He could have been anybody, if not for the red baseball cap with the letters *HTCC* stitched across the front. Holy Trinity Catholic Church. It wasn't some random guy, it was Hector.

Juarez pulled into his regular parking place and watched him in his rearview mirror. Hector pivoted toward the pickup and, ever so slightly, made the sign of the cross.

Okay. As meetings with Hector went, this was a little unusual. But Juarez knew Special Agent Hector Flores well enough to know that if he'd driven his ass all the way down here from Houston, he had a good reason. And if he was trying to be secretive about it, he had a *damn* good reason.

Juarez adjusted his rearview mirror, gave Hector a brief nod, and went aboard his boat, pretending to pick something up. Two minutes later, he was back in the Silverado and heading across town to Holy Trinity Catholic Church, his and Hector's childhood stomping grounds.

By the time he pulled into the church parking lot, he'd figured out the significance of Hector's visit. Juarez was under surveillance. How could he not have known? And for Hector to have come here, this was more than just some rookie agent sitting in a car. His phones must be compromised, too.

Juarez entered the church and took a moment to let his eyes adjust to the cool darkness. Out of habit, he dipped his fingers in holy water and crossed himself before making his way down a side aisle. He stopped at a shadowy niche, where a statue of the Virgin perched on a pedestal surrounded by flickering white candles. An old woman sat in the pew closest to the statue, either deep in prayer or asleep. Juarez stopped a few rows behind her and sat down to wait.

Several minutes later, Hector slid into the pew directly behind him. After a brief silence, Juarez heard him pull out the kneeler and arrange himself as if he were praying. Given all the shit they'd done as kids together, Juarez nearly laughed.

"What brings you home?" he muttered to Hector.

From the corner of his eye, Juarez saw him shake his head. "Marco, brother, you're in some serious shit."

"Tell me something I don't know."

Hector didn't say anything for a while, and Juarez waited patiently. He was probably scoping out the church to make sure no one had followed them inside. Finally, he seemed comfortable.

"I hear you been asking about Armando Ruiz," Hector said. "You're starting to make a lot of people nervous."

"What do you know about Ruiz?"

"I know that he's dead."

Juarez bit back a curse. There went one of his best leads. "Are you sure?"

"Killed in prison. Most likely by a fellow inmate connected to the Saledo family. Seems some people considered Ruiz's big mouth a liability."

So Paloma and her partner's deaths were definitely connected to the Saledos. That explained which cartel Garland was laundering money for.

But it didn't explain Hector's presence hundreds of miles away from the Houston field office where he worked.

"Marco, man, I need you to listen to me. Your sister was a beautiful girl. A smart girl. It isn't right, what happened to her. I understand you being angry, man."

Juarez scoffed. *Angry?* He had no fucking idea. "Cut the shit, Hector. Why'd you come here?"

He sighed heavily. "You need to back off, man. Back way the fuck off. Let law enforcement investigate, okay?"

"Law enforcement?" Juarez clenched his teeth. "The SAPD hasn't investigated *shit* in more than a year. I'm just supposed to sit back and let them handle this?"

"The bureau's involved, too, Marco. They have been since the beginning."

"Oh, yeah? And you expect me to believe they give a rat's ass about Paloma?"

"You're right." Hector lowered his voice as an old lady shuffled up the aisle and kneeled in front of the statue. "They don't give a rat's ass about Paloma. But they *do* care about her partner."

Juarez was so startled he nearly turned around. He tried to keep his voice down. "Ben was a fed?"

"Yeah, working undercover," Hector said. "He was on the task force investigating the Saledos."

Shit. That explained a lot of things, like why the SAPD investigation hadn't gone anywhere. The FBI had probably stymied it because they didn't want to draw attention to their agent. Just the fact that the bureau had planted someone in Paloma's squad confirmed Juarez's suspicions that something was rotten up there.

"Fuck," Juarez muttered.

"Pretty much."

Juarez sat there a minute, trying to rein in his temper. On one hand, he wanted to thank Hector for finally bringing him into the loop. He could probably lose his job just for being here like this.

But on the other hand, he wanted to kill the guy for withholding the information for so long.

"How's your mother, man?" Hector asked him now.

Juarez gritted his teeth. "The same."

Hector leaned closer. "Don't make her go through this again. You hear what I'm saying? Let the task force handle this from here. You leave it alone."

Hector crossed himself and got up from the kneeler. "You hearing me?"

Juarez looked straight ahead as the woman near the statue lit her candle. She had deep lines etched around her eyes, and she reminded Juarez of his mother.

"Marco?"

"I hear you, man."

"Good." He touched his shoulder briefly. "Take care of yourself."

And then he was gone.

Feenie stumbled over the threshold into the motel room. The air conditioning was set to arctic, and the place smelled like stale coffee.

Three men were inside, two talking on cell phones and one seated cross-legged on the bed with a notebook computer in front of him. They all wore dark slacks, button-down shirts, and ties, and their eyes tracked Feenie as Rowe ushered her into a chair.

"We got any water?" Rowe asked the room at large.

Someone opened a mini-fridge near the television cabinet and tossed him a plastic bottle. Rowe plunked it down in front of her before disappearing into the bathroom.

Feenie unscrewed the cap and tried to take a sip, but her hands were still shaking, and water dribbled down her shirt. Rowe reappeared with a damp towel and handed it to her.

"You might want to clean up those scrapes," he said.

"Thanks." She wiped the dust and blood from her cuts. Then she glanced up at Rowe. In jeans, a windbreaker, and sneakers, he looked casual compared with his colleagues. The jacket seemed absurdly out of place in the summer heat, but maybe he wore it to hide the holster.

Rowe took a seat across from her at the table, glanced at his watch, and jotted some notes down on a yellow legal pad. Then he launched into some questions about her actions leading up to the shooting. Had she received any strange phone calls earlier that day? Had she noticed anyone suspicious lurking around? As she answered the series of questions, she clasped her hands and tried to get the shaking under control.

Suddenly, the door burst open, and a young man entered the room, followed by a white-haired guy with a bulbous nose. He wore a dark suit and tie, unlike the younger guy, who wore a variation on Rowe's jeans-and-windbreaker theme. Everyone's posture straightened, and the cell phones disappeared, so Feenie guessed White Hair was in charge.

"I'm George Purnell, FBI." He extended a hand.

She shook it, sensing this was a name to remember. "I'm Francis Malone."

"I know." He slid her pink handbag in front of her. Then he pulled up a side chair with tacky orange upholstery and sat beside Rowe. "I take it you've met Special Agent Rowe?"

She snorted. "Met him, yes. If being tackled to the pavement constitutes a meeting."

Purnell frowned at her. He thought she was being inappropriate.

"Sorry," she mumbled. "I'm a little . . . flustered at the moment." She reached for her water again, becoming intensely aware of the many pairs of male eyes focused on her damp T-shirt. She changed her mind about the water and crossed her arms.

Purnell cleared his throat. "Ms. Malone, do you know who was shooting at you back there?"

"I was kind of hoping *you* would."

Purnell leaned back in his chair, clearly disappointed with this answer.

Rowe turned and gestured to the four agents behind him. They filed out of the room, and Feenie felt slightly more at ease when they were gone.

"Unfortunately, we don't," Purnell said. "The shots came from an alley behind an abandoned building, and we haven't located any witnesses yet who saw the suspect. Police are canvassing the area now. You sure you have no idea?"

Great. The FBI was just as clueless as she was. Wonderful news.

"I mean, someone's been following me," she said. "I know that. I just don't know who it is. He drives a—" *Oh, God.*

Purnell leaned forward. "A what?"

"Nothing. I noticed a tan Blazer following me a while back, but I guess that was you guys."

Purnell flicked a glance at Rowe, and Feenie could almost hear the silent reprimand.

"Did he have a getaway car?" Feenie asked.

"We don't know."

She stared at Purnell, feeling more frustrated than ever. Maybe it was just a delayed reaction to being shot at, but her fear was quickly morphing into something else. Something with teeth.

"Do you want to fill me in on what you *do* know?"

The agent didn't seem perturbed. "Ms. Malone, we're on a task force investigating, among other things, your ex-husband."

"I put that together, thanks."

"We need to ask you some questions about him," Purnell said.

"Go ahead. I have nothing to hide." At least, she didn't think she did. Maybe she should ask for a lawyer. But she didn't know anyone not connected to Josh, except the guy she'd hired to handle her divorce.

He'd turned out to be an expensive disappointment, and Feenie still harbored suspicions that he'd taken money under the table to botch her case. She'd be better off on her own.

"Do you need to read me my rights or something?" She hoped they'd think she was bitchy and litigious.

"You're not in custody."

"I'm not?"

"No. You're free to leave whenever you want." Purnell tipped his head to the side appraisingly.

"Not before I ask *you* a question," Feenie said. "Why am I under surveillance?"

Purnell didn't answer. Rowe slid the legal pad in front of him, and he pulled some glasses from his pocket and positioned them on the end of his nose. He resembled Feenie's father reading the Sunday paper, and she guessed he was about the same age.

"Ms. Malone, you were married to Josh Garland for, what, about five years, was it?" Purnell asked.

"Yes."

"And how long have you been divorced?"

"Officially? About a year and a half. We were separated for six months before that."

He took out a ballpoint pen and scrawled something on the pad. "No children?"

She blew out a breath. "No."

"And you still reside at the house on Pecan Street? The one you lived in while married to Josh Garland?"

"Yes," she answered. She looked at Rowe, but his face was a blank mask. "No offense, but these questions seem a little basic. Don't you guys have all this already?"

The side of Rowe's mouth ticked up, but Purnell ignored her. "And you and your ex-husband no longer see each other socially?" Purnell continued.

"No."

"What about business? Are your finances still intertwined?"

"Definitely not. Feel free to check, if you don't believe me."

Something in his expression told her he already had. They were investigators. They probably had a three-inch file on her already. But she knew what they were doing. She employed the same technique whenever she interviewed people for a story. It was simple: Start with easy, comfortable questions, and make sure you know the answers. Watch people's mannerisms as they respond. That way, when you get to the questions that count, you can tell if they're lying.

"Can we cut to the chase, please?" she asked. "Surely you must have something to ask me that you don't already know."

Irritation flickered over Purnell's face. "Okay. Ms. Malone, how would you characterize your relationship with Marco Juarez?"

"What does that have to do with Josh? Or my being shot at?"

"We're just trying to understand the circumstances here."

She gulped. "We're . . . friends, I guess."

His look sharpened. "Friends? Are you romantically involved?"

Did mind-blowing sex count? "Uh . . . I guess so."

"Okay. So, given that you're romantically involved with Mr. Juarez, would it be fair to assume that you're helping him with his investigation?"

She didn't like where this was going. "I thought you wanted to talk about Josh?"

"We do. And Juarez. Could you answer the question, please?"

"Yes, I'm helping him."

"Is that what you were doing at Cecelia Strickland's house today? Helping Juarez?"

Feenie bit her lip. "I was visiting my friend."

"Ms. Malone, since you're romantically involved with Mr. Juarez, I assume he's filled you in on his personal connection to your ex-husband."

Her stomach tightened. "What personal connection?"

"He never told you about Paloma?"

"Paloma?"

"Paloma Juarez?"

Dear God, he was married. She should have known.

"I don't really know anything about . . . her."

Purnell's eyebrows went up, but she got the impression he wasn't that surprised. "Really? Well, we should enlighten you. Paloma Juarez was Marco's sister."

Sister. Thank you, God.

"He believes Josh Garland had her murdered."

"What?"

"Several years ago, Paloma Juarez was working on the vice squad in San Antonio. She was investigating a smuggling ring with ties to your ex-husband when she disappeared. She and a federal agent who was working undercover. We believe they were abducted and killed. Together."

Feenie glanced at Rowe, then back at Purnell.

"Marco's sister. Was murdered by Josh. Is that what you're saying?"

Purnell shrugged. "We doubt Josh Garland actually carried out the murder. We have reason to believe he hired someone. Now Mr. Juarez, it seems, is trying to track that person down. It's quite possibly the same person who shot at you today."

She tried to get her mind around it. Marco had a sister, one who had died. He hadn't told her much about his family, and she'd tried to respect his privacy. Now she felt incredibly stupid. *His* family was the one that had lost a loved one because of Josh. It was all connected—his sister, his investigation, his obsession with Josh.

His obsession with *her.*

She slumped in the chair, too shocked to speak. She'd been played all along. Once again, the dumb blonde.

"Marco Juarez has spent the past two years fixated on his sister's death," Purnell told her. "The official investigation didn't go anywhere, because we didn't want it leaking out that we had an agent involved. So Mr. Juarez took it upon himself to start snooping around."

She stared at Purnell, still too stupefied to talk.

"Let me get to the point. We believe Marco Juarez is using you to get to Garland. But his primary objective isn't Garland at all; it's his sister's killer."

That snapped her out of her silence. "You don't think he wants Josh? That's crazy. He's collected evidence. He's—"

"We didn't say he didn't *want* Garland. Just that Garland isn't his only goal. You see, we think he's hoping your ex-husband will give up his sister's killer. Juarez wants revenge and probably a body. Garland could provide the first, at least partially, but not the second."

"So . . . he wants to track down the man who actually murdered her so he can find out what happened and recover her remains?" Her mind flashed back to the day of Rachel and her mother's funeral. She knew how important those rituals were. "Can you blame him?"

"Not really. If that's all he wants. But he's jeopardizing our investigation in the process."

"How?"

Purnell looked her over, then turned and nodded at Rowe.

"We believe Juarez may be getting to a breaking point," Rowe said. "He's becoming impatient. Everything he's worked for is finally coming to a head. We believe he might use the information he's collected so far to blackmail Garland into giving up his hit man. After that, we don't know what he'll do. Maybe he'll kill Garland. Maybe he'll go after Garland's hired gun. Unfortunately, if he eliminates either of them, we're faced with a major setback."

"The contract killer is likely to be one of our best witnesses against Garland," Purnell said. "And we need Garland to connect the dots between the other suspects we're investigating."

Was this why Marco was so adamant about not turning to the authorities? For once, it made sense. Marco had his own agenda, and it went way beyond seeing Josh behind bars.

"Okay," she said slowly. "Why don't you just arrest Josh? Put him in jail and charge him with a crime? I've got a laundry list of possibilities."

Feenie saw the muscle in Purnell's jaw jump. She'd hit on a touchy point. "We can't do that yet," he said. "We need Garland to continue business as usual for a while so we can get to some people even higher up the food chain."

"Yeah? Like who?" She was pretty sure they wouldn't answer this, but she was too curious not to ask.

"You ever hear of Manuel Saledo?" Purnell asked.

"No. Should I have?"

"His name was in the news a few years back in connection with something called Operation Money Trace. His brother's in a federal prison now, but

Manuel's still in Mexico. Seems he's taken over the family business."

"I don't know the man," Feenie said. She needed to find out if they knew that Saledo's business involved exploiting young girls. "So, this 'business as usual' strategy. Just what type of *business*—"

"The drugs, the child trafficking, the money, all of it," Purnell said.

They knew about the girls. It was the one good thing she'd heard out of his mouth.

But why weren't they doing something about it? She squeezed her eyes closed. It was all so complicated. So sleazy. How did she get entrenched in all this? She opened her eyes.

"Why not just tell Marco to get out of your way?"

Purnell leveled a look at her. "We have our reasons, Ms. Malone. It would work better if you'd influence Juarez for us. Get him to ease off a little, just for the time being. And tip us off if he plans to do anything rash."

"You want me to spy on him for you? What makes you think I'd do that? He's my *friend*." The words made her feel sick, because they were so far from the truth. He'd lied to her. He'd used her. Still, she wouldn't spy on him. The last thing she wanted was to be used by yet another party, even if it was the FBI.

"Accessory to murder's a serious crime, Ms. Malone," Purnell said.

"Is that a threat?"

"It's a reality. And you may want to remind your

boyfriend that he could be looking at life in prison or even the death penalty if he does anything stupid."

Feenie gulped. Surely Marco wouldn't go after a professional hit man. Then again, if the guy had killed his sister, who knew what he'd do?

"And in light of today's events, we should encourage you not to trust him," Purnell said. "It appears as though he's using you as bait to lure his sister's killer out of hiding."

"That's ludicrous. He's been trying to protect me."

"Where was he today?" Purnell asked.

Feenie started to say something, then bit her lip.

"If our agents hadn't been nearby, you most likely would have been killed. Probably by the same hit man who killed Paloma Juarez."

"You make it sound like . . . Are you telling me you know who he is?" She couldn't believe it.

"We have a pretty good idea, yes."

She wanted to smack him, right in that big, fat nose. "So arrest the guy! What are you waiting for?"

"It's not that simple," Purnell said. "The suspect's very elusive. We've been looking for him for months, and we still haven't found him."

"Well, why aren't you looking for him now instead of talking to me? This is a waste of time!"

"We've got agents working the scene as we speak," Rowe said.

"I assure you, we take this all very seriously," Purnell added. "As I said earlier, this is a multiagency operation. We've got three years and thousands of man-hours tied up in it. We'd like nothing more than to arrest Garland and his associates and put them away. But we need your help. And you're in the unique position of being close to Marco Juarez."

Now, *there* was a crock.

"Hate to break it to you, but you're on your own," Feenie said. "I've been lied to and used by just a few too many people, and I've had enough."

"Ms. Malone—"

"I mean it!" She stood up and snatched her purse off the table. "I don't want any part of Josh or Marco or any of this. I'm done."

"Unfortunately, it's too late for that. You're involved, whether you like it or not." Purnell pushed his chair back and got to his feet, followed by Rowe. "And you'd be wise to help us apprehend these guys, Ms. Malone, or you could end up their next victim."

CHAPTER

17

"Ma'am, I told you, you need to be on the *other* side of the yellow tape. Please step back."

"I want to know who's in charge here!"

John McAllister recognized the voice and whirled around. Sure enough, Cecelia Wells—Cecelia *Strickland*, dammit—stood just inside the crime-scene tape surrounding the *Gazette* entrance. She was arguing with one of the uniforms, who apparently had interpreted her blond hair and petite stature to mean she was a pushover. The cop was attempting to steer her outside the cordoned-off area, but she yanked her arm away from him.

"Get your hands off me! Who's your boss?" she demanded. "I want to talk to him right now!"

John's gaze skimmed her. Instead of tennis clothes, today she wore denim shorts and a bikini top.

Fuck. Her perfect breasts were practically spilling out of the thing. He glanced around. Every male in the vicinity had made the same observation.

"Cecelia?" He walked toward her, trying to block the view.

"McAllister!" She rushed over and grabbed his arm. "Where's Feenie? What's going on?"

"Don't worry, she's fine." From the corner of his eye, he saw the officer she'd been talking to glaring at him. John made it a point to avoid pissing off local cops whenever possible. "Let's get out of the way, and I'll tell you what I know."

She continued to grip his arm as he maneuvered her to the edge of the crime scene, lifted the tape, and let her duck under. He ushered her into the alley next to the building.

"I heard there was a shooting?" She looked as if she was about to lose it.

"There was, but no one got hurt," he said. She didn't take her hand off his arm, and he wasn't about to do it for her. "From what I've gathered so far, it sounds like someone fired some shots at Feenie when she was leaving the newspaper office about three-thirty."

"Three-*thirty?* My God! That's right when I dropped her off. Is she okay? Where is she?"

Those glistening green eyes combined with her death grip on his arm made it difficult to concentrate.

Cecelia had dropped Feenie off at three-thirty. So Feenie had been arriving at the building when the shooter fired, not leaving it. That put a different spin on things. How had the shooter known where to find her? Feenie wasn't in the habit of working on Saturdays.

"McAllister? Is she at the hospital?"

"The officials I've talked to say she's being interviewed at a safe location. And that she isn't injured." He purposely omitted the fact that those officials were FBI. The information would probably freak her out, and he didn't want her involved in this situation any more than she already was.

"Who, besides you, knew Feenie would be working today?" he asked. "She doesn't normally come in on Saturdays."

Cecelia's eyes widened at the question. "God, you're right. I hadn't thought about that. As far as I know, no one knew she'd be here but me and Marco Juarez. Feenie took a break to come over for a visit. But then I brought her back, and she said Marco was picking her up later."

John hadn't seen Juarez anywhere.

"Whoever was in the newsroom knew she was here," Cecelia added.

John had already checked that out. The only people in today were Grimes, the features editor, and a couple of the sports reporters. John found it pretty tough to believe one of them would have tipped the shooter off about Feenie's whereabouts.

Cecelia watched the police work the crime scene, clearly getting more distraught by the minute.

"My God," she said. "I can't believe Feenie was here getting *shot* at while I'm off buying beer!"

A few of her tears leaked out. It was amazing, really. He'd seen her keep her cool under exceedingly stressful circumstances, but just the thought of what *hadn't* happened to her friend made her cry.

"Are you okay?"

She swiped at her cheeks. "Yeah, I'm just ... all this is a little intense, you know?"

He stepped closer and put his hand on her shoulder to comfort her. She smelled like coconut oil. Jesus. He needed to get out of there.

"McAllister!"

He jerked his head up. The cop who'd been talking to Cecelia was charging toward him. "Does your friend there drive a blue Explorer?"

He looked at Cecelia. "You drive an Explorer?"

"What? Oh, yes. Sorry." She turned around, breaking contact with his arm. "I guess I'm parked in the middle of the street."

She turned back to face him. Her cheeks were wet, but she smiled. "I need to go. Thanks, McAllister."

Juarez screeched to a halt next to Feenie's white Kia and sprinted toward his boat. He saw movement aboard and readied his gun. But it was Feenie, and she was alone.

"Where the hell have you been?" he thundered.

When the cops told him she'd been shot at, he'd practically had a heart attack right there on the sidewalk.

Feenie, on the other hand, looked strangely calm for someone who had just dodged three bullets. She stepped off *Rum Runner* and onto the pier, and he noticed the duffle bag slung over her shoulder.

"What are you doing?"

"Leaving. What does it look like?"

"What do you mean, leaving?"

She brushed past him without a look. "Leaving. Taking leave. Packing up. Moving out. Hitting the road—"

He grabbed her arm and pulled her back around.

"Don't *touch* me."

"Feenie, come on—"

"I mean it!" She jerked her arm free and glared at him.

He watched, amazed, as she stepped backward. *What the hell?* He tucked his gun back in its holster.

"What's this about, Feenie?"

"That's a great question. You tell me. You drop into my life, offer to help me. Next thing I know, I'm in your house, I'm in your *bed*. I'm feeding you information right and left, and what are you feeding me? A pack of lies, that's what!" She stepped forward and jabbed a finger into his chest. "I'm sick of being lied to!"

"Feenie, slow down. What—"

"You know the worst thing, Marco? The worst

thing is you could have told me. I would have understood."

Her eyes welled up. Here it was, the tearful breakup scene he'd been dreading. It always happened sooner or later when he got involved with a woman, but damned if he understood what was causing it right now.

"Feenie . . ." He took a deep breath and tried to get the exasperation out of his voice. "Would you just tell me what happened?"

She stepped closer and lowered her voice. "I know about your sister, Marco. I know about Paloma."

He set his jaw and tried to control the flare of temper that shot up every time someone mentioned her name.

"What does Paloma have to do with you?"

"Quite a bit, apparently. Especially since you've been using me to draw out her killer."

"Is that what you think? You think I'd do that?"

She smiled ruefully and patted his cheek. "I don't think, Marco. I *know.*" The smile vanished. "Now, get out of my way before I use one of those moves you taught me."

He raised his eyebrows.

"I mean it. I'm mad as hell. Don't mess with me right now."

He stepped back and watched her throw her bag into the Kia. Then she got in and peeled away without a second glance. He'd pissed off a lot of women in his time, but this was a new height, even for him.

He'd let her cool off...for about five minutes. Then he'd go talk to her.

The Kia disappeared, and he realized he didn't know where she was going. And she'd been in a killer's sights just hours ago. *Goddamn it.* She should be here. With him.

"Shit," he muttered, boarding his boat. He was going to need his GPS again, this time for Feenie's car.

He walked through the cabin, surprised at how bare the place looked without her clutter everywhere. No sandals by the door. No toothbrush on the sink. No lacy things drying on the towel rack. His gaze wandered to the bed.

She'd left something for him with a sticky note attached. It was the concealed weapons permit he'd given her.

Marco,
   I'm keeping your gun for now, but you can have the permit. The FBI guys tell me it's phony.
                    —Feenie
P.S. You've got an audience, so don't do anything stupid.

So she'd talked to the feds. Perfect. That explained where she'd gotten the idea he was using her as a lure. It was just the sort of scheme they'd cook up.

So they wanted to turn her against him. Now, why

would they want to do that? What good would it do the feds if she dumped him on his ass?

He crumpled the note and tried to think. She was pissed. Royally. She'd go crying to Cecelia or her father. Except that she wasn't really the cry-on-your-shoulder type. When she got upset, she pushed people away.

She'd go home.

And that's what the feds wanted. They planned to isolate her, then step back and wait. And now that they knew she was a target, they'd be ready this time. *He* wasn't using her as bait, *they* were.

Fuck that. Feenie needed his protection, and he was going to give it to her, whether she liked it or not.

Feenie lounged by the pool in her terry robe, enjoying an iced coffee and a burst of pride.

Her first Sunday feature.

She'd interviewed dozens of students and teachers for the story, and it had turned out even better than she'd hoped. She'd done her best to put people at ease, and her status as a Northside alum probably had helped. After interviewing kids from various cliques, teachers, coaches, and parents, she'd pulled it all together and given readers an in-depth look at the social dynamics of a high school. Her article provided a glimpse into the world of high school athletics—the competition, the hazing, the peer pressure. And Drew's photographs, which occupied a two-page color spread in the Sunday A-section, were the cherry on top.

She felt good, confident, even elated. If Grimes didn't promote her now, he was an idiot. She'd already decided that if he didn't give her the job she'd earned, she'd march right into his office and ask for it. She had enough faith in her abilities now to stand up for herself.

She wouldn't be walked on. Not anymore.

The high-pitched buzz of a table saw filled the air, and she cast a glance over her shoulder at the house. Marco's friend and his crew had come out on Saturday as promised and put in a full day on her kitchen. Feenie had given Carlos most of her last paycheck as a deposit and worked out a plan for the rest. She'd pay interest to stretch the payments out over three months, but she didn't particularly mind. It was the best she could do if she didn't want to rely on Marco's charity. And she wanted to avoid that at all costs.

"It's about time you did somethin' about that eyesore."

Feenie turned around. Mrs. Hanak stood on the patio in a periwinkle blue pantsuit.

"Morning, Mrs. Hanak. You headed to church?"

"Yes."

"Pretty shoes."

Mrs. Hanak frowned down at her periwinkle slides. She considered it a sacrilege to wear pants and flat shoes into the house of God, but a bad hip and varicose veins had persuaded her to break with sixty years of tradition. Still, she always dressed up the look with a fake white chrysanthemum pinned to her lapel.

"Thanks," she said. "Did your friend leave?"

Feenie put down her paper. "What friend?"

"Marco What's-his-name. He was here last night when I went to bed."

Feenie lifted her eyebrows. "Here as in *here?*"

Mrs. Hanak tipped her head to the side. "Well, not *here,* exactly. Down the street. His pickup truck was parked in front of the Millners' from seven until at least ten, when I went to bed."

Feenie masked her irritation. It would take some pretty intense spying to notice someone's truck parked halfway down the block all evening. But that was just Mrs. Hanak's style. Marco, on the other hand, came as a surprise. Why would he stake out her house all night? He didn't strike her as the obsessed-jilted-lover type.

"He's gone now," Feenie said firmly.

Mrs. Hanak sniffed. "Too bad. That one's a hunk."

After Mrs. Hanak left, Feenie heard a car pull into the drive. She looked over her shoulder, expecting Marco's Silverado, but instead she saw a familiar gray Buick. A towering, silver-haired man climbed out of the car and stalked up the drive, not even pausing to glance at the workers hammering away on Feenie's roof.

"Hi, Dad," she said, getting to her feet. "What are you doing here?"

He stopped in front of her and crossed his arms. Feenie lifted her chin and braced for a blast of criticism.

"Are you all right?" he asked instead.

"I'm fine."

"Why didn't you call me? My own daughter's involved in a shooting, and I have to read about it on the Internet?"

Since when did her dad surf the Internet? "How on earth—"

"I tried calling, and your phone's not working." He raked a hand through his hair, and she could tell he was rattled. "What's going on, Feenie?"

She sighed, regretting her decision not to call him last night. But it wasn't as though she'd actually been injured, and she hadn't wanted to worry him. The strategy had obviously failed, though, and now he was not only worried but angry with her, too.

"Have a seat, Dad. I guess I should fill you in."

He pulled up a patio chair and waited for her to elaborate. She watched his face, thinking about how much to tell him. He looked distressed, and he'd probably been frantic for the two-hour drive down to Mayfield.

"How'd you run across this on the Internet?" she asked.

"That McAllister fella did an article about the shooting."

"You read the *Gazette*? *Online*?"

"I signed up for an electronic subscription after you told me 'bout your promotion," he said. "How else am I supposed to get your articles? Port Aransas isn't in your coverage area."

Feenie leaned back in her chair, astonished. She had a hard enough time visualizing her computer-phobic father using the Net. But it was even harder to imagine him following her career.

"I had no idea," she said.

"Yeah, well, I figured you didn't. Otherwise, you woulda called me instead of making me read about it. This has something to do with Josh, doesn't it?"

Leave it to Frank Malone to get right to the heart of the matter.

"He's in a lot of trouble right now, and I've been helping do some research into it. I guess he found out I was involved."

He looked down and muttered a curse.

"It's okay, though. You don't need to worry. The FBI has me under surveillance, so I think I'll be safe from here on out."

His gaze shot up. "The FBI? Goddamn it, Feenie! What's that son of a bitch gotten you into?"

She closed her eyes, wishing for the millionth time that this would all just go away. She didn't need this. And her aging, worry-prone father sure as heck didn't need it, either.

She reached for his hand. "Dad, really. It's okay. I can't tell you everything, but you have to trust me when I say I'm safe now." She hoped she sounded more convinced than she felt.

He regarded her warily. "You got a gun in the house?"

Guns. Of course.

"I have my .22," she said. "Plus, a friend of mine lent me his .38. He's been giving me lessons."

Her dad shifted in his chair and looked uncomfortable. "A friend, huh? What, like a roommate?"

She smiled. In his clumsy way, he was inquiring about her love life. But how could she possibly explain? She didn't even understand it herself.

"No, he's not a roommate." *Not anymore.*

Her dad looked skeptical.

"Look, he's just . . . he's a friend, okay?" Although that was being generous. He wasn't really a friend at all. And he definitely wasn't someone she planned to sleep with. Ever again. "But he's a former cop, and he's helped me learn to protect myself. Plus, the FBI is watching."

His frown deepened, and she realized she wasn't necessarily helping matters. Her dad was a man of action. He didn't like leaving things up to other people.

"You could help me, too, if you want," she said. "How about we go to the firing range where I've been practicing? You could give me some pointers."

He stood up. "All right. Let's get going, then. No sense wasting time."

For the first time since his arrival, her dad looked somewhat relieved. Feenie's guilt subsided.

"Thanks. Come inside and have some coffee while I get dressed." She stood up and gave him a peck on the cheek. "And I'm sorry you had to come all the way down here. I really didn't mean to worry you."

He patted her awkwardly on the back. "Parents always worry. You'll understand someday when you have kids."

Yeah, right. Motherhood had never seemed farther off on her horizon.

She led her dad toward the back door, but he stopped to gaze up at the workers placing shingles.

"You lost the pecan?" he asked.

"Yep. Lightning bolt."

"Now, that's a shame." His gaze shifted to Feenie, standing there on the stoop, holding open the screen door. He cleared his throat. "So this friend of yours. Any chance I'll get to meet him while I'm in town?"

Feenie left Chico's feeling sweaty, spent, and completely invigorated. She never would have believed punching bags and medicine balls could give her such a high, but tonight she'd loved every minute of it. It was her third workout without Marco. In his absence, Chico's brother Eduardo had swooped in to help coach her on free weights—as part of her one-month trial membership, he'd said. They both knew that was just a euphemism for free use of the gym, at least until Feenie's finances got back on track, but no one seemed to mind. Chico probably thought it was good for business to have a few women around the place.

Clutching her pepper spray, Feenie headed for her car. She'd had her gun and her spray close at hand ever since her meeting last Saturday with the FBI.

Footsteps sounded behind her, and Feenie quickened her step. Despite the sweat, the hair on the back of her neck stood up. When the footsteps sped up to match her own, Feenie took a deep breath and whirled around.

"McAllister!" she yelped, nearly bumping into him.

"Shit." He grabbed her wrist. She'd been an instant away from dousing him with pepper spray. "Put that away."

"What are you doing here? God, you scared me!"

He smiled. "I can see that."

She stuffed the spray into her purse. "You always stalk women in parking lots, or is this a special occasion?"

"I was looking for you. The stalker gig was filled." His gaze veered toward a black pickup parked at the back of the lot.

Marco. Again. She hadn't spoken to him in four days, but she'd seen him at least a dozen times—parked down the street from her house, parked near the *Gazette* when she left work, even loitering around the grocery store when she went shopping. He wasn't making much of a secret of following her, unlike Agent Rowe, whom Feenie had spotted only once—just a fleeting glimpse as she'd driven to work this morning. So the FBI was tailing her discreetly, while Marco was practically broadcasting his mission with a megaphone. Just what was he up to?

"How about a Cuba libre?" McAllister asked, drawing her attention away from the Silverado. "And if you're hungry, I'll buy you some buffalo wings."

She sighed. "I'm trying to cut back, actually. All this working out has me kind of on a health kick."

"Okay, but I don't think anyplace around here sells wheat germ. Want a frozen yogurt?"

She glanced again at the pickup and could almost feel Marco's eyes boring into her. He didn't like McAllister, and he was probably jealous. Watching her leave with him would get under his skin.

"Yogurt sounds perfect," she said.

Fifteen minutes later, they were seated in a booth at Hal's Helado. The place offered two flavors of frozen yogurt and twenty kinds of ice cream. Feenie had ordered a chocolate banana split.

McAllister nodded at her bowl. "That's some health kick you've got going there."

She licked a dollop of whipped cream from her spoon. "It's got potassium," she pointed out.

He slurped his double-chocolate shake. "I haven't had one of these in years."

"I believe that. Fact, I've never seen you drink anything besides beer and coffee."

He shrugged. "My body's a temple. I let other people worship it."

Feenie rolled her eyes. "I can see why you're such a hit with women. So what's this about? You didn't bring me here to flirt."

His smile faded. "I need to talk to you."

"Uh-oh."

"About a story I'm working on involving your ex."

"Uh-oh again." She shoved her bowl away and took a deep breath. "Okay, hit me."

"A woman came into the paper last week. Wanted us to look into doing an article about the Mayfield Food Bank. I remember you saying you used to work there."

"That's right. Who was the woman?"

"Ana Rivas. You know her?"

"Sure," Feenie said. "We were in charge of organizing the lunch service back when the food bank had a soup kitchen. I didn't realize she was still working there."

"She is." McAllister sipped his shake. "She's got all these complaints because the food bank's been taking in a lot more donations lately, but they haven't increased the number of families they're serving in the valley. Actually, according to this lady, they're cutting back. She thinks someone's skimming off the top, but she doesn't know who."

"Well, I know they're cutting back," Feenie said. "They don't serve hot meals anymore. They just provide nonperishable groceries to needy people. Why'd

Grimes give this to you? This isn't really the police beat."

"You haven't heard the interesting part yet. Grimes asked Rivas if she'd reported her concerns to the cops, and you know what she said?"

"What?" Feenie was getting a fresh feeling of dread in the pit of her stomach.

"She said she relayed her suspicions to her son-in-law, who just happened to be with the Mayfield PD. But that was months ago, and nothing got done about it. Take a wild guess what her son-in-law's name was."

"*Was?* No way. Not Brian Doring?"

"Ding, ding, ding." He smiled. "You're good, Malone. We should team up more often. I'll have to tell Grimes."

"You think Doring was murdered because of the food bank?"

"Right again," he said. "Or at least, I think it's possible. Originally, I thought he might be taking bribes to look the other way on this smuggling operation, and maybe someone offed him because he got greedy. But now I think he was just asking a few too many questions about the food bank."

"Whoa," she said. "That's pretty severe. How do you know Ana Rivas is even right about her suspicions? And what does all this have to do with Josh?"

McAllister pulled out a file and slid it toward her. "I think Josh is using the organization as a front to launder money. I want you to take a look at these re-cords and give me your opinion."

Feenie opened the file. It contained a printout from a computerized check ledger. She didn't recog-nize the format.

"Where'd you get this?" she asked.

"Rivas printed it out from the PC in the food bank's office."

"I don't know if I'm going to be much help. When I worked there, I never dealt with the books." She scanned the figures. The numbers practically leaped off the page. "Jeez! Do you know how much money they're bringing in?"

"A lot, I know. I thought it looked weird for a non-profit with only one salaried employee."

"This is crazy," she said. "There's no way they're getting this kind of cash. I used to be in charge of the annual fund-raising auction. Our goal was twenty thousand. This shows twice that coming into the ac-count in only a month's time."

"Lower your voice," he muttered.

Feenie glanced around, but luckily, most of Hal's other patrons were high-school kids.

"Sorry," she said quietly. "It's just . . . I can't believe this. And the debits are crazy, too. Nine thousand four hundred to Alvarez Groceries? Eighty-nine hundred to Sun Valley Market? That's insane. Especially if they haven't expanded the number of families they're serving. How far back do these big deposits go?"

"They started almost three years ago. Mid-August, I believe." He smiled. "You really think I've got something here, huh?"

"I do. But I don't see how all this ties to Josh. Unless—" She glanced up at him. "It's the payee, isn't it? One of these grocers is Josh's uncle."

"Right again. I'm impressed."

Feenie closed the file. "Wow."

"That about sums it up. And now that you've corroborated my theory, I'm a few steps closer to running a story on everything. I need to nail down some more sources, but it's coming together."

"You say this started three years ago in August?"

"Yeah."

Feenie tried to recall anything unusual going on in August three summers ago.

"Did you see anything weird in July?" she asked.

"I don't think so. Why?"

"Nothing," she said. She and Josh had traveled to Mexico in mid-July that year, although she couldn't think what the significance might be. She slid the file back to him. "Are you going to share your information with the cops?"

"Not the local ones. I don't want to end up like Doring."

She unzipped her purse and rummaged around.

"I think I still have a business card for one of the FBI guys I talked to after the shooting incident. Yeah, here it is. His name's Rowe." She passed him the card.

"Thanks," he said. "It may not matter anyway, because listen to what else I found out. I've got a source on the grand jury who says they just started hearing testimony about a prominent Mayfield citizen."

"Gee, I wonder who that could be."

"I wonder. It's all just rumor, but this source has been pretty reliable in the past. Maybe Josh will get indicted soon."

He checked his watch. "Shit. I've got to go. I just need one more thing from you."

"I'm all ears."

He took a deep breath. "Tell me about Cecelia Strickland. She still volunteer at the food bank?"

"Not anymore. She volunteers for the Red Cross now. It's a pretty big commitment."

McAllister watched her intently.

"You won't find her fingerprints on any of this," she told him. "Not a chance in hell."

But McAllister didn't look convinced.

"Look, I know you don't know Cecelia, but I do. She's been my best friend for almost twenty years. And this is the very last thing she'd ever get involved with. I promise."

"I'm glad to hear you say that," he said. "Now, do me a favor and quit telling her things, will you? The more she knows about Josh's situation, the more she's at risk."

Feenie folded her arms. "I'm aware of that, but thanks for the advice."

He looked away.

"She's married, you know."

He didn't say anything.

"Happily. To a really nice man."

He raised an eyebrow.

"What's that supposed to mean?" she demanded. "You don't think he's nice?"

"I didn't say that."

"So what's with the attitude? You've been checking him out, haven't you?"

"You bet your ass. He was tight with Garland a few years ago. And he was his accountant at one point."

"That was before my divorce. When Josh and I split up, Robert quit working for him."

"Something about him just . . . I don't know. Shit." McAllister rubbed his hand over his face and scowled. "What's a woman like Cecelia doing married to a loser like that, anyway?"

Cecelia had plenty of reasons for marrying Robert, and they were private. "Are you checking up on Robert for your story or for personal reasons?" she asked.

"Both."

Great. Terrific. The king of playboys had the hots for her best friend. But at least he was being honest about it.

"What else did you find out?" she asked.

He shrugged. "Nothing interesting. He's never had so much as a parking ticket, he pays his taxes, he's never been in trouble with anyone, from what I can tell. I couldn't get crap on him."

"Me, neither."

He looked surprised.

"What? Cecelia's like family to me. Of course I checked him out. But there's nothing there. So leave her alone, okay?"

He stared at her, his expression carefully blank.

"I mean it, McAllister."

"I know you do."

Feenie sighed, resigning herself to the fact that he was going to make a play. But Cecelia was a big girl. She could take care of herself and any unwanted advances that happened to come along.

"Let's go," McAllister said. "I've got some stuff left to do at the newsroom."

When they exited the ice cream shop, Feenie spotted Marco's Silverado parked just across the street.

"You go ahead," she told McAllister. "I'll catch a ride with him."

He frowned at the truck. "You sure?"

"Yeah, it's fine."

Marco had the windows rolled down and was watching her, looking bored. She sashayed across the street and leaned her forearm on the door.

"Hi," she said casually. "Working late?"

"Yeah. You?"

"Yep."

He scowled in McAllister's direction. She'd been right—he *was* jealous.

"You mind giving me a lift back to Chico's? Since you're following me anyway?"

"Hop in," he said, starting the truck.

They rode in silence through town, and he took a circuitous route, as usual. When they finally pulled into the parking lot, she turned to face him.

"You can stop doing this, you know. The FBI has me under surveillance."

He didn't speak.

"Fine, suit yourself," she said. "But you're wasting your time."

"Am I?"

She looked at him closely, but his face was emotionless. Damn him and his mind games. "Are you trying to scare me? What, you think I'll come running back to you just so I can have a free bodyguard and some cheap sex? Hate to break it to you, Marco, but it wasn't that great."

He laughed at that. "Yes, it was, and you know it."

"Speak for yourself."

He leaned across the console and cupped a hand around her neck. His eyes dropped to her mouth, and she froze. He was going to kiss her. And she wanted him to.

"Feenie?"

"Huh?"

He brushed a thumb over her lower lip, and her heart felt as if it would pound out of her chest. "You've got chocolate on your mouth, *guera.*"

His seductive smile widened into a grin. He was

laughing at her. She felt tears stinging her eyes, and she reached for the door handle, but he grabbed her arm.

"Hey." His face was somber now. "I know you're pissed at me, but I want you to listen. You can't trust the FBI, Feenie. Do you hear me? They're way more concerned with bagging their man than protecting you."

She looked at him, incredulous. "Are you even *hearing* yourself? You're such a hypocrite! All *you're* really concerned with is your vendetta."

Anger flared in his eyes. It was one of the few emotions he didn't hide well.

"Do you deny it?"

He didn't respond, and she jerked her arm away. "Good night, Marco." She opened the door. "Have fun sleeping in your truck."

Two hours later, Feenie sat at her kitchen table feeling slightly amazed.

She'd been right.

The big deposits into the food bank's account had started shortly after one of her trips down to Mexico with Josh. And not just any trip—an unusual trip. During their marriage, they'd frequently gone across the border for mini vacations. They'd shopped, snorkeled, gone diving. But this trip had been different.

For starters, it was the only time she could remember going on vacation with Josh and not staying at a fancy resort. They'd flown into a rinky-dink airport and stayed at a less-than-remarkable hotel. It was nowhere near up to Josh's typical standards. No room service. No fitness center. No golf course within miles.

And then there had been the diving. Marginal, at best. Josh and Feenie were both certified scuba divers. They'd gone diving all the time, at all the best vacation spots, and they were accustomed to being impressed. But not that time. The whole weekend had been a dud, really. Yet Josh hadn't complained. Looking back, Feenie realized recreation may not have been high on his list of priorities.

She recalled the stop they'd made on the way to meet the diving boat. She'd spent half an hour sweating in the rental car while Josh had checked out an investment opportunity, or at least that's what he'd called it.

The memory was vague—an unremarkable weekend three years ago—but it was coming back now. She recalled the winding gravel road they'd taken, the dilapidated warehouse where he'd parked the car. She didn't remember much else, but for some reason, she thought it was on the water.

A barge. She'd seen a barge. The place was definitely on the water. Some kind of loading dock, most likely.

She hadn't asked many questions at the time— Josh was always investing in some real estate deal or another, and the details bored her to tears. She simply remembered being hot and irritated and impatient to get to the dive shop.

Now Feenie studied her passport. It had been stamped numerous times during her visits to Mexico and the Caribbean, but only one stamp was from July three years ago: Punto Dorado. She jotted the name on a sticky note. It had to be the place. Feenie combed through her bookshelf until she came across an outdated world atlas. She located the page for Mexico and hunched over it. Punto Dorado was near the coast, as she'd suspected. And it wasn't too far from Texas. They could have taken a car, but instead they'd flown. Why, she had no idea.

She glanced at the clock. Just after midnight. And she'd bet money Marco's truck was still stationed outside her house. She was still angry with him, but she couldn't help admiring his tenacity. It was nice knowing he was there, if only for Mrs. Hanak's benefit.

Feenie went into her closet and looked for her backpack. It was getting late, and she had a lot left to do tonight. She had to shower, gather supplies, and make preparations. Most important, she had to figure out a way to lose Marco.

As she pulled the bag out of the closet, she dialed McAllister on her cell phone.

"Hey, it's Feenie," she said when he answered. "How badly do you want this story?"

He laughed softly on the other end. "Sweetheart, do you even have to ask?"

CHAPTER
18

Juarez slid into a space at Rosie's and watched Feenie cross the parking lot. In jeans and a bouncy ponytail, she looked ready for a typical day at work.

But he knew better. She looked nervous. And he bet whatever was making her anxious had something to do with the meeting she and McAllister had had last night.

She was up to something. He just didn't know what.

He followed her into Rosie's and watched her slide into a booth toward the back. With Cecelia, dammit. There went his hopes of joining Feenie for breakfast. Their conversation the previous evening had ended the no-talking phase, and he was ready to smooth things over. Preferably naked, but he'd talk to her across a table if he had to. *Then* he'd take her home and get her naked.

He watched her talk to Cecelia. At least she wasn't with that reporter. McAllister had a reputation, and Juarez didn't like him around Feenie. In fact, if he saw him around her again, he was pretty sure he'd have to rip the guy's head off.

He took a seat at the bar. He was testy. And jealous. And frustrated. All because of her.

Hell, he missed her. He could acknowledge that. The sex had been amazing, whether she wanted to admit it or not. He wasn't ashamed to want her back in his bed.

But it was more than that, he realized, and she probably did, too. That's why she was torturing him like this. She was proving a point. When she finally decided she'd proven it, he'd get her back.

"Hola, Marquito. Migas otra vez?"

Rosie smiled across the counter at him. He asked her for a plate of *huevos rancheros* and engaged in the typical banter about his mother and Kaitlin. Rosie poured a steaming mug of coffee and gave her usual instructions to send his mother her regards.

"Claro," he answered, taking a sip. He glanced toward the back of the restaurant.

She was gone.

"Fuck!"

He rushed past the empty booth, past the bathrooms, and shoved open the back door. Several busboys stood near a Dumpster, taking a smoke break.

"Vieron a dos mujeres?"

The guys looked up. One of them cupped his palms in front of his chest, and the others snickered.

"Sí!" Juarez said. *"Adónde fueron?"*

The boy pointed toward the parking lot. He scanned the row of cars. The white Kia was still parked at the back, but Feenie was gone.

McAllister's Jeep hit another pothole as they traveled through downtown Punto Dorado for the third time.

"Are you sure we've got the right town?" he asked.

"Positive." Feenie unfolded the cumbersome map and studied the area another time. It had to be near here. *Had* to. The sleepy seaside community had only one highway that paralleled the coast. They'd driven up and down it three times now, but Feenie had failed to spot the familiar dive shop.

McAllister passed an abandoned dwelling that, judging by the weathered wooden sign out front, might once have been a seafood restaurant. He pulled into the gravel parking lot of a motel with a vacancy sign permanently affixed to the roof. The tourism industry in Punto Dorado seemed to be on life support.

"Lemme see the map," McAllister said.

Feenie gladly handed it over and waited for him to admit that he couldn't make any more sense of it than she had.

Someone tapped on the Jeep's plastic window, and she jerked her head around. Two brown-faced boys stood alongside the Jeep, holding their hands out.

"Don't open your door," McAllister told her, tossing the map in back. And then to the kids, *"Vengan acá!"*

He held up a ten-dollar bill, and the children rushed to the driver's side. McAllister opened his door and exchanged some words with them in Spanish.

She studied the kids' faces as they talked to him. They couldn't have been more than eight years old, ten at the most. Their clothes were grubby and torn, and their cheeks looked hollow. McAllister must have said something funny, because both kids laughed. Then he passed them the ten and closed the door.

"About two kilometers south, next to a pink cantina," he reported.

He made a U-turn, and a few minutes later, they passed the dive shop. It didn't look all that familiar, but it was the only one in the area. They were on the outskirts of town now. The motels and tourist shops had thinned out, replaced by scrub bushes and the occasional ramshackle dwelling. Her shoulders tensed as she looked up and down the highway for any gravel roads.

"This seem familiar?" McAllister asked.

"A little." She hoped she hadn't brought him here on a wild goose chase. It was entirely possible this trip was a waste of time. Even if she could find the place where Josh had taken her, who knew what they'd find there?

They passed several primitive roads, all leading away from the water. The one she wanted would lead toward it. She'd seen a barge, too, which meant there would have to be some sort of shipping channel nearby, a place for boats to dock, as they obviously couldn't just pull up to the beach.

The road bent westward, and the landscape become marshy. She spotted a bridge up ahead, spanning the mouth of a river. As they neared the bridge, a gravel road came into view. A wooden sign posted nearby said "Alvarez Distributing."

"There!" Feenie said. "I think that's it!"

McAllister passed the sign without slowing, probably so as not to draw attention to the Jeep.

Feenie surveyed the place. The chain-link fence topped with barbed wire was new, but this was it. It had an electronic gate, and behind it, the road curved toward the water and disappeared into a clump of trees. *Shoot.* How would they get past the gate? McAllister passed the turnoff and pulled over just before the bridge. The ground was soggy, and cattails grew in abundance by the water's edge.

"Be careful," she said. "You don't want to get stuck."

He pulled off the road and eased between some shrubs. The plants were slanted and misshapen from the strong winds blowing off the gulf. Tucked among the bushes, the Jeep would be fairly well hidden from the casual passerby.

"Four-wheel drive, honey." He smiled at her. "Aren't you glad you brought me along?"

She was, more than he knew. Not only had he helped her ditch Marco at Rosie's and lose any FBI tail they might have had on the way out of town, but his Spanish had been useful. Plus, he was a man, and six feet two inches of towering, muscled male might come in handy if she should find herself in a dicey situation.

Feenie hoped it wouldn't come to that. Their mission was pure information gathering. They were planning to scope out the place, take some photographs, and possibly even talk to a few locals to see what kind of business, if any, was supposedly being conducted on this piece of property. The food bank was cutting huge checks to something called Alvarez Distributing here, but that could mean anything.

McAllister pulled a pistol out of his scuffed brown cowboy boot and checked to see if it was loaded.

"I was wondering why you wore jeans," she said.

He tucked the gun back inside the leather. "You ready?"

"One sec." She unzipped the fanny pack she'd brought, which was clipped around her waist. She packed it with a few necessities from her backpack: gun, Mace, cell phone, the camera she'd borrowed from Drew.

"You look like a tourist with that thing on," McAllister said.

"That's the plan." She smiled. "If someone asks me what I'm up to, I'll just pretend to be lost."

She slipped some money into the pocket of her jeans shorts, along with her passport. Then she decided to clip the Mace to her belt loop, so she'd have it within easy reach.

"Ready," she said, rubbing the sweat off her forehead with the back of her arm.

McAllister clasped her shoulder. "Stick to the plan, okay? Don't draw attention to yourself. And if anyone approaches, let me do the talking."

"I will." She patted his hand. "McAllister... thanks for coming. It means a lot to me."

"No problem."

"I have to ask you something. Do you know what *guera* is?"

He frowned. "What? Like in Spanish?"

"Yeah."

He smiled. "Did Juarez call you that?"

"Yes. What's it mean?"

"It's like 'blondie.' Someone fair." He looked at her closely. "You need to be careful here, Malone. He's not going to give you what you want, you know."

She didn't reply. It was too late to be careful.

"Malone?"

"Come on, let's go," she said, pushing her door open and ending the conversation.

They got out of the car and locked it. They crossed

the road and walked briskly back toward the gravel driveway, taking care to stay close to the bushes.

"Give me your camera," McAllister said. "I'm going to sneak over and get a photo of that sign. Try to keep out of sight, okay?"

Nodding, she unzipped her pack and handed him the camera. After he disappeared into the foliage, Feenie ducked behind a wind-whipped palmetto and checked out the entrance again. There didn't appear to be a secondary gate. No easy access. She glanced from the electronic gate to the fence. Even if she could climb it, the barbed wire on top looked menacing.

"Hey, babe."

Her skin bristled at the familiar voice. "What are you doing here?" she hissed.

Marco stood a few yards in front of her, well camouflaged in the dense thicket of leaves and branches near the fence. He wore brown cargo pants, a black T-shirt, and some type of lace-up military boots.

"Following you," he said.

She hustled toward him, glancing over her shoulder to make sure no one was watching. "How did you find me?"

He gave her a half-smile. "I told you before, you're easy to track."

Her cheeks warmed. How could he have tailed them? "But how did you—"

"You left an atlas on your kitchen table with a sticky note on it. Once I got to town, it wasn't hard to find the two lost Americans cruising around."

She gaped at him, too infuriated even to yell at him, which wouldn't have been a good idea anyway, as she was trying not to get caught trespassing.

"So," he said, eyeing the fence. "Where are we, and why are we here?"

She had two choices: stand there and argue with him and then let him follow her, or let him follow her.

"We need to get past the gate," she said. "Any ideas?"

A truck rumbled up the highway and slowed near the gravel road. Marco pulled her closer to the bushes.

"Just one," he said, watching the gate open.

"I thought of that already. There's a security cam."

"Good catch. Okay, I've got another way."

He unzipped one of his many pockets and took out the most elaborate pocket knife she'd ever seen. He quickly flipped open some pliers. "We make our own gate."

"Well, what do you fucking know?" McAllister strolled over and handed Feenie the camera. "It's a Mayfield reunion."

Marco stared at him, and McAllister stared right back. Feenie could feel the hostility crackling between them—two alpha males who obviously disliked each other. Feenie figured the animosity had its roots in the news article about Marco's drug bust.

McAllister turned to Feenie. "I'm going around

the north side of the property. I want to get a view of the place from the water's edge, see if there's any boat traffic." He raised his eyebrows in a silent question, and Feenie knew he was wondering about Marco. "You want to come with me?"

"She's staying with me," Marco said.

Feenie rolled her eyes. "I'll stay here," she told McAllister. "We're going to explore inside the fence."

"Okay, then let's meet back here in thirty minutes." He gave both of them a hard look. "Stay outta trouble."

When McAllister left, Feenie zipped the camera back into her pack and turned to Marco. He'd crouched down near the chain-link fence, and she squatted beside him.

"Those pliers don't look strong enough to . . ."

Her voice trailed off as he held a long blade of grass up to the wire mesh. Was he testing for a current? Nothing happened, so he tossed the plant aside and touched the fence with the pliers. In minutes, he'd cut out a two-foot square.

He pocketed the tool and stood back. "Ladies first."

She crawled through the hole, snagging the back of her T-shirt as she went. He unhooked the fabric and followed her through.

"Now what?" he asked.

"We're looking for a building. Beige, I think. Corrugated metal."

"And what are we hoping to find there?"

She shrugged. "I don't know, really. I think we'll know it when we see it."

He looked her up and down. Sweat beaded at his temples, and his T-shirt was plastered to his chest. It had to be a hundred degrees out and a hundred and fifty percent humidity.

"You came all the way down here, and you don't know what you're looking for? You guys could get shot, and no one would even blink an eye. The law around here's pretty lax."

"Look," she said, exasperated, "I didn't invite you to come, okay? So spare me the lecture. I think we'll find evidence here. Josh bought this place just before he started moving money through the food bank."

"The food bank, huh? And this is what you and Johnny Boy were talking about last night?"

"Yes! Now, can we look around, please? I don't know what's here, but I think it might be worth seeing."

He shrugged. "Good enough for me." He took his gun out, checked the clip, and tucked it back into his pants. "But follow my lead."

She fell in behind him, and they picked their way through the vegetation. Looking past the leaves, she saw a row of parked cars and two beige buildings made of corrugated metal.

"Which one?" he asked.

"I don't know. The newer one, maybe? It's closer to the water."

He set off for the newer-looking building. The other had broken windows and some graffiti scrawled across one of the walls. It didn't look very secure, so she guessed whatever it housed wasn't that valuable.

They skirted the parking area, trying their best to stay out of sight. The front door to the building lacked a security camera, but workers streamed in and out, carrying crates and boxes. Some were dressed in T-shirts and jeans, some just in shorts. Many had shirts or bandanas tied around their heads, probably to absorb the copious amounts of sweat that streamed off everyone in this heat. Feenie's gaze veered toward the back of the building, where several men milled around near a forklift, smoking and spitting in the dirt.

"We need another door," Marco said. "Stay behind me."

They crept to the other side of the warehouse, but no other doors came into view. Luckily, Feenie spotted an open window. Unluckily, it was at least ten feet off the ground.

"Hoist me onto your shoulders, and I'll peek in," she said.

Marco gave her a look that said "Get real."

"I'm serious. Hoist me up there, I'll get the lay of the land, and then we'll decide what to do."

He hesitated.

"It'll just take a minute. You really want to go in blind?"

He muttered something in Spanish and headed for the window. Thanks to four summers of cheerleading camp, she was on his shoulders in seconds. He wobbled underneath her, and she was reminded that she weighed more now than she had in her pom-pom days.

"Grab my ankles to steady me," she instructed. "Am I hurting you?"

"No," he said gruffly. "What do you see?"

She peered through the window. Her eyes adjusted, and she was looking into a second-floor room. The warehouse had a loft, apparently. File boxes and crates filled the space. Something hummed off to her right, where a man was standing next to a document shredder. He was young, twentysomething at most, and his clothes were soaked with perspiration. He stuffed page after page into the machine, oblivious to his audience. Behind him, a rotating fan churned the air and created little paper tumbleweeds.

"It looks like an office and storage room," she whispered down. "On the second floor of the warehouse, I think."

"Any people?"

"Just one. I'm going in for a better look."

"*Goddamn* it, Feenie!" Marco staggered backward, but it was too late. She'd already grabbed the windowsill and pulled herself over—*thank you, medicine ball*.

"I'll just be a sec!" she whispered.

He stared up at her, his face reddening with fury.

She ducked behind a box of files and took a good look around.

It looked like a storage room, but it felt like an oven. Sweat streamed down her back as she nudged aside the top of one of the crates and peeked inside. Canned goods. She read the labels: corn, pineapple, peaches. She picked up a can and gave it a shake. It sounded like fruit, but who knew? Maybe it contained some type of contraband. She unzipped her fanny pack, which she wore in front for easy access, and stuffed it inside. She noticed the gun. Now might be a good time to have it handy, especially since Marco wasn't nearby. She tucked it in the back of her shorts and hoped she wouldn't shoot herself in the butt.

The man in the office pivoted toward her and entered the storage room. She crouched behind a tower of boxes as he shuffled around. When his footsteps receded, she peered out. He'd hauled another box into the office and was shredding again.

The entire loft area overlooked a large warehouse. Some sort of hulking machinery occupied one side of the building. A canning machine, maybe? Whatever it was, it was sleeping at the moment. Men bustled past it, carrying boxes and crates and stacking them on pallets near a giant garage door. A forklift moved the pallets onto the bed of an eighteen-wheeler.

A patch of green water was visible just beyond the truck. And a pier. She saw a couple of giant cleats for tying up boats but no boats in sight. Her gaze fell on a row of crates lined up by the door. They were stacked four high, and a pair of feet in red sandals poked out from the far side of the row.

Women's sandals.

The minutes ticked by as Feenie waited for the crates to disappear. Men loaded them systematically onto the truck in a process that seemed to take forever. Finally, someone picked up a crate, and Feenie saw a woman with long dark hair seated near the door. Actually, she looked more like a girl. Given her position, though, she couldn't have been the owner of the shoes. As more crates disappeared, more girls became visible. When the entire row of crates had been loaded, Feenie counted six girls seated in a row.

Now what? Any moment, those children could be hauled away like the rest of the cargo, headed for God knew where.

She pulled out the camera and snapped a few shots of the girls. Then she took several pictures of the crates surrounding her in the storeroom. The photographs wouldn't look like much without an explanation, but she'd worry about that later. She had to get back to Marco now so they could reconnect with McAllister and come up with a plan for the kids. She turned to leave.

And smacked right into the paper-shredder guy. He didn't look happy.

She reached for her .38 just as he pressed the cool, black barrel of a pistol against her temple.

• • •

What the hell was taking so long? Juarez kept his gaze trained on the window. He should have expected this. He *had*, actually, but then he'd fallen for those damn puppy-dog eyes.

He caught a flash of movement at the edge of the window and waited for Feenie to reappear. She didn't, which meant she was in trouble. *Shit.* He ducked behind an oleander bush just as someone leaned out the window. The guy made a visual sweep of the area and said something into a walkie-talkie.

When the guy disappeared, Juarez emerged from the bushes and crept around to the waterfront side of the building. The area was crawling with people, but he had to get inside. Right now. He might be able to pass himself off as a worker, but Feenie sure as hell couldn't.

He had to get her out of there, and he had to do it fast.

Feenie sat on the concrete, surrounded by blackness. She had no idea how much time had elapsed since she'd been shoved into the graffiti-covered warehouse, but it felt like hours. Sweat trickled down her arms, stinging the cuts at her wrists. The man hadn't been gentle with the rope. Her ankles were on fire, too, burning whenever she shifted positions. The gag tasted like dirt and had absorbed every drop of saliva in her mouth. She needed some water soon, or she'd probably pass out.

She craned her neck around and tried to see what

lay behind her, beyond the rows of crates and metal drums. The only light was a beam of yellow coming through a broken window pane high up near the ceiling, but that didn't help much. A truck rumbled outside, its sound receding as it moved away from the compound. Truck four. She'd been counting them since she'd been dumped here. Four trucks had come and gone, and still neither McAllister nor Marco had come for her.

Where are they?

She shut her eyes and tried to think about something less worrisome, like how desperately she needed water. Anything was better than wondering what must have happened to keep them away.

She should have stayed with Marco, but, as usual, curiosity had won out over good judgment. Now she was trapped and alone, with no idea what lay in store for her. The guy from the warehouse hadn't spoken English, but his meaning had been clear.

She was in trouble. Big time. Someone higher up would be coming soon to deal with her. He'd taken her fanny pack, shoes, and keys before pushing her into the warehouse and tying her up. If she tried to escape, or even move, she'd be shot.

The last message had been communicated with the butt of his semiautomatic pistol. Feenie wasn't eager to test the sincerity of his threat.

After the departure of the second truck, she had tried to look for a way out. Giant metal drums lined the back of the warehouse, and the only entrance to the place looked at least twenty yards away. Her bindings made it nearly impossible to move, and the door was probably guarded or locked. Or both. But she had to try. The time between trucks was stretching out. The din of voices outside had quieted. The place was clearing out, and the thought of being left behind terrified her.

She had to find Marco.

Maybe he was trapped somewhere, too. Otherwise, he would have come by now. And what about McAllister? Something had happened to them both. Something awful, she just knew it.

She'd never forgive herself for coming up with this stupid, stupid idea.

She got on her knees and tried to stand up, which was impossible because of the way her ankles were tied. Maybe if she did a somersault, she'd have enough momentum to—

Her attention swung to the door as it creaked open. Someone was coming, striding briskly across the concrete. She knew the gait and the silhouette, even though he was backlit and she could hardly see his face until he crouched in front of her.

"Feenie, Feenie, Feenie. What are you up to now?"

Josh reached for her cheek. She jerked her head back.

"You've got a nasty cut here, Feen. You should take better care of yourself."

He stood up, and she got a nose full of Polo Safari. She wanted to retch. He wore Italian loafers and dress slacks—still playing the dapper attorney, apparently. He stared down at her with those flinty gray eyes.

"You're a real pain in the ass, you know that?"

She mumbled against the cloth.

He patted the front of his sport coat and retrieved a small Swiss Army knife from the pocket. He cut the bandana tied around her face and threw it aside. Progress. At least she could talk.

"You say something?"

"So I've been told," she croaked.

He looked down at her. "I bet your detective can't keep up with you, either. What's his name? Manuel? Miguel? José?"

She refused to take the bait. Instead, she coughed and tried to expel the dust from her lungs.

"Not much of a PI, but then, neither are you. Did you really think you'd bring me down with your little investigative-reporter bit?" He knelt in front of her again and stroked a finger over her nipple. She winced, and a smile spread across his face.

"Maybe he's good in bed. Is that it? Brings out your wild side? I always knew you had one, but you were too prissy to admit it." He stood up again, grinning now. "I should thank you, come to think of it. If you'd been any good, I wouldn't have decided to broaden my sexual horizons. I might still be turning in time sheets at that damn law firm. The import business's much more lucrative."

"You're going to jail, Josh." She hoped he didn't hear the quiver in her voice.

"Now, where'd you get that idea? Is that what your *sources* tell you? That I'm being indicted, maybe? Well, I've got news for you, Feenie. And feel free to quote me on this: It doesn't matter. I'm invisible now. No one knows where I am or where I'm going, and I've got so much money socked away, I don't ever have to come back."

She balked. "What about your father? Is he going, too? He has a heart condition. I'm sure life on the run will be great for his health."

His face hardened. She'd hit a nerve.

"And what about your mother, Josh? You plan to just leave her behind to explain your crimes? She's doted on you your entire life, and this is how you treat her?"

He set his jaw. "Don't pretend to know my family, Feenie. You were never one of us. My parents always told me I was marrying down, and I should have listened."

He spat on the ground in front of her and turned around.

"Where are you going?" she yelped.

He whirled back, clearly delighted by her panic. "Oh, I'm *sorry*. I've got a plane to catch. This place is empty now, except for you. But hey, don't worry. I've hired someone to keep you company. I've told him to shut you up. Permanently."

Her stomach clenched. "You don't even have the guts to do it yourself? You brought your hit man down here to do it for you? You always were a spineless shit!"

He smirked. "You mean Brassler? You think I'd call him down from El Paso just for your sorry ass? He charges twenty K a pop, Feenie. I reserve that kind of cash for *real* obstacles. Like nosy cops, not pissant reporters. You have an inflated ego. Always have."

His smile widened. "I've got better plans for you." He took a pack of cigarettes from his breast pocket and tapped one out. Then he struck a match and held it to the end. After taking a drag, he exhaled a long stream of smoke.

"Still dreaming about fire, Feenie?"

Juarez was getting desperate. He'd scoured the warehouse without finding a trace. Then he'd run into McAllister, and the reporter had gone pale at the news that Feenie was missing. Juarez had sent him into town to try to get help from the local police. And in case they seemed reluctant to get involved, Juarez had given McAllister Hector's phone number to use as a last resort.

Then he'd reentered the compound. After ripping his T-shirt and tucking his gun into his boot, Juarez had posed as one of the workers and checked every truck on the premises. No sign of her. He'd checked the second warehouse, too, and nothing. The only place he hadn't been was the boat tied up by the dock, but it had just arrived.

Now oozing with frustration and sweat, Juarez stacked a crate onto the bed of an eighteen-wheeler and scanned the area. The place was emptying, and it wouldn't be long before someone noticed he didn't belong. He had to find her soon.

A gust of wind moved through the compound, kicking up dust and stirring the vegetation around the buildings. Something shiny gleamed through the trees—just for an instant—then it was gone.

Metal. There was another building.

Feenie struggled against the bindings, pushing the rope at her wrists with both feet. Blood covered her hands, and the pain was excruciating, but she didn't care. Josh had locked the door behind him. If she didn't break through the bindings, she didn't have a shot in hell of getting out alive.

She heard footsteps near the entrance and froze. Was he back? Or had Marco finally come? The door remained shut. Gravel crunched along the side of the warehouse. Someone was circling the place. *Doing what?* God, could they be pouring gasoline? She imagined her skin on fire, smoking and crackling and turning black. She imagined the smell, the sound.

She had to get out.

She positioned both feet between her wrists and strained against the rope with all her might. Her skin tore as the rope inched over her hands. A sob burst out of her as she yanked her hands free. Ignoring the blood streaming from her cuts, she stooped over and frantically went to work on her ankles.

Smoke. She didn't see it, but she smelled it. The acrid fumes were unmistakable, the stuff of her nightmares.

Her fingers trembled as she fought with the bindings. Finally, the knot came loose.

Then a gunshot sounded, and the door burst open.

Juarez saw blood and ran toward her. "Are you hit?"

"No! We have to get out!"

Smoke filled the warehouse as he pulled her, limping, toward the door. He eyed the metal drums. Shit, what was in *those*? He didn't want to stick around and find out.

He stepped over the body near the doorway—the guy who'd started the fire. He looked about sixteen, and for an instant, Juarez regretted shooting him. But the kid had pulled a gun, and he'd forgotten everything except making it to Feenie. After yanking her through the doorway, he knelt down and checked the kid's pulse. Faint but detectable.

"Can you walk?" he barked at Feenie.

She nodded. "Where's McAllister?"

"He went for help. Get away from the building!"

She hobbled toward a clump of trees. Holding his gun with one hand, Juarez grabbed the laces of the kid's boots with the other. He followed Feenie across a wide swath of grass, dragging the kid behind him.

They stopped about fifty yards away from the warehouse.

Feenie slid to the ground near a tree. Blood streamed down her hands, and her shoeless feet were smeared with red. Ditching his gun, Juarez kneeled in front of her and carefully took her forearms. The blood was trickling from abrasions on her wrists. Messy but not fatal.

"Are you okay?" he asked.

She stared up at him and nodded numbly. Then her eyes focused on something behind him. Juarez followed her gaze to a black Suburban as it halted by the open warehouse door. Garland jumped out, cursing, and started toward the door. He seemed to notice the trail of blood leading from the building and whirled around. He spotted them and fumbled inside his jacket. Juarez reached for his gun, but it was gone. *Fuck!*

Then Feenie was on her feet, the Glock trembling in her hands.

"Get down!" He lunged for her, and a shot rang out.

CHAPTER

19

Marco pulled into the parking lot and cut the engine. Feenie stared, dazed, at the blinking neon sign. The parking lot was nearly empty, so they must have a vacancy.

"Wait here," he said.

She nodded. She couldn't have moved if she'd wanted to. Her muscles were limp, and every joint ached. She examined her bandaged wrists. They were beginning to throb now—the anesthetic was wearing off. The doctor had given her several shots before stitching up her torn skin. Twenty-two stitches in all.

Josh had been wheeled into the same emergency room, such as it was. Even with shaking hands,

Feenie had managed to put a bullet in his thigh. She'd caught a glimpse of him handcuffed to a gurney and accompanied by a fleet of Mexican officials. His entourage also had included a few Americans. McAllister, apparently, had made it into town and contacted the FBI.

Special Agent Rowe had been the first to arrive at the ER. He'd winked at Feenie across the hospital beds, and she'd burst into tears.

George Purnell had taken her statement. She'd answered his questions in a dull monotone as she watched the doctor stitch her wounds. In, out, in, out, the needle had traveled through her flesh.

Then Purnell had disappeared, and Marco had materialized at her side. He'd watched her closely, not saying much, until her discharge papers finally arrived. Some money changed hands. When Marco stuffed the forms into his back pocket, she'd noticed the Glock tucked into his waistband. Security in small-town Mexican hospitals seemed a bit lacking.

He'd piled her into his truck and driven to the nearest motel. It was a dilapidated row of rooms situated next to a bait camp. A sign nearby—this one in English—advertised deep-sea fishing trips.

A young American-looking couple exited one of the rooms. Feenie watched, mildly interested, as they held hands and walked to their car. When was the last time she'd held hands with someone like that? The guy opened the woman's door and kissed her before helping her in. They looked like newlyweds on a budget honeymoon—flushed, happy, probably going out for a late dinner after a couple of hours in the privacy of their cheap motel. Feenie felt a twinge of jealousy as they pulled away.

Marco's door squeaked open.

"Where's McAllister?" she asked. She suddenly realized she hadn't seen him since the hospital, where he'd been talking to Purnell and some of the Mexican authorities.

"On his way back." He tossed a room key onto the dashboard and drove the truck across the lot. "I told him I'd get you home." He glanced at her. "He was kind of a dick about it. I think he likes you."

Feenie sighed and stared out the window.

Marco parked at the very end of the lot, in front of room twelve. He got out, came around to her side, and opened the door. Without saying anything, he scooped her into his arms and backed against the door to shut it. When they got inside, he laid her gingerly across the bed.

"Don't move," he said, and disappeared into the bathroom. The pipes hummed and whistled behind the door.

Feenie eased back against the pillow and surveyed her surroundings. The place was decorated in a beach motif, with light blue paint and a wallpaper border of faded sand dollars. The threadbare bedspread probably had been a matching blue at one time but was bleached white near the window. Dusty miniblinds covered the glass.

A shaft of light shone from the bathroom as Marco came out.

"I made you a bath." He reached down to lift her, but she sat up on her elbows.

"I can do it," she said. "I'm not an invalid."

She walked to the bathroom, trying not to limp. He followed her into the cramped room and stripped off her T-shirt.

"I can *do* it," she repeated, swatting his hands away. One look at her skin under the fluorescent light had her grimacing. She had bruises scattered across her rib cage and brown bloodstains on her bra. Her hair had become a mass of frizz. Not a very appealing look. She'd just been through hell, but still, she had her vanity. She didn't want him seeing her like this.

"I'm fine," she said, holding the doorknob. She hoped he'd take the hint and leave her alone.

He clenched his jaw and walked out.

In the privacy of the tiny bathroom, she ditched the rest of her clothes. She couldn't stand the sight of herself in the horrible light, so she flipped the switch and surrounded herself with darkness. She felt better immediately. She dipped a toe in the water. He'd made it hot but not scalding, and she felt grateful as she lowered her body into the bath, trying to block out the pain as the water touched her cut ankles. The doctor had instructed her not to get her wrists wet, so she propped them on the side of the tub and let the water envelop her.

She must have dozed off. She awoke to the sound of running water and the smell of something sweet. Shampoo? Marco knelt beside the tub, silhouetted against the glow of the bedroom. He worked a fragrant lather into her hair and massaged her scalp.

"That feels nice," she murmured, unable to muster the energy to be embarrassed. He'd seen her naked before, and at least it was too dark for him to get a good look at her bruises. The water from the faucet warmed the bath, which had grown cool. She must have dozed longer than she'd thought. Her wrists and ankles were feeling better.

"Lean back," he said, and helped her dunk her head under. After rinsing out the foam, he pulled a towel from the bar by the door. It was hardly bigger than a dishcloth, but it was all they had. She got out of the bathtub and he squeezed the water from her hair and patted it with the towel. She combed her hands through it, wondering how bad it was going to look tomorrow without conditioner to tame her curls.

Marco had turned down the bed, and now he eased her back against the cool white sheets. A halo of light came from the sole lamp on the table by the door, and she noticed a McDonald's bag sitting next to it.

"You went out?"

"We needed some things, and I thought you might be hungry." He smiled faintly. "I got you a Happy Meal."

She closed her eyes and dropped her arm across

her face. She wouldn't cry. It was just a hamburger, for God's sake. "Thanks," she muttered.

The mattress sank as he stretched out next to her. She felt naked. Vulnerable. She *was* naked. If he touched her, she would definitely cry. He picked up her hand, and a hot tear slid down her cheek.

She opened her eyes and turned to look at him. He was propped on an elbow, staring down at her. His eyes looked softer than she'd ever seen them.

"Sorry," she said, wiping her cheek.

He kissed her. She tensed at first, but he didn't seem to care. He kissed her long and thoroughly until her tension slipped away. She draped her bandaged arms around his neck and pulled him closer. He was warm. Strong. Solid. She didn't want to let go. His mouth trailed down her neck, settled for a moment at her breast, and then moved tenderly over her bruised torso.

"Why did you come for me?" she asked quietly.

His hands stilled on her hips, and he glanced up. Would he admit that he cared about her? Would he tell her he loved her? She knew, after today, she'd been wrong about him. His vendetta mattered to him, yes. But she mattered to him, too. He'd been ready to take a bullet for her, and he would have, if she hadn't shot Josh first.

She combed her hands through his hair as he looked at her. But he didn't answer her question. Instead, he turned his head into her hand and began kissing her fingers, one by one, careful not to touch her bandages as he sucked the sensitive tips. He watched her as he did it, and she'd never felt anything so erotic in her life.

She didn't care about confessions anymore. Whatever he wasn't saying, he could keep it to himself, at least for now. Now she just wanted to forget about everything that had brought them here and just *be*.

She closed her eyes as he moved down her body. The heat of his mouth took over, winning out over all her aches and pains. His complete gentleness brought a different kind of pain—a tight lump that clogged her throat, refusing to go away. But somehow she found a way to ignore that, too. Her mind drifted, shutting out everything but that exact moment, the rasp of his zipper, the sound of his clothes hitting the floor, the warm feel of him next to her. Soon they were skin to skin, her legs twined around him, as her body slid into oblivion.

Gray bands of light seeped through the blinds and made a pattern of stripes across the bed. She nestled back against him, liking the weight of his arm around her waist.

"Marco?" she whispered.

"Hmm?"

She turned toward him. His eyes were closed, and he was smiling slightly.

"What?"

"You called me Marco." He opened his eyes, and the smile widened.

"So?"

"So, you've been calling me that since that night on my boat. Before, you always called me Juarez."

She frowned. She hadn't noticed.

"I like it," he said, tucking a curl behind her ear. His finger trailed over her side. She knew without looking that he was tracing her scar. It was pink and jagged, shaped sort of like a sickle. Josh had hated it. He'd urged her more than once to have a plastic surgeon remove it, but she never could bring herself to do it. It didn't seem right to erase something like that.

"Tell me how the accident happened," Marco said.

She shifted onto her back and looked at the ceiling. He had to be well acquainted with her background. He probably had a file on her somewhere, like the FBI. Like everyone, it seemed.

"You know everything about it, don't you? That's why you never asked."

He sat up on an elbow. "I don't know about it from you. Just what I read in the police report."

She sighed. This wasn't an easy topic for her. "It was Fourth of July weekend. We were coming back from a barbecue at some friends' ranch. Late afternoon. Hit-and-run driver."

He continued to trace her scar. "And this?"

"From the car door. My dad pulled me out, then went back for my mom and Rachel, but their side of the car was crushed pretty badly. Then everything caught fire."

Everything she'd just told him had been in the police report. He seemed to want more than that, though, so she tried to reach deeper, into that part of herself she rarely talked about.

"You read about grief, about these stages. Shock, denial, anger, all of that. You know what I'm talking about?"

He was silent. Either he didn't know, or he couldn't admit that he was grieving. *She* knew he was. She'd sensed that about him from the beginning, she just hadn't recognized it for what it was.

"I stumbled around for so long," she continued, "I guess it was like a whole year or something, and all I could feel was anger. After the funeral was over, that's all I felt."

"What? Like anger at yourself for surviving?"

"No." She paused. "More like anger toward Rachel. I felt like she'd taken my mom away, like we divided up my parents, and she'd ended up in heaven with my mom, and I got stuck in real life with my dad. With all his long silences. And stuck in that house where we used to be happy, and we couldn't be happy anymore. I thought I was going to suffocate, you know? And I blamed Rachel. I swear, I hated her guts. For the longest time."

His hand rested at her waist. "How do you feel now?" he asked.

She thought about it for a few seconds. "Sorry, mostly. That I never got to know her. At least, not as an adult. I think we would have been real close, like me and Celie are." She looked at him. Intimacy was a two-way street. "Tell me about Paloma."

He flinched, just an instant, but she caught it.

He cleared his throat. "She was twenty-eight. Five years out of the academy. She'd worked her way onto the vice squad in San Antonio. Then one day, she disappeared."

His voice sounded tight, controlled.

"And you're certain it had to do with her work?"

He looked away. "The police concluded she'd run away with her partner, but that's bullshit."

"How do you know?"

"Because the guy was engaged, for one thing."

"So? That doesn't mean Paloma might not have been in love with him." Or maybe even lust. But Marco probably had a hard time seeing his sister in such a light.

He shook his head. "I doubt it. But even if she was, she'd never leave Kaitlin."

"Kaitlin?"

"Her daughter, the one whose picture you saw. She's six now, lives with my mom."

Feenie remembered the pretty little girl in the photograph on his boat. No wonder he was obsessed.

"Do you really believe Josh killed her?" Her stomach knotted as she waited for the answer. Marco's eyes had gone cool.

"He's responsible, I know that. But he didn't actually kill her."

"How can you be sure?"

He looked at her a long moment. "Because Paloma disappeared the day we met. Your husband was in a hotel in Mayfield with a paralegal from his office. I saw the security tapes."

Her throat tightened. The day of the phone call. She hadn't realized the timing.

"He checked right back in after you kicked him out of the house, too," he said. "Stayed for weeks. His time's accounted for."

"And you know this how?"

"Two years of investigating, plus my contact at the bureau. Everyone said it was a hired hit, and I'm almost certain it happened down here."

"Do you wish I'd killed him?" she asked. She hadn't aimed to kill Josh. Her bullet had shattered his femur, disabling him, but not permanently. "Do you wish *you* had?"

He clenched his teeth. "Killing's too good for him. A guy like him'll suffer more in prison. It's the best revenge I can think of. That and being deprived of all his money." He rubbed the bridge of his nose, as if he was trying to fight off a headache. "I'm just sorry I didn't get a chance to talk to him first."

"You mean torture him? Make him give you a lot of sordid details about your sister? You think that would make you feel better?"

"Yes," he said, without emotion. He sat up and leaned against the headboard. "I've got some unanswered questions."

Feenie closed her eyes. She'd been dreading this.

If she told him what Josh had said, he'd go straight to El Paso to hunt down the hit man. Marco could end up dead or, at the very least, behind bars.

"Finding the killer isn't going to bring Paloma back, you know. It won't give Kaitlin back her mother."

She watched him stiffen, and she knew she was treading on hallowed ground here.

"She was my kid sister, Feenie. I'm not just going to forget about her."

He wouldn't look her in the eye, and to Feenie, that spoke volumes. Maybe he *was* forgetting. Maybe he *wanted* to forget it, to get on with his life, but he felt ashamed.

"She deserves better," he continued. "My family deserves better."

"I'm not saying you should forget about her. But what about letting go of all this rage you carry around? What about letting go of this obsession with how she died?"

His looked at her scornfully. "I'm an investigator, Feenie. I want to know what happened. How do two trained detectives just disappear? The guy was an FBI agent, for Christ's sake. And how did Garland find out Paloma and her partner were onto him? And who blew her partner's cover with the SAPD?" His brow was furrowed in frustration. "I think there's a mole somewhere, maybe someone in the bureau's San Antonio field office. Or maybe someone on Paloma's squad. I haven't figured it out yet."

Feenie couldn't believe this. "What, now you want *another* person to go after? Marco, this is endless. She was investigating awful, unscrupulous people. You can't hunt down every one of them and make them pay."

"I don't want every one of them," he said firmly. "I want the one who killed Paloma."

"But . . . it's been two years. Don't you think it's time to move on?"

He shot off the bed and grabbed his crumpled cargo pants off the floor. "Oh, like you?"

"What?" she asked, sitting up and tucking the sheet around her.

"You've had eighteen *years* to get over it." He yanked on his pants and T-shirt. "And you're still having nightmares. At least your sister wasn't murdered. At least you had a funeral."

Her jaw dropped.

He jammed his feet into his boots and stalked to the door.

"Don't act like you've got some monopoly on grief!" she shouted. "My sister was murdered, too, if you ask me. And so was my mom. The guy didn't even stop! He was probably drunk out of his mind. You think I don't have unanswered questions?"

His hand stilled on the doorknob, and he took a deep breath. "I'm getting some breakfast," he said calmly. "Want anything?"

"No."

"Fine. Be ready when I get back."

• • •

They shared the four-hour drive in silence. His anger had dissipated by the time they reached the border, but hers hadn't. He could tell, because she kept her arms crossed over her chest and her cheeks flushed every time she looked at him. When they finally reached Mayfield, he drove straight to Pecan Street.

"Your house is finished?" he asked, pulling into the driveway. It was their first scrap of conversation since the border checkpoint.

"Yes."

"I've got some things to catch up on at the office. I'll call you later."

She stared at her lap. "His name's Brassler."

"What?"

"Brassler. Josh said it, but I don't know if I heard him right."

"When did he tell you this?"

"Before the fire," she said, not looking at him. "He said he paid twenty thousand, that he didn't mind spending that on a nosy cop. But he wouldn't waste that kind of money on me."

His hands tightened on the steering wheel. Brassler was his man. He'd been pretty sure, but hearing it confirmed was like a kick in the gut. And the price. *Goddamn it.*

"Thank you." He tried not to choke on the words. "But I already had a name."

Her gaze shot up. "You knew?"

"I was pretty certain, yeah. But it's not enough.

The guy's like smoke. He operates on both sides of the border, but no one's seen him in well over a year. I've been back and forth searching for him, but I need more to go on."

She looked at him, and for the first time, he got it. She was afraid. Afraid for *him*.

"I won't get hurt," he told her. "I know what I'm doing."

"No one's bulletproof, Marco."

What could he say to that? She was right, but he'd long ago stopped caring about the risk.

He reached out and stroked a finger over her bandaged wrist. "I'll call you later," he said.

"You don't have to."

"I will."

Instead of calling, he showed up. She couldn't suppress the smile when she saw him standing on her front porch that evening.

"Look at you," she said, eyeing the collared shirt and unripped jeans. He still wore the scuffed bomber jacket, but she'd gotten used to it now that she understood the reason for it. "You even shaved."

"Can I come in?"

"Of course," she said, swinging the door open. She looked down at her grimy T-shirt and jeans. She'd been cleaning her house earlier, trying to use up some of her nervous energy.

He stepped inside. "I came by to see if you wanted to have dinner."

"Dinner."

"Yeah. I want a steak. You game?"

Her gaze skimmed over him, and her heart started to melt. "You mean, like a date?"

"Yes." He cleared his throat. "I'd like to take you out. If you're not still mad at me. Or even if you are still mad, I'd like to take you anyway."

She tried not to smile. He was courting her and clearly uneasy about it. Her heart melted some more. "I'd love to."

"Good. Let's go."

"Wait."

"Wait what?"

She shut the door behind him. "I can't go out like this. Look at me!"

He stepped back and looked her over. "What? You look fine."

She rolled her eyes. "Please, I'm a mess. If you're going to take me to dinner, the least I can do is get pretty."

He quirked an eyebrow. "What happened to all that feminist stuff?"

"Feminism doesn't mean I have to go out looking like a drowned cat. Lemme change, okay?"

Twenty-five minutes later, she'd showered, slapped on some makeup, shimmied into a cherry-red tank dress, and managed to style her hair. The bandages at her wrists made her look like she was under suicide watch, so she slipped on a gauzy black shirt and tied it at her waist. Not perfect but definitely better.

He watched her with a predatory glint in his eyes as she came down the stairs.

"Thanks for waiting," she said.

He pulled her against him and kissed her neck, and she knew he was about to suggest they go upstairs.

His cell phone buzzed, and he checked the number. "Hold on," he muttered, letting her go. "Juarez."

She went to get her purse from the kitchen, and when she came back, he was off the phone.

"That was Peterson." His face looked grim.

"What?"

"They've tested the .45 Josh had on him when he was arrested."

"And?"

"And the rifling marks match the slugs they recovered from Martinez's and Doring's autopsies."

She could tell that wasn't all of it. "What else?"

"It's also a tentative match to a bullet they found embedded in the wooden planter by the *Gazette* building."

She stared at him a minute, stunned into silence. Josh had killed two men in cold blood and tried to kill her. *Twice.* He'd pretty much told her in Punto Dorado that he hadn't contracted out her murder, that he'd wanted to do it himself, but somehow she felt shocked.

"Wow," she finally said.

He stepped closer and took her hand. "You okay? We could skip dinner and just stay in tonight."

She scoffed. "What? And miss our first date? I don't think so." She wanted to get out of the house, to be around people and noise and forget about Josh. "Let's go."

"You sure?"

She forced a smile. "Absolutely. You invited me on a date, and I intend to take full advantage. Where are we going, anyway?"

"I was thinking Harbor House Grille."

Whoa. Expensive *and* romantic. The place actually had tablecloths and a wine list.

"Sounds perfect." She kissed him, trying to distract both of them from the phone call. He returned the kiss, and she knew she'd half succeeded.

Her alarm went off the next morning at six, but she was already awake. She'd been lying there for hours, not sleeping.

Marco stirred next to her. "Turn it off," he grumbled, pulling the pillow over his head.

She silenced the clock, pulled on her robe, and went to the window. The morning was gray, just like her mood. She glanced at her bed. The sight of him sleeping there made her chest ache.

She loved him. She wanted to tell him, but she couldn't. It was the last thing he'd want to hear, and under the circumstances, telling him would just open her up to more hurt.

He was going to leave. There was no getting

around it. If not today, he'd leave tomorrow. Or next week. And as soon as he went after Brassler, everything would be over between them. He'd either get himself killed, God forbid, or he'd be guilty of something that would follow him the rest of his life. The rest of *her* life.

So why bother telling him how she felt? At least now when he broke her heart, he wouldn't actually know he'd broken it. She'd have a scrap of pride left, however small.

She watched Marco sleeping and wanted to tell him anyway. A tiny corner of her mind had started hoping that maybe, just maybe, he felt the way she did. And maybe they could have a relationship, a future together.

She went into the bathroom and turned on the shower. When she emerged ten minutes later, the bed was empty. Feenie put on her robe and followed the aroma of coffee down to her kitchen, where she found him leaning against the counter reading the paper. He was fully dressed, holster plastered to his side as usual.

"You made coffee?"

"That's for you," he said, shrugging into his jacket. "I've got to get going."

"You don't even want a cup?"

"Nah, thanks anyway."

Trying not to feel slighted, she went to the front door and opened it.

"I'll call you later," he said, kissing her forehead.

She took his hand. "There's something I have to tell you."

Her heart squeezed. She could still back out. She could make something up. He'd never know.

"What?" he asked.

She couldn't lie to him. She led him well away from the house to the driveway, where he'd parked his truck. Marco had swept the house for bugs after it had been ransacked, but she didn't know the extent of the FBI's surveillance. She rose on tiptoes and kissed him under the ear. "El Paso," she whispered.

"Huh?"

"That conversation we had yesterday. He's in El Paso."

She stepped back to look at him. His eyes were hard, black.

"You sure?" he asked.

She shrugged. "It's just something I heard. You know, yesterday."

He gazed over her shoulder, down the street. If he saw someone there, he didn't react.

"I'll call you," he repeated. He sounded distracted this time, and her heart sank.

"You're going, aren't you?" He wouldn't look at her. She shifted into his line of vision. "Marco, look at me. Are you going?"

He met her gaze briefly, then glanced away.

She pictured him dead in some parking garage like Martinez, and all her pride vanished. "Please don't go. Please? I know you want to. I know you think you can't *not* go. But you can. You can stay here with me."

He winced at that, and she felt as if he'd slapped her. He didn't love her. Just the thought of staying with her made him cringe.

He glanced at her face and seemed to realize he'd done something wrong. "Shit," he muttered, looking down. "Feenie, don't do this—"

"I'll come with you," she blurted. Maybe she could buy some time and find a way to talk him out of whatever he had planned. "Please? I won't get in your way. I just . . . I just want to be near you."

There. She'd said it. Well, not the love part, but pretty damn close. Any semblance of pride she might have had was long gone.

He looked down and shook his head.

"Please?" God, she was begging now. She was begging this man to stay with her—something she'd never thought she'd do—and she didn't care.

He looked over her shoulder again. And that's when she felt it, like a rush of cold air, the actual moment when his emotions turned off. And she realized she'd pushed him too far. She'd begged him to give up his goal, to stay with her, to take her with him. She was clinging, and now he was going to run away.

"We'll talk later," he said without feeling. He slipped on his shades.

"Sure, whatever."

"Take care," he said, and got into his truck.

She stood alone on her driveway and watched him go.

Juarez pulled into Rosie's and headed straight for the kitchen. He found her there, bustling around, giving instructions to the breakfast crew.

"Can I use your phone?" he asked. Rosie knew English, but she didn't like to let on. She gave a slight nod toward the office.

He ducked into the cramped little room and picked up the phone. He needed a line that wouldn't be tapped. After talking with a private detective he knew in El Paso, Juarez returned to the front of the restaurant and ordered a plate of *migas* and some coffee. He lingered a minute, until he was sure his tail was waiting for him in the parking lot. Then he plunked a twenty onto the counter and drove to his office.

• • •

Rowe flipped open his cell.

"We lost him," Stevenski said.

"You want to repeat that?"

"I don't know how it happened," his partner said. "I personally followed him to the boarding area."

Rowe bit back a curse and swerved the Blazer into the parking lot. He stopped but didn't cut the engine. In this heat, with no air conditioning, he'd surely have a heat stroke. "What did Purnell say?"

Stevenski cleared his throat. "I, um, haven't told him yet. I was hoping you'd make the call."

Great. Now, in addition to locating Juarez, Rowe had to cover his partner's ass. He could sympathize with Stevenski's plight, though. The young agent was still on Purnell's shit list because the Malone woman had given him the slip when she went to Punto Dorado.

"You're sure it was the right flight?" Rowe asked.

"I saw the reservation myself. Flight one seventy-two into Tucson. Eleven-twenty a.m. He bought an electronic ticket from his office computer, but he never got off the plane."

"And you watched him board?"

Silence.

"Shit, tell me you saw him get on the damn plane."

"Not exactly. But he was in the boarding area—"

"*In* the boarding area isn't the same as *on* the plane!" Rowe thumped his head back against the seat. This case was going to sink his career.

"What do you want me to do?"

"Check the passenger manifest. Chances are he's not on it, but check anyway. Then look at the tapes from the security cams in the airport garage. My guess is he's left already."

"Okay. We've got a guy staking out the detective agency in Tucson. Do you want me to have him interview the contact? Contact's name is Ortiz."

"Ortiz is a decoy," Rowe explained, struggling for patience. His partner said nothing, and Rowe knew he was reviewing the way Juarez had played him.

Rowe sighed. "Who's Ortiz work for again?"

"Sonoran Investigations," Stevenski said. "They're a small shop on the outskirts of town. Juarez called Ortiz from his office this morning, asked him to run down everything he could on Brassler. That was just before he bought the e-ticket. Should we interview this guy?"

Private investigators often helped each other with cases that crossed state lines, and they usually got paid for their trouble. But the chances of the decoy knowing Juarez's real whereabouts were minuscule. Still, it wouldn't hurt to ask. They were grasping at straws now.

"Yeah, do that," Rowe said. "And when you're done, review phone calls. Flag anything suspicious, and get back to me. He's on the move, we just have to find out where."

"You got it."

"I'll call Purnell. But no more fuck-ups, or we'll both be sorry."

"I understand."

Rowe flipped shut his phone and stared out the window. If he didn't bring Brassler in soon, the guy was going to wind up with a bullet in his back. And they really needed some information only he could provide. So far, Garland had been a disappointment. He'd been interviewed nonstop since his arrest, and he'd refused to give up anything, even after the murder charges had been added. Rowe believed adding those charges so soon had been a tactical mistake, but, of course, no one wanted his opinion. Now the bastard had dug in his heels, refusing to divulge crap while his defense attorney played hardball.

They needed Brassler more than ever, and time was running short.

"Where are you, Juarez?" Rowe muttered, steering back onto the highway and heading for HQ.

He'd faked a trip to Tucson, so where was he really going? Somewhere much closer, probably. The girlfriend surely knew something, but she wasn't talking. And nothing interesting had come from watching her house. Juarez was too smart to contact her directly, but he'd communicate somehow. The guy was whipped. Rowe recognized the signs.

He didn't call.

She'd known he wouldn't, but knowing didn't take the sting away. Feenie drove by the marina a few times, but his truck was gone. She left several messages on his voice mail, which he didn't return. With each passing day, the tension built. She tried working it off at the gym, but that didn't help. Ditto for the firing range and work. The knot between her shoulder blades was becoming unbearable.

On the second Friday with no word, she went to Rosie's and found Cecelia already seated in their favorite booth, reading a newspaper.

"Any word from Marco?" she asked as Feenie slid in across from her.

She shook her head.

Cecelia folded her paper and put it on the table. Like everyone else, she'd been tracking the story through McAllister's articles in the *Gazette*. Today's headline was about Josh's uncle, who had been arrested yesterday after the joint task force raided his grocery stores.

"How are you holding up?" Cecelia asked.

"Okay, I guess."

"This article says Josh has an alibi for the *Gazette* shooting," Cecelia said. "Apparently, there's proof he was at his law office across town at the time."

"On a Saturday?" Feenie hadn't had time to do more than glance at the morning paper. Or maybe she just hadn't made time. She'd been trying her best to get everything Josh-related out of her mind.

Trying but failing miserably.

Cecelia tapped her finger on the newspaper story. "According to this article, there's a security video showing him entering his law office just before three—"

"How are *you* doing?" Feenie asked, cutting her off. On Wednesday afternoon, a couple of FBI agents had shown up at Cecelia's house to interview her about her connection to Josh. At the same time, another team of agents had arrived at Robert's accounting office, where they'd interviewed Robert and subpoenaed all the firm's records related to their now notorious former client.

"I'm okay," Cecelia said. "Robert's a little freaked out, though. He swears the records are all in order, that if anything, they'll clear his name. But his partners still don't seem too happy about this. I think they're going to ask him to resign."

"But why? He didn't do anything."

Cecelia shrugged. "I guess just the hint of suspected impropriety is too much for them. They're pretty uptight about negative publicity."

Feenie never realized the ripples this thing would have. It seemed everyone she knew was affected one way or another. "That sucks."

"Yeah." Cecelia faked a smile. "So, how about we drop the subject for an hour and talk about something else?"

The waitress came by, and they ordered margaritas. They started chatting, but then McAllister appeared, obliterating any hope they might have had of having a normal conversation. He sported his typical button-down, wrinkled chinos, and scruffy hair. The combination should have looked sloppy, but somehow on him it came off as sexy.

"Hey, ladies. Mind if I join you?"

"As a matter of fact—" Feenie demurred.

"Not at all," Cecelia said, smiling up at him.

Before Feenie could scoot over, McAllister slid into the booth next to Cecelia. Then the waitress came by with their food and asked McAllister if he wanted anything.

"I'll have the taco plate. And a water." He gave Feenie a pointed look. "I don't like to drink on the job."

What a load of bull. They both knew he spent most of his lunch hours at Eddie's Pool Hall. "What are you doing here?" Feenie asked, not caring that it sounded totally rude.

"Same as you guys. Having lunch."

"We were just talking about how we *didn't* want to discuss the Garland case," Feenie said. "So if you're planning to talk about it, I suggest you get another table."

Cecelia gave her a puzzled glance, obviously having no clue why she was being such a bitch.

He shrugged. "Fine by me. Let's talk about something else." He turned to Cecelia. "Feenie tells me you work for the Red Cross. That must be interesting. I'm thinking about writing a story about their efforts with displaced hurricane victims."

Oh, *please.* It was a ridiculous ploy, but he managed to keep Cecelia engaged for the entire meal.

Finally, they paid the bill and made their way to the parking lot. McAllister pulled out a pack of cigarettes as Feenie hugged Cecelia goodbye.

"You got a minute?" he asked Feenie, who turned around to glare at him.

"What was that? I told you, she's married. Go find someone else to play with!"

"I wanted to give you a heads up," he said, ignoring the comment. "Word is, the feds are looking for your boyfriend. Any idea where he might be?"

"No."

He lit his cigarette and took a drag. He exhaled the smoke, looking at her intently. "You need to work on your poker face."

"I have *no* idea. I haven't heard from him, okay?"

"Okay. But you might want to think about getting a message to him. The FBI knows he's gunning for someone—I don't know who, but I think they do. And they're watching. Just thought you might want to pass it along."

He took out his keys and headed for his Jeep, leaving her standing there fuming.

"Excuse me," a voice said.

Feenie turned around to see a short, plump woman standing behind her. Her dark brown hair was curly and streaked with gray. She looked vaguely familiar. "Yes?"

The seconds ticked by as the woman stared. She wore a floral print skirt and a neatly pressed black blouse. A crucifix rested on her ample bosom. She had kindly brown eyes, but for some reason, they made Feenie uneasy.

"Can I help you?" Feenie asked impatiently.

"You don't know me." The woman's voice was hesitant. "But Rosie says you know my son."

Y ou're Marco's mother?"

The woman smiled faintly, but it didn't reach her eyes. They looked immensely sad. "I'm Maria Juarez."

Feenie held out her hand. "Feenie Malone. It's nice to meet you."

They had one of those awkward, woman-to-woman handshakes. God, now what? What could she say to this woman? That because of her, her son had gone after a dangerous fugitive? The woman already knew something was amiss, or she wouldn't be standing there.

"I need to talk to you. Can we sit?" Maria nodded at a bench by the restaurant entrance.

"Sure."

Feenie perched stiffly on the end of the bench and watched Maria.

"Marco talks to you, yes? Spends time at your house?"

"Uh, not lately," Feenie said. "I haven't talked to him in about two weeks."

Her brow furrowed. "But he calls you, yes? Have you heard from him soon?"

"You mean recently? No, I haven't."

She looked crestfallen. Her hands tightened around the strap of her handbag, and she took a deep breath.

"If I hear from him, I'll tell him to call you," Feenie said.

Maria nodded and unzipped her purse. She wrote an address and phone number over a coupon for frozen dinners, then handed it to Feenie. "You can reach me there. Anytime. And if Marco calls, please tell him to call home."

"Is everything all right at home?" Feenie asked. "Is Kaitlin okay?"

"*Sí, sí.* Kaitlin is fine." She smiled slightly. "She keeps asking for Marco, and I don't know what to tell her."

"I'm sure he'll call soon," Feenie said.

Maria forced another smile. "You could call me—how you say?—a worry wart? All my children say I'm a worry wart."

Feenie bit her lip. "I wouldn't worry, if I were you. He's probably just busy."

Maria stood and fingered the beads at her neck. "*Bueno,*" she said. "Thank you so much."

Cecelia was going to be sick. She stared at the television and knew she was going to throw up. Or faint. Or possibly die.

It couldn't be true.

Yet it was. The evidence was staring right at her, irrefutable, on the screen. She'd found the tape in Robert's closet when she'd gone looking for ... what? She didn't know. Evidence of an affair? Evidence of fraud? He'd been acting strange lately, almost secretive. Yet less than an hour ago, Celie had actually felt guilty for snooping, for doubting her husband, for even entertaining the possibility that the FBI might be right to ask questions about his association with Josh. She'd thought there was a teeny *tiny* chance he'd have some sort of papers linking him to Josh's operation. Or maybe she'd thought she'd find nothing, and she could put her fears to rest finally and stop feeling alienated from her own husband.

Less than an hour ago, she'd felt guilty for doubting him, for not being the faithful, trusting wife she'd always been.

And now this.

The black-and-white footage showed a bird's-eye view of a familiar office lobby. It was Josh's lobby, the lobby Cecelia had been in dozens of times when Feenie had worked there. Cecelia had walked through those same glass doors, past that same fake ficus tree, and approached the same reception counter where Feenie had sat. On a typical weekday, she'd find Feenie on the phone, the lobby around her swirling with attorneys and support staff and delivery men.

But that lobby was deserted in this footage, taken on a recent Saturday afternoon. Cecelia rewound the tape and watched it a second time.

The date and time stared at her from the bottom of the screen: May 16, one-fifteen p.m. Not a soul in sight. She fast-forwarded through the tape, slowing as it approached three o'clock. The lobby remained empty. Three-ten. Still no one. Three-thirty came and went, and still nothing. She fast-forwarded through until six p.m. and saw no one, not a single person, enter or leave the building. Whatever tape Josh's lawyers had produced to give him an alibi, it hadn't been this one. And *this* one was the original. *This* one was real. She knew it as surely as she knew that she'd found it on the top shelf of Robert's closet.

With a trembling hand, she picked up the portable phone from the coffee table and dialed Robert's number. He was working late, or so he'd said. The refrain was so familiar, she'd stopped questioning. He was working late. Too late for dinner. Too late for sex. Too late for talk, or argument, or anything that would explain what something like this was doing in his possession.

His voice mail clicked on. She hurled the phone against the wall.

She had to get out.

She ran up the stairs, two at a time, and yanked open the hall closet. She pulled out an overnight bag and tossed it onto her bed. She flung open her dresser drawers, grabbed handfuls of clothes, and stuffed them into the bag. Then she wrenched her cosmetics drawer open and emptied its contents atop all the clothes. She zipped the duffle, carried it into the hallway, and pitched it down the stairs. As an afterthought, she raced back into the bedroom and grabbed her migraine prescription from the bedside table.

She went downstairs and peered out the front window. No headlights coming down the street. No Accord pulling into the driveway. She snatched her cell phone from the desk in the hallway and punched Feenie's number.

Voice mail, dammit. Didn't anyone answer their phone anymore?

"Feenie, it's me. You're not going to believe this." Her voice caught. "Um ... I need to talk to you." Where was her goddamn purse? She headed for the kitchen. "I found—"

Robert stood in the doorway. He held his computer case in one hand and his keys in the other. She jumped back, crashing into the doorjamb and dropping the phone.

"Hi," he said. "What's going on?"

She stepped backward. "You're home."

He deposited his computer and keys on the sofa

and loosened his tie. Cecelia glanced over his shoulder at the television, and her heart skipped a beat. A frozen image of Josh's lobby filled the screen.

Robert walked over and kissed her cheek. "Sorry I'm late. Have you eaten dinner?"

Had she eaten? Dinner. Meatloaf and potatoes. *You lying bastard.*

"I'll fix you a plate," she said instead. She walked into the kitchen, listening for his footsteps behind her as she scanned the counter for her keys. They were there, by her purse. Any second now, he'd look at the television and demand an explanation. Any second now—

His footsteps sounded on the stairs.

"What happened in here?" he called down from the bedroom. "It looks like a tornado whipped through."

"I'm . . . I'm organizing my dresser."

Cecelia rushed into the living room, ejected the videotape, and jammed it into her purse as she crossed the kitchen. She glanced frantically out the breakfast-room window. Robert's Accord had blocked her in. She scurried back into the living room, snatched his keychain off the sofa, and raced for the back door.

Feenie dumped her mail onto the kitchen counter and sifted through it. For the first time in months, the sight of bills didn't bring on a stress headache. She was catching up with the help of her new salary. Her house was safe from foreclosure, at least for now.

The promotion to full-time news reporter hadn't given her the lift she'd expected. It was a boost to her self-esteem, sure. Her first real job, the first time she'd really stood on her own two feet. But something was missing. Feenie's gaze wandered to the patio, devoid of trikes and roller skates, the swimming pool's surface placid in the evening light.

She was alone.

She hadn't minded before—at least, not really. Kicking Josh out had been such a relief, in many ways, she hadn't spent much time focusing on how empty her house felt with all its unused rooms and un-played-in corners.

She should call her father. Their relationship had warmed since his visit to Mayfield. To Feenie's surprise, her dad had begun e-mailing her several times a week. His messages were filled with commentary about her stories, mostly, but sometimes he'd intersperse other tidbits—what he'd been up to that weekend, how the fishing was going, the obligatory reminder to get her oil changed or check her tires. And Feenie always wrote back. She never would have imagined revitalizing their relationship over the Internet, but somehow it worked for them. It wasn't as if they were having gut-wrenching heart-to-hearts, but for her father, it was progress. She decided to pay him a visit soon. July Fourth was coming up. It was always a tough holiday for them both, but it would be easier if they spent it together.

She shuffled through the stack of papers, separating the real mail from the junk. A postcard fluttered to the floor.

Feenie stooped to pick it up. *Chihuahua.* The picture showed a waterfall spilling over some craggy rocks. She flipped it over, but there was no message. Just her address—no name—written in neat block letters.

He was alive.

She tipped her head back and closed her eyes. *Thank you, Lord.*

She studied the card more closely. At least, he *had* been alive eight days ago when the postcard was mailed. From Chihuahua. What was he doing in Mexico instead of El Paso, anyway? She probably didn't want to know. But maybe he'd come home soon. And when that happened, maybe he'd want to pick up where they'd left off.

Sure. As if that was really possible. This obsession would either kill him or, if he was lucky, merely land him in prison. And then she'd spend the rest of her life pining away for a man who wore an orange jumpsuit. Her ex-husband? No, different jumpsuit. This was the *other* man she'd loved who had ended up in jail.

God, she really knew how to pick 'em. Well, he'd picked *her.* He'd made her fall in love with him, and then he'd thrown away any future they could have had together by going to El Paso. Or Mexico. Or wherever the heck his sick revenge quest had taken him now. *If,* of course, he was still alive.

She shoved the postcard into the pocket of her jeans and opened the refrigerator so she could stare blankly at its contents. What was she doing? She wasn't even hungry. She shut the fridge and opened a cupboard. A box of Pop Tarts caught her eye. She fished a foil-wrapped pastry out of the box and decided she needed a beer with her dinner.

A pounding on the window made her spin around. She crossed the room and opened the back door. "Celie! What are you—"

Cecelia pushed her back into the kitchen and slammed the door. She flipped the bolt and yanked the curtains together.

"What the—"

"Call 9-1-1!" Cecelia ordered. "I think he might have followed me."

"Call . . . *what?* Who followed you?" Feenie tossed the Pop Tart onto the counter.

"Robert!" Cecelia dragged her into the living room. "Stay here. No, maybe you should go upstairs. You have a gun, right? Where is it?"

Not waiting for an answer, Cecelia sprinted to the front door and threw the deadbolt.

"What—"

"Where's your phone, Feenie? We need to call 9-1-1!"

Feenie stood, dumbstruck, as Cecelia raced back

into the kitchen. "Shit, your phone's still out, isn't it? *Fuck!* Where's your cell?"

That got Feenie's attention more than any of the previous blather. Cecelia rarely cursed. She reappeared with Feenie's cell phone in hand and started towing her up the stairs.

"Don't tell me this thing's not working! Oh, God, you're kidding, right? Your battery's *dead?*"

At the top of the stairs, Feenie shook Cecelia's hand off her arm. "What's going on? You're scaring me here."

She looked up from the phone. Her hands were shaking. "I found a tape. In Robert's closet. Of Josh's law firm."

"O-*kay.* And this matters why?"

"It's a tape, Feen. A surveillance video. From the day you were shot at!"

"I'm still not following—"

"Josh's alibi is fake! Robert has the real tape! And I found it, and I left the tape case out on the coffee table, so now he probably *knows* I found it! And I was coming here to tell you, and I think he might have followed me!"

The doorbell rang.

"God, that's him! Feenie, go get your gun. Is it under your bed? I'm going to sneak out the back and see if I can find a phone. Is Mrs. Hanak home? She has a separate line, right?"

Feenie's heart was thudding now, but she didn't

want to panic. Two hysterical women would not be good, especially if one of them was armed.

"Hold on a second, okay? Are you sure about this? I mean, could there be some other reason—"

"Like what, huh? Robert just *happens* to have a surveillance tape of Josh's office for the same block of time you *happened* to get shot at? And Josh just *happened* to use a tape like that for his alibi? Except his tape shows himself strolling into the office on Saturday afternoon just before the shooting? Think, Feenie!"

Okay, when she put it like that . . . "But you really think . . . *Robert?* Would try to—"

The doorbell rang again.

"Get your gun, Feenie. I'm going to find a phone."

Rowe plopped a Mr. Goodbar onto the counter and took out his wallet.

"Espresso with that?" The young woman at the register gave him a warm smile.

This place was one of the many convenience stores trying to cash in on the Starbucks craze by serving three-dollar coffee. It wasn't bad, either, and Rowe was pulling the night shift.

"Sure, why not? A double, please."

She prepared a cup while he pulled out his money. After securing the lid, she pushed the cup toward him, along with two creamers and a packet of Equal. He'd started coming here only a few days ago, but already she'd noticed how he liked his coffee. For some crazy reason, that made him feel good. The woman had pretty brown eyes and a ready smile and always went out of her way to be nice to him. He was probably older than she was by at least a decade, but maybe she still found him attractive. Some women liked a little gray at the temples. Plus, he kept in shape, even when he was on the road.

A group of rowdy teenagers entered the store, and she cast a nervous look in their direction. Who was he kidding? She was nice to him because she was observant. She'd probably noticed his holster and knew he was in law enforcement.

"Here you go." He slid his money across the counter. She rang up just the candy bar and gave him his change.

"Come back again, now," she said.

He nodded and walked out, staring down the teens as he left. He got back into the Blazer and sipped his coffee for a few minutes as he waited for the kids to leave. They bought some soft drinks and drove away, and Rowe waved at the cashier as he started his car.

His cell phone beeped, and he flipped it open. "Yeah?"

"We got activity at the girlfriend's house," Stevenski reported.

"Is it Juarez?"

"Nope. But something's going down."

Shit. "All right. I'm on my way." He checked his watch. "ETA four minutes."

CHAPTER

22

The doorbell rang again. The chime was followed by pounding fists. Feenie crept down the stairs and searched for a place to hide the .22, which wasn't easy, because she barely had any furniture. She leaned it against a corner in the empty dining room and walked toward the door.

"Feenie, open up." It was Robert's voice on the other side of the door. "I need to talk to Cecelia."

She didn't respond, and he started down the porch and across the yard, as if he was going around to the back. Cecelia was back there somewhere, probably in Mrs. Hanak's apartment by now.

Feenie hurriedly undid the latch and yanked open the door. "Wait! Robert? What's going on?" Maybe she could just play dumb, pretend Cecelia wasn't here.

Except that her Explorer was sitting in the driveway. Parked right behind Robert's Accord. She'd come in Robert's car?

"Where's Celie?" Robert charged toward her, his eyes wild, his cheeks blotchy. She'd never seen him like this. The perpetually cool accountant had gone postal.

But his hands were empty. He wasn't armed.

"She's not here," Feenie said, taking a step back.

Robert glanced at the driveway. "Oh, yeah? Where is she, then? Come on, Feenie, I have to talk to her. I know she's in there. I just want to talk."

Should she ask him inside to stall for time? Or just keep him talking there on the porch? Before she could decide, he shoved past her into the house.

"Cecelia! I need to talk to you."

Feenie followed him, leaving the door open. "Robert, really. It's not a good time. Could you just—"

He ignored her and went into the kitchen. He came back out almost instantly, holding Cecelia's purse. He strode toward Feenie and tossed it at her feet.

"Where is she?"

"Um, I don't—"

"I'm right here." Cecelia stood in the kitchen doorway now. "Don't do anything stupid. I've called the police."

"*Goddamn* you!" he roared. "What were you thinking?"

Feenie inched toward the .22. It was only a few feet away, but she didn't want to get too close and draw attention to it.

"Let's all just relax here, okay?" Feenie tried to sound calm, like the mediator on the playground. A little tiff among friends. "Let's just sit down and talk."

But there was no place to sit, and even if there had been, neither Robert nor Cecelia looked even remotely ready to make nice.

"It's over, Robert," Cecelia said. "I found the tape."

He grabbed her arm. "It's not what you think, Celie. Josh just asked me to hold on to it for him."

She glared at him. "When did he ask you, huh? Did you visit him in *jail?* You know what I think? I think you were hiding that tape for him because you made him another one. That's what you were doing holed up with all your video equipment, wasn't it?"

"Celie—"

"And you know what else? I think you told Josh where to find Feenie that day. How could you do that, Robert?"

No way. Had he really told Josh where to find her? Feenie eyed the gun.

"Just listen," he pleaded. "You have to—"

"I'm telling the police! You're a liar—"

"Stop it!" He shook her arm. "Don't you dare do this to me. Don't you *dare!*"

Feenie stepped closer to the gun, hoping they'd be too distracted to notice.

But Robert dropped Cecelia's arm and stepped away. He ran his hands over his face, which was sweating now, and took a deep breath. "Okay, just think about this, Cecelia. Just *think*. If you tell that to the police, they're going to arrest me. They're going to charge me with conspiracy to commit murder. I'll go to jail. Is that what you want? What about the family we're trying to have? You could be pregnant. What about that?"

Cecelia crossed her arms over her chest. "Nice try, but I won't lie for you, Robert."

His shoulders sagged, and he looked at the floor. Then he drew back his hand and *smack!* Cecelia was on the ground. He lunged for the purse at Feenie's feet, snatched the videotape and the keys from it, and raced out the door.

Feenie scrambled to Cecelia's side. "Are you okay?"

She nodded, clutching her jaw. "I called the police." As she said this, sirens sounded in the distance.

Tires squealed outside, and Feenie didn't know whether they were coming or going.

Gunshots sounded, and Feenie leaped to her feet. Who was shooting? She glanced out the front window. The Explorer was still in the drive, but Robert had taken the Accord, leaving trench marks across the neighbors' lawn.

"You girls okay?" Mrs. Hanak stepped through the kitchen doorway, clutching her pearl-handled pistol.

The sirens were wailing at full volume now, right

in front of the house. Feenie looked out the window again and saw two police cars, along with a tan Blazer. Special Agent Rowe barreled up the sidewalk.

"You should put your gun away," she told Mrs. Hanak. "The police are here."

"Hmph!" She stuffed the pistol into the pocket of her robe. "A day late and a dollar short, if you ask me. Your burglar already got away. I tried to shoot out his tires, but my aim's not what it used to be."

John McAllister swerved into a space behind one of the police cruisers and jumped out of his Jeep. In three strides, he was across Feenie's lawn, elbowing his way through the crowd of cops and agents who were milling around talking and taking notes.

"Where is she?" he snapped.

Feenie stopped speaking to a young officer. She frowned at John, sighed, and gave a slight nod toward the house.

He spotted Cecelia on the porch. She was curled up in the swing, her legs tucked under her as she stared off into space.

He took the stairs slowly, not wanting to startle her. "Cecelia?"

The flicker of warmth in her eyes when she saw him made his breath catch.

"Hi." Her voice was quiet, but she smiled slightly. "News travels fast, huh?"

"Night editor called me from the paper. He'd been listening to the police scanner." He touched the chain holding up the swing. He wanted to sit down next to her, but maybe she needed some space.

After getting word of gunshots fired at Feenie's address, John had sped across town, making calls the whole time and trying to get the lowdown on what had happened. Finally, he'd reached a cop on the scene, who was able to give him the nutshell version. Feenie Malone and Cecelia Strickland were involved, yes, but no one was hurt.

The fifteen-minute drive had taken about fifteen years off his life.

He looked at Cecelia now, sitting motionless on the swing. *Fuck it.* He sat down beside her.

She didn't seem to mind his being there. Now that he was closer, he noticed the cut on her upper lip. He wanted to kick the living shit out of her husband.

"You okay?" he asked.

She sighed and looked out over the lawn. "I've had kind of a rough day." She shifted her gaze to meet his. "How about you?"

He laughed dryly and looked down. He took out his pack of Camels and tapped out a cigarette. "Ah, I'm okay," he said, lighting up. "Better than you, at least."

She scoffed. "Hey, what's the big deal, right? My husband's a crook. My marriage sucks. But I'm a tough cookie, right? I can take it."

She was trying to be light, but the look he gave her in response was deadly serious.

"I know you can," he said.

He watched her face as understanding dawned. He knew the exact moment when she recognized him. Then her eyes welled up, and she looked away.

"I *thought* I'd seen you before," she said. "It's been bugging me for weeks. You covered my rape trial, didn't you? Back when I was in college?"

He exhaled a stream of smoke. "Yes, I did."

"I don't remember your byline."

He studied her expression. She seemed determined not to cry, and he remembered that same look from many years back. "I didn't write about it," he told her. "I was an intern that summer at the Austin paper. I took some notes, mostly, and the guy covering courts wrote everything up."

She reached for his cigarette. While she took a drag, he got out another one for himself.

"Thanks," she said. "I haven't had one of these in a long time."

He looked at the ground again, then back up at her face. She was, quite possibly, the prettiest woman he'd ever seen. Even prettier than she'd been a decade ago in that courtroom, giving testimony about her worst nightmare come true. As her story had unfolded on the witness stand, he'd understood for the first time what bravery was about. This petite young woman was made of stronger stuff than any man he'd ever known. She had his complete respect . . . and something else he couldn't quite pinpoint.

She looked away from him. "So, what now, McAllister? I guess you need a few quotes for your story tomorrow?"

He felt a pinch in his chest. "That's not why I'm here."

Her eyes veered back to his face, and for once, he didn't try to mask what he was feeling. He reached over and took her hand. "I just thought, I don't know, maybe you needed a friend."

She sniffled a little and looked down at their joined hands. The diamond on her finger winked back at him.

"Thanks," she said. "I could use one right about now."

The following evening, Feenie parked in front of a white stucco cottage with a red tile roof. All the houses on the block looked similar—front doors shaded by narrow porches, laundry hanging from clotheslines that crisscrossed the tiny backyards. Feenie got out of the Kia and made her way across the lawn, sidestepping the soggy patch of grass where an inflatable kiddie pool had been emptied and abandoned. She stood before the screen door and rang the bell.

Barks erupted from within, and a shaggy yellow head appeared on the other side of the screen. The dog's bark sounded menacing, but his frantically wagging tail gave him away.

"Hi, puppy," Feenie cooed. The tail shook faster.

Someone turned down the cartoon that had been

blaring in the living room, and a girl with a long dark braid came to the door. She wore a purple bathing suit with a rainbow of glittery stars scattered across the front.

"Who is it?" she asked politely, tugging at the dog's collar. He sat down next to her, eyeing the visitor, tail thumping against the floor.

"I'm Feenie Malone. Is your grandmother home?"

As she said this, Maria appeared. Her eyes brightened immediately, and Feenie felt a tug of guilt. Maria whispered something to Kaitlin, who went back to her cartoons, taking the dog with her. The screen door squeaked open.

"Yes?"

"Hello, Mrs. Juarez. I just wanted to stop by—"

"You've seen Marco?"

"Well . . . not exactly. But I have something for you."

Maria ushered Feenie inside the house and motioned for her to sit on a worn brown recliner. Feenie sat on the edge and dug the postcard out of her purse. She handed it to Marco's mother.

"I got this in the mail yesterday," she said. "I'm not certain, but I think it's from Marco."

Maria nodded, running her finger over the hand-written address.

"I'm not too sure what he's doing in Chihuahua," Feenie said. "Do you know if he knows anyone down there?"

She shook her head. The grave expression on her

face made Feenie think Maria knew exactly what Marco was doing.

"I wanted to show you the postcard, but I don't think Marco would want you to keep it lying around." He'd want to protect his mother. If the police ever stopped by to ask about him, Maria could truthfully tell them she hadn't heard from her son. Feenie hoped it would never come to that, but a feeling of dread had been building inside her.

Maria passed the postcard back to Feenie. "You keep it. Marco sent it to you."

Feenie tucked it into her purse, deciding to get rid of it before she got home.

Kaitlin was watching Feenie now with solemn eyes.

"Do you like to swim?" she asked the girl.

Kaitlin nodded. The dog nestled its head in her lap.

"Maybe you can come over sometime. I have a pool in my backyard. I love going in it, but it's more fun with two."

Kaitlin looked at her grandmother, who nodded slightly. "Okay," she said.

Feenie stood up. Her gaze landed on the mantel above the faux fireplace, where dozens of photographs had been arranged.

Maria smiled. *"Mis hijos,"* she said, nodding toward the pictures.

Feenie stepped to the mantel and examined the photographs. She counted five different faces, all bearing the same family resemblance. In one picture, Marco stood next to a slender brunette in a police uniform, his arm hooked playfully around her neck. She held up a shiny badge.

"Isn't she beautiful?"

"Yes, very," Feenie said.

"Kaitlin looks like her." Maria smiled over at her granddaughter, who didn't look up from her show.

"Well . . . I need to be going."

"Thank you for coming," Maria said, walking her to the door.

Feenie smiled and stepped out. "No problem. And I mean it about Kaitlin. She's welcome anytime."

The next morning, Feenie sped down Main Street, running a succession of yellow lights. She didn't want to be late for her first monthly editorial session as a full-time reporter, but it appeared unavoidable. The meeting started in two minutes.

"Shoot," she said, screeching to a halt at a red. She might have run that, too, had it not been for the trio of pedestrians on the corner. As they crossed the intersection, she took a moment to put on some lipstick.

A truck in the rearview mirror caught her eye. She whipped her head around and stared at the black Silverado parked a block away from Rosie's. He was *back?* Her stomach clenched, just as a chorus of horns sounded behind her.

She swerved into the left-turn lane, made an illegal U-turn, and doubled back. She slowed as she passed the truck. The toolbox and dust-coated running board looked right. She checked the license plate. It was him.

She circled the block and pulled into the *Gazette* parking lot. Her worry about the meeting had disappeared.

How long had he been back? Why hadn't he called?

She'd spent weeks telling herself he hadn't called because he was too busy, or trying to keep a low profile, or maybe he was in a place without cell-phone reception. Now he was right here in Mayfield, and he still hadn't called? She checked her cell phone. No messages.

She tried to ignore the ache in her chest as she went into the office. She managed to put in a solid day typing up stories on her computer and casting furtive glances at her desk phone, but it didn't ring. When she exited the building late that afternoon, the ache returned.

She went about her normal routine, running errands, making dinner, stopping by the gym for an hour to work out. As she went through her fitness routine, she kept her eye on the doorway, half expecting Marco to stroll in. He didn't.

Two more miserable days ticked by, and as Feenie left the office Friday evening, she decided to hell with it.

She called him and was bumped straight to voice mail.

He didn't want to talk to her. Whatever she'd thought they had going between them had been in her imagination. It took some mental acrobatics for her to arrive at that conclusion, but she did. He didn't feel anything for her; she'd simply misread the signals. They'd had one date and sex about a dozen times. It didn't make them engaged. Everything had been casual, no strings.

Or even worse, *nothing* had been casual. Everything between them had been carefully orchestrated. It had been about her feeding him information, and now that she had no more to offer, he was finished with her.

Feenie's phone buzzed just as she started her car, and she hurried to answer it. He'd seen her call come in, and he was calling her back.

"Hello?"

"You have to come over, Feenie." It was Cecelia, and her voice was wobbling.

"Is Robert back? What's going on?"

She heard a shaky breath on the other end. "The FBI just left. They spent half the day here executing a search warrant. I swear, Feenie, I think I'm gonna lose it."

"Just sit tight, Celie. I'll be right there."

As she raced across town, she tried to put Marco out of her mind. She couldn't let her world revolve around a man who didn't want her. Her best friend's life was falling apart, and she had to be there to support her. And then there was Feenie's father, who was facing another grim anniversary all alone in Port Aransas. She kept meaning to call him and set up a visit.

She had people who needed her, even if Marco didn't.

After a tearful sleepover at Cecelia's, Feenie returned to her house feeling emotionally beat and more than a little hungover. No one had heard from Robert in weeks. Federal agents had reason to believe he'd left the country, and he was now considered an international fugitive. Feenie had stayed up most of the night talking to Celie about her problems, but they hadn't solved a one of them.

Back in her own kitchen now, Feenie made a strong pot of coffee and a list of chores to fill her Saturday. She'd start by calling her dad. Then she needed to get a haircut and stop by the grocery. Her weekend was shaping up. After a few sips of coffee, she felt positively positive. Really.

And then she fetched the paper.

The wire story at the bottom of the front page made her choke:

Police Unearth Body of Slain Officer

Mexican authorities in Punto Dorado uncovered the body of a missing San Antonio woman this week, solving a two-year mystery. The remains, which were found inside a garbage bag, were identified through dental records as those of Paloma Juarez, a Mayfield native. The twenty-eight-year-old police detective was reported missing by family members two years ago. A second set of human remains found in a second garbage bag buried nearby is still being identified.

Feenie read on. According to sources inside the SAPD, the break in the case was an anonymous tip received late Wednesday. The tip prompted a team of forensic specialists from both sides of the border to focus on a particular patch of land near an abandoned fruit-canning plant just outside Punto Dorado. Investigators had not yet determined the cause of death and were still combing the area—

The phone shrilled. Feenie snatched it up.

"Hello?"

"Have you seen the paper?" It was McAllister.

"I'm reading it. Why didn't you call me?"

"I didn't know about it. It came over the wire last night just before press run. The night editor dropped it in."

She skimmed the rest of the story. Following an autopsy, the body would be released to the family for burial. The San Antonio police were planning a memorial service next week.

The story didn't mention the undercover FBI agent who'd gone missing with Paloma, but Feenie suspected the other remains would be identified as his.

The article also didn't mention Josh.

"Feenie? Are you there?"

"Yes."

"I said, do you want the interview?"

"What?"

"Because of the local angle, Grimes wants a story about the family. I'm on my way over there now to do the death knock. You want to come?"

"No." The mere idea made her cringe. It was too personal. "Leave me out of this one."

"Are you sure?"

"Yes."

"Okay. I hear it's a circus over there already. The TV guys have it. If the family clams up, will you put in a call for me?"

She hesitated a moment, her journalistic instincts warring with her sense of decency.

"I'd really like to get some time with the girl."

"She's only six, for God's sake! Leave her alone!"

McAllister paused. "Okay, but if they stonewall me, I'm coming to you."

"Fine. Just stay away from Kaitlin."

Feenie glided through the water. A full hour at Chico's had failed to cure her frustration, so she'd hoped a dip in the pool would help.

It hadn't. Her nerves were frayed. She'd spent all week at the *Gazette* trying *not* to get involved in the Paloma Juarez story, but she couldn't get away from it. Reporters had staked out Maria's house, all hoping for emotional sound bites or a glimpse of Kaitlin. For several days, all media outlets had carried the tragic tale of the murdered policewoman. Then, just when interest began to fade, it was revealed that her grave had been discovered on land owned by a Mexican corporation with ties to prominent local attorney Bert Garland. The storm of coverage became a full-fledged hurricane. Local TV stations had carried little else in the way of news for days. Feenie felt sick about what the Juarez family must be going through, but what could she do? She couldn't put a muzzle on every media organization in South Texas. The family would just have to wait it out. In the meantime, Feenie felt ashamed to be a reporter.

She hitched herself onto the side of the pool and blew out a breath. She'd been fretting for hours, but she still hadn't decided whether to attend Paloma's funeral the next day. She wanted to show her support for the Juarez family, but she didn't know what to say to Marco. He still hadn't called. And what if he misread her intentions and thought she was there to take part in the media feeding frenzy? She could just see his look of contempt if she approached Kaitlin. He'd hate her.

"Hi."

She jerked her head around. Marco stood on her patio, his hands shoved into the pockets of his familiar leather jacket. In the near-darkness, she couldn't read his expression. Not that light would have helped. He was amazingly talented at hiding his emotions.

She got to her feet. "Hi. What are you doing here?"

He stepped toward her. She had the urge to throw her arms around him, but it was accompanied by an equally strong urge to slap him.

"I needed to see you," he said.

Her breath rushed out. What was that supposed to mean? He'd been in town at least two weeks without calling.

He stepped closer, until he was just inches away. Stubble covered his jaw, and his jacket smelled smoky, as if he'd been in a bar. She recognized the look in his eyes, and her pulse picked up.

"Marco—"

He kissed her, and whatever she'd been about to say flew out of her mind. He tasted like bourbon, and he felt different. Rough. There was meanness in the kiss. Finally, he let her go.

"How was your trip?" she asked.

"I got what I needed."

She stepped back from him. So he'd done it. He'd killed a man in cold blood. She understood his motive, but what she didn't understand was how he'd gone through with it. He'd spend the rest of his life hiding from it. And what if what he'd done caught up to him? Whatever future they might have together would always be in jeopardy. He was so selfish, she wanted to scream.

She stalked to the back door. He caught up to her and slapped a hand on it before she could turn the knob.

"I said I need to see you."

"Yeah? Well, I don't need to see you."

"Yes, you do." He yanked her to him. He felt hard, and his breath smelled sweet.

"You've been drinking."

"So?"

"So I can't talk to you right now." She tried to wrench her arm away, but he tightened his grip.

"What's to talk about? I said I need to *see* you. Now."

He pulled her closer. The light from the kitchen fell over his face, and she got a clear look at his eyes. Maybe it was the alcohol, but for the first time, she could see what it was he couldn't say. He was hurting. Needy.

She looked down. "Marco, this isn't a good idea."

He dropped her arm. "Do it anyway."

Of course. Easy for him to say. Anger flared inside her as she thought of all the ways he'd hurt her, all the nights she'd gone to bed worried he could be dead somewhere. She *loved* him, and all he wanted from her was sex. And he probably only wanted that because he was too drunk to remember to stay away from her.

She stepped back and turned to leave. Again, he grabbed her arm. And something in her just broke.

"Don't *touch* me!" She whirled around and punched him in the chest, hard, with the side of her fist. It felt amazingly good, and she hit him again, this time with both fists. "You're a selfish bastard, you know that?"

He wrestled her hands to her sides and wrapped

his arms around her, squeezing her so tightly she couldn't hit anymore, so tightly she could hardly even breathe. She was trapped there, against his chest, as she struggled to keep the tears from coming.

Finally, he loosened his grip a little. She took a ragged breath, and the next thing she knew, he was kissing her. Hard. And she could taste the anger on his tongue.

Or maybe it was her anger. She kissed him furiously, nipping his mouth and clawing at the buttons of his shirt. She heard him fumbling with the doorknob and felt a cool drift of air as the door swung open. She stumbled backward over the threshold, dragging him with her.

Later, she lay beside him, watching him sleep. Her gaze skimmed over the tousled hair, the two-day beard, the hard planes of his chest. He looked drained, exhausted. If she had to guess, this was the first sound sleep he'd had in weeks.

She propped herself on her elbow and peered into his face.

"Marco?"

In the moonlight, he looked harmless. It didn't fit his personality, but there it was. He was so full of contradictions, it drove her crazy. Enraged one minute, calm the next. One second laughing, deadly serious moments later. How was she supposed to read a man like that? A long-term relationship with him would drive her nuts. She'd never know where she stood, especially since he wasn't big on talking. But she could get around all that, if only he'd let her in.

She needed to know what had happened. The details would be appalling, but still she had to know.

"Marco?"

The steady rise and fall of his chest told her he was fast asleep.

"I love you," she whispered. "You can tell me about it later." She rolled onto her back and tried to sleep.

CHAPTER

23

Juarez had imagined the day a thousand times, but somehow it had always been raining.

No chance of that today. Ninety-eight degrees and sunny, ninety percent humidity. An insane day for a black suit, but his mother had insisted. Thinking of the hell he'd been through to make this day happen, dragging his only suit out of hiding was a minor inconvenience.

Still, it was *hot*. And his head was throbbing from way too much Jack Daniel's the night before.

Juarez slipped off his jacket and draped it over his arm. He'd wear it for the mass. If he put it on now, he'd be drenched by the time the service started.

Cars filed into the parking lot, snaking between giant potholes. Juarez tugged at the knot of his tie and watched Ricky approach the church. His brother wore his Army dress uniform like a second skin. Even without it, his ramrod-straight posture and close-cropped hair would have tagged him as military. Not a wrinkle in sight, and the creases in his pants looked sharp enough to cut butter.

"Aren't you hot in that thing?" Juarez asked.

Ricky shrugged and propped a gleaming dress shoe on the curb. "I'm used to it," he said.

Juarez felt a shot of jealousy. He'd been used to it, too, once upon a time. The starched shirts. The spit-and-polish. Sometimes he missed being a cop. He'd loved the job, but he could never go back. Especially now.

"I thought Mom was riding with you," Juarez said.

"Tony's bringing her. He has tinted windows. He thought it'd be better with the media and all."

Juarez scowled at the line of cameras staked out near the church entrance. Having seen the paper, he wasn't surprised. Today's headlines had only heightened the drama of the long-awaited funeral. "Won't do any good. The buzzards'll just swoop down when they get out."

Ricky nodded. "Yeah. But Manuel's riding with them."

Juarez's oldest brother, Manuel, was built like a Hummer and looked as friendly. He and Tony would handle things. They were a good team. They ran a roofing business together in Corpus Christi and made good money at it.

None of his siblings had ever tied the knot. Everyone had expected Paloma to get married when she got pregnant with Kaitlin, but she'd refused. She'd said the father wasn't marriage material, and she'd been right. The guy had barely spent five minutes with Kaitlin, even after Paloma's disappearance. At least he'd had the decency not to show up today. Not yet, anyway. A reunion with her absentee father was the last thing Kaitlin needed right now.

A dark green Suburban pulled into the parking lot, and the TV reporters sprang into action. They clustered near the curb, blocking the path between the lot and the church entrance.

"Looks like they made the car," Juarez muttered.

Ricky sighed. "Somebody probably saw them leave the house and called ahead. You think Kaitlin's okay?"

She emerged from the Suburban, clinging to Manuel like a life raft. She wore a navy-blue dress and a tidy braid with a white bow at the end. Juarez swallowed the lump in his throat.

A hearse approached the church. Two of Juarez's uncles stepped forward, both wearing white carnations in their lapels. The pallbearers.

"Looks like our cue," Ricky said. "You ready?"

Juarez shrugged into his jacket and dug a flower out of his pocket. His mother had passed them out to her brothers and each of her sons earlier that morning.

Juarez set his jaw. "Ready as I'll ever be."

Feenie sat in her car, sweltering. Hair clung to her neck, and her feet already felt slimy in her patent-leather pumps. She was wearing her only black dress, which was linen—luckily—but stifling nonetheless.

She hated black, always had. The feeling had only intensified after she'd watched the parade of mourners at her mother and sister's funeral. She remembered wanting to wear pink that day, because it was her mother's favorite color, but her father had insisted on black, saying it was a sign of respect.

She opened her black handbag and dug out a lipstick. With painstaking care, she painted her mouth, then blotted the excess on a tissue.

She was stalling.

If she didn't leave soon, she'd be late. Yet she couldn't bring herself to start the car. Marco had slipped out of bed before dawn and left without a word. She wondered if he regretted coming over last night. She wondered what he'd say to her at the funeral, if anything. Maybe he'd want to pretend last night hadn't happened. But it had. He'd been a willing participant—intoxicated, yes, but not so much so that he didn't know what he was doing.

He'd known exactly what he was doing.

Sighing, Feenie shoved her key into the ignition and backed down the driveway. She hit a bump and realized she'd forgotten to bring in the morning paper. She put the car in park, opened the door, and snagged it off the ground. Her article about Mayfield's recent housing boom had been slated for page one today. It was a good story, and she wanted to see what kind of play Grimes had given it.

She was stalling again. She pulled the rubber band off the paper and unfolded it in her lap.

She read the banner headline, and her heart skittered.

Ten minutes later, she slid into a parking space at Holy Trinity Catholic Church. Most of the mourners had already gone inside, but a crowd of media milled around near the entrance. A TV reporter with perfectly coiffed hair and a somber pantsuit stood before a camera. Feenie recognized her from the NBC affiliate in Corpus. McAllister stood behind her, interviewing a police officer. Feenie strode toward them, noting the SAPD insignia on the officer's uniform.

"I have to talk to you, McAllister."

He shot her a glare as he scribbled in his notebook. "Just a minute."

"Now!" she snapped.

His eyebrows arched, and he flipped his pad shut. "Thanks for your comments, sir," he said to the officer. Then he turned to Feenie. "What the fuck?"

"Why didn't you call me?"

"What do you mean?"

"The Brassler story. What do you think I mean?"

He crossed his arms. "I thought you wanted to be left out of it. Anyway, I drove by your house last night, and Juarez's truck was there, so I thought you knew."

"Well, you thought wrong. Who called in the tip?"

"It was anonymous."

She rolled her eyes. "Don't bullshit me. Who called in the tip?"

"Who do you think? It came from an Internet café in Reynosa." McAllister grinned. "I hear he even sent a map."

She bit her lip. "When was the arrest?"

"Yesterday morning. Didn't you read the story?"

"I skimmed the lead."

He feigned shock. "You *skimmed* it? That was some damn good journalism. I have to tell you, Malone, I'm a little insulted."

She shoved her purse under her arm. "It's hard to read when you're doing eighty down Main Street. We need to get in there. The mass is beginning."

He waggled his eyebrows at her. "Late start this morning?"

"Oh, shut up."

They entered the church just as the priest started speaking. All the pews were filled, mostly with dark-haired, dark-dressed mourners. Feenie scanned the rows, recognizing a few familiar faces—Rosie, Chico, some local cops. A group of San Antonio police officers filled several pews in front of Feenie. They wore black armbands. The reporters had flocked to the opposite side, conspicuous with their recorders and notebooks. At least someone had had the sense to ban cameras. Feenie's gaze settled on the white-haired clergyman with the stern expression. He didn't look like someone who would put up with any sort of irreverence on his turf.

Her gaze wandered to the front pew. She recognized Maria sandwiched between two oversized men, then Kaitlin, then a man in an Army uniform, and then Marco.

He didn't turn around. His stare remained fixed on the casket, even while everyone around him bent their heads, whispering and passing tissues. When the priest offered communion at the end of the mass, Marco stayed behind, hunched over the kneeler, while the rest of his family stepped forward and took the sacrament. She couldn't tell if Marco was praying or crying. Either way, she guessed it was the closest he'd ever come to showing his emotions in public.

After the mass, Feenie's row was nearly the last to exit. She stepped into the blazing sun, shielded her eyes, and glanced at the parking lot. A line of cars with headlights on had already rolled away from the church, headed for the cemetery.

"Need a ride?"

She turned and saw McAllister. Riding in his Jeep would trash her hairstyle, but it would give her a chance to pump him for information. She could pick her car up later.

"Sure," she said.

As soon as they were moving, she started pelting him with questions.

"What kind of shape was Brassler in?"

McAllister cast her a sidelong glance. "Not good, from what I hear. He's in a Mexican hospital at the moment, with a round-the-clock guard. As soon as he's back on his feet, they'll probably extradite him."

"Extradite him? But how? Why? Wasn't the murder in Mexico?"

McAllister shifted into fourth gear, speeding to catch up to rest of the procession. "Probably. But he's wanted for more than a dozen murders, most of them in Texas. Plus, the FBI's gotten involved, and they're determined to get him back ASAP. They've really turned up the heat with the Mexican authorities."

"Will he . . . die?" She dreaded the answer. Depending on what type of shape Brassler was in at the time of his arrest, Marco could still be brought up on murder charges.

McAllister tipped his head to the side. "Mexico won't extradite him to face the death penalty."

The death penalty? Feenie frowned. "I mean, could he die from his injuries?"

He gave her a curious look. "A broken arm isn't fatal last time I checked."

"A broken . . . ? But I thought you said he was in the hospital?"

"Shit. You didn't read anything I wrote, did you? He *is* in the hospital. But that's just until he dries out. The guy's a walking bottle of tequila. Had the DTs so bad he couldn't even go before the judge yesterday."

"You mean he's an alcoholic?"

"Been on the downhill slide for years now, apparently." McAllister turned left and rolled past some wrought-iron gates. He parked the Jeep behind a news van with a peacock logo on the side. Feenie sat, bewildered, as he made his way around to open her door. "Now that he's in custody, the feds have a mile-long list of things to try him for. The Juarez murder is right at the top."

If they can ever prove it.

"But if he's such a mess, how do they know he killed Paloma?" she asked.

He smirked. "That's an excellent question, Malone. And I think I see someone who might know the answer." He pulled a mini-tape recorder from his pocket and pressed the red button.

"Morning, Mr. Juarez. Is it true you told authorities where to find your sister's killer?"

Feenie gasped and whirled around. Marco stood behind her, glowering. He snapped the recorder from McAllister's hand and hummed it into some bushes.

"Fuck off," he snarled.

McAllister had the good judgment not to push it. He was lucky *he* hadn't been tossed in the bushes.

Marco pulled Feenie aside. "What are you doing here?" he asked.

She looked over his shoulder at the knot of mourners on the lawn. "Aren't you supposed to be with your family?"

"What are you doing here?" he repeated.

"I came because . . ." Her gaze drifted to the reporters standing near the news van. Marco glanced at them scornfully before shifting his attention back to her.

"I'm not with the press, Marco, I swear. I came because—"

"I *know*. I mean, why are you *here?* Why aren't you with me?"

She blinked at him.

"Come on." He took her hand and led her to a row of folding chairs beneath a huge pecan tree. Paloma's casket sat on a carpet of fake grass, surrounded by wreaths and floral arrangements.

Before Feenie could protest, Marco steered her into the second row and seated her between himself and a stooped gray-haired woman who was weeping and holding a string of beads in her shaking hands. Marco's mother, who sat diagonally in front of Feenie, held a similar string, but her hands were still.

A hush fell over the crowd as the priest began to pray. The pecan tree rustled in the breeze, blending with the sound of his voice. The sweet fragrance of lilies wafted over her. She felt oddly soothed by it all and wondered what Marco was feeling.

Her gaze settled on Maria. She sat inert, holding her beads, as the priest chanted over the coffin. Her cheeks were dry.

Feenie thought about the incredible lengths Marco had gone to to make this ritual possible. She wondered if it had been worth it. It appeared to have brought his mother some peace, and she hoped it had brought him some, too.

She glanced over at him, sitting next to her all decked out in his crisp black suit. Her gaze landed on the white carnation pinned to his lapel. Everything about him looked so formal, so stilted, so un-Marco. But this ritual wasn't about him, she realized. It was about Maria, and Kaitlin, and paying some long-overdue respects to a young woman who'd died a horrible death trying to do something good.

She'd been twenty-eight. Nearly Feenie's age. And she'd been someone's mother. Someone's daughter. Someone's sister.

Marco stirred beside her.

Suddenly, Feenie felt his grief. It had been wrapped in anger so longer she'd hardly glimpsed it. But it swept over her now, like the scent of the lilies.

I'm sorry, she wanted to say. *I love you, Marco, and I'm so, so sorry.* But she didn't say anything. Instead, she squeezed his hand.

When the service ended, Marco stood up and hugged the old woman beside Feenie. Then he bent down. "You ready?" he whispered.

"For what?" Feenie whispered back.

"To meet everyone."

Before she could answer, she was engulfed by a crowd of people. Marco introduced her around, each time calling her his "girlfriend." The Juarez brothers passed before her in a blur of nods and firm handshakes. All three had Marco's intense, dark eyes, and she could feel them scrutinizing her.

Finally, Marco pulled her away from the group. He tucked his arm around her waist and led her toward the street.

"They weren't so bad, were they?"

She didn't know what to say. Shock couldn't begin to describe how she felt at the moment.

He stopped and touched a hand to her cheek. "You all right? You look pale."

"I'm fine, I just . . . I feel like an intruder. Don't you need to be with your mother right now?"

He kissed her forehead. "She's okay. Trust me." He cast a glance at Maria, who was surrounded by throngs of friends and relatives. She held her beads, as well as the cross that had lain on Paloma's casket. Her face remained serene as people paid their respects. It seemed to Feenie she was comforting them, not vice-versa.

"She hasn't been this okay in years," he said.

Kaitlin peeked out from behind Marco's legs.

"Uncle Marco?" Her voice was barely audible.

He scooped her up. She cupped her hand and whispered something in his ear. He answered her in Spanish, then shot Feenie a questioning look.

"You invited Kaitlin swimming?"

"Yes." Feenie smiled before she realized what he was thinking. "Oh, but not today!"

Kaitlin's face fell, and she gave Marco a doe-eyed look.

Feenie's heart melted. "Any other day is fine, sweetie. I'm sure your grandmother—"

"Would think it was a great idea," Marco said. "Let's go."

He plopped Kaitlin to the ground and took her hand. She smiled up at Feenie triumphantly. The little girl was smart and beautiful and clearly had Marco wrapped around her little finger.

Feenie laughed. "Okay. I guess I'm up for a swim."

Marco patted his niece's shoulder. "Go tell Grandma you're coming with us."

She trotted off. Marco pulled Feenie against him and hugged her tightly. "Thanks for coming," he said into her hair.

"I wanted to." She was glad she'd summoned the nerve to do it. She still felt guilty for taking him away from his family, but he didn't seem too concerned about it. Maybe he needed a break. Or maybe Kaitlin did.

An hour later, they sat together on the edge of the pool, watching Kaitlin and her dog, Duke, frolic. Feenie had shed her pantyhose and heels. She dangled her feet in the water and sipped lemonade as the hum of cicadas filled the air. Marco had ditched his jacket and tie, rolled up his sleeves, and popped open a Corona. Kaitlin's delighted shrieks echoed across the water. The little girl and her dog were in heaven.

"This is nice," Marco said.

Duke paddled over and delivered a soggy tennis

ball, which Marco promptly threw toward the deep end.

"He likes to swim!" Kaitlin said gleefully. "Just like me!"

"We'll have to bring him over more often," Marco said.

Feenie's chest tightened. She hoped he would. Now that he was back, she never wanted him to leave again.

"You want to tell me what happened?" she asked softly.

He looked at her, and his smile faded. "Not really."

She sipped her drink, trying not to look hurt.

"But I will." He stroked a finger over her knuckles, not meeting her gaze. He cleared his throat. "When I finally tracked him down, it was pathetic. The guy was a wreck."

"Where'd you find him?"

He looked away and kept his voice low, probably to prevent Kaitlin from hearing. "Some nothing town down in Chihuahua. An investigator I contacted in El Paso put me on the right track. Said he'd heard of this rich American down there who was retired from all sorts of serious shit. Ex-military. Said he'd lived in El Paso for a while. It fit, so I checked it out."

Duke delivered the tennis ball again, and Marco threw it across the pool. Kaitlin squealed.

"Once I had a starting point, it didn't take me long to find him; it was a small town, and everyone knew who he was. I caught up to him in a bar. Think he practically lived there. Anyway, he was wasted. Totally. Didn't even resist or anything. Followed me straight into the alley behind the bar."

"Is that where you broke his arm?"

Marco's eyes narrowed.

"Hey, I'm not judging. I'm just asking," she said. "I need to understand what happened."

"That's where I questioned him."

There was a euphemism. "And then?"

He sighed. "And then I hauled him to the local jail. Paid them a few hundred bucks to lock him up on some trumped-up charge for a few days while I came back here and made a deal with the feds."

"I thought you e-mailed them from Reynosa?"

He flashed a smile. "You believe everything you read in the paper?"

She ignored the jab. "What kind of deal?"

He paused. "Well, I had to give it some thought. I'd always counted on getting rid of him, so I hadn't looked at all the possibilities. After I decided to change my plan, I wanted to make sure he didn't get some kind of immunity in exchange for testimony."

"And?"

Satisfaction flickered in his eyes. "And he won't. No matter what he knows. Turns out the feds hate him as much as I do, and they've got plenty of evidence. He'll never see the outside of a prison."

Marco was in the clear. He could get on with his life. *Their* life. She stared down at her lap, afraid that if she looked at him, he'd read everything she was thinking. He'd read marriage vows, and baby strollers, and Christmas mornings with a house full of people. He'd run for the hills, she felt sure.

He picked up her hand. "So ask me."

"Ask you what?"

"Why I wimped out."

She looked up at him. "You don't need to be ashamed of it. I think what you did took a lot more courage."

He rolled his eyes. "It wasn't courage. It was selfishness, pure and simple."

"How's that?"

"I knew no matter how careful I was, there was always the chance I'd get caught. I know from being a cop, people always leave a trail. I knew the risk, but I'd never cared about it until now." He was watching her intently, and she held her breath. "I looked at this guy, and I wanted to squeeze the trigger, but I kept thinking about you. About how I'd rather spend my life with you than rot in some jail cell."

He gazed out at the pool. "And then I thought about Kaitlin." His voice broke on her name, and Feenie squeezed his hand.

"It's okay to cry, Marco."

He cleared his throat and waited a few beats.

"She's already lost her mom, and she's pretty attached to me. I don't know. I couldn't do it. I couldn't throw everything away. And even if I could, it wouldn't bring Paloma back. So I came back here."

He looked at her again, his eyes tentative. "And ever since I got home, I've been trying to think of a way to tell you . . . to make you understand, I don't know, the way I feel about everything. About you."

Feenie's heart hurt. But it was a good hurt, the kind she'd been waiting for for a long time. She watched Kaitlin and Duke splash around in the shallow end, making waves and disrupting the hot stillness of the afternoon.

She smiled. "You know, this is the first time I've watched a child play in my pool. I like it. This is a great yard for kids."

He shook his head. "Shit. You don't listen, do you?" He leaned closer and looked her right in the eye. "Feenie, I love you."

"I know," she said, smiling. "I love you, too." And then she kissed him.

When she pulled away, the silence stretched out. She knew he had something left to say, and she wasn't going to do it for him. She'd accepted that he wasn't a talker, but this was one moment when he needed to find the words.

He cleared his throat. "So. Like I said, I love you."

She couldn't repress a laugh. "Yeah, I heard you."

"Since you feel the same way about me, I think we should, you know, get married."

She grinned at him, loving the discomfort on his face and the fact that he'd gotten over it for her. "Married, huh?"

He narrowed his eyes, as if he thought she was

making fun of him. "Yes. I think you should marry me." He nodded firmly and looked away. And the next time he glanced at her, his face was wary. "Don't tell me you want some live-together bullshit. I want *kids* with you, Feenie. I want everything."

"Marco, it's okay. I want everything, too."

He sighed, obviously relieved. "Why didn't you just say so?"

"Because." She smiled. "I needed to hear *you* say it."

POCKET BOOKS
PROUDLY PRESENTS

ONE WRONG STEP

LAURA GRIFFIN

Available in paperback in May 2008
from Pocket Books

Turn the page for a preview of
One Wrong Step. . . .

CHAPTER

I

Celie Wells dropped the fire extinguisher on the floor and gaped at her kitchen through the cloud of yellow dust. How come they never showed scenes like this on the Food Network?

Her lungs tickled. Coughing, she waved away the superfine particles that floated around her. God, she'd made a mess. And a racket. She should probably notify the building super about her little accident.

She eyed the disemboweled smoke detector on her kitchen floor and decided against it. If anyone from the building's management saw her luxury unit in its current state, she could kiss her hefty security deposit good-bye. And the damage wasn't permanent—nothing a little Spackle and touch-up paint couldn't fix.

She picked up the portable phone, battling the urge to do what she normally did when disaster struck, which was call her mom. Virginia Wells was great in a crisis, and she would be delighted to learn that her domestically challenged daughter was actually baking.

But Celie wasn't in the mood for a lecture, and that's just what she'd get if she told her mother she'd set her kitchen on fire while baking goodies for the Bluebonnet House Easter party. It wasn't that her mother disliked battered women's shelters per se; she just didn't believe it prudent for a thirty-one-year-old divorcée to work at one.

Celie wasn't up for the debate tonight. Her self-esteem had taken a hit already when the cheerful, scrumptious bunny cake she'd lovingly created had morphed into a charred, inedible pancake inside of her oven. *Throw together a festive Easter party in six simple steps!* the glossy magazine had proclaimed from the check-out line. Celie's radar should have been on red-alert when she read step one: *Create a tasty bunny cake that doubles as a fun centerpiece!*

Celie dumped the nontasty, unfun bunny cake into the sink. Even her disposal rejected it.

She sighed. When it came to cooking—or anything remotely domestic, for that matter—she was totally inept. It was ironic, really, considering that her lifelong ambition had been to settle down, make a home, and raise a family. Her uselessness in the kitchen was just one more sign that the Suzie Home-maker gene had missed her.

She was being hormonal again.

She fetched the broom from the hall closet and began sweeping up the snowy mess all over her floor. She'd made it through this entire hellacious week without a meltdown and she wouldn't lose it now, not over a stupid bunny cake. If Feenie were here right now, she'd be laughing, not on the verge of tears.

The portable phone rang. Celie glanced at the caller ID and confirming for the umpteenth time that her best friend had mental telepathy.

"Hi, Feenie, what's up?"

Feenie Juarez lived five-and-a-half hours away down in Mayfield, Texas, but she and Celie talked so much, she may as well have lived next door.

"Just calling to see how your meeting went. Did you get the director to recommend drug treatment for your kid?"

Feenie always called the children at Bluebonnet House "her kids," and Celie hadn't gotten around to mentioning that it bothered her.

"No." Celie leaned her broom against the counter and took a clean mixing bowl out of the cabinet. "But I *did* get roped into being in charge of the Easter party tomorrow."

"You're kidding. Don't tell me you have to cook."

"You got it." She started measuring ingredients again. Darn it, she was out of baking soda. She'd borrowed that first teaspoon from her neighbor across the hall, but she dreaded the thought of going back there. That woman could talk the ear off a cactus.

"Hey, do you know anything about cake baking?"

she asked hopefully. Feenie was no domestic diva, but she'd come a long way in the months since she'd been married. Just last week, she'd been making homemade tamales for her husband.

"I know two things," Feenie said. "Betty and Crocker."

Celie sighed, and then explained what was going on, omitting the part about the four-foot flames that had leapt out of the oven and scorched her ceiling.

"I can't believe you're making something from a magazine," Feenie said. "Are you masochistic or just nuts?"

She eyed the April issue of *Living* sitting open on her counter. The photograph showed a rabbit-shaped cake with jelly bean eyes, licorice whiskers, and fur made of shaved coconut, tinted pink of course. Her gaze shifted to the singed heap at the bottom of her sink.

"A little of both," she answered, glancing out the window. Even if she hadn't been wearing threadbare plaid pajamas and waiting on a take-out delivery, she didn't relish the thought of braving west Austin's hilly streets in a driving rainstorm.

Especially at night. Celie steadfastly avoided going out alone after dark.

"The good news is I figured out where I went wrong," she told Feenie. "The bad news is I don't have any more baking soda, and I want to give this recipe another whirl. Is there something I can substitute?"

Feenie snorted. "You're asking *me* for cooking tips?"

"Well you mentioned the tamales, so I thought maybe—"

"It was a nightmare. I was up to my elbows in corn husks for days, and the final product tasted like soggy Fritos. Next time Marco wants homemade Mexican food, he can hit up his mom."

"Oh." Celie felt deflated. In the morning her boss expected her to put on an Easter party for twenty-six kids, some of whom had never even received a birthday present. She wanted to do something special and memorable, but the prospects were growing dimmer by the minute. And the thought of picking up a package of generic, grocery store-bought cupcakes depressed her. Celie's mother never would have resorted to such a thing.

"Get over it," Feenie said, reading her mind. "The kids'll be fine. Set 'em up with some chocolate bunnies, and they'll think you hung the moon."

"So what are you doing home, anyway?" Feenie asked. "I thought you had a hot date with that grad student."

And there it was—the real reason for the call.

"I'd say 'hot' is an exaggeration," Celie said. "Think Will Ferrell without the jokes."

"Well, didn't he ask you out for coffee tonight? What happened?"

Celie plopped down on the couch. "I told him we'd take a rain check. With this party tomorrow, I didn't have time."

Actually, she'd gotten cold feet. Celie hadn't been on a date since before Google was invented, and she felt woefully out of touch with modern standards. What if this guy wanted more than just coffee? What if, say, he wanted to come back to her apartment afterward and jump into bed together? Celie didn't do recreational sex. Even when she'd been married, the recreation part had been pretty lacking.

"Celie."

"Hmm?"

"That's chickenshit, and you know it. Who doesn't have time for coffee?"

Celie heard cooing on the other end of the phone and decided to divert the conversation. "Olivia's awake?"

"Yeah." Feenie's tone mellowed. "She's just having one last feeding before bedtime. At least I hope it's bedtime. Last night we were up every hour between midnight and six."

No wonder Feenie sounded crabby. "You must be exhausted," Celie said.

"I'm okay. Liv's just colicky, bless her little heart."

Feenie could hit the kill zone of a paper silhouette from fifty yards away with her .38, but motherhood had turned her into a complete softy. Celie had spent a few days down in south Texas after Olivia's birth, and Feenie had been a total sap. Celie had actually caught her getting misty-eyed over reruns of *Seventh Heaven*.

Celie felt a pang of envy, and then hated herself for it. Feenie deserved to be happy. She'd been to hell and back over the past few years.

Feenie must have sensed what the silence meant.

"So, this cake thing," she said, changing the subject. "Here's my advice: toss the Martha Stewart mag in the trash and stop by the grocery store on your way to work."

The buzzer sounded, and Celie got up to grab her checkbook off the kitchen counter. "My dinner's here. Lemme let you go."

"I mean it, Celie. Pick up some Easter candy and quit torturing yourself. Those kids adore you, with or without cake."

Celie punched the intercom button. "Yes?"

"Ms. Wells, we have a delivery down here—"

"Send him right up!" And then to Feenie, "All right, all right. I'll talk to you tomorrow."

After hanging up the phone, Celie wrote a check to Shanghai Garden. On her way to the door, she glanced in the bathroom mirror to make sure she looked halfway decent. She didn't. Her dark-blond hair was dusted with flame retardant and globs of batter decorated her pajama top. Plus she wasn't wearing a bra. She grabbed a denim jacket off the hook in the foyer and shrugged into it just as the doorbell rang. Out of habit, she patted her pocket to make sure she had her pepper spray handy before going to work on the numerous locks. As she flipped the first latch, she peered through the peephole, expecting to see a stranger in the hallway holding a carton of Chinese food.

But the man who stood there looked all too familiar.

Celie's hands froze. She backed away from the

door and darted a frantic glance around the apartment. Where had she put the phone? The bell rang again, and then the doorknob rattled. God, was it possible he had a *key*? She took out her pepper spray.

"I can hear you in there, Celie. Open up, okay? I just want to talk."

Yeah, right. Did he think she was crazy? She held her pepper spray in a death-grip as she bit her lip and tried to decide what to do.

"Celie, please?" The familiar voice made her chest tighten. Guilt, anger, regret—the emotions battled inside her.

"I just need to talk to you," he repeated.

Guilt won out.

Instead of locating her phone and calling the police, she found herself moving toward the door and reaching for the locks. Methodically, she undid them all until only one deadbolt remained. She waited a beat, giving herself one last chance to heed the warnings blaring in her head. Then she turned the lock and pulled open the door.

Her ex-husband stood before her holding a drooping bouquet of flowers and a baseball cap. He wore a tattered UT windbreaker, ratty sneakers, and wet jeans that clung to his gaunt frame. He desperately needed a haircut.

Not to mention a methadone fix.

"Hello, Robert," she said. "Rumor has it you're dead."

Love a good story?
So do we!

Don't miss any of these bestselling romance
titles from Pocket Books.

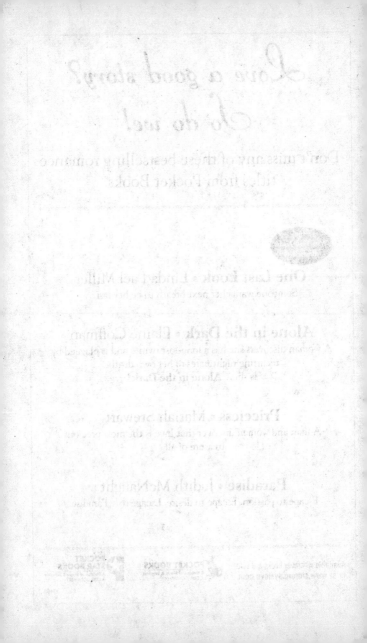